Also by Chris Roberson

Novels
Voices of Thunder
Cybermancy Incorporated
Any Time At All
Here, There & Everywhere
Paragaea: A Planetary Romance
The Voyage of Night Shining White
X-Men: The Return
The Dragon's Nine Sons (due 2008)

Series
Shark Boy and Lava Girl Adventures: Book 1
Shark Boy and Lava Girl Adventures: Book 2

Set the Seas on Fire

Chris Roberson

SOLARIS

For my parents.
They taught me how to read,
so this is all their fault.

First published 2007 by Solaris
an imprint of BL Publishing
Games Workshop Ltd
Willow Road
Nottingham
NG7 2WS
UK

www.solarisbooks.com

Trade Paperback
ISBN-13: 978-1-84416-488-2
ISBN-10: 1-84416-488-8

A CIP catalogue record for this book is available from the British Library.

Designed & typeset by BL Publishing

Acknowledgements

As with everything I do, this book would not have been possible without the love, support, and encouragement of my wife, partner, and friend, Allison Baker. I also remain grateful to my friends Lou Anders and John Picacio, who continue to inspire me, each in their own way. And to my daughter, Georgia Rose Roberson, who sometimes lets me pick what we watch on television.

Part I
Sea Wanderings & Strange Meetings

October, 1792

THE DAY WAS clear, and warm considering the lateness of the year, so the tutor had convened the morning session out in the garden of the Jacobean manor, the three children seated on stone benches arranged in a semicircle near the fountain, their Latin grammars balanced on their knees. The tutor remained on his feet, pacing back and forth before them, hands clasped in the small of his back, scarcely looking at his pupils as he gave each verbs to conjugate, nouns to decline. The children, with evident disinterest, answered as they could, their attentions clearly elsewhere.

But if the pupils did not display much interest in their tutor, there was another in the garden who did.

Hidden in the shadows of an outbuilding, a short way off, the boy watched. The gurgling of the fountain obscured most of the tutor's words at this distance, but the boy was scarcely interested in Latin grammar, at any rate. Instead, he was watching how the tutor moved. The boy had seen him engaged

in swordplay only days before, and now studied his movements to see if anything in the tutor's manner betrayed his
martial prowess. Before the demonstration he'd inadvertently
witnessed earlier in the week, the boy would never have taken
the man for anything but what he seemed—a somewhat dour
household retainer who affected severe, and one might even
say puritanical, dress. Now, the boy knew better. This was no
mere servant; this was a duellist.

The pupils were two brothers—three and four years older than
the boy's eleven years, respectively—and a sister—a few years his
junior. The boy had seen them on rare occasions, of course, having grown up only a short distance away, but more than a
hedgerow and a few hundred yards separated him from them. His
own father was a lecturer in antiquities at Christ Church, Oxford,
who raised three children of his own on meagre means, while the
pupils' father was a member of the gentry, with aspirations of
becoming a peer.

The boy had heard his father contend that Geoffrey Fawkes
made entirely too much of distant family relations to the Fourth
Duke of Marlborough—and that he was an insufferable boor to
boot. It was rumoured, at least around the boy's household, that
Fawkes had purchased his land and holdings with a fortune made
through illicit trade, though nothing was known for certain, and
Fawkes would doubtless have denied any such accusations, desperate to appear in all respects a proper gentleman. Reportedly,
Fawkes had gone recently to the College of Arms, and submitted
his application to the Earl Marshal for his own coat of arms. But
even the boy, at his age, knew that it would take more than letters patent to make Geoffrey Fawkes a gentleman, with or
without the king's seal.

The boy's mother, who with her phlegmatic Dutch temper tended not to speak ill of the neighbours—at least not within her
children's hearing—had once been so incensed by a remark of

Fawkes's when passing in the road that she had declared him nothing more than a churl, and never spoken of him again.

Fawkes's male offspring appeared to have inherited their character from him, as there was something undeniably churlish in their manner, and in the insouciant way in which they answered the tutor's questions. Their sister, for her part, may have drawn more on their mother, answering in a quiet but clear voice the questions put to her, but for all the boy knew she might in other circumstances be a terror.

The lesson was interrupted by the children's nurse appearing at the garden walk, calling the children inside for their midday meal. The pupils looked to the tutor eagerly and, when he excused them with a nod of his head, they carelessly threw their books aside and ran for the house, more a pack of hungry strays than the children of the manor's lord.

The tutor lingered, gathering up the pupils' things.

The boy saw his opportunity and took it. Marshalling his courage, he stepped out from the shadows of the outbuilding, and followed the flagstone-lined path through the garden to the fountain's edge. His heart pounded, thundering in his ears, and his hands trembled at his sides. The boy was by nature a retiring child, preferring to keep himself to himself, and was typically beset by nerves when addressing adults in even the most normal of circumstances. Now, he found himself scarcely able to set one foot in front of another.

The tutor continued to gather and arrange his pupils' papers and books, and did not look up, even when the boy came to a halt only a few short yards away. The boy raised a hand ineffectually and then dropped it back to his side. He opened his mouth to speak, then closed it when he found he couldn't remember any of his carefully rehearsed words.

Finally, the boy simply cleared his throat, a contrived and unconvincingly unnatural noise from one so young. It had the desired effect, though, as the tutor set his stack of books down on a stone bench, and turned to face the boy.

"Yes?" the tutor asked, a quizzical half-smile tugging up one corner of his mouth.

"E-excuse me, s-sir?" the boy managed, but just barely.

The tutor clasped his hands together behind his back and regarded the boy, his head inclined slightly to one side. "You have my undivided attention, young master." When the tutor spoke, there was a slight but unidentifiable accent to his words. "What is the matter?"

"I..." the boy began, uncertainly. "That is to say, I... Well, if you'll forgive me, I came to ask whether..." He stopped and swallowed hard. Steeling himself, he said in a rush, "Does the offer to instruct me in the art of the sword still stand?"

The tutor remained motionless and quiet for what seemed an eternity, the half-smile immobile on his lips. Finally, he blinked slowly and answered. "When last I made that offer, you showed little interest in accepting. Why now the change?"

The boy opened and closed his mouth again, and shuffled his feet. Then, as though it required all of his energy and attention to do so, he shrugged.

The tutor scowled and shook his head. "That's the sort of response I might expect from the gentry"—he cast a quick glance towards the house—"but I might have expected a scholar's son to have learned how to speak."

The boy felt a blush of shame rising in his cheeks, hearing in the tutor's words an echo of more accustomed scolding. How often had the boy's father taken him to task, saying his mumbling befitted a menial and not the member of an educated household?

"Well? Why do you now wish to learn the use of the sword?"

Rather than answering, the boy responded with a question of his own. "Sir?" The boy narrowed his eyes, thinking there was something familiar to the tutor's accent. "Are... are you French?"

The tutor's half-smile wavered momentarily, and the boy felt a thrill of fear at his back. It seemed all his parents had talked about, these last few weeks, was the news that the French had abolished the monarchy and established a republic. Revolutionaries terrified the boy, not least because he so often found himself agreeing with one or another of their tenets, which would place him in some peril were he ever to admit it out loud.

"No," the tutor finally answered, shaking his head. "I am not French, though I lived there for a time, and traces of that tongue may occasionally be heard in my words. I most recently was abroad in lands governed by King Frederick II of Prussia, but I can affirm that I was born within the shores of these British Isles, and consider myself a loyal subject of the British crown."

"Oh," the boy said simply, relieved.

"I have answered your question, young master. Now do me the courtesy of answering mine."

The boy composed his thoughts and, taking a deep breath, answered. "I wish to lead a life of adventure. I wish to explore. I want to go places no one has ever been, see things never seen. But I'll need to protect myself, I've decided. Who knows what dangers I might face?"

The tutor smiled, perhaps a little sadly. "Who, indeed?" He paused, and seemed to consider something for a moment. Then he sighed and nodded slowly. "So, not content to remain safely at home, you would range the world in search of excitement, at your side a yard of steel as surety. And to me you come seeking instruction in its use."

The boy stifled the urge to shrug. "Y-yes, sir."

Unclasping his hands, the tutor rubbed his chin, thoughtfully. "And are you prepared to dedicate yourself to the task?"

The boy nodded, eagerly.

"This is not a path to be trod lightly," the tutor continued. "If you step on, you must walk it until you reach the end. And the goal is not to be won lightly, but years will pass before you can play the prize."

"The prize, sir?"

The tutor's smile widened, fractionally, nearer full three-quarters now than half. "Surely you've read of old King Henry's Noble Science of Defence, in all your dusty manuals of fence?" When the boy's expression made clear that he hadn't, the tutor continued. "It was Henry VIII, of course. Not content with driving a schism between England and Rome, once he had established the Church of England and dissolved the monasteries, he set about creating a new school."

"You mean Christ Church?" the boy asked.

The tutor shook his head, smiling. "He established more than one, I'll admit, but that's not the one I mean. No, though it was peopled with 'scholars', 'provosts', and 'masters', this was a school of steel, not of letters. But it was not a school entered without careful consideration. It took a minimum of seven years before an incoming scholar could apply for the rank of provost, and a further seven before he could contend for the Master's Prize."

"Seven?" The boy's eyes widened. "And a further seven?"

The tutor chuckled. "And that seven years and seven was not ended without occasion. In playing the prize, as it was called, an applicant had to take on not only his own master, but all masters in the region, once each with six different weapons. The examination could last for days, and was performed upon a scaffold erected in the marketplace, where crowds gathered for hours on end to watch."

The boy was crestfallen. "Fourteen years?" he repeated. "Would it... does it really take fourteen years to learn the sword?"

The tutor laughed, clapping his hands together. "Young master, I've been studying the art my whole life—a longer time than a boy your age could imagine—and I am still learning."

"Very well," the boy said unenthusiastically, resigning himself to spending more years than he'd yet been alive in the effort. "If that is the cost of it…" He paused, and a worried expression flitted across his features. "But what is the cost?" he added eagerly. "What fee will you charge for the service?"

"My current employer sees to my present needs"—the tutor glanced to the manor house—"giving me a roof beneath which to sleep and my crust of bread for supper. So all I ask is that you devote yourself to the task. I think you'll find that will be cost enough."

The tutor reached down and picked up the stack of books and papers from the stone bench.

"Do you accept the terms?" he asked, tucking the books under his arm.

The boy thought for a moment, and then nodded, resolute.

"Then consider the lessons begun. And we'll begin with the proper salute. Or, in this case, the introduction. I don't believe on our last meeting we reached the exchange of names." The tutor stuck out his right hand. "My name is Giles Dulac."

The boy regarded the proffered hand, as though unsure how to respond, and only after a long hesitation reached out and clasped it with his own. "Hieronymus," he replied. "Hieronymus Bonaventure."

Chapter One
First Sighting & Engagement

IT WAS MIDDAY when the galleon was sighted, no more than ten miles windward of the frigate. At an unspoken signal from the captain, the first lieutenant ordered the sails hauled, heading into the wind as much as was advisable. The frigate, though less manoeuvrable than the galleon, was the swifter of the two and, if the wind held, promised to overtake her within hours. The crew, called to quarters at the first sighting, were anxious for the excitement, the last months of sailing having ground into numbing monotony, and they kept their stations around the decks and in the rigging in stoic silence. The wind was chilled beneath the bright sun overhead, carrying both the threat of rain and the hint of spices from within the galleon's hold, and darkening storm clouds boiled on the northern horizon.

As the two ships drew nearer together, the captain and the first lieutenant stood at the railing on the quarterdeck, spyglasses trained on the galleon.

"She's riding low in the water," the captain observed, eye to the lens, "her gunports barely kept dry. Think of the weight in silks, spices, and gold in her hold to drag her so low."

The first lieutenant, for his part, considered it just as likely that bad Spanish seamanship and an excess of ballast had left the other ship so heavy laden, but he kept his opinion to himself. The captain hadn't solicited dissenting views, or confirmation of his own deductions, and the first lieutenant had learned months before that the captain was not one to accept unsolicited advice; or solicited advice, in many cases, if it came to it.

The captain breathed a dramatic sigh, barrel chest expanding beneath his threadbare blue coat, and compacted the spyglass with a metallic snap.

"She's a pretty prize, and no doubt," he said, balling his left hand into a fist and pounding it against the railing in eager anticipation. "She'll do."

The treasure which the captain deduced would be found in the hold of the galleon, in his eyes, far outstripped any potential dangers the frigate might face in opposing such a manoeuvrable and well-armed ship. In private discussions, the first lieutenant had disagreed with these arithmetics, considering the risks too dear a price to pay, whatever the outcome. A man of duty to the bone, however, he wouldn't dream of voicing these concerns while on deck and in earshot of the crew.

"Well?" the captain demanded, an edge in the word.

The first lieutenant was startled from a brief reverie, but the image of men made red ruin by grapeshot lingered as he turned to address the captain. It seemed that after his final pronouncement on the suitability of the galleon, the captain had expected some response. The first lieutenant's silence had been taken as tacit criticism.

"Aye, sir," the first lieutenant hastened to say, nodding reluctantly. "As you say."

He watched as the captain grinned, revealing the chipped tooth that marred the left forefront of his smile. In the fleshy darkness revealed beyond the gap, the first lieutenant could see reflected only the grapeshot-ruined crewmen of his imagining. It was an apt image, he knew, the able seamen of the frigate gnawed to pulp by the appetites and fears of a captain who saw his best days behind him, and saw stretching out before him endless days of half-pay and wretched obscurity. The galleon, once captured, would ensure that the captain would see better days in the years to come, though purchased at a price.

The first lieutenant turned his attention back to the spyglass, and the galleon visible beyond. He counted the gunports along her hull, barely dry or not, and the carronades lining her deck.

Too dear a price, he told himself; too dear a price by half.

THE FRIGATE WAS nearly alongside the stern of the galleon, the latter with the wind on her beam, when the first shots were fired. Too far off and at too oblique an angle for the twelve-pounders on the frigate's port side to be effective, or yet for the larger guns on the starboard side of the galleon, a Spanish crewman took the opportunity to fire off a shot from his musket. While the ball plunked harmlessly into the sturdy hull of the frigate a few handspans below the quarterdeck railing, the brief barrage had the effect of setting the frigate's crew on their guard, anxious to begin.

The winds had picked up in the interim, still blowing from the north, but with increasing force as the storm approached. The captain had ordered the topsails reefed by two bands, diminishing the frigate's speed. As the galleon had been forced to do the same, however, the winds bearing down on her as much as on her pursuer, the difference was held in balance.

The waves beat against the hull of the frigate as the two ships pulled within range, the motion of rising up and plunging down again at every crest and trough forcing the crewmen to hold tight the railings and riggings. The second lieutenant on the gun deck drove his men hard, to ensure both that the guns were ready and in position at the captain's command, and that the flames in the match-tubs would still be alight when the moment came to fire, despite the spray blowing in through the open gunports.

Finally, the distance between the two ships closed, and the battle was joined.

The first volley poured forth from the frigate in a black cloud of acrid smoke that was whipped by the wind up into the faces, noses, and eyes of the crewmen on deck. Nearly half the thirteen twelve-pound guns on the port side had spoken, and when the wind had finally cleared the smoke from view, it could be seen that almost all of them had found their mark on the galleon. The second lieutenant had ordered his men to aim low on the galleon's hull, and the crashing sounds and pockmarked holes that appeared just above the waterline on the galleon's gun deck were testament to his marksmanship.

The galleon replied with as many of her larger guns as she could muster into position, twenty-four-pounders by the look and sound of them, but aimed high across the frigate's prow rather than at her hull, the first shots finding their way through the rigging and spars to splinter the mizzenmast less than eight feet above the deck. The remainder of the shots crashed through the railings, and crewmen, indiscriminately.

The first lieutenant, who reflexively gripped the hilt of his scabbarded sword, watched as the quartermaster's mate, unlucky enough to position himself in the path of twenty-four pounds of leaden destruction, dissipated from the shoulders up into a blood-coloured mist. The quartermaster, his attention diverted, shrugged with annoyance when the lifeless arm of his mate fell across his back, the headless form slumping to the deck. The mate had always been a clumsy oaf, and it would be after the battle, during the storm that followed, that the quartermaster would learn he hadn't simply tripped and staggered.

The first broadsides concluded, the captain barked orders for the quartermaster to steer the frigate in even closer. He wanted to capture the galleon, not sink her, and the second lieutenant's successful initial volley had increased the chances of losing his prize to the depths. They would sooner board her, and take the galleon by force of arms. The first lieutenant, the taste of smoke and blood already on his tongue, stepped quickly to the captain's side, a hand on his superior's elbow.

"At least let us fire the second volley, sir," the first lieutenant said, his words a harsh whisper. "The remaining guns are primed and ready to fire, and the rest will be so again in moments."

The captain scowled, his hunger for the gold driving him, but reluctantly he conceded it best the galleon was tenderized a bit further before the meal began.

"But instruct Mister Jeffries to fire higher, damn his eyes!" the captain shouted, chasing the first lieutenant from the quarterdeck and towards the hatch. "If he sinks that ship, he goes down after her!"

The first lieutenant nodded and leapt the railing to the waist of the ship to duck down the hatchway. Barrelling down the steps, he rushed to the second lieutenant's side and took hold of the junior officer's elbow.

"Have your men aim high, Mister Jeffries, but fire at will. The captain won't have her sunk, but by God cripple her."

A silent look passed between the two in an instant, and each knew the other man's thoughts. Though they might have had their occasional differences, neither wanted to end his career, or his life, in taking unnecessary risks, whether for personal gain or some distantly imagined national benefit. To sink a prize ship and live was better than to die needlessly on her decks in an attempted capture.

"Raise up, boys!" the second lieutenant shouted in response, his chin over his shoulder. "Aim across her decks. Fire!"

Clapping his junior on the shoulder, the first lieutenant bounded back up the steps to the open air. In the brief moments he'd been below decks, it seemed as though twilight had fallen. The sun had almost vanished from the skies, dark clouds roiling overhead. The winds were three times as fierce and strong as they'd been just minutes before, and the rain had begun to fall. The storm entered the fray.

THE HOURS OF the battle that followed were not ship against ship, but men against the elements, and the victor was neither the frigate nor her galleon prey, but the storm itself. It raged from the north, a seemingly endless tumult that lashed at both ships with wind, rain, and wave, driving them first apart, then further south.

The frigate, her mizzenmast gone and her mainmast shattered to splinters above the maintop, fared a little better than the galleon, so it seemed at least to the frigate's crew as long as the other ship was in sight. The sails of the frigate's foremast reefed in, and the gunports closed, they had only a few holes torn into her hull to contend with, which the carpenter and his mate set to repairing immediately. That the same shots which pockmarked the hull had also splintered the lumber and spars kept to repair and replace damaged masts was a concern the crew would keep until after the storm had passed.

The galleon, hull scored by the frigate's broadsides, sails billowed taut by the fierce winds and refusing to be reefed, was driven ahead of the storm at speed, her crew no doubt working feverishly at the pumps to keep her from filling up completely. Finally, the storm, the rains, and the waves seemed to swallow her up, and the frigate could see her no longer.

The captain stayed at the railing of the quarterdeck for long hours after the galleon disappeared from view. He claimed to be directing the efforts of the quartermaster at the helm, but in reality he waited in vain hope that his prize might again appear, and not have vanished forever beneath the waves. Like Odysseus, he'd have lashed himself to the mast if he could, but in the end the first lieutenant persuaded him to retreat below deck to rest, leaving the first and second lieutenants to marshal the crew in weathering the storm.

While the merely wounded were taken below to the sheltering orlop deck, the casualties had been dragged to the splinter of the mainmast. When the body of the quartermaster's mate, laid out lifeless on the deck along with the other fallen crewmen, was washed overboard by a high-mounting wave, the first lieutenant considered it justice of a sort. The crew had paid deposit on the captain's treasure with the lives and limbs of their fellows, and if the prize were lost it was only fitting that the price paid should follow it down.

The first lieutenant added the strength of his arms to those of the quartermaster in wrestling the helm in line, but the storm demanded that the ship be driven south, and nothing the men on board could do could gainsay it. The storm blew south, and the ship rode on ahead.

Chapter Two
The Ship & Her Crew

THE FRIGATE, WHICH now ran before the storm, battered and abused by wind and wave, was hardly the trim warship that had left Plymouth some eighteen months before, nor yet that which sailed from Bombay harbour the following autumn, newly dispatched on his majesty's service in the far reaches of the East Indies.

His Britannic Majesty's Ship, named the *Fortitude*, was a fifth-rate frigate, so classified due to the number of guns she carried. Thirty-two guns total, comprising twenty-six twelve-pounders, divided equally on the port and starboard sides of the gun deck, four six-pounders positioned on the quarterdeck, and two six-pounders on the forecastle. In addition she carried some half-dozen carronades not included in the count, distributed both fore and aft.

A three-masted vessel, of which only one mast had survived the skirmish intact, she was roughly 130 feet long on her gun deck and thirty-five feet wide, with her lowest gunports opening only seven feet above the waterline. Had she her full complement of men, water and provisions aboard, all three of which had been in short order since Plymouth, she would draw an average of seventeen feet, little enough that she could come in fairly near any coastal shelf, but still sufficient to demand careful soundings with the lead-line when approaching shore.

Her ship's complement was intended to number nearly 300 souls, officers, crew, and Marines together, but since taking on additional men in Bombay harbour some eight months before the total number was barely half that: 150 men, all told, including the captain, two lieutenants, three midshipmen, the ship's surgeon, the master, the quartermaster, the carpenter and a detachment of thirty Royal Marines, officers and privates included. The remainder were able seamen, most having been impressed into service, but a handful who'd volunteered for the position, eager to put down the Emperor Bonaparte and his allies.

Most of the men, and the Marines, and the better part of the officers, after a year and a half at sea and away from home, would in their more sullen moments admit to preferring any end to the hostilities, however unfavourable to the British crown, so long as they could return home, to dry land and their families. Most had never met a French native in their lives, nor a Spaniard, nor a Dutchman, and had only the most tenuous grasp of the politics that had set Europe ablaze, and pitted Britain against France for longer than any of them cared to recall. Now, in the spring of 1808, far from home or news from home, many felt themselves prisoners of the sea, and considered the storms that bashed and battered the ship's hull merely mistreatment at the hands of their jailer.

The first lieutenant, however, was not among them, neither those who longed for home, nor those who considered themselves helpless victims of fate and state. He had volunteered for service in His Majesty's Navy, though it had broken his father's heart, and had done so driven by twin forces, pushing him from land and pulling him towards the sea: Duty, and Boredom. Bored on land, and with the prospect of the academic life that his father had planned for him, he wanted to seek adventure. Duty-bound to serve his king and country, he chose to seek that adventure in the defence of his nation, helping to secure naval superiority during the current crisis. It was, in the end, the only natural course for him to follow.

Lieutenant Hieronymus Bonaventure had from childhood listened to his mother tell stories about her own father, her accented and lyrical voice speaking in hushed whispers against the possibility that her husband might overhear. The young Hieronymus had marvelled at the idea of sailing to the opposite side of the world, where trees grew upside down and rain fell up, and where men in ornate robes carried grand great swords in their sashes. Compounded with these were the tales his own father had pressed upon him, stories of Greek and Roman adventurers and heroes, sailing to the edges of the world and finding the islands of the dead and of dreams, fighting monsters born of dragon's teeth and bearding one-eyed giants in their own lairs.

It was hardly any wonder that, as soon as he'd reached his majority, and said final farewells to his siblings, Bonaventure had left his studies at Oxford on the spot and marched to the harbour to present himself for duty as a midshipman. His last few coins going to purchase his uniform and provisions, he'd been offered a berth on a gunship, and left the shore behind.

Now, some years later, striving against the odds to maintain control of the storm-wracked frigate on the waves, Bonaventure had only one complaint to offer as regarding his occupation. He was bored.

Chapter Three
Below Decks

HIERONYMUS BONAVENTURE STAMPED below decks, water sluicing off the sleeves of his greatcoat. Working his way aft, he paused to strip off his coat and hang it on a peg, and running long fingers through his doused brown hair opened the door to the gunroom.

The second lieutenant, William Jeffries, and Ned Symmes, a midshipman, were seated on benches in the flickering, dim light of the lantern swinging overhead, the bones of the evening meal sliding back and forth on the pitted table before them. On Bonaventure's entrance, a sardonic grin split the second lieutenant's face, and he nudged the midshipman in the ribs, indicating their superior.

"If it isn't our own 'Hero'," Jeffries began, teeth glinting white in the lantern light, "returned from his battles with Poseidon himself. How goes the war?"

Stripping off his jacket, and dropping it to the table, Bonaventure slid onto the bench opposite the other two, a customary scowl on his face.

"Need I remind you, Will," he answered, "that I am your superior officer, with a mandate to report any insubordination to the captain, and to the Admiralty itself should the need arise?"

Jeffries started to frame his usual response, his grin not waning a fraction, but Bonaventure silenced him with a wave of his hand.

"That said, I'll restate my only standing order," Bonaventure continued, in mock-wearied tones. "You may address me, in moments of equal fellowship such as these, as 'Hieronymus', or as 'Mister Bonaventure', should you be of a more formal mind, or as 'sir' in an absolute pinch, but if you persist in calling me by that detestable diminutive I'll persuade the captain to have you called before the mast, and attend to the flogging duties personally."

"I'm afraid I'm experiencing another of my intermittent bouts of partial deafness, 'Bonnie', and didn't quite get all of that," Jeffries answered. "How about you, Ned? Did you follow that quite lengthy discourse?"

The midshipman smiled sheepishly and nodded.

"Yes, Mister Jeffries, sir," he said, the timidity he'd yet to lose still tainting his voice, "I did."

"Then at least this ship can count one respectable officer among its complement," Bonaventure added, dragging over an opened bottle of wine and splashing a liberal amount into his mug. Before drinking, he poured three parts brackish water over the one part wine, and took a long pull with a grimace. The bottle was one of their last, and had been nursed along with water for months, the dilution increasing with each passing week.

"Besides your noble self, of course," Jeffries said, smiling still.

Bonaventure reached up two fingers and touched the brim of an imagined bicorn hat in mock salute.

"How sails the ship?" Symmes asked, ending the momentary banter.

"Still like storm-tossed driftwood," Bonaventure answered. "Before your fellow midshipman relieved me as officer of the

watch, I spent another four hours helpless in the face of the elements. The jury-rigged mast we've contrived in place of the main
is holding up well enough, considering the circumstances, but the
winds and waves, even after nearly a week, are sufficient to best
our most directed efforts. We are like a man climbing a hill by
taking a step back for every two steps up. We make headway, but
we're fighting every inch of the way."

"And the captain?" Symmes continued. "I haven't seen him..."
He paused, eyes down-turned, as though he'd overstepped his
bounds. "That is, he's not been—"

"He's not been very much in evidence, Ned is trying to say,"
Jeffries finished, interrupting. "He's been quite busy entertaining
dear Doctor Beauregard." He jerked a thumb towards the captain's cabin above. "Though I should say Beauregard is more
likely entertained by the captain's rum than with the captain's
recent black moods."

Bonaventure scowled, his eyes flashing uncontrollably to the
braces and planking above that separated the three officers from
their master and commander. Such talk was well enough when
taken in the proper spirits, but to a less charitable listener could
be construed as mutinous.

"I'm sure our captain, while having his own concerns at the
moment," Bonaventure answered, "is as aware of our present circumstances as any three of us combined. Remember, gentlemen,
this ship, and the conduct of her crew, is a reflection of our captain and his leadership, and I for one would not relish the thought
of exchanging places with him."

"Here here," young Symmes offered, hoping to mend any
breach of protocol he might inadvertently have made.

"Well said, our Hero," Jeffries answered. "A consummate
politician to the last. Parliament lost hope for a brighter future
when you deigned to join His Majesty's Navy, I should think." He
paused, and then added, "But, in the interests of fairness, it must

be admitted that, were you and he to exchange positions, you would likely not find yourself here at the same impasse. Is that not the case?"

"What?" Bonaventure said. "Have I some preternatural control over the elements of which I am unaware? Could I, if in command, stand upon the ship's deck and shout the winds to stillness, or the waves to calm?"

"No," Jeffries answered, through a smile with no trace of humour, "but you would likely not have taken off against the galleon in the first place, and found yourself, your ship and your crew battered in the distant mid-Pacific reaches."

Bonaventure's scowl deepened momentarily, lines etched in his face, but in an instant his expression softened, and he nodded reluctantly.

"Possibly," he admitted, hesitantly. "But possibly not," he hastened to add. "Our mandate, as I have it from the captain himself, was to sail from Port Jackson in New South Wales, north past Timor into Dutch-held waters, and to harass and impede traffic and commerce amongst the French allies to the extent that such action is achievable and circumspect."

"Ned," Jeffries interjected, "mark you how our own first lieutenant can speak the Admiralty's own tongue? Why, I'd believe I'd seen an official dispatch come to life."

Bonaventure ignored the jibe, friendly or not. He and the second lieutenant had served some time together, and Bonaventure had learned it best not to take the offered bait in certain instances. Tempers wore thin on the open seas, the endless vistas and cramped confined spaces having the effect of splintering a man's thoughts, leading him to unsavoury conclusions. Bonaventure saw his bosom companion Jeffries teetering on the edge of such a precipice, and had no desire to push him over into it.

"As I've said," Bonaventure continued, "our captain's orders were to harass and impede traffic and commerce, and he made the considered judgement that preventing the annual shipment of goods from Manila in the Philippines to Mexico was within that mandate."

"And would mean a considerable large prize as well," Symmes chimed in.

"Exactly so," Bonaventure added, unenthusiastic.

"And the fact that Manila does not fall within the confines of nor the jurisdiction of the East Indian station," Jeffries pressed, his temper beginning to flare, "and that the middle of the twice-cursed Pacific Ocean is nowhere near Dutch-held waters, did not enter into these calculations at all?"

"I'll remind you, *Mister* Jeffries," Bonaventure replied in a harsh whisper, "that you have sworn an oath to obey any order given you, whether you understand the reasoning of it or not. And, further, that in addition to whatever other cargo it might carry, a ship this size holds in its hull any number of ears, and that the bulkheads dividing us from the remainder of the crew or them from us are not quite so thick as one might sometimes hope."

Jeffries opened his mouth as though to reply, but thinking better of it, swallowed any answer unsaid. His own gaze flitting for an instant overhead, and then to the cabin door, which led to the ship beyond, he nodded slowly, his manner calming.

"I'm sorry, Hieronymus," he said finally, his tone softer. "I... I've just been fatigued, of late."

Symmes, eager to see the brief confrontation ended, nodded eagerly and added, "As have I. I've slept most fitfully the last week, if at all."

Bonaventure smiled slightly, and the atmosphere in the room relaxed.

"You both can claim fatigue if you like," he answered. "As for me, I'd give anything for this blasted rain to stop, and for something, anything of interest to befall us." He paused, and then added, "Short of the ship sinking, naturally, and all of us drifting down to our watery graves."

The other two gave answering smiles in return, and passed the diluted wine from hand to hand. They talked well into the night, the better part of a watch, keeping the darkness and their demons and fears at bay with the light of the swinging lantern and their fellowship. They'd sleep better that night, if only a little, some small few of those demons exorcized.

Chapter Four

All Hands

THE MORNING AFTER the storm finally broke, the winds having died down and the seas very nearly becalmed, Captain Northrop Ross made an unaccustomed appearance above decks with the ship's surgeon, Doctor Eugene Beauregard, in tow. Unaccustomed of late, in any event, since the captain's retreat below decks following the loss of the Manila galleon. For more than a week, Captain Ross had spent his days shut away in his cabin, again accompanied by the dutiful Doctor Beauregard, the former appearing beyond the bulkhead infrequently at best, the latter staggering out to the head whenever generous drams of the captain's brandy had run their course.

It was just past eight bells when the captain appeared on deck, Lieutenant Bonaventure serving as officer of the watch. Bonaventure, after a brief moment of awkward surprised silence, relinquished the windward half of the quarterdeck to the captain, and moved to stand by the master's mate on the leeward side of the helm. Doctor Beauregard, for his part, listing only slightly more noticeably than on his best days, stood one pace beside and behind the captain, hands held together tightly in the small of his back.

"Mister Bonaventure," the captain began, finally speaking after a few long moments spent surveying the decks and the makeshift spar mast. "Kindly call all the men on deck, if you please."

"Aye, sir," Bonaventure answered, nodding his head a fraction. He took three long strides to the deck's railing, leaned over and called down to the nearest midshipman, "All hands on deck, Mister Symmes."

Young Ned nodded eagerly, touching three fingers to the brim of his hat, and hurried to instruct the quartermaster to blow the order on his silver pipe. The quartermaster, Jacob Macallister, taking his position near the bones of the mainmast, performed his duties admirably, even accounting for the discord introduced by his newly appointed mate's inexperience with the tuning of his own pipe. The new quartermaster's mate was every inch the able seaman, but he would have some considerable distance to cover before he adequately filled the shoes of his departed predecessor.

There were close to three minutes of bustle and confusion before all the men were on deck, those still convalescing below decks the only ones excused. Three minutes was over two minutes worse than the crew's best time, but their officers had been lax in their drills since the storm began, a fact that left Lieutenant Bonaventure gritting his teeth in self-recrimination. In the time that Bonaventure had served with Captain Ross aboard the *Fortitude*, the captain had not been above calling his officers to task for keeping too loose a rein on the hands, but on those rare occasions the captain had rarely resorted to anything more severe than a tongue lashing. After the stress of recent days, however, Bonaventure was not sure to what lengths the captain might go, were he stirred to wrath. In addition, the thought that he might, on the one occasion when he was left in virtual command of the ship, have inadvertently let the men go slack did little to lighten Bonaventure's mood.

"Men," the captain began when the crew had assembled, standing ramrod straight at the railing's edge, looking out over the hands like a judge overlooking a jury, or a minister over his congregation. "I want first to recognize your valiant efforts during the recent troubles, and to assure each of you that your contributions have not gone unnoticed. It was a battle hard fought and won, and though in the mouth of victory our reward might have eluded us, Poseidon himself taking the prize for his own, let it not be said as a result that our victory was one whit less complete." The captain paused for a moment, allowing a ragged cheer rising from the men to fill the brief intermission.

"The task before us now," he continued, "is no less arduous, and no less the valiant struggle. Our dear ship, our own home upon the waves, has been hard hit by shot and storm, and demands repair. As our own Doctor Beauregard might have it, the patient is in need of rest, and of recuperation." There was polite laughter at this from the ship's surgeon, followed by a meagre ripple of courteous amusement from the officers and a few of the crew. "The onus is upon us, then, to find a suitable hospital bed upon which our patient might convalesce." Again, polite laughter; less forthcoming than before.

"After a thorough study of all extant charts and maps of this region of the ocean Pacific, I have determined there is no suitable landing to be found anywhere within two weeks' sail, even with the ship at peak performance. In her depressed state, I daresay we would be some months at sea without sight of land, and in that time our reserves of food and water would run out." The crew shuffled nervously, looking from one to another. Bonaventure, a pace from the captain's elbow, had to stifle the urge to shuffle a bit nervously himself. If the captain's goal were to invigorate the spirit of the men with enthusiasm, he would do well to reconsider his oratorical approach.

"But take heart, men," the captain went on. "There are, to the south and west of us now, huge stretches of ocean never yet charted, never yet sailed by white men. It is my hope... no, my fervent belief, that if we sail into this *mare incognita* we will find precisely the sort of landing site for which we are looking, and will get the old girl once again shipshape and on course for more familiar waters." The captain paused, and balling his right hand into a fist pounded it into the outstretched palm of the left, a motion familiar to his officers. "Well, men? What say you?"

Another cheer erupted from the men, less restrained and more sincere than the last. The captain smiled, and turned to the first lieutenant.

"Dismiss the men, if you please, Mister Bonaventure." With that, the captain made for the hatchway below, Doctor Beauregard following in his train, and returned to his cabin below decks.

Bonaventure passed the orders onto Mister Symmes, who passed them on to Macallister, who piped them to the crew. When the men had dispersed, chatting excitably with each other and in high spirits, the second lieutenant slipped to Bonaventure's side, leaning in close.

"Where exactly are we sailing?" Jeffries asked in a whisper, his brows knit tight.

"Oh, didn't you hear?" Bonaventure answered, feigning an indifference he hardly felt, his expression carefully composed. "*Mare incognita*. The unknown sea."

Chapter Five
Lessons

DESPITE THE HEADY mix of excitement and trepidation that prevailed on board after the announcement that they were to be sailing into uncharted waters, naval standards dictated that the daily life of the ship continue unabated. As a result Lieutenant Bonaventure found himself below deck in the gunroom that afternoon, wrestling for the attention of the three midshipmen.

It was ironic, though hardly amusing, that Bonaventure should find himself in the role of schoolmaster, should find himself thrust into the very position in flight from which he originally went to sea. He was sure that his father, if he knew, would find it a kind of poetic justice, an example of *hubris* in the classical sense, proof that one cannot escape one's destined fate, and that in the end the skeins knit for our lives will weave true, no matter how much we might try to change the warp and woof.

His father would also consider it just, Bonaventure was sure, that he would face three so unwilling students, on this of all days. Students not unlike those Bonaventure himself had known at school, who on the last day before the Christmas holidays could scarcely be contained in their seats. The midshipmen, Symmes,

Horrocks and Daniels, seemed each a pent-up torrent of energy, eager to be anywhere but in the dusty confines of the gunroom studying their lieutenant's exams.

Bonaventure, for his part, tended to agree with them, being despite his anxieties more willing to be up on deck gazing on unknown waters than down in the bowels of the ship consulting charts and texts. As a commissioned officer in His Majesty's Navy, however, he was bound to do his duty, and one of those duties was to prepare his junior officers for their futures at sea. This preparation included familiarizing them with the rudiments of seamanship, navigation, and command, in the hopes that one day they might pass muster by examination at the hands of the Admiralty, and be promoted in the ranks accordingly. So, Christmas holidays or seas of unknown waters be damned, they would stay below and study.

"Now then, Mister Horrocks," Bonaventure continued, "the next question is to you." He paused briefly, consulting the text of *The Practical Navigator* from which the examination would be culled. "Let us say that you have been sent down into the hold to retrieve a topsail. How do you know, there in the dark, a mainsail from a foresail, or a main topsail from a fore topsail?"

The midshipman, Horrocks, shifted uneasily on the bench, his face screwed tight in concentration. A valuable member of the crew, able to perform tasks well when given neatly defined boundaries in which to act, in Bonaventure's view he lacked a certain inventiveness necessary to a successful officer.

"Erm, that is," Horrocks began, glancing from the planks above to the bulkhead before him as though to draw inspiration from the wood's grain. "I suppose I would... that is—"

"I believe I know," cut in the excitable Daniels, the midshipman to Horrocks's left. He sat with his back straight and his shoulders back, as though expecting an admiral's inspection at any moment. In his relatively brief experience with the man,

Bonaventure had found him to have an almost uncanny ability to remember facts and figures, and an almost complete lack of capacity to put any of that information to practical use. The man was little more than a parrot, remembering sounds and aping them back, with no comprehension of their meaning.

"I'm sure you do, Mister Daniels," Bonaventure replied. "Well, Horrocks? Any last moment revelations? Very well, then, Mister Daniels," Bonaventure said, unable to prevent all traces of wearied reluctance from his voice, "if you could enlighten us?"

"If it has three bowline cringles it is a mainsail, and if it has but two it is a foresail," Daniels began, for all the world like he was reading the text from memory. Bonaventure, who knew the answer himself from practical experience, could not help himself opening the book to the relevant passage, and marvelling as he read silently along with the junior officer's letter-perfect recitation. "If it is marled abaft the foot rope it is a mainsail, and if before it is a foresail. If a main topsail it has four bowline cringles, and if a fore topsail it has but three. All topsails are marled to the rope," he concluded, "because the foot rope is served."

Bonaventure nodded wearily, closing the book on his thumb.

"Exactly so," he admitted, though he knew that if he were to send Daniels that very instant to fetch such a sail, in light or dark, he'd as likely come back with a splintered spar as the correct bit of cloth.

Bonaventure smacked the closed book against his thigh, twice, and for a brief moment gnawed at his lower lip. It was an accustomed action when restlessness threatened to overtake him, and by his count he still had better than an hour to go before the studies might be dismissed.

"Mister Symmes," he finally said, turning to the third midshipman, "let's put aside the questions of our text for a moment, and turn our attentions to our recent shipboard activities. Now, in the course of the lieutenant's examination, you might likely be posed a hypothetical identical in every particular to our encounter with the northern storm this week past, so it seems suitable to pose a question to you regarding just such a circumstance. Let us say that you are, as we were, chasing from the wind, and find that your main topmast is carried away, either by shot or gale-force wind. How would you then proceed?"

Symmes looked thoughtful for a long moment, composing his answer.

"Well, sir," he began slowly, "I would first haul up the mainsail..." He paused, and Bonaventure nodded. "Then I'd send up crewmen to the top with a rope, to grab hold of that part of the mast hanging down, then cut the lanyards of the main topmast shrouds, and..." He paused, his eyes focused on the middle distance.

It seemed to Bonaventure that the young officer, though he appeared to know the correct answer, had become preoccupied with some other thoughts, thoughts that overtook him and drove the prepared answer from his mind.

"Well, Mister Symmes," Bonaventure finally prompted. "Go ahead."

"Your pardon, sir," Symmes answered, shaking his head to dispel the reverie, "but I wonder if I might ask a question before continuing." He paused, then hastened to add, "One not directly related to my answer, of course."

Bonaventure set the book down on the table in front of him, and crossed his arms over his chest.

"I don't see why not," he answered. "Go ahead."

Symmes nodded, darting a glance sidelong to his fellow midshipmen at the bench, and then with eyes downcast continued. "Well, sir, I suppose you could say that I'm... curious about these seas we sail. That storm we suffered the week past, the one you were mentioning..."

"I remember," Bonaventure answered kindly.

"Well, sir, I haven't been long at sea, just these last eighteen months, and I suppose I haven't seen a fraction of the things as have you and the captain, but sir, I've never even heard of a storm quite so vicious as that. You'll forgive me saying such foolishness, sir, but I could swear that the sea herself had risen up from her bed and sworn to drag us down into her embrace. It was as though wind, rain and wave had come after us with intent, perhaps blaming us for some transgression of which we're all unaware."

Daniels, at Symmes's elbow, snickered behind his hand, but Bonaventure silenced him with a glance.

"I'm sorry, Mister Symmes," Bonaventure said, "but I'm afraid I haven't yet heard a question."

Symmes looked up from under his sandy brows at Bonaventure and nodded his embarrassment.

"Sorry, sir," he answered. "I guess my question is, of the seas you've sailed, which is... which is the worst, sir?"

"What you mean to ask, I gather," Bonaventure replied, "is whether *this* is the most quarrelsome water upon which I've sailed."

Symmes nodded in agreement.

"Well," Bonaventure said, smiling slowly, "I'm afraid that I can't answer on the grounds that I reject the validity of the question."

The three midshipmen looked at him blankly for long seconds.

"What I propose, gentlemen, is that there is no such thing as discrete 'seas', and that while you might compare conditions in one region as opposed to another, that taken as a whole the attempt to contrast one ocean against another is a fool's bet."

Still the blank stare from the midshipmen, growing even blanker.

"Allow me to illustrate my point." Bonaventure reached to his throat, unfastened the top three buttons of his shirt, and drew out a small round pendant on a woven necklace. The pendant was spherical, just over an inch in diameter, and covered in sharkskin dyed a deep blue. The sphere was bisected by a brass equator, at one point of which was positioned a sickle-shaped latch, and opposite it delicate brass hinges.

Bonaventure held the pendant up for their brief inspection, and then with a deft manoeuvre opened the latch and swung open the sphere. Revealed within was an ivory ball, the exposed portion of which was covered in engraved and stained representations of the Earth's continents. Carefully tipping the open sphere to one side, Bonaventure neatly caught the falling globe in his outstretched palm, and held it up before the confused gaze of the midshipmen for their inspection.

"Behold," he said, "our watery home."

The midshipmen leaned in closer, each nodding absently that the globe in question did seem a fair representation of their planetary abode.

"This, my fine gentlemen," Bonaventure continued, "was a gift to me from my dear departed mother. Her father, my maternal grandfather, had been a cartographer while still living, employed by Dutch merchants to chart the courses to far distant Japan. My mother, as a result, grew to be something of an amateur cartographer herself, and instilled in me a love of maps and their makings. This diminutive globe, manufactured by the London firm of James Newton, is said to be the smallest of its kind, commissioned especially by my mother that I might be able to carry it with me always." He paused, smiling, and shook his head. "You'll have to forgive me, gentlemen, but I appear very nearly to have lost the thread. The point I was making concerned the world itself, and not merely its representations in miniature.

"Regard the Earth," he continued, reaching out with his free hand and rolling the globe back and forth on his outstretched palm. "Though our world is constant and unchanging, our perception of it is perhaps more malleable than any of us might care to admit. It's barely four decades since the inestimable Captain Cook proved for once and all that the southern continent, supposed by his predecessors necessary to counterbalance the weight of the five continental cousins to the north, did not exist. Up until that moment, however, any map or globe you might have been able to find would have displayed a vast *Terra Australis Incognita* filling every empty nook and cranny of the world's southern regions. Now, our ignorance dispelled, see what we find."

Bonaventure picked up the globe between finger and thumb, angling the sphere towards the midshipmen, the South Pole presented. The midshipmen sat in confused silence, eyes on their first lieutenant.

"Well," he asked again. "What do we find?"

Symmes, recovering himself partially, looked at the proffered globe, and answered, "Water?"

"Precisely," Bonaventure answered. "Water. No massive unknown continent, not even hidden archipelagos of islands, just water. And on this hemisphere, dividing the old world from the new?" He turned the globe a quarter turn to the north, and held it before Horrocks's nose.

"Water?" Horrocks answered uncertainly.

"Exactly." Bonaventure turned the globe a half-revolution along its equator, and moved to stand before Daniels. "And on this, dividing the lands of the Americas from Japan and the lands beyond, dividing East Indies and West?"

"Water," Daniels replied, with assumed assurance.

"Yes, water," Bonaventure said. "Now tell me, gentlemen, to which degree should I turn this globe to reveal the point at which this water is divided from this, or that from that?" A chorus of silent and blank stares greeted him. "Perhaps the question is unfair, as I believe there is no answer. Turn the globe however you will, you find that the waters continue in an unbroken band from one pole to the other, encircling both hemispheres. There is, I put to you, but one ocean, one great world ocean, around which the lands we know are arranged like a necklace of stone and tree. A true *orbis terrarum*, the circle of lands of which the ancients spoke, and which we are just now rediscovering to be the truth."

"Dear God no," came a voice from behind, "he's not on about this again, is he?"

Bonaventure turned, his evangelistic zeal still burning in his eyes, to find Lieutenant Jeffries leaning against the bulkhead at the entrance to the cabin.

"His never-ending crusade," Jeffries continued, waving a hand merrily, "to convince all junior officers of His Majesty's Navy that the term 'Seven Seas' is semantically incorrect, and that the notion of one ocean versus another is simply a conspiracy of cartographers."

Bonaventure glowered good-naturedly. Reluctantly, he returned the globe to its housing, the pendant again hidden beneath his shirt-front.

"Something like that," he allowed. "It doesn't hurt, Mister Jeffries, to expand one's conceptions from time to time."

"Of that I'm sure," Jeffries jibed, a smirk on his face. "In that case, I beg a moment of your time to expand another of your conceptions. The captain sends his compliments, and requests that you join him in his cabin. He wants an accounting of the last week's logbook from you."

Bonaventure sighed, and turned to the midshipmen seated around the table.

"We'll continue this tomorrow, gentlemen," he said. "You are dismissed to return to your duties."

Bonaventure moved past Jeffries in the doorway, the latter pulling a comical face as he went through. When he had gone, Jeffries turned to the midshipmen himself.

"Don't worry too much about all that," he said, a kind older brother taking pity on harried siblings. "I can without a doubt guarantee that none of that will be on the lieutenant's exam."

The midshipmen, as one, breathed a heavy sigh of relief, and trooped from the room.

Chapter Six
A Pleasant Day

THE WEEKS ROLLED slowly by, the crippled ship inching her way south and west into the unknown. The weather was with them, and the wind held, but each morning greeted the crew with an endless expanse of silver sky above and blue sea below, and each evening said its farewell in the same hues. No brown or greens disturbed the composition of the view; the seamless horizon remained unbroken by land.

Each day hands were sent to the highest perch on the foremast, to spend all the hours of daylight scanning the far horizon, but except for the occasional cloud formation misreported as misty mountaintop their efforts proved fruitless. Still the captain and his officers spurred the crew on, all idle hands turned to drills, swabbing duties, or the general maintenance and upkeep of the still-battered ship.

On the fortieth day of keeping to their south-western course, a weary voice cried down from the cap atop the foremast. The call was that land had been sighted, though the disaffected tones of the crewman indicated that he doubted the evidence of his own eyes after so many days at the task. The speed with which the officers and other hands responded to the news suggested that they, too, feared another in an endless series of climatic decoys, the region appearing rife with mountain-seeming clouds.

"So, Will?" Bonaventure said beneath his breath, retrieving his spyglass and moving to the forecastle railing. "What do you think today, hmm? Cumulus or stratus?"

"I'd sooner reply evergreen or deciduous, Hero," Jeffries answered, "if it's all the same to you."

Bonaventure scowled, more from reflex than annoyance, and bringing the glass to his eye trained it in the direction indicated by the crewman aloft.

"Damn me," he spat, his voice a harsh whisper. "Damn me!" he added, more forcefully. He lowered the spyglass for an instant, as though he might better see the far horizon with his naked gaze, and then returned the glass to his eye, gnawing his lower lip in anticipation.

Jeffries lounged against the railing, his attention on a shoal of fish coursing along in the wake of the ship's prow. Snapping the spyglass shut, Bonaventure tapped the metal tube sharply against the junior officer's knuckles, demanding his attention with a smile.

"It looks like the answer is deciduous," Bonaventure said, "though in these climes it's sometimes hard to tell."

Jeffries goggled at him for a moment, confused, then unceremoniously snatched the glass from his superior's grasp. Turning his attention to the horizon, he scanned left and right through the lenses, finally stopping at a point a few degrees to port.

"I'll be a rum-soaked lubber," Jeffries breathed.

"That you will," Bonaventure answered with a smile. "Come on, we must tell the captain."

The two officers, excited beyond measure, scampered in their childish glee like powder monkeys aft to the quarterdeck, composure and propriety forgotten at first sight of land. When the news had been relayed, Captain Ross seemed almost to crack in two, the carefully composed demeanour he'd worn since his reappearance weeks before melting like ice on a summer's day. Bonaventure almost believed he saw tears well in the captain's eyes, though he'd never mention it to his shipmates.

Little more speed could be coaxed from wind and sail, but the crew marshalled their strengths to wheedle every additional knot possible. At the best estimates of the officers, they had perhaps a few hours until landfall, until they could drop anchor and take the boats ashore. The prospect of dry sand and firm ground upon which to walk was a tempting prize for them all, more valuable now than all the gold in all the galleons at sea.

Some hours still distant from the island, which now seemed an arcadia fringed with greenery, its purple mountain peaks haloed in downy clouds, another cry came down from atop the foremast, this time of a different sort.

Bonaventure and Jeffries, returned to their accustomed spot on the forecastle railing, looked at each other with confusion.

"Did he say that he spied a boat?" Jeffries asked, brow furrowed.

Bonaventure nodded absently, and then cupping his hands called up to the crewman aloft.

"Where away?" he shouted.

The crewman, by signals, indicated a point some few degrees to the starboard of their present course, nearer the *Fortitude* than their island destination.

Bonaventure again trained his spyglass on the distance, though this time with an unaccountable feeling of sinking within him rather than the excitement he'd known just a few hours before. He'd come to recognize his body's own reactions, and to use them as a barometer of his situation when rational means failed him. The sensation he currently felt, in times past, had been a sign of foreboding, an indicator of dark clouds on the horizon.

"It's a boat, and no doubt," Bonaventure said aloud, more for his own benefit than for Jeffries's. If the second lieutenant had not lost his own spyglass overboard during a brief battle in the Indian Ocean the year before, he wouldn't be forced to rely on his superiors for their observations. "Approaching the island from the south."

"Natives?" Jeffries asked, hanging by Bonaventure's elbow.

"No," Bonaventure added, his hands gripping white-knuckled on the spyglass's housing. "Not unless the natives of these regions dye their skins white and go sailing in Spanish fore-and-aft launches."

"Well, then," Jeffries answered, mirthlessly. "And it was promising to be such a pleasant day."

Chapter Seven
Code of Conduct

"YOUR ORDERS, CAPTAIN?" Bonaventure stood at Captain Ross's side, his hands gripping the quarterdeck railing. The captain, peering through his spyglass first at the sighted land on the horizon, then at the Spanish launch, then back again, mouthed wordlessly, his brow furrowed.

Bonaventure caught his lower lip between his teeth to stifle any further questions, his superior's silence fanning the fires of impatience and anxiety that already burned within him. Resisting the urge to pace back and forth, he gripped tighter the railing.

"Captain?" he finally asked, louder than he'd intended, unable to refrain himself any longer. "Your orders?"

Ross lowered the spyglass to his side, and Bonaventure saw at last the expression on his captain's face. Wide-eyed, nearly trembling with barely controlled fury, Captain Ross was in the grips of what seemed a maddening bloodlust, his ire directed at the meagre boat of the Spaniards. Bonaventure half expected the captain to order the gunports opened, and a broadside fired against the helpless craft. That the Spanish boat could now be seen to be sailing under a white flag of truce was, Bonaventure was sure, the only thing that stayed the captain's hand.

"Mister Bonaventure," the captain seethed through clenched teeth, never taking his eyes off the boat in the distance, "we are officers of His Majesty's Royal Navy. No matter our personal feelings, nor whatever just cause we may have to act, we are bound to follow certain codes of conduct while in the service of the Crown."

"Of course, sir," Bonaventure answered, uneasily. The captain was speaking as much to himself as to his junior officer, the first lieutenant knew, and was surely in no mood for debate.

"That being the case," the captain continued, "we have no choice but to parley with the Spanish dogs, offer whatever succour we are able, and only then proceed on to the completion of our appointed tasks." He paused, and added in an angry whisper, "May God Himself damn us."

"Aye, sir," Bonaventure replied. With no further comment from his captain, he gratefully turned away and stepped towards the helm, where Jeffries waited with the quartermaster for their orders.

"Make for the launch, Mister Macallister," Bonaventure instructed the quartermaster, "best possible speed. She looks to have been on our own course, headed towards that island, but having spotted us came about."

"And now just sits there, idle," Jeffries observed. "Hatching some plot, do you suppose?"

"She seems more like someone who's run a long distance and flagged before reaching their goal," Bonaventure answered. "I've seen only one man on her decks so far, as best as I can reckon, and he's done little more than lean against her mast, looking back towards us. It could be that, having come so near their island destination, and seeing in us a possible alternative goal, they've opted instead to stop halfway between and consider their options."

"Dago bastards," the quartermaster spat, "ya can't trust 'em." Bonaventure answered him with a cocked eyebrow, and the quartermaster hastened to add, apologetically, "Beggin' your pardon, sir."

"Well, Macallister," Jeffries cut in, "there's at least one amongst the officers who might well agree with you." He inclined his head towards the windward side of the deck, where the captain stood silent, his only motion the trembling of white-knuckled fists at his sides.

"That's enough, gentlemen," Bonaventure answered, cutting off any further discussion with a curt nod. "Mister Macallister, you have your orders."

"Aye, sir," the quartermaster answered, eyes downcast.

"Mister Jeffries," Bonaventure continued, turning to the second lieutenant, "with the exception of something so unforeseen as our ship's sudden sinking into the briny depths, we are in short order to have some level of diplomatic discourse with our enemies, and following on closely are to make landfall on what may well be an inhabited and previously unvisited island. In both of these cases our rules of conduct are quite clear."

"Sir?" Jeffries answered, confused.

"Your appearance, Mister Jeffries," the first lieutenant explained with a slight smile. He indicated the junior officer's threadbare breeches and patched and re-patched jacket. "You look as though you'd be more at home in the bowels of a coal-ship's hold than on the deck of one of His Britannic Majesty's men-of-war."

The second lieutenant replied with a smile of his own. "Well, then, sir," he answered, "you hardly look the Lord High Admiral yourself." He indicated the missing buttons on Bonaventure's jacket, and the sad state of his own breeches.

"That's as may be," Bonaventure grinned. "Perhaps we should each pluck the spars from our own eyes before angling for the splinters in others's, eh?"

Bonaventure stepped to the railing overlooking the ship's waist, and called for the nearest midshipman to have the captain's man ready the captain's best jacket and hose. At their current speed, the *Fortitude* would overtake the Spaniard within the next two hours, and whatever would come, be it salvation or doom, the officers would need to look their best.

Chapter Eight
Whence the Launch Sailed

THE *FORTITUDE*, HER crew dressed in their relative finest and standing watch on the quarterdeck, came alongside the Spanish launch as the sun overhead reached its zenith. At very nearly that precise moment, as through orchestrated by nature herself, the winds from the north-west flagged, leaving the seas almost becalmed and the ship and boat frozen in their respective positions. That this could be considered an inauspicious omen for their meeting was not voiced aloud, though by their looks a number of the crew seemed to share that opinion.

"Ahoy the boat," called Captain Ross from the railing, raising his hand in a half-wave to the man leaning against the launch's mainmast. Even at this near distance, the crew of the frigate could see no others on the deck of the launch, unless one counted the vaguely man-shaped lump in the prow.

As if in answer, the man against the launch's mast turned a fraction towards the frigate, pulling free his arm which had cradled the spar of the mast, and in the moment that his face was in full view of the frigate he crumpled lifelessly to the deck, a marionette with its strings cut. He struck the deck with a groan and a solid thump, audible even over the yards separating the two craft.

The captain, impatient, turned to his first lieutenant and snapped off an order.

"Take the jolly-boat and a detachment of Marines and board her, Mister Bonaventure. If that Spaniard or any others still live, bring them back with you. If none live, scuttle her and we'll be on our way."

"Aye, sir," Bonaventure answered. Motioning Midshipman Horrocks to his side, the first lieutenant ordered that the jolly-boat be lowered from the ship's deck to the water, and that the commanding officer of the Marines select a handful of his men to accompany him in the crossing.

In the restless few minutes that passed, the crew watched and waited for any sign of life from the Spanish launch. By the time Bonaventure clambered over the frigate's side, a musket-wielding Marine already stationed between every crewman rower on the jolly-boat, there had been no perceptible movement on the other craft.

The minutes needed to row the short distance to the launch were very nearly more than Bonaventure could stand, and it demanded all of his restraint to keep from diving overboard and swimming ahead at speed to the craft. To encounter an enemy ship in unknown waters was event enough, but compounded with the odd state and limited number of the boat's crew it was a profound mystery. More, that a boat so ill-designed for long sea voyages should be out sailing so far from any civilized outpost, only served to deepen the mystery further.

Finally, the jolly-boat was within arm's reach of the launch, and Bonaventure again cried out his ahoy, standing astern while the Marines watched intently, hands wrapped tight around their muskets. No answer came.

All thought of dignity or propriety forgotten, Bonaventure reached up, grabbed the upper rim of the launch's hull, and hauled himself up bodily. Working his legs over with ease, he came to rest on the deck of the launch and looked around him, baffled. The first of the Marines, rushing to join the first lieutenant in any potential danger, thudded to the deck beside him and joined him in an open-mouthed gape.

Aside from the crumpled form of the man lying against the foot of the mainmast, and the huddled shape of another crewman in the prow, the deck of the craft was empty. No other crew, no supplies, no implements or provisions. Just the two men in an empty boat on the open sea.

Bonaventure's first thought was that the man in the prow was already dead, and worried that the other near the mainmast might just have joined him. But, as he watched, the man at the foot of the mast stirred an inch, and worked his lips as though to speak. Bonaventure rushed to his side, kneeling down and placing a hand on the man's shoulder. Up close, Bonaventure could see that these two had been at sea without fresh water for some time. The lips of the weakened man were swollen and cracked, limned with dried flakes of salt, and his eyes were puckered and red.

"Whence have you sailed, man?" Bonaventure asked, his words loud and slow, as though he were speaking to a simpleton or one hard of hearing.

Leaning in close, bringing his ear as near as possible the man's lips, Bonaventure listened hard.

"*Infierno*," the man wheezed, in the voice of the dying. "*De infierno.*"

Bonaventure pulled back, and looked at the man for a long instant. Swollen lids closed over the man's eyes, and he slumped further onto the deck.

"You there," he called to the commanding officer of the Marines. "Have your men take this one aboard the jolly-boat, and check the other for signs of life. When we're back on board the *Fortitude*, I'll have crewmen return to tow this hulk alongside us."

"Aye, sir," the Marine replied, and began to turn away to relay the first lieutenant's orders. He paused midway, and turned back towards Bonaventure. "Those words he said?" he asked. "What did they mean?"

Bonaventure worried at his lower lip before answering.

"Well, I'm afraid my Spanish isn't as good as our Mister Jeffries," he answered, "but unless I'm mistaken, this man just informed me that this launch has sailed from Hell."

The Marine, eyes widening, looked at Bonaventure with his mouth hanging open. Then, swallowing hard, he snapped off a weak salute, and rushed to pass along the first lieutenant's orders.

Chapter Nine
The Spaniard's Recovery

Once the ship's surgeon Doctor Beauregard had the opportunity to look over the two Spaniards, he announced that one of them would, after a few hours's rest and ample water, regain consciousness and be able to speak for some short period of time. This was the man who had first been seen leaning against the launch's mast, and who by the cut of his clothes seemed at the very least a low-ranking commissioned officer. The other, who had been found huddling in the prow, barely alive, was farther gone than his companion, and Doctor Beauregard was unable to say with any certainty whether or not he was likely to regain consciousness.

It was hoped, among the officers, that as soon as the healthier of the two men was awake and rational they would be able to get from him an accounting of the state in which the launch had been found. The winds still becalmed, the frigate was unable to make significant progress towards their island destination without resorting to towing the ship along behind rowing-boats. As a result, the hours following were spent dispatching a prize crew comprised of a handful of crewmen led by Midshipman Symmes to take possession of the Spanish launch. Towed alongside the frigate, the prize crew were kept busy examining in closer detail the state of the craft, and in making what repairs and corrections they could.

Finally, when it seemed to the *Fortitude*'s crew as though they could wait no longer for answers, the first of the Spaniards recovered sufficiently from his exhaustion and thirst to answer a brief series of questions. Of the officers on board, Bonaventure had little Spanish at all, the captain was somewhat conversant but hardly fluent, and the second lieutenant, Jeffries, was near enough a native speaker to count. It was said that he'd learned the tongue the better to carouse the streets of Madrid when a younger man, and the better to negotiate business with ladies of easy virtue, but when at sea a man's experiences on land were best seldom mentioned.

It was several tense moments before Jeffries was able to calm the Spaniard, who'd awoken from a delirious slumber to find himself surrounded by his enemies. He at first assumed that he must still be dreaming, still drifting in his delirium on the open boat. Only after plying him with another flask of water, and some meagre rations of fruit, was Jeffries able to convince the Spaniard first of their reality, and second of their good intentions.

The Spaniard, once he was calmed and communicative, introduced himself to Jeffries, and through him to Captain Ross, as Bernal Alvarez y Aguilar, a commissioned officer in the Navy of His Most Catholic Majesty Ferdinand, the King of Spain. His companion, who still drowsed near death a short distance away, was Fray Gonzalo Diaz, a Franciscan lay friar.

Using Jeffries as intermediary, Captain Ross asked the Spaniard how a Spanish officer and Franciscan monk came to be adrift on the South Pacific reaches without provisions, water, or arms in an open boat.

The Spaniard Alvarez explained that he and the friar had until recently been among the crew of a Spanish ship, and only within the last weeks taken to the seas in the launch.

The captain, his growing impatience increasingly evident, demanded to know on what ship had they sailed, and how they came to leave her. Had the ship sunk? Or the crew mutinied? If the former, why had so few survived on the launch, and if the latter, why set adrift only these two?

The Spaniard, his eyes grown wide as he listened to Jeffries translate the captain's question, began ranting feverishly before the second lieutenant had even finished. So energetic and enthusiastic was Alvarez's answer that Jeffries soon lost the thread of it, and was forced to wave the Spaniard silent in his desperation.

"Well, man," Captain Ross demanded of Jeffries. "What is he saying? Which was the blasted ship, and what's become of it?"

"It was the *Nuestra Señora de Burgos*," the second lieutenant answered, and then translated, "Our Lady of Burgos." He paused, his eyes narrowed. "It was a Spanish galleon bound from Manila for Acapulco, which was fired upon by an English frigate nearly two months past, though the battle was interrupted by a fierce storm from the north."

"Hang me," Doctor Beauregard muttered.

"The very ship we thought foundered, her treasure lost," the captain said nearly in whispers.

"Not so lost as it might have seemed," Lieutenant Bonaventure said.

The captain, suddenly animated, took three steps forwards at a rush, leaned over Jeffries and grabbed him by the elbow in a vice's grip.

"Does it still sail?" the captain shouted. "Is it even now afloat?"

Jeffries, wincing slightly at the pressure of the captain's grip on his arm, glanced at the wide-eyed and frightened Alvarez, and then back to his captain.

"That, I'm afraid," he answered, "I've not yet determined."

The officers crowded round, and in response to Jeffries's calming tones, the Spaniard began answering his questions one by one.

Chapter Ten
A Strange Tale

THE DAMAGE DONE by the *Fortitude* to the Spanish galleon, as Alvarez explained to Jeffries, had been every bit as extensive as Captain Ross and his officers had supposed. Scored by shot in her hull below the waterline, she'd begun taking on water immediately, the crew forced to work the pumps ceaselessly to keep her afloat. That her masts were intact and her sails largely unharmed proved to little advantage, as the force of the storm bearing down on them prevented the crew from taking in the sheets even a single reef, and the ship was left completely at the mercy of the elements.

In the hours and days that followed the moment at which the two ships lost sight of one another, while the frigate struggled against the fierce winds with her single mast and sails, the crew of the *Nuestra Señora de Burgos* slaved at the pumps to keep the bilge from flooding. Even after fothering the hull, stretching a spare sailcloth underneath the ship that sucked into the gaping wounds between ship and sea, the intake of water was slowed but still continued. Those crewmen and officers who weren't at work baling out the seawater were employed in trying to furl the sails and slow the ship's speed, or else huddled below decks joining in the near endless prayers being read by the Franciscan friar Diaz.

Finally, as it had for the English frigate some distance to the north, the storm left the galleon at relative peace. Exhausted, waterlogged and barely afloat, the galleon had been driven to uncharted waters to the south, her meagre provisions largely destroyed in the skirmish and storm, and her hull kept from swamping only through the tireless efforts of her captain and crew.

After consulting his charts and seeking the advice of his officers, the Spanish captain, Bartolomé Velásquez de Leon, had come to much the same conclusion as his erstwhile nemesis Captain Ross. Deposited by the storm too far distant to reach any charted island in her present state, the galleon was left with little alternative but to strike out into the unknown, hoping to stumble across some suitable landing at which to effect repairs. The crew, with as much enthusiasm as that of the *Fortitude*, had cheered the pronouncement, and counted eager rosaries at Fray Diaz's insistence.

Though hopes faltered and rosaries were counted less ardently in the days and weeks that followed, still with no sight of land, the crew attended to their duties. The officers, among them Lieutenant Bernal Alvarez y Aguilar himself, did their level best to set the standard their subordinates were expected to follow, adhering rigidly to the Spanish Navy's regulations and codes of conduct, never allowing even a hint that their captain's plan would not succeed. When, finally, land was sighted, it was all Alvarez could do to resist the urge to jump up and down and whoop his delight; after all, it should appear that it was only natural, the captain succeeding in accomplishing just what he'd stated could be done.

The island the galleon had come upon, while not the most welcoming of temporary habitats, was sufficient for their needs. Small, measuring perhaps no more than a dozen or so miles in circumference, the island was almost a perfect cone flattened on top, a rocky mound dotted around the periphery by stands of tall forlorn trees. Circumnavigating the island, Captain Velásquez found the most suitable landing, that beach least marked by stone outcropping and nearest the trees. Sending a scouting party ashore, the captain ordered the ship's carpenter and his mate to begin planning repairs immediately, and led the officers in preparations to beach the ship.

Repairs were begun immediately after the galleon was brought safely on land, the galleon's cannon, shot and cargo brought out of her hold to lighten her and make the work that much easier. There was little doubt now that the island was volcanic in origin, though now safely dormant. The first scouting party had brought back word of a system of caves lacing the island, which surely had been produced by the passage of hot gases during the volcano's last eruption. At the captain's direction, the galleon's precious cargo was transferred to the largest and most easily defensible of these caves, and the cannon arranged both in front of the cave mouth and at strategic points around the island's circumference, pointed out to sea. Though there was little risk that they would be attacked while on the island, the captain and his officers agreed that their best course lay in preparing for the worst possible scenario.

As work on the ship continued, the majority of the crew were at their liberty on the island, which offered little that might hold their interest. There were no game animals on the island to speak of, no natives to entertain with their favours, and the only rum that which they'd brought along with them, which was still closely rationed by the officers. After a few slow days spent lounging on the sandy beaches, or fishing in the preternaturally still waters at the island's edge, when the captain announced his new work programme the majority of the crew grumbled behind their hands, but were secretly relieved.

The officers, for their part, assumed at first that the work assigned to them and the crew by the captain was an attempt to keep the men from going slack and lazy, make work to hold their edge. That was Alvarez's initial conception, and so he fell to his work as befitted an officer of the Spanish Navy.

First, the captain ordered that all trees on the island be felled, even those not needed for the galleon's repair. He next ordered that these be planed into lumber, suitable for building, and that the resultant materials be used in the construction of massive fortifications at the mouth of the cave system. The cannon and carronades, positioned originally on the rocky ground at key points around the island, were to be installed in sentry towers of wood and stone, which the men were to collect for this purpose. This done, the men not assigned watch at the sentry towers or the cave fortifications were to be drilled in hand-to-hand combat and tactics by the officers during every waking hour.

It first occurred to Alvarez, while supervising the construction of the cave fortifications, that the introduction of sturdy wooden pickets and walls would make more difficult the task of transferring the stored cargo back to the ship once the repairs to the galleon were complete. Then, upon seeing the completion of the sentry towers, he thought the difficulty of returning the cannon to their positions on the ship was doubled if not trebled by placing them so high off the ground in such solidly constructed towers. It was not until the captain ordered that lumber needed for the completion of the cave fortifications be first brought from the store of lumber needed for the repair of the ship, and then prised from the sides of the ship herself, that Alvarez realized without doubt that their captain had no intention ever of leaving the little volcanic island.

Though it was treason to breath a word of his concerns, Alvarez went to each of his fellow officers in turn, couching careful questions on their views of the captain's actions and motivations. To a one, they announced simply that they, too, saw no reason ever to leave the island, and that it only made sense to fortify their position as best they could. Alvarez was shocked. Growing frantic, thinking some form of disease or madness had come over the crew, he went on to question the non-commissioned officers and ranking crewmen, even the better part of the crew itself, and among all of them found only two who shared his concerns, and who could even conceive of ever sailing back to Spain again. They were Fray Gonzalo Diaz and the carpenter's mate Francisco Munoz.

At Alvarez's insistence, the three met in secret in the dark of night, on successive evenings, trying to devise a way to return their captain and his crew to sanity. Their schemes and approaches, attempted by light of day, proved fruitless and feeble, the remainder of the ship's crew growing more insistent in their madness each day.

Just as the trio was convinced in their desperation that matters could grow no worse, the galleon disappearing from view plank by plank, things took a darker turn. While the madness that had fallen on their mates had seemed at first to affect only their judgement and ability to reason, it began more and more to affect their personalities and actions, and worse yet seemed slowly to mark them physically as well. The other members of the galleon's crew became distrustful, aggressive, and their skin took on sallow tones. At first, the suspicions and resentments of the affected crewmen seemed directed only at one another, scuffles and fist-fights breaking out regularly during the course of their assigned duties, but gradually the mass of them turned their attentions to Alvarez and his fellow conspirators.

That the trio of them were unaffected by whatever malady had gripped their mates singled them out as a threat to the continued well-being of the crew. What began as stern reprimands from the captain for their lack of enthusiasm for his goals, and harsh whispers from the officers and crew for their laggard pace of work, quickly threatened to escalate to violence. Wherever the trio went, either alone or together, they were met with glowering looks and hands tightened white-knuckled on axe-handles or knives.

In the end, Alvarez, Diaz, and Munoz were left convinced that their only option lay in flight from the island. Having failed to redeem even one of their former colleagues from the island's madness, they could with clear conscience take to the seas in the distant hope of their own survival. However, the only one of the ship's craft still seaworthy was the bare launch, only some thirty feet in length and with no sheltering hold against the sun's rays. What was worse, the whole of the ship's provisions and supplies had been relocated within the fortified caves, and was kept under heavy guard at all hours of the day and night. The trio devised a plan to keep back a portion of their rations for several days running, water and food, in the hopes that they might store up enough to keep them alive at sea. Whether the plan would have worked proved a moot point, as circumstances contrived to force their hand.

One hot morning, when the trio of conspirators had saved only a few skins full of water and a handful of meals's worth of food, Alvarez and the others rested in the shade of the galleon's hulk, some distance from the other members of the crew. As the madness had worsened, the three of them had taken to spending more and more of their time in each other's company, each cherishing the sense of security the others offered.

A party of the affected crewmen approached the ship and the trio, led by Captain Velásquez. Alvarez at first assumed that they were yet another workgroup, sent to plunder further materials from the corpse of their former ship. Seeing the swords and axes held menacingly in each hand, however, he quickly realized this was hardly the case.

The armed crewmen encircling the trio, the captain announced that Alvarez and the others had only two choices. They could either stand with the crew, and devote themselves to the protection of the captain's cargo, or else be put down on the spot. The captain's precious store of firearms, kept now under guard at the caves, was too valuable a resource to be wasted on recalcitrants such as they. The sharp edge of a sword or axe would be enough justice for them.

Alvarez, so he reported, was left frozen on the spot. His nerves frayed thin in the preceding weeks, he found that he was unable to act when forced to a decision. Fray Diaz, for his part, clutched at his crucifix and mumbled prayers to the Holy Virgin. Munoz, the carpenter's mate, was quicker to act.

Taking up his own axe, which had been lying in the sands at his feet, Munoz screamed a shout of bloody vengeance, and lay into the assembled crewmen. Taking one mate on the bit of his axe-blade, and wrenching it free to face down the next, Munoz shouted over his shoulder for his comrades to make good their escape. He claimed he expected to follow as soon as he was able, the reactions and movements of the maddened crewmen seeming to have been dulled by the effects of their malady, but for his sins Alvarez confessed that he hadn't believed him.

Taking the opportunity that their friend had purchased at the risk of his life, Alvarez and Diaz raced ahead of the pursuing crewmen, around to the far side of the galleon to the sandy beach where they had left the launch ready. Its prow already nosed into the water, its sails wrapped but able to be unfurled with the release of a scant handful of ropes, the launch lacked only the remainder of their hoarded provisions and water to make her seaworthy. In their haste, though, and not expecting the bloody decision of the maddened captain, the majority of the saved rations of the trio were still kept safely in a hidden nook, halfway the distance between the galleon and the caves, with only two partially full skins stowed on board the launch.

Bare moments ahead of the axe- and sabre-wielding madmen, Alvarez and Diaz reached the launch and shoved her out onto the water. She was fully afloat only seconds before the crewmen reached the water's edge, and even with the furious rowing of the two men at her sides, the launch had not moved far enough from the beach for safety. Alvarez was sure that the armed men would simply wade into the surf, climb on board and kill the pair where they stood.

The captain, however, had other ideas. Rushing to the scene, he forbade his men to step foot in the water, on pain of death. He hardly needed to have bothered, it seemed, as when Alvarez looked back, the crewmen had made no move to follow them beyond the water's edge, even before the captain's approach. It was as though water had become something that they could not bodily abide, and it was this that proved the pair's only salvation.

The captain shouted that muskets were to be rushed from the cave fortifications, the value of putting down the escaping pair apparently brought equitably in line with that placed on the precious shot. Alvarez urged the friar to row harder, pulling further out of reach of the shore, but still watched for any sign that Munoz lived and might join their escape. The captain disappeared behind the far side of the galleon, out of view of the seaward launch, and returned on the heels of the men rushing from the cave with the muskets.

As the crewmen took careful aim with the firearms, the captain held aloft his bloody trophy, the severed head of their compatriot Munoz. Blanched and breathless, Diaz and Alvarez rowed harder, their lives in their hands, and as the shots from the beach plunked into the water and the sides of the ship harmlessly, they pulled finally to a safe distance.

At sea, the sails unfurled and steering them slowly to the north and west, the pair on the boat kept silent, unwilling or unable to voice their thoughts on their survival prospects. Their only hope lay in the uncharted waters ahead, and in finding a haven there. Despite their best efforts to ration their resources as long as possible, the two half-full skins were eventually emptied, and they were left with no water. Their lips cracked and their throats gone dry with thirst, they carried on, ignoring the rumblings of hunger from their bellies. The friar counted his rosary endlessly, but in the end gave up even that. It was as though God Himself and all the saints in heaven had forsaken them, and each man spoke only to convince the other that Hell surely existed, and that it lived on the rocky island with their former mates.

Chapter Eleven
A Brief Conference

WHEN THE SPANISH officer had finally slipped back into unconsciousness, unable to answer even one more of Lieutenant Jeffries's questions, Captain Ross and his officers, accompanied by Doctor Beauregard, left the Spaniard to his rest and reconvened in the captain's quarters.

"His story is credible enough," Lieutenant Bonaventure began, "given the evidence at hand. The state of the launch and her passengers in their obvious distress."

"But what can you say about the supposed madness that overcame his crew?" Jeffries asked. "Do you credit that aspect of his account?"

"I suppose that it could have been some sort of ill-humour borne by the island's water," Doctor Beauregard answered.

"But have you ever heard a similar report, doctor?" Bonaventure asked. "And why should this man and his two fellows be immune to the effects?"

"To your first question, I have to say that no, I have not," Beauregard replied. "As to the second, I have no answer to offer, except to say perhaps that it was their faith that sustained them."

"An odd remark for a man of science," Jeffries observed.

"And one that takes in only an aspect of the information at hand," Bonaventure added. "The friar, we can assume, is a pious enough man, but there was little in Alvarez's account that would lead me to suspect that he, or the other, was any more faithful than those affected."

"It could be a ruse," Jeffries answered. "Some plot by the Spaniards to lead us astray or prompt us to lower our guard at some crucial moment."

"But to what end?" Bonaventure said. "And why go to such lengths? To convince us that the galleon's captain and crew have gone mad and fortified themselves on some distant island? What use would that be to the Spanish?"

"One supposes that it could be this man himself who is mad," the doctor put forth. "We have, after all, only his account of the events in question, and it may well be that he took leave of his senses, abducted this unconscious man, friar or not, as his hostage, and made away from the island in the stolen launch."

"For that matter," Jeffries added, "we have no practical proof that such an island exists at all. Only this man's say-so, and if we doubt his credibility we must doubt the whole of his account."

"No," Bonaventure said, chewing his lower lip, "I think we have to take some aspects of it on faith. And besides, he hardly seems a madman to me; bewildered, perhaps, and driven by circumstance to the fringes of sanity, but not insane. Tell me, Mister Jeffries, as you could better understand his speech, did he by word or sign suggest to you that he was in any way less than sane?"

Jeffries thought for a long moment, and then shook his head.

"No," he answered. "He seems as sane and hearty as you or I would be, given the circumstances."

"Then I don't see that we have any choice but to proceed under the assumption that his story is a statement of fact," Bonaventure answered. "Until such time as the other man regains consciousness and can corroborate his story."

"Assuming that the other man survives," Jeffries added.

"Which is far from a certainty," the doctor said.

"Enough," the captain barked, pounding on the table with a balled fist. He'd not spoken since they'd left the Spaniard sleeping, but had kept silent, his face wrinkled in concentration. "This island exists, and the treasured prize which is rightfully ours is secreted there. We'll effect our repairs on this nearer landing, and then with this Spaniard's help proceed to his former position and capture the cargo."

"But suppose this Alvarez has no intention of helping us?" Bonaventure asked. But before the captain or any of the others could answer the silence was broken by the sound of knocking at the cabin door.

"Come," the captain barked, and Midshipman Daniels appeared in the doorway.

"Your pardon, sir," Daniels announced, "but Mister Horrocks sends his compliments, and instructs me to inform you that a flotilla of boats has sailed from the sighted island, headed in our direction."

"Order the quartermaster to beat to quarters," the captain answered, hurrying from the cabin and pushing the midshipman before him. "You men," he called back over his shoulder to the assembled officers, "to your posts."

Chapter Twelve
Ship's Nails

FROM THE DECK of the *Fortitude,* the officers watched as the small fleet approached. Double-hulled canoes, single hulls with outriggers, larger craft surmounted by flower-strewn arches, some dozen craft large and small were paddling towards them, each so filled with men and women that it seemed sure to capsize at any moment.

"They're an eager bunch, I'll give them that," Jeffries remarked, whistling low. "I should hope not eager for our heads," he added sombrely.

"I... I don't think those ladies are wearing any clothes," Midshipman Daniels stammered.

"They're clothed appropriately for the climes, I assure you," Midshipman Horrocks answered admiringly.

"That's right," Jeffries said with a snap of his fingers. "Daniels, my boy, you've not had the pleasure of landing on one of these little South Pacific jewels, have you? Your former tour restricted to the unfriendly and unwelcoming North Atlantic reaches." He clapped the younger man on the shoulder, grinning. "Ah, the times you'll have."

"That's enough, men," Bonaventure scolded, with good nature. "This is quite likely the first contact these people have had with any white men, and I remind you all that you are British officers."

"Just keep an eye on the nails, Hero," Jeffries chided.

Both midshipmen were confused, as was apparent by their expressions.

"Allow me to explain," Jeffries continued. "The first ships to come this far into the Pacific, either from the west past Timor or from the east round the Cape, found themselves in an unexpected world of... shall we say, sensuous pleasures?"

"We shall not," Bonaventure answered, blushing slightly. "The natives proved friendly, and generous with their favours, is all."

"I should say so," Jeffries replied. "It seems that the Pacific natives, having no familiarity with the finer products of civilization, would go to any lengths to procure a small piece of glass or bit of iron. They began trading their oh-so-generous favours for nothing more than ship's nails, if you can believe it, a single small length of metal for a night's attentions."

"No," Daniels said with a breath.

"Oh, yes," Jeffries answered. "In no time, the crew on one of those early ships had plundered their ship's stores of every nail they could find, and then proceeded to pluck the nails right from the hull of the ship itself. One after another, bartered with the *friendly* natives."

"Almost foundering the ship in the process," Bonaventure added, shaking his head. "By the time the ship's master caught wind of it, the ship had near as damn it fallen to pieces, and only by placing armed guards on the ship at all times and restricting any and all contact with the native ladies were they able to keep the ship afloat."

"I'll be damned," Horrocks said in a low voice, turning his hungry attention towards the approaching flotilla, and the waving women with flowers woven into their flowing hair.

"You may well be, Mister Horrocks," Bonaventure said, "if I ever catch wind of you abusing ship's resources in any such way. The same goes for the rest of the crew, and have no doubts. The first time any tools or implements, even so much as a single nail, goes missing, I'll have you all confined to quarters when not actively employed in repairs on the ship."

The two midshipmen looked longingly at the boats paddling towards them, and then averted their eyes with a shared sigh.

"Ah, my boys, don't look quite so down," Jeffries chided with a smile. "After all, there's many things aboard ship that are metal, as have nothing to do with the ship herself." At this, Jeffries reached out a hand and rapped one of the brass buttons on the front of Horrocks's blue jacket.

The midshipmen, realization dawning, smiled broadly.

"Mister Jeffries," Bonaventure said with a barely suppressed smile, "you are nothing if not a cad."

"Thank you, sir," Jeffries answered, waving his hand in a mock salute. "I do my best, sir."

The captain, who'd gone to his cabin to change into his best uniform after checking the progress of the flotilla, returned to the quarterdeck. Even after a year and a half at sea, and more than his fair share of hardship, he still cut the figure of the model British commander while in his finest.

"Come on, men," he said to the assembled officers, polishing a gold button with the cuff of his jacket, "let's do our best for the Crown, shall we, and make a good impression on the natives."

The midshipmen and Jeffries, in light of their previous conversation, were forced to stifle inappropriate laughter when seeing the delicate care the captain took of the metal objects on his person, to say nothing of his desire to make an impression on the natives. Bonaventure froze them with a glare, and the four officers followed the captain to the railing.

The flotilla was but moments away. Bonaventure hoped that the frigate would fare better on this island than the comatose Spaniards below decks had done on theirs, but only time would tell.

Chapter Thirteen
Language Barrier

THE FIRST CRAFT to reach the *Fortitude*, more martial than most in the flotilla that followed, was a double-hulled canoe carrying nearly two dozen men. Better than half the crew were on their knees in one of the boat's two hulls, paddling, while the remainder stood sure-footed amongst them, armed and wary. Some carried long wooden staves, others war clubs edged with shark's teeth, a few held stone knives, but all wore cautious expressions on their dark, tattooed faces.

As they drew nearer, those on the frigate's decks could see that the dark, spiralled tattoos covering each man's face in varying and diverse patterns spread down over their chests, arms and legs. In some cases the tattooing was so thorough that it seemed that the men were fully clothed, and not exposed nearly naked with only a brief loincloth and decorative necklaces as covering.

Captain Ross, his hands held out palms first in an attitude of willing non-aggression, hailed the craft from the quarterdeck railing.

"Ahoy the canoe," he called out. "We have no quarrel with you good people, and wish only to open lines of communication and exchange."

On the canoe, a small collection of the forward-most warriors huddled in conference, with frequent glances up at Captain Ross as they spoke. Finally, one among them, a leader of sorts it seemed, cupped his hands in front of his mouth and shouted an answer.

"*No hea koe? To kewhea tou moukere?*"

The captain nodded, dumbly, and gave a weak smile and wave in reply. While the tattooed warrior repeated his questions, the captain half-turned towards his officers and whispered out of the side of his mouth.

"Does anyone have any notion what sort of nonsense the man is babbling?"

Bonaventure and the others shook their heads in silent reply, and the captain turned his attention back to the canoe.

"We no wanting trouble," the captain answered, speaking slowly and in loud tones, trying a different tack. "We trade pretty baubles for supplies, yes?"

Bonaventure, hiding silent laughter behind his hand, felt a touch on his elbow, and turned to see that Macallister the quartermaster had approached from his post at the helm.

"Begging your pardon, Mister Bonaventure, sir, but I think I might be able to help."

"Yes, Mister Macallister?" Bonaventure prompted, eager to turn his attentions back to the intercourse with the natives. "What is it?"

The quartermaster tugged at his collar, eyes shifting nervously.

"Well, sir," he began, "a few years back, I served on a ship out of Ceylon with a fella who'd been brought in by a press-gang down in New Zealand, you see, and we worked the rigging the same shift, day after day, for some twenty month. Couldn't shut up, this rotten bastard, you'll pardon me saying so, with never an interesting word to share. It hammered at me, it did, listening to him go on without stopping, night and day, for almost two years running. He finally got put down by grapeshot fired from a French warship, if you can believe it, and God forgive me but if I shed tears when we rolled him in his hammock and put him over the side, they were tears of sweet relief."

"Yes, Mister Macallister?" Bonaventure sighed. He'd grown used to the quartermaster's typically circuitous answers, but there were more pressing matters in this instant.

"Sorry, sir," Macallister answered. "Anyway, this New Zealand fella, he'd been a whaler out of Okiato on the North Island, and had done a fair deal of trade with the local blacks, and he'd picked up their lingo and such. During those whole twenty months at sea with the bastard, he spent the better part of every day and too much of every night nattering on in that speak, telling me what words the folks there used for what other words I'd have used, and so forth. Well, damn me but that I didn't pick up a bit of it myself, and heard it every night in my sleep for years after, his voice droning on and on about what they call a boiling pot in New Zealand, and what they call a cloud, and what they call a woman—"

Bonaventure cut him off, impatient, with a wave of his hand.

"Right," Macallister answered, eyes averted. "Like I said, I picked up this New Zealand lingo, and from where I stand, what those boys in the canoe are spouting sounds as near as damn it."

Bonaventure looked from the quartermaster, to the increasingly frustrated warriors on the canoe, and back again.

"You mean to say that you can understand them?" Bonaventure said, his mouth gaping.

"Well, sir, I can't say it's exactly the same as what I've heard, but close enough that I can get the gist of it."

"Well," Bonaventure shot back eagerly, grabbing the man by both shoulders and shaking him. "What are they saying?"

Macallister swallowed hard.

"They want to know where we're from, sir," the quartermaster answered in a rush. "They want to know which island we sail from."

Bonaventure grinned, and without thinking drew Macallister into a bear's hug, pounding him on the back. Remembering himself, Bonaventure straightened his arms, pushing the quartermaster away, but refused to release his hold on the man as though he might scamper away before he'd outlived his usefulness.

"They can't have said just that," Bonaventure said, looking over the quartermaster's shoulder at the warriors, who'd now fallen to arguing amongst themselves, taking turns in attempting communications with the captain, one after another. "What about it, man? What else have they said?"

Macallister frowned, and knitted his thick eyebrows together.

"Well, sir, I could follow a part of it, but not all the words are the same, or else that bastard from New Zealand didn't know the half of what he said. The only other bit I think I followed was when the big one was announcing who he was... you know, sir, like knights and champions in olden times are said to have done, listing off where they're from, who sired them on their mothers, who they've killed before—"

"And?" Bonaventure prompted, trying to steer the man away from digression. "Who is he?"

"I didn't catch the name, sir," the quartermaster apologized. "Not his name, at any rate, but I think I did get the name of the island. No words I knew the English of, but I got which ones were the name. Sounds something like the New Zealand word for 'abound', if you can believe it. *Kovoko*, he said. Or maybe *Kovoko ko te'maroa*, if the words after I didn't know are part of the name as well."

"Well," Bonaventure answered with a half-smile, "that's something at least. Come along, Mister Macallister. I believe you've just volunteered for translation duties."

"Aye, sir," the quartermaster replied, saluting. He followed the first lieutenant to where the captain stood shouting red-faced at men who couldn't understand a word of his rantings. It took some time to calm him down, but Bonaventure knew it would be worth the effort.

February 1795

IT WAS LATE afternoon when Hieronymus Bonaventure arrived for his lesson at the disused carriage house, not far from his parents's home. He was running late, as usual, and Giles Dulac was there waiting for him, as always, already standing on the makeshift piste at the centre of the packed dirt floor, sword in hand.

"Considering that the only fee asked of you is your devoted attention, young master, I wonder that your habitual tardiness does not bespeak some lack of commitment to your studies."

"I'm sorry, sir," Hieronymus said, changing from his woollen coat into a jacket of heavy canvas. "My father was taking me to task for a... disagreement I had with Cornelius this morning."

Dulac answered with a weary sigh. "You and your brother will share a roof for some years to come, and so must come to some accord. The only alternative is that one of you should manage at last to kill the other, which solution I don't recommend."

"It is an attractive notion." Hieronymus gave a sly smile, as he slipped the padded plastron over his head and shoulders, and drew the heavy leather gloves over his hands. "At least then I could be reasonably sure that my books and papers would remain where I put them, and not be later found strewn across the floor with a nine-year-old boy's fingerprints outlined in jam upon them."

"Ah," Dulac said, nodding with mock solemnity, "but what of your sister, Claudia?"

"Not to worry." Hieronymus picked up his own sword, tucked his wire-mesh mask beneath his arm and took his place on the piste opposite his instructor. "She doesn't like jam."

In response, Dulac raised his sword in a quick salute, and without another word came en garde.

Hieronymus returned the salute, pulled the mask over his head and fell into position, legs bent with his feet shoulder-width apart, front foot pointed straight ahead, back foot sideways. His sword arm was held loosely before him, point towards his opponent, his back hand held up behind his head.

The sword still felt strange in his hand. He'd been studying with Dulac for more than two years, but had only within the last month begun to fence with an actual sword, and not an iron bar twice a sword's weight. Two years of swinging a few feet of iron, his muscles protesting daily, all the while desperate to move on to more advanced studies. Since he'd shifted from the iron to a proper sword, though, Hieronymus had to admit that Dulac had been right, and that training with the excess weight greatly eased his facility in handling the real thing.

Today, he was using a French foil with no crossbar, constructed of fine Toledo steel, with a ball blunting its point, and even weighted down with a padded plastron, leather gloves and wire-mesh mask, after the dead weight of the iron bar for so many long months it felt as though he were holding nothing at all.

"Begin," Dulac said, patiently waiting for Hieronymus to make the initial attack.

Hieronymus went into a lunge, which Dulac easily parried, and while Hieronymus tried to retreat, Dulac quickly riposted, scoring a touch to the middle of Hieronymus's bicep. Even through the thick sleeve of his canvas jacket Hieronymus could feel the sting of the hit. He'd been hit there so often in recent days that he had developed a seemingly permanent bruise, gone past purple to a greenish-yellow, a viridian circle surrounded by a rim of sallow flesh, like a miniature ringed target.

Dulac recovered his position, and regarded Hieronymus through narrowed eyes. "Again."

Resisting the urge to rub his stinging bicep, Hieronymus returned to the en garde position, and began his next attack.

For the next quarter-hour, the carriage house echoed with the ring of crossed swords, the clash of steel. Attack. Parry. Riposte. Attack. Parry. Riposte. And with hit after hit, the bruises on Hieronymus's pale flesh multiplied beneath the padded plastron.

When Dulac had first taken Hieronymus on as a pupil, he'd ordered him to forget everything he thought he knew of swordplay. Hieronymus had spent some years assembling a small personal library of fencing manuals, and had studied them with single-minded intensity, gaining a whole new vocabulary of terminology but, Dulac insisted, little insight. It hardly mattered that Hieronymus could use terms like *imbrocatta*, *stocatta*, or *punta riversa*; if his muscles didn't know what those movements felt like, then the words were useless.

So it was that Dulac's training had focused on movement, not on vocabulary. Hieronymus scarcely knew what any of the techniques he'd so far learned would be called in Mr Angelo's famous fencing academy in Soho Square, and while it was perfectly clear that Dulac did know, it was just as clear that Dulac put little stock in the knowledge. Just how Hieronymus's instructor, to all outward appearance a humble tutor of Latin, had come by such a mastery of swordplay remained a mystery; however, it was obvious to Hieronymus that however Dulac had come by his skill with the blade, it had been through practical application and not through the trivial pursuit of a sport. At some point, in the past about which he wouldn't speak, Dulac had lived by the sword.

"Don't watch the blade," Dulac barked, drawing Hieronymus's attentions back to the moment. "Watch my eyes. They'll tell you everything you need to know of my movements."

The lessons continued. Attack. Parry. Riposte. And bruises piled upon bruises.

Finally, Dulac called an end to the bout. "Enough!"

Dulac motioned for Hieronymus to remove his mask. The instructor seemed about to hurl his foil to the ground in frustration, but instead just fixed his pupil with a hard stare.

"In the salles d'armes of Paris, before the Revolution, the maîtres would have ousted you from the building after so poor a showing. And I'll admit I'm tempted to follow suit. Your mind is clearly not at the task. So what occupies your thoughts?"

Hieronymus stifled the urge to lower his gaze and shuffle his feet, and instead, as Dulac had taught him, looked his instructor in the eye and spoke in as clear a voice as possible. "I'm not certain, sir."

"Hmph. But you'll agree with me that your thoughts are not on your efforts, I take it?"

Hieronymus drummed his fingers on the wire-mesh of his mask for a moment before answering, nervously. Finally, he said, "No, sir. That is, yes, I agree that I'm not concentrating."

"Very well," Dulac said with an indulgent sigh. "Perhaps a brief interval will allow you to collect yourself, and then we'll try again."

Glad for the respite, Hieronymus set his foil and mask on the floor, and took long draughts from the jug of water sitting near the wall. He tried not to meet Dulac's eyes, as shame and guilt warmed the back of his neck.

The truth was that Hieronymus knew precisely what was occupying his thoughts, and distracting him from his fencing. But Dulac had long months before insisted that he forget such matters as soon as he entered their makeshift salle, and the punishment for infringing upon this restriction was an additional series of strenuous and time-consuming muscle-toning exercises.

Even in the face of such punishment, though, Hieronymus found himself almost entirely unable to control himself and, after nearly emptying the jug of water, turned back to Dulac. In as casual a manner as he was able, he said, "Have you heard the latest news?"

Dulac, who was intent on cleaning the blade of his foil, glanced up, his left eyebrow cocked. "Oh," he asked, though it was clear he knew perfectly well the answer. "What news would that be?"

"Of the capture of the Dutch fleet by the French army," Hieronymus said, excitedly. "Under the command of Jean Pichegru, it appears, the French crossed the frozen Zuyder Zee river and seized the ships trapped in the winter ice." So animated did he get, as he recounted the anecdote, that he seemed nearly ready to dance a jig. "It marks the first time in history that a navy has ever been captured by an army."

Dulac treated him to a half-smile. "I wouldn't be so sure of that, young master. History is a considerable deal longer than you might expect, and the catalogue of past events, now all but forgotten, is nearly endless. You would be surprised at what strange things have happened before, and will happen again." He paused, significantly, and added, "But am I mistaken, or was there not some stricture against discussing wars and news of wars during our sessions?" Though Dulac's tone was on the whole playful, there was clearly steel beneath his words.

"Oh, I beg your pardon, sir!" Hieronymus answered in a rush. "But... but it's all too... Well, sir, just this week we've heard the news of the fall of the Netherlands to the forces of the French. And one of my classmates says that his uncle saw Statholder William's arrival in Dover with his own two eyes."

Dulac sighed. "Little more than a decade since William V of Orange lost the latest Anglo-Dutch War to the English, and now he flees behind their coattails for protection."

"My mother says that the Netherlands has been virtually a vassal of King George ever since the war, scarcely less a puppet state than this Batavian Republic set up by the French, and that William was only able to control the Patriots amongst his own population through the intercession of Prussian troops." Hieronymus paused, and with his eyes lowered went on in a subdued voice. "That's what my mother says, at any rate, based on what news she has from her own father."

Dulac pursed his lips in an expression of sympathy. "So your grandfather is well, and weathers the recent troubles?"

Hieronymus nodded.

"His name is Cornelius, too, isn't it?" Dulac asked.

"Yes," Hieronymus answered. "Or near enough. Cornelis van der Waals. My brother was named for him, after a fashion. Just as I was named for my father, Jerome, I suppose."

"A cartographer, wasn't he?"

"He made maps for the Dutch East India Company." Hieronymus raised his chin, his tone suggesting pride commingled with awe. "Of the coastlines of Japan, and charts of the sea-lanes to and from there." He paused, and a cloud passed for a moment across his features. "Better that I'd been named for him, and Cornelius for our father. My brother is the studious one, suited to follow in our father's footsteps, not me. But father wants me to pursue the career of the scholar."

"So what career would you prefer, then?" Dulac narrowed his eyes, looking close at his pupil.

"I don't know," Hieronymus said, with a shrug he couldn't suppress. "But I know I don't want to spend my life confined to a dusty library. I want to see the world!" He began to pace the floor, hands curled into ineffectual fists. "Mother says that I have her father's temperament, passed down through her. Father says that I have the fidgets, and need only discipline to make of me a scholar."

"And what do you say?"

"I don't know," Hieronymus repeated, wearily. "Sometimes I don't know if I'll ever get to leave home."

Dulac tactfully failed to point out, as he'd done many times before, that Hieronymus was not yet fourteen years old, and had scarcely reached the stage where leaving home was an imminent proposition. Instead, a momentary silence stretched between them, in which the tutor regarded his pupil with an amused expression.

Finally, Dulac chuckled. "So, young master, you are not much of a *diseuse de bonne aventure*, after all."

Hieronymus didn't understand, as his look made evident.

"Do I take it you don't know the meaning and history of your own surname?"

"Oh," Hieronymus said. "I had always understood it to be a cognate to the Italian *buonaventura*, or 'good luck'."

"Perhaps." Dulac nodded. "But in French, *dire la bonne aventure,* or 'to speak the good adventure', means fortunetelling."

Hieronymus's mouth reformed in a moue of distaste. "So my name is French?"

Dulac laughed at his pupil's consternation. "I'm not sure of its ultimate origin, but so far as I know, the name Bonaventure originates in the Varadeaux region which, you may be happy to know, while it was formerly a possession of France, is now under the control of the Prussian king. But whatever its roots, it is a name of which to be proud."

Hieronymus blew air through his lips, making an undignified noise. "I see no reason to take pride in my name."

"Oh, no?" Dulac mimed surprise. "Then perhaps you should count yourself lucky that you are not able to share those sentiments with Etienne Bonaventure, who served king and country in seventeenth-century France, in the days of Louis XIII and Richelieu. I doubt a musketeer of his calibre would take so kindly to the casual dismissal of a name he bore proudly? Or perhaps Amandine Bonaventure, opera singer and swordswoman at the turn of the eighteenth century, who affected male dress and counted men and women alike amongst her conquests, both martial and amorous?"

Hieronymus's eyes opened wider as he parsed that last statement. "Men and women?"

"She was as willing to face either sex with her blade, and just as willing to welcome either to her bed."

If possible, Hieronymus's eyes opened even wider.

"And what of Achille Bonaventure, who in the sixteenth century explored the new world with Jacques Cartier, journeyed to the kingdom of Saguenay, and helped found La Society de Lucien? Did he fight and bleed only to have his good name dismissed so casually by his namesake?"

"I don't know."

"And perhaps you'd like to..." Dulac paused, his words choked off, and a brief expression of pain flitted across his features, before vanishing again. Regaining his composure, he continued. "And perhaps you'd like to explain yourself to Michel-Thierry Bonaventure."

Dulac fell silent again, for a brief moment, and his gaze drifted to the middle distance.

"Who was he, then?" Hieronymus asked, somewhat overwhelmed.

"Michel-Thierry was a mercenary with whom I served in the DeMeuron Regiment. And he was my friend."

Hieronymus's breath caught in his throat. There was a quality to Dulac's voice that he'd not heard before, and this marked the first occasion on which Dulac had revealed anything of his life before their initial meeting.

"What is that? The DeMeuron Regiment?"

Dulac turned and looked at Hieronymus, wearing a strange expression, almost like he was seeing the boy for the first time.

"The regiment is a Swiss company of mercenaries, its name taken from that of its founder and first commander, the Comte Charles de Meuron, veteran of the regiment D'Erlach and the Swiss Guard. During the majority of my tenure with the DeMeuron, the regiment was in the employ of the VOC, better known in English, I suppose, as the Dutch East India Company."

Hieronymus felt like he was a beat or two behind, slow to catch up to the pace of the revelations. "So you... you were a soldier?" If so, it confirmed many of his suspicions about his instructor.

"For a span," Dulac admitted, his tone subdued, "and not for the first time. But I'm in no hurry to be one again, and never will, if I can help it."

Hieronymus puzzled through what Dulac had said. "But you are British. How did you come to serve a company of Swiss mercenaries?"

"I was recruited in the region of Varadeaux in 1782, as was my friend Michel-Thierry. We served together four years, seeing action on three continents, countless islands and seemingly half of the world's oceans." Dulac fell silent once more, and again his gaze drifted to the middle distance, lines forming around his eyes, perhaps the sign of some dimly remembered pain.

So Dulac had begun his soldier's career when Hieronymus had been scarcely a year old. Hieronymus found it difficult to imagine what the younger Dulac must have been like. Whatever the details, it was clear that Dulac's experiences as a mercenary had marked him in some way, and though there were no scars evident on his skin, perhaps there were other forms of scarring, more subtle and yet more indelible still.

"What happened to your friend?" Hieronymus asked at length. "What became of this Michel-Thierry."

Dulac turned, and for a long moment looked at Hieronymus in silence, studying him closely. "He died needlessly," Dulac finally said, breaking the silence with an air of finality that suggested that was an end to the topic.

Something seemed to pass between them, in the silence that followed, and Hieronymus wondered whether there was something he was expected to say, or to do. But before he could act, whatever the case, Dulac leapt to his feet, snatching up his foil.

"But enough of such sombre topics," he said, striding back to the piste, forcing a bright tone into his voice. "While we do our warming-up exercises, to limber our limbs, I'll tell you a bit about my days in the DeMeuron. You mentioned Japan earlier. Once, Michel-Thierry and I were seconded to a VOC delegation from the Chamber of Enkhuizen, and sent to act as little more than bodyguards to a bureaucrat on the artificial island of Desjima."

Dulac sliced his foil through the air with a whistling sound, while Hieronymus tugged on his gloves and fitted his mask over his head.

"Tell me, young master," Dulac went on, "in your mother's stories of her father, have you ever heard mention of the word *rangaku*?"

With a shake of his head, Hieronymus allowed that he hadn't. Then, while he went through a series of lunges, thrusting his sword hand forwards and throwing his other back for balance, his instructor examined his technique and explained.

"It is the Japanese word for 'Dutch learning', and is used to mean any knowledge derived from the west. As you are doubtless aware, for hundreds of years the island of Japan has been closed off from all contact with the outside world, with one notable exception, namely, the Dutch, who are allowed to maintain a 'factory', or trading post, on Desjima, an 'island' of wood constructed in the bay of Nagasaki. Mind that foot, young master, you continue to turn it inwards and you'll regret it in the long run. Desjima is intended to act as a buffer between the Japanese and the base barbarians of the west, and as such the Dutch are prohibited from passing over the narrow bridge from the wooden island onto the Nagasaki shore, and the Japanese are banned from entering Desjima—except of course for the ladies known as *yūjo*, though perhaps your ears are still too young to hear about them. Keep that back leg straight in the lunge, or you lose your support. There are occasional exceptions to these restrictions, scholars periodically allowed onto the island of Japan for one reason or another, and of course the perennial visit of the Dutch legation to the court of the shogun."

A familiar half-smile tugged up one corner of Dulac's mouth, and he paused for a moment, chuckling to himself.

"That is where Michel-Thierry and I come into the story, and where the problems begin. Now, let's try a few bouts, and see if your attentions are with your efforts."

The pair took their positions facing each other on the piste, saluted and then closed, crossing swords. As they fenced, Dulac continued to speak, perhaps testing Hieronymus's concentration, perhaps just not willing to leave off, interspersing his anecdote with instruction.

"The head of the Dutch factory is called *opperhoofd*, and carries the equivalent position in the Japanese hierarchy to that of a *daimyo*, a rank something like an English duke or count but with considerably more power. Like the daimyo, once a year the opperhoofd was called upon to journey to Edo, to pay obeisance to the Japanese ruler, the shogun, and to present him with gifts—which gifts the Shogun had invariably selected in advance, so that the legation served as little more than freight-carriers with bespoke goods. Try to expend as little effort as possible to redirect the point of my blade. Here, begin a simple attack and I'll demonstrate."

Hieronymus thrust his sword's point forwards, and Dulac simply swivelled his wrist, describing with his own foil a small circle around Hieronymus's blade, turning it aside.

"Always an economy of motion. Never engage in flourishes or wasted effort, but apply only the resources necessary to the task. Again. Now, as I said, Michel-Thierry and I had been seconded as a security detachment to Desjima, and when it came time for the opperhoofd's annual pilgrimage to the shogun's palace, we were selected to escort him. You see, the opperhoofd had made some enemies among the Japanese gentry, those who quietly opposed the shogun's policies, and while these malcontents were hardly eager to rise up against their own ruler, they could with greater ease take out their frustrations on foreign dignitaries. As a result, shortly before the legation was set to depart from Desjima, word was received that assassins had been hired to take the opperhoofd's life. However, by Japanese law only civilian members of the opperhoofd's staff could go on the pilgrimage, and so Michel-Thierry and I were forced to pose as the opperhoofd's scribe and the factory doctor. That Michel-Thierry's penmanship was horrible would have been apparent even to Japanese unable to read the letters, and so he was selected instead to play the part of the doctor. You should anticipate, and attempt to turn a defensive manoeuvre into an offensive one. Try to feint the first parry to draw out the attack, and then use the second parry as your real parry for the riposte. That's it, now again. So it was that on a bright spring morning the opperhoofd, Michel-Thierry and I set out from Desjima on the long journey to Edo, under the watchful eyes of our escorts, the shogun's own warriors. The journey took days, in which Michel-Thierry and I were constantly vigilant, never sure from what corner danger might present itself, or in what guise death might come for the opperhoofd. Finally we reached the Nagasakiya, the residence prepared for the legation, where we were to wait until summoned."

Dulac took a step back, barely winded from his exertions, while Hieronymus felt his heart pounding in his chest, the blood rushing in his ears, trying desperately not to pant.

"Keep that elbow tucked in. Your arms and legs seem always to want to rush away from your body, but your thrust loses its impetus if your arm is out of line. As it happened, our stay in the capital lasted for more than two weeks, during which time we waited on the shogun's pleasure, and busied ourselves as befitted the Dutch legation. Michel-Thierry, as the supposed doctor of the legation, was expected to meet with the local practitioners, to exchange techniques and the like, while the opperhoofd met with merchants in an attempt to negotiate better terms for the VOC, with me at his side keeping careful record of the interaction. That's it. Now, we'll see what happens when the attack falls just short, but your attacker does not withdraw. I regret that I was unable to see Michel-Thierry's star turn as a doctor myself, but then I was busy keeping careful watch over the opperhoofd, look-ing out for any sign of danger, and so had to forgo the pleasure. Finally, we were called to court where, after presenting our gifts, we were expected to perform Dutch dances and songs for the shogun." Dulac chuckled. "I don't know that 'O Dag, O Langgewenste Dag' has ever had a sorrier interpretation than that we gave it, but nevertheless I maintain that I remained in tune, whereas Michel-Thierry would likely not have been able to pronounce a convincing Dutch vowel if his life depended on it. In any event, the opperhoofd paid proper homage to the shogun, and received a token gift of plum wine in exchange, and then we were sent on our merry way back to Desjima."

Dulac, without missing a beat, returned en garde, parried and then immediately riposted, at which Hieronymus dropped into a squat and thrust with his sword, all in one motion. As he'd hoped, Hieronymus managed to drop completely beneath the point of Dulac's foil, and scored a slight but undeniable hit on Dulac's chest with the point of his own foil.

"Good, good," Dulac said, nodding in admiration. "A risky move, but a useful one. But remember to keep your bell guard high, which should provide the maximum protection against your opponent's point hitting your top shoulder."

Hieronymus, now thoroughly winded, took off his mask and put his hands on his knees, struggling to catch his breath.

"What..." he began, raggedly. "What happened with the opperhoofd? And the assassins?"

"Hmm?" Dulac blinked for a moment, confused. He'd clearly lost the thread of the story amongst the details, fondly remembering his lost friend. "Well, as it happens, the assassins were simply smarter, and had infiltrated the staff of the shogun. When we returned to Desjima, the opperhoofd toasted his safe return with the plum wine given him by the shogun, and promptly dropped dead on the spot."

"Poisoned?"

"Poisoned. Which, I suppose, should serve you well as an illustrative example. When dealing with the unknown—whether fencing an unknown opponent, entering a strange land, or dealing with a person or people unfamiliar to you—remember one thing: that the unknown is exactly that. Not known. The moment one assumes that he understands that which he doesn't, he is inviting disaster."

Part II
A Fateful Haven

Chapter Fourteen
Nightmare or Dream

IN THE YEARS since he first went off to sea, both on the decks of the HMS *Fortitude* and any number of ships besides, Lieutenant Hieronymus Bonaventure had been fortunate to find precisely the brand of excitement and adventure in search of which he'd left home. This excitement was leavened, of course, by weeks and months of relative boredom, long ocean voyages composed almost entirely of repetitive duties and unbroken scenery which one could hardly call "exciting." Nevertheless, despite the occurrence with almost clockwork regularity every few months of some stripe of pulse-quickening adventurous danger, Bonaventure reminded himself on odd occasions that there was still one experience he could not claim: that of first contact with some alien culture or race.

As a young boy, head filling with tales of adventure both real and imagined, Bonaventure had read a popular account of Captain James Cook's voyages to the far side of the world, from the momentous first voyage to the ill-fated last. The accounts of brown-skinned and well-formed islanders, with their pagan beliefs and outlandish practices, left a deep impression on the young Hieronymus. His dreams were filled with emerald islands and inviting natives waving from sandy beaches on which no white man had ever trod, while his nightmares were plagued by reefs and storms and cannibals in close pursuit, hungry for their first taste of European flesh.

By the time he'd reached his age of majority, though, and put off to sea, it seemed to Bonaventure as though the day in which a man might encounter some unmolested aboriginal culture had passed. Captain Cook, and those like him, had filled in the blurred edges of the map, and left as their legacy to Bonaventure's generation a comprehended world. No dragons crept along in the distant corners of the globe Bonaventure wore around his neck, nor were there men with heads below their shoulders or only one huge foot used for shade in the shining sun. It was an ordered world the pendant represented, and it was an ordered world on whose seas Bonaventure sailed. There were scant few peoples, scattered either in forests, deserts or far oceans, who had not yet been touched by the long-reaching hand of the British crown and its rivals, and Bonaventure had given up hope that he might himself set foot on some undiscovered or exotic land.

Finding himself now at his captain's side, facing a towering island warrior, tattooed-black and naked but for a brief loincloth around his waist and a war club in his hand, Bonaventure fancied his childhood dreams and nightmares were rushing from out of the past, racing to be made real in the present. He couldn't yet see which of the two would win the race, whether the dream or the nightmare would become the reality, the welcoming islander or the fierce cannibal.

Bonaventure hoped for the one, preparing himself for the other.

Chapter Fifteen

First Contact

KING GEORGE HIMSELF, holding court at Buckingham House or Kensington Palace, could not have presented a more regal figure than the island ruler whose solemn features greeted Captain Ross and his officers warily. Seated upon a rude throne of carved wood, wearing a wrap of rough brown cloth around his middle, with a cape of woven feathers hung across his shoulders, this native king was every bit the equal of any king or queen in Europe. Bonaventure thought so, at any rate, as did Second Lieutenant Jeffries by his look. Macallister, the quartermaster who was serving as interpreter, seemed to vacillate between stark terror at the prospect of ending up a cannibal's entrée, and world-weary indifference at the thought of encountering yet another island of nubile and welcoming young ladies, while the ship's surgeon quavered silently at the rear of their party. Captain Ross, for his part, though he performed his duties to the letter as the circumstance demanded, seemed barely able to mask his own perceptions of the island "king" and his court, a sneer only half-hidden behind every smile. Bonaventure hoped the natives wouldn't notice, or would think it some cultural idiosyncrasy if they did.

At the side of the wooden throne, interposed between the visitors and his king, stood the tall tattooed warrior who'd first set foot on the decks of the *Fortitude*. His initial dialogue with the captain, through the agency of Macallister's knowledge of a cognate language, this partial translation enhanced by liberal use of hand gestures and non-verbal expressions, had gone well enough. Well enough, at least, that Captain Ross and his officers were convinced that they'd be given a fair hearing by the island's authorities, and not immediately dressed for the fire pit and spit. After a lengthy conference of signs and liquid foreign sounds, the tall warrior had indicated that Captain Ross was to follow him to the island, there to meet with his chief.

Once the warrior had returned to his double-hulled canoe, and driven his countrymen paddling back towards their island home, Captain Ross ordered the sails unfurled, and the ship sailed on towards their haven.

The island proved to house an almost perfect natural port, a wide bay encircled on one side by sandy beaches, and on the other by high cliff walls, the bay's mouth shielded from the fiercer waves and currents of the South Pacific by twin lines of rocky outcroppings that grew from either edge of the bay, reaching towards one another like arms, leaving only a narrow defile of seaway between them. Cautiously entering the mouth of the bay at reduced speed, taking constant soundings to ensure that the ship would not run aground, Captain Ross was satisfied that the depth of the water at the bay's extremities was sufficient for the frigate's draw, and ordered Bonaventure to have the anchor lowered and the jolly-boat readied to ferry them to the shore.

Ross, along with his officers, the ship's surgeon Beauregard, and their translator Macallister, accompanied by a detachment of armed Marines and rowers, clambered into the jolly-boat and made for the shore. Met there by the familiar tattooed warrior, they were escorted across the sandy beach and into the tree line, following a wide trail to a clearing in front of a long wooden structure. Narrower than it was long, with a thatched roof that arched in gentle curves overhead, the only entrance to the building appeared on its shortest end, facing the clearing. Immediately in front of this entrance stood a wide platform or stool, of wood carved in the likenesses of grotesque creatures, one fierce grimace or toothy grin above another. Arranged in a wide semicircle facing the mouth of the clearing was an assortment of islanders. A further number of tattooed warriors, fierce siblings to the captain's escort, were positioned at the ends of each of these two arms, mirroring the natural defences of the island's bay, most armed with war clubs or sharpened sticks held in tight two-fisted grips. Nearer the long wooden structure was arranged a collection of older men and some women, nearly all as thoroughly tattooed as their war club-wielding honour guard, their hair and beards hoary with age. Clustered around and behind these two contingents were a few dozen women and children, the youngest among the women and the oldest of the girls whispering to one another and laughing behind their hands, pointing out some feature or other relating to these strange new visitors.

Captain Ross's party having reached the focal point of this lens of islanders, their guide motioned them to remain in place while he continued on to the structure's entrance. Once there, he rapped sharply once on the wooden beam of the entrance's lintel with his war club, and then took a few paces back to stand before the wooden platform.

After a few long moments of curious anticipation on the part of the visiting crewmen and continued whispers from the women in the crowd, a hand thrust back the hanging drape that served as the door to the wooden structure, and two ancient men appeared.

The first, wearing a feather cape over his shoulders and leaning on a carved wooden staff, seemed the relative younger of the two. Approaching the twilight of his days, he still presented an imposing figure, barrel-chested with massive tattooed-blue arms. The other, with an abbreviated headdress of woven animal hide dyed a dark blue circling his brow, was slighter in build, but seemed quicker on his feet, with an amused glint in his eye and a lightness in his step.

The ancient in the feather cape stepped up onto the wooden platform, and gracefully sat with his legs folded under him, the carved staff resting across his knees. The other in the blue headdress hopped up onto the platform beside him, and sat down at his side.

"*To wai eni kauiwi?*" the first ancient began, addressing the warrior escort but indicating the visitors with a wave of his hand.

"*Taumoana, ariti,*" the tall warrior answered in a loud voice. "*Kiara me taitoro.*"

Captain Ross, keeping his eyes on the two ancients on the platform, half turned to the quartermaster at his side and spoke in a low whisper from the corner of his mouth.

"What are they jabbering about, man?"

"The one there, prettied up with the feathers, he looks to be their headman, their king, and he's asking this fellah who we are. This fellah with the big club is telling him back that we're wanderers and explorers."

The captain bristled.

"Blast it," he said, his voice beginning a slow crescendo from low whisper to normal speaking tones, threatening to continue on to shouting, "he should say we are naval officers, and emissaries of His Majesty King George."

"Well, sir," Macallister answered nervously, whispering fiercely and scratching his neck, "if this lot is anything like those I've heard of over in New Zealand, the only word they've got for anything like navy officer is 'warrior', which means either that bruiser," he indicated the tattooed warrior with a jerk of his chin, "or somebody come from another island to steal their pigs and women. They're going to know we aren't the one, and I wouldn't want them thinking we're the other. As for our own king, meaning no offence, sir, but I don't think they'll give a tinker's damn about him either."

"The gifts, sir?" Bonaventure whispered, leaning in between them, his hand never straying far from his sabre's mount. Catching the captain's attention, he glanced over to where Lieutenant Jeffries stood with a heavy wooden chest held in his arms. "Tokens of our esteem...?" he prompted.

"Very well," the captain answered impatiently. He took a step forwards, and snapped for Macallister. Raising his chin and locking eyes with the island headman, he began to speak in a loud voice, as though addressing the chief directly. "Be so good as to tell these people that we first mean them no harm, and that we further have brought for them gifts as a token of our esteem, and as a sign of our wish to communicate to them the goodwill of our sovereign king, George the Third of England."

Macallister shuffled nervously, clearing his throat.

"Well?" the captain asked after a few moments of silence, his eyes still on the chief and a half-hearted smile pasted on his face. "Go on."

"Erm, well, I suppose," the quartermaster stammered.

"Speak, Macallister, damn you," Bonaventure prompted, fingers brushing the handle of his sword.

The quartermaster took a deep breath, and in halting tones said aloud, "*Kaore raruraru. Matou koha kai a ringa.*"

At this, Jeffries walked forwards a few paces in front of the party, and setting the chest down on the hard-packed dirt opened the lid. Inside glinted shaped pieces of glass, a brass tube originally a component of a long-broken spyglass, a bolt of cloth, and various other sundries.

The island king and his fellow ancient, their faces stone, leaned forwards to peer at the chest, still a few yards away. At a barked order from the king, the tattooed warrior walked to the chest, and after inspecting the sides and handles carefully, picked it up and carried it within reach of the throne.

While this examination proceeded, Bonaventure stepped up to Macallister's side, resting a hand on his shoulder.

"Is that it?" Bonaventure said. "Haven't you more to say?"

"Um, no?" Macallister answered, shaking his head slowly.

"What was it you told them, in so few syllables?"

"Well, as I told you before, sir, I know quite a few of their words, I reckon, but I've never had much call to speak the lingo myself. So I just put together what words I knew out of the captain's little talk, and hoped it would do."

"Well, they haven't come clubbing for us yet, I'll give you that," Bonaventure answered. "But what words did you know to translate? What did you say, precisely?"

"I said, 'no trouble, we have gifts in hand'," Macallister answered.

Looking over to the throne, where the two ancients were busying themselves with their examinations of the chest's contents, their antics with cloth, mirrors, and brass drawing ripples of laughter from their assembled countrymen, Bonaventure nodded.

"Seems sufficient communication, I would say."

Chapter Sixteen
A Fine Sight

ON THE MORNING to follow, there would be work enough for every crewman. A stockade had to be built, both to offer protection against any change of heart on the part of their so-far cordial hosts, and to house the ship's stores of foodstuffs, weapons and ammunition, any one of which was worth twice its weight in gold. The ship, once relieved of the burden of its cargo and cannon, would be raised bodily from the water by a system of pulleys and rigs they'd construct on the over-cropping cliff-tops, and the carpenter would direct the men in the needed repairs. Teams of men would be sent inland to fell trees sufficient to plane replacement spars and planks, others would be sent to haul fresh water back in barrels. They had the work of months before them to get the ship back in fighting trim, months before they'd again put to sea.

This first night, for one brief moment, all of that would be forgotten. All but a handful of the men given their liberty and gone ashore, those sad few left behind to serve as a skeleton crew guarding the ship, the crewmen were barely restrained from sprinting flat out to the native festivities. The island king, after putting his figurative imprimatur on the gifts Captain Ross had presented, insisted that the visiting crew be fêted in high island style on that very night. The captain, eager that repairs should begin, reluctantly accepted the headman's invitation, and ordered that all crewmen be put at their liberty, with the exception of a few benighted unfortunates.

That Midshipmen Symmes and Horrocks were among this unlucky number, the former left in command of the captured Spanish boat, the latter in temporary command of the *Fortitude*, did little to deter their fellow junior officer, Mister Daniels, from enjoying the full measure of the event. So much so, in fact, that Lieutenant Bonaventure on more than one occasion was forced to remind Daniels of his responsibilities as a British officer, both his duty to set a good example for the crewmen who served under him, and to the higher standards of the British race when meeting with an aboriginal people. These rebuffs, growing increasingly harsh as the evening wore on, did not save Daniels from an excess of food, spirits and merrymaking that left him, the following morning, with an aching stomach, a splitting headache and a reprimand that kept him on board ship during all similar functions for the coming month.

The sad case of Daniels aside, the rest of the crew fared well enough during the impromptu celebrations, Quartermaster Macallister especially. Having found himself elevated in social standing, at least temporarily, by dint of his linguistic skills, Macallister delighted in his constant proximity to the captain and his trusted senior officers, and drew great pride from this opportunity to take part in such high-level decisions.

"Honestly, now, Macallister," Jeffries asked him, for example. "Am I to eat this mess, or use it for caulking up holes in the hull?"

"Oh, you eat it, sir," the quartermaster answered without a hint of irony. "Though I suppose it would do for caulk in a pinch."

Jeffries boomed out a laugh, and slapped Macallister on the shoulder.

"Now that, Hero," he said, turning to Bonaventure, "is a man of resources."

"Thank you kindly, sir," Macallister answered, and turned back to his bowl of mashed breadfruit paste.

"The crew seems in high spirits," Bonaventure observed, chewing contentedly on a wedge of coconut meat. From where he, Jeffries and the quartermaster sat in a line, the rest of the frigate's complement could be seen ranged around the circle of firelight, the flickering flames casting lingering shadows across grinning faces and leering expressions.

"Hmmm," Jeffries answered, sucking a dollop of the breadfruit paste from a fingertip. "You'd almost forget that they might just as easily have starved in another few weeks, if we hadn't struck ground."

Bonaventure took another bite from the coconut, and nodded.

The entertainment to that point in the evening having largely consisted of appreciative glances at the island ladies who brought endless servings of coconuts, breadfruit paste and roast boar, the crew were transfixed when a new player took the stage. Approaching through a break in the ring of feasting crewmen, the newcomer was an imposing figure, a feathered crown on his head, and a paddle-like spear some fifteen feet in length in his hand. Around his waist he wore a length of brown cloth, which was braided in long fringes that hung down in front and behind, belted with a woven cord from which dangled a green stone knife on a tether. In the firelight, the jet black tattoos which began at his eyelids, rising up onto his forehead to part and cascade down his cheeks and onto his shoulders and chest, seemed to shift and move across his brown skin almost as though they were alive, flat black snakes coiling on his willing flesh.

Striking the butt-end of the spear against the flagstones around the fire-pit's base, the newcomer commanded the attention of all present with a silent glance. Holding still and quiet for a long moment, demonstrating his full control, he finally began to speak. The assembled crew of the frigate, officers and captain included, sat listening in respectful silence, not understanding a word.

"That's the old duffer from today," Jeffries whispered in Bonaventure's ear. "You'd hardly know it under all the flimflam, but that's him all right."

"I do believe you're right," the first lieutenant answered. "This little display, no doubt, is to establish clearly for our benefit his martial prowess, just in case we get any ideas." Bonaventure wiped coconut milk from his chin, and then reached over to tap Macallister's outstretched foot.

"Macallister," he said in a low voice, "what's he saying?"

"Hard to say, sir, but I reckon it's something to do about their glorious conquests and such, and their long road to get here from wherever they come."

Bonaventure nodded thoughtfully.

"I assumed as much," he answered. "So, Macallister, what do you think? Is the old man there, who interviewed our captain today, the king of these people as we suspected?"

"Well," the quartermaster equivocated, scratching his neck, "I figure the others called him *ariti*, or near as damn it, and the closest word I know in the New Zealand lingo to that means something like 'head chief', or 'highest chief', so I figure king'll have to do for it."

Bonaventure nodded again.

"I have to hand it to you, Mister Macallister," the first lieutenant continued, "you've done a fine job as our intermediary so far."

"Thank you, sir," Macallister answered, blushing.

"That said," Bonaventure continued, "and I want this to be taken as no sign of any lack of trust in your continued performance, but I'd like you to teach me what you can of the natives's language, both what you know for certain and that which you only suppose. In the duration of our stay here, at least until such time as we can instruct some of their number in some level of conversational English, it would be useful if more than one of us could speak to them directly. I'd hate for a work crew to be halted in their efforts if you happen to be unavailable to communicate with the locals on their behalf."

The quartermaster sat up straighter, a barely suppressed grin playing at the corners of his mouth.

"Be happy to help, Mister Bonaventure, sir," he answered quickly. "Anything you want to know, I'm your man."

Without warning, the island king stopped short his recitation, and again struck the flagstones with the spear, once, then again. Throwing back his head, he let out a loud whoop, mouth wide and tongue waving, and struck a third and final time at the stones.

As though in answer to his cry, a small army of warriors, all tattooed and armed with spears of their own, leapt over the heads of the crewmen from the darkness beyond the firelight, landing within spear's reach of the central fires. The visitors from the frigate tensed, some crying out, some screaming for mercy, sure that the cruellest trick had been played on them, and that the island warriors were ready now for their cannibal feast.

Bonaventure, hand flying to the hilt of the sabre at his side, half rose to his feet before he got the full measure of the situation, and relaxed back on the ground. He passed word on either side that the men were to calm themselves, but to stay alert for any later developments. The assembled warriors had not leapt on stage to club the fatted crewmen as entrées for their gruesome suppers; they were the entertainment, come to provide dinner theatre.

Arranging themselves in serried ranks, spears held across their tattooed chests, the warriors began a sort of martial dance, guttural chants accompanying their movements. At their head, in his striking barbaric finery, was the tall warrior who'd escorted the captain and the others from the ship, and acted as their intermediary with the island king. While they danced, spears crashing against the stones at their feet and fists thumping on their muscular chests, the tall warrior seemed to keep his eyes fixed on Bonaventure and the officers, his brows furrowed.

Bonaventure shifted uneasily. He wasn't sure what the undivided attentions of the fierce warrior suggested, but the grim expression on the tattooed face did little to set the first lieutenant's mind at ease. Resisting the urge to draw his sabre and do a bit of martial dancing of his own, Bonaventure let his gaze wander from the fierce warrior and over the assembled crewmen and natives around the firelight.

It seemed, as his attention was drawn to the far side of the circled assemblage, that the warrior's were not the only pair of eyes fixed on Bonaventure during the celebration. A graceful figure of a woman, not long since a girl, stood near the edge of the group, looking directly at Bonaventure. In the brief moment in which their eyes met, Bonaventure had the impression of long, fine hair, open and honest almond eyes, the smooth lustre of brown skin, long limbs, and a slim waist. As quick as a blink, however, the woman realized her gaze was returned, and opened her mouth in a sudden "o" of surprise.

Bonaventure leaned forwards, as though he might communicate with the woman through the barriers of their two languages and the dozen yards between them. The sudden appearance of the tattooed warrior's snarling visage in his line of sight, the orbit of the martial dance having brought him between Bonaventure and the woman, sent the first lieutenant's head jerking back defensively. The warrior continued his dance, thumping and crashing, his eyes never leaving Bonaventure, and no matter how much the first lieutenant leaned to one side or the other, the warrior's body still blocked the view of the circle's far side.

By the time the warrior had moved on, and Bonaventure's view of the other side was unobscured, the woman had disappeared.

The dance ended, the chanting stopped, and the warriors leapt back out of the circle and into the darkness, accepting stoically the puzzled applause of the visiting crewmen.

"That was a sight, wasn't it?" Jeffries asked, leaning in close to Bonaventure.

"That it was," Bonaventure answered, his attention on the darkness beyond the fire's light. "That it was."

Chapter Seventeen
The Sermon

WHEN THE WARRIORS had completed their martial dance, and stamped and chest-thumped their way single file from the circle of firelight, a new player took the stage. The old man glided in serenely from the fringes of the gathering to stand before the fire-pit, facing the captain and officers. He was dressed in island finery, a wrap of dark brown cloth draped over one shoulder and belted at the waist, a necklace of shark's teeth hanging around his neck, matched by a pair of larger teeth dangling one from each earlobe. Around his forehead was wound the same blue woven headband he'd sported earlier, though now it featured in addition a pair of brilliant blue feathers, one hanging suspended at each temple, looking almost like donkey's ears. In his hand he carried a green stone knife, twin to that carried by the island king in his belt.

"That one," Bonaventure whispered, tapping Macallister's foot. "What role does he play, do you suppose?"

"They call him *tohuna*, which sounds near enough the words I've heard on other islands for priest, or witch doctor."

"The local clergy, then?" Jeffries asked. "Is he come to give us his blessing? Some barbaric benediction?"

"You might be right," Bonaventure answered. Eyeing the knife in the priest's belt, he added, "Though I shudder to imagine the native ceremonies of baptism."

"Body and blood," Jeffries answered, grinning darkly. "Perhaps we'll be the offering at some cannibal communion."

"Don't blaspheme," Bonaventure shot back, on seeing Macallister tense at the second lieutenant's words. Bonaventure himself, if he could be said to have a religion, was somewhat of a free-thinker; he knew, though, that despite their sinful ways the majority of the crewmen were still loyal adherents of the Church, who were apt to view such sacrilege as an invitation for divine intervention and misfortune. Whether God truly existed or not, it seemed to be the prevailing view best not to offend Him. Likewise, for that matter, better not offend any other gods or goddesses who might be listening, proper homage paid to Neptune being just logical insurance against his potential existence.

Jeffries was about to frame an answer, sharpening his wit and tongue, when he was interrupted by a long string of syllables from the island priest.

Unlike the king before him, who'd declaimed in a loud booming voice, punctuating with his striking spear, the priest spoke in more dulcet tones, fluid and lilting. In the passage of long seconds, his speaking took on the sound of chanting, then the chanting the air of song, discordant and strange to the ears of his European listeners but song nonetheless. Bonaventure and the others, even Macallister unable to understand a syllable, sat in rapt attention, entranced by the sounds of the old man's voice.

While he spoke, or chanted, or sang, the old man pointed to the sky, first with one hand, then the other, then both in concert, indicating one quarter of the heavens or another. Then his arms moved in wide circles, seeming to encompass the congregation of natives and visitors, the village of huts beyond, the entire island and the whole of the world itself.

In the tones of the old man's recitation, Bonaventure fancied that he could hear the notes of birdsong, the rustle of wind in leaves, the sound of waves lapping against stone. In his mind's eye, he could picture a pristine portrait of nature wild, a perfect harmony of sun and sand, wave and sky. Listening harder to the incomprehensible words, he imagined that he could hear the music of the spheres echoing back to him, a celestial chorus of nature joining in with the old man's song.

It took Bonaventure a moment to realize that the island priest had begun to move, walking slowly around the circuit of the fire-light, his hands moving in rhythmic patterns before him in time with his song. When he'd made a complete revolution, reaching again a point directly in front of the officers, he stopped, and turned to face the crackling fire-pit.

The priest reached out his arms, hands held over the fire, the flames reaching up to lick gently at his down-turned palms. His song reached its gentle crescendo, and as the last syllable drifted away on the wind he clapped his hands together once over the flames.

Suddenly, as though the fire itself were providing the finale to the old man's song, the flames leapt thrice their previous height into the night sky, sending out a shower of sparks that glittered like dying stars in the air overhead before drifting back dwindling to earth. The flames guttered and shrank back into themselves, but not before flaring into the unmistakable image of a bird in flight. In a heartbeat, the fire had returned to its normal proportions, and the old man's song was done.

Bonaventure blinked hard, brilliant spots of colours flaring behind his eyes, ghostly impressions of the fire's bright lights. He was certain that he'd only imagined the things he'd seen, that a gust of wind had fanned the flames momentarily to new heights, and that his reveries had only suggested the illusion of the bird of fire. Glancing around at his fellow officers, though, and the crewmen positioned around the circle of light, Bonaventure saw etched on each face the same mask of wonder and shock that he knew he wore himself. A trick, then, conjuror's artifice, no more unusual or inexplicable than those he could see on any London street-corner.

The island priest, eyes raised to heaven, folded his arms slowly across his chest, and lowering his eyes to the ground at his feet walked solemnly from the circle of firelight. When he had gone, the blanket of silence that seemed to have fallen over the congregation was lifted. The native girls again attended to the needs and wishes of their now-baffled guests, the older island men and women pestering those nearest them with unanswerable questions in their unintelligible tongue. The crewmen, some reluctantly and some with relief, turned their minds back to the feast and the generous attentions of their hosts. Only Bonaventure, his portion of roast boar going cold on the plate of woven fronds at his feet, watched the way the old priest had gone, his eyes narrowed.

Chapter Eighteen
The Doctor's Secret Passion

THE MORNING FOLLOWING found the crew of the *Fortitude* beginning the work of restoring the frigate to her prior fit state. Lieutenant Bonaventure, after receiving the first report of the day from the officer of the night watch, went below decks to check on the health of their Spanish guests.

Of the two, the lay friar Diaz had so far not regained consciousness, but instead still dreamed uneasily in his death-like stupor, expressions of pain and terror drifting across his sleeping face like clouds passing before a midnight moon. His companion, Alvarez, was in nominally better health, but still just short steps from death. Rousing briefly from his fitful sleep, he seemed to register Bonaventure's presence with a shifting of his eyes, but said nothing, turning his face towards the bulkhead until the lieutenant left him to his solitude.

The ship's surgeon, Doctor Beauregard, was on his way to check on the Spaniards himself when he met Bonaventure in the passageway. Beauregard had been delayed the better part of an hour, forced to hear and attend to any number of internal and intestinal complaints from the ship's crew, the majority suffering

only from distended bellies the result of nothing so much as glut-
tonous eating at the previous night's fête.

"Good morning, Mister Bonaventure," the doctor huffed,
reaching up a hand to right his wig. He was red-faced, or rather
with a redder face than was usual, his breath near to panting.

"The same to you, doctor. You seem in something of a hurry. Is
anything the matter?"

"Only in a hurry to discharge my day's duties, sir, and eager to
be at my liberty on this island. I have leave from the captain to
spend whatever time not required of me by my obligations on the
island itself, my time spent as I see fit."

The lieutenant could not help but let slip a sly grin.

"And how might you see fit to spend your time, Doctor Beauregard?" Bonaventure asked, knowingly.

The doctor regarded him with a blank stare, uncomprehending,
and then understanding dawned.

"Ah," the doctor answered, smiling, "not in the manner you
suspect, I imagine. No, my days of bacchanalian excess are far
behind me, I'm afraid, even if there wasn't the Mrs Beauregard
and her mother to consider. No, truth be told, I'm something of
an amateur botanist, and the mere thought of an island such as
this, untouched by civilized hands, untrod by civilized feet, is
enough to make me sleepless with anticipation."

"Doctor Beauregard," Bonaventure answered, "I'm genuinely
surprised. I had no idea you harboured this secret passion."

"Ah, yes," the doctor replied in breathy tones. "Since I was a
small boy, and first read Joseph Banks's account of his travels in
the South Seas with Captain Cook, I could imagine no greater
thrill than to discover some heretofore unknown species of flora.
Who could know what mysteries might lie locked within those
never-seen leaves and stems? Some panacea might well one day be
found, a cure to all of man's infirmities hammered out from the
petals of a paradisiacal flower. In truth, it was in large part my

love for botany that led me to the study of medicine, learning the origins of so many of the tinctures we now take for granted. To think that, on this heathen isle, I myself might find something that would contribute both to our ever-growing knowledge of the natural world, as well as to the greater medicinal good of us all, is a staggering thought."

"You've certainly persuaded me, doctor," Bonaventure answered with a smile. "I caution you, though, if the captain has not already done so, that it would be unwise to ramble around this island haven of ours unprotected. As gracious as our hosts might presently seem, there's nothing to say that their mood might not one day turn, and I'd hate to think of you on your own among them were that to occur."

The doctor's face fell, and he began to rub his thick-fingered hands together rapidly, as though warming them against a sudden cold.

"But..." he began, "that is..."

"Don't worry a bit, doctor," Bonaventure assured him. "I'll see to it that one of the ship's complement, either a Marine or one of our more trusted crewmen, is assigned to you at your discretion, to serve as your protection during your island visits."

The doctor beamed his thanks.

"In fact," Bonaventure continued, "I might serve in that capacity myself, as soon as I have the luxury of it. I've always had a passing interest in the natural sciences, and would certainly be interested to tour this new-found land of ours with an expert like yourself as a guide."

"Splendid," the doctor answered, clapping his hands together. "You'll see, Mister Bonaventure. A world of mystery and beauty is beneath your very nose in a place like this. You have only to look for it."

"I have no doubt," the lieutenant smiled. "No doubt at all."

Chapter Nineteen

The First Lieutenant's Unease

IT WOULD BE another week before Lieutenant Bonaventure could make good his promise to serve as the doctor's escort on an island ramble, a long, hard week. Leaving the second lieutenant, Jeffries, to oversee the removal of cannon and cargo from the frigate, Bonaventure had led a detachment of able seamen and Marines a short distance to the foot of the towering cliffs on the eastern edge of the island's bay. The seamen were to assist him in the construction of a fortified stockade, for the protection of the crew and their provisions during the duration of their stay, and the Marines were, by and large, to keep watch over the seamen. The temptation of desertion was never so strong as when a ship was anchored at such a paradisiacal setting, and the Royal Navy was well able to justify the expense of feeding and boarding a few dozen Marines on board a man-of-war if the alternative was the loss of half her crew at every South Sea landing.

The first stage of construction required that a large number of trees be felled, that these trees then be dressed for use as lumber, and that they finally be collected together at the building site to be worked into place. The strongest and stoutest pieces of lumber thus produced were set aside for use in the construction of the winch mechanism that would be used to hoist the frigate out of the water, the ship's carpenter making daily rounds to inspect the quality of the wood the crewmen procured.

The removal of such a large number of trees, even on an island as relatively large and thickly wooded as this, left noticeable swaths cut clean through the normally verdant island cover, like patches of mange on the hide of a sickly dog. Though the native authorities had given the crew leave to make use of whatever natural resources they required, after a few days's work the full impact of the frigate's needs became clear to the islanders, and opinions on the matter of full access began to shift. It was only through the personal and frequent intercession of Captain Ross himself with the island's king, to say nothing of the liberal application of additional gifts, that the work was allowed to continue. Nevertheless, as the first week wore on, and the stacks of planed lumber grew taller, the labouring crewmen and their foreman Bonaventure found themselves with an audience of natives that swelled daily in size, until by week's end the men found it hard to carry out their duties without first having to mutter a by-your-leave to some island matron or gaggle of children who hounded their heels.

Bonaventure, who since the firelight celebration of their first night had suffered an inescapable feeling of unease whenever on the island's shores, found it increasingly difficult to maintain his composure in the face of the obstructions. On the one hand, in his blacker moments, he considered the native islanders little more than pests, to be shooed away like flies so that necessary work could continue; on the other hand, in his secret thoughts, he envied the islanders their life of relative leisure, and their freedom to spend the day watching others at work without having to turn a hand to work themselves. The first lieutenant had spent very little time in the South Pacific, but from his conversations with officers and crewmen on this and other ships, he'd come to view the islands there as, if not paradise themselves, then at least the only place on this mortal coil where a man was likely to find a life approaching the elysian. To spend one's day as one saw fit, in a climate neither too hot nor too cold the year round, in a place where when hungry one was forced only to reach up and pluck food from overhanging trees, was in the eyes of many the nearest one might come to heaven on earth. A more typically restless spirit himself, Bonaventure nonetheless felt the tug of this ideal himself from time to time, not least when straining under a heavy load of lumber, sweat blinding him, his hands rubbed raw red and blistered.

It was perhaps this temptation, Bonaventure supposed, more than any other factor, that generated in him this feeling of uneasiness. Having decided early in life the course he was to follow, a life which demanded constant movement and stimulation, it was not surprising to him that the thought of an existence of decadent indolence might be psychically unsettling. He was, after all, a self-professed man of action, and his spirit rebelled even at the thought of a few months's forced immobility on a remote island haven.

In quieter moments, more honest with himself, Bonaventure knew that this was a lie, or if not a lie at least only a partial truth. He'd been forced by circumstance before to play a waiting game, resting his weary bones on shore or at anchor for weeks, even months at a time, and never before felt this sense of disquietude. There was something else at play on the island, working below the threshold of his attentions. He couldn't help but trace the sensation to the hour of the firelight celebration the islanders had held in their honour, though he had no notion what specifically had been its cause. Could it have been the strange chanting song of the island's priest, and the impressions left indelibly by it on the lieutenant's mind? Or the waking dream of the bird of fire, glimpsed at the song's conclusion? Or the other waking dream, seen likewise through the fire, earlier in the evening?

Bonaventure could not be sure. He'd rarely been good with problems of internal landscapes, especially his own, which perhaps was what led him to be so much involved in the world around him. Never one to dwell overmuch on the struggles within, he'd focused instead on the struggles without, letting his own internal conflicts work themselves out in time. It was for this reason—more than any other, Bonaventure knew—that things with his father had ended as they had, and that he was not closer to his own siblings. Bonaventure was a man who could face any external challenge, any opponent, but who found it at times almost impossible to be alone with his own thoughts.

Driven to his work to escape a burgeoning feeling of unease, then, by week's end Bonaventure was a mass of blisters and bruises, pricked out like a hedgehog with splinters, coughing sawdust in clouds from his lungs. On the evening of the seventh day, the palisades complete, the lion's share of the stockade's interiors in place, Bonaventure was called aside by the quartermaster, alongside whom he'd been working the week prior. In the opinion of the quartermaster, the first lieutenant needed a day of rest, if not for his own good health then for that of those in his command. The crewmen who'd worked with axes, saws and planes the week through were as bone-tired and weary from their exertions as Bonaventure plainly seemed to be. The only person who seemed unaware of the lieutenant's exhaustion was the lieutenant himself. The quartermaster warned that, if the demands on the men were not relaxed at least for one day, the officers might well have a mutiny on their hands, and he was only half-joking to say so.

Bonaventure, reluctantly, agreed to a break, both for himself and the crewmen under him. Work would halt for the eighth day, to commence again the ninth. The doctor, in earshot while tending to a minor cut incurred by a labourer at the business end of an errant axe, rushed to the first lieutenant's side and insisted that Bonaventure spend this decreed day of rest on a gentle island ramble with him and the young Midshipman Symmes. Bonaventure was left with little choice but to accept.

Chapter Twenty
Another Eden

THERE WAS SOMETHING unmistakably Adamic about Bonaventure's first extended excursion into the island's wilds. The resemblance of the island to the Eden of Genesis, no doubt, contributed to this, but more so the process of discovery, and of naming. Walking alongside the young Midshipman Symmes, a few paces behind the strangely energetic Doctor Beauregard, Bonaventure felt in some ways as though he were charting out the boundaries of a fresh-minted creation. Only the weight of the brace of flintlock pistols snugged into his belt, a necessary concession to their requirements for safety, disrupted the purity of the illusion.

"There, Mister Bonaventure, do you see?" In his excitement, the doctor had spun around on his heel, rushing back to grab the first lieutenant by his elbow, almost tumbling face first onto the grassy path halfway along. "There!"

Bonaventure, who found the doctor's enthusiasms somewhat less than contagious, did his best to follow behind, trying to determine what in the indicated direction had so captivated his companion's interests.

"I'm not certain I follow, doctor," Bonaventure answered. "I see only a rather unremarkable growth in a rocky crevice."

"That's it precisely!" the doctor replied. "See the dichotomously branched green stalks, with the slight fringe of leaves. What does it put you in mind of, I ask you both?"

"Um, a little plant?" Symmes answered uncertainly.

"A pixie's broom, I suppose," Bonaventure added.

"Ha," the doctor barked, clapping the lieutenant on the shoulder. "Very observant, very perceptive. The plant is *Psilotum nudum*, of the phylum *Psilophyta*, and is commonly referred to as the 'whisk fern', so your mention of a miniature broom is not far off the mark. The *Psilotaceae*, as every schoolboy knows, are comprised of leafless and rootless terrestrial or epiphytic homosporous, protostelic vascular plants, of which the 'whisk fern' is but one. They are commonly found growing in sandy or rocky regions, and are among the native flora of the south-eastern portions of the North American continent. I've read an account of a Dutch botanist which places them in the regions surrounding New Holland in the Australian landmass, but I've not seen any substantial evidence in support of his claim."

The majority of the day, so far, had proceeded in precisely this manner. The trio of intrepid explorers, the doctor in the lead, ambled across beaches and through stands of towering trees, across shadow-dappled clearings and forbidding rock outcroppings, all in pursuit of plants, lichens and mosses that would pass completely without notice under most ordinary circumstances. The majority of the examples thus stumbled across instigated a lecture from the doctor, of varying lengths, on subjects with which both Bonaventure and Symmes were convinced no schoolboy in Britain could admit even a blushing familiarity, despite the doctor's continual statements to the contrary.

Symmes, it seemed, agreed to accompany Doctor Beauregard on these forays motivated both by a desire for some measure of solitude—the company of only one or two others being preferable to that of the combined crew at either of the two ongoing worksites—and out of what seemed a general good regard for the ship's surgeon himself. Bonaventure, in addition to keeping his word given perhaps rashly the week before to Doctor Beauregard below decks, found that the element he enjoyed most about the excursion was the sensation of personal movement.

Shackled, mostly figuratively, to the decks of a seagoing vessel for weeks and months at a time meant that the longest walk Bonaventure could under normal circumstances take was precisely the length from stem to stern. The notion of walking in a straight line, unencumbered, in excess of an hour, was paradise enough in and of itself. To do so accompanied by cool breezes, the soft music of rustling leaves, and the promise of the occasional fresh fruit or swallow of spring-fresh water, served merely as added incentive.

The price paid, however, involved listening to the doctor's impromptu lectures on the phylum, genus, and species of every plant they chanced upon, and responding when appropriate.

"Interesting," Bonaventure replied, kneeling down a brief moment to inspect closer the whisk fern.

"Yes," Symmes added, rubbing his neck, "really, really interesting."

The doctor, satisfied with the enthusiasm of their responses, made some quick notations in his notebook, and continued down the path. Following along behind, the midshipman turned to the lieutenant, seeming eager for some other level of discourse.

"Mister Bonaventure, sir, the locals wouldn't be calling it a 'whiskey fern', would they?"

"I shouldn't think so," Bonaventure answered smiling. "Not excepting some remarkable coincidence."

"What do you suppose they call it, then?" the midshipman continued, pressing the matter. He had the air of one who pursues a conversation in which he has no interest, preferring it to the alternative. As the alternatives in this case were silence, and another potential lecture from the doctor, even a conversation as uninspiring as that in which he found himself would do for the moment.

"I wouldn't know," Bonaventure replied. "Mister Macallister's lessons on the linguistic cognate Maori have not extended as far as horticulture, nor would I assume him to be particularly well versed in such matters. The bulk of his instruction so far, in fact, beyond simple greetings and basic noun and verb combinations, appears to be restricted primarily to items of the female anatomy, which I doubt will be terribly useful in negotiations with the natives."

Symmes snickered, and a blush rose momentarily on Bonaventure's cheek.

"Not," he hastened to add, "useful in the types of negotiations in which I'm likely to find myself."

"As you say, sir," Symmes answered, hiding a smirk behind his hand.

They walked on a while longer, passing at least two other ferns of interest, a type of ropy ivy and what seemed to Bonaventure a wholly unremarkable lichen. The sun having reached its zenith overhead, the doctor suggested they rest in the shade of a palm grove for a short while, to which Symmes wholeheartedly agreed.

"I hear running water," Bonaventure said, still standing while the doctor and midshipman had arranged themselves in some semblance of comfort on the soft grasses. He pointed to a stand of trees a few yards off. "Over in that direction."

"Hmm, yes, well," the doctor replied in his typical professorial tones. "I've chanced upon a number of freshwater springs on the island so far, several of which feed into the streams and rivers which inch towards the island's bay."

"Fresh springs," Bonaventure repeated, his eyes fixed on the stand of trees, and the imagined water beyond. "Imagine it."

After months of subsisting on increasingly algae-filled water, poured in small measures from the wooden casks on board, the thought of an endless supply of clear water, free of algae or brine, set Bonaventure's mouth watering. He'd drunk deep from the casks brought back by the scouting parties when they'd first made landfall, and had made free use of the island's resources in the week since, but hadn't yet had the pleasure of cupping water fresh from the source with his own bare hands. This was an opportunity too rare to miss.

"Mister Symmes," he ordered, pulling one of the pistols from his belt and passing it and a pouch of powder and shot to the midshipman, "I'll leave you in the company of Doctor Beauregard. I'll be back shortly, but not before I've seen one of these springs with my own eyes. Should you encounter any difficulty, shout after me, and failing that fire a shot into the air. I'll come running."

"Aye, sir," Symmes replied, taking the pistol with all the solemnity of a captain receiving his first command.

Touching a finger to the brim of his hat as he passed the doctor, Bonaventure ambled towards the stand of trees with an easy gait. He walked slowly, savouring the anticipation, taking deep breaths of fresh island air and rolling his head around his shoulders, easing tension. The strange feeling of unease that had been plaguing him for the past week seemed to dissipate, if only in part, and he revelled in the sensation of tranquillity, even if it were only temporary, if not even illusory.

By the time he'd reached the stand of trees, the sound of water burbling in the near distance had grown louder and more distinct. Pushing through the heavy foliage of the trees, he could see between the parting leaves and fronds a silver glistening ribbon, like a thread of liquid sunlight laid out across the island's sands.

It ran from his left towards his right, towards the south and, as the doctor had suggested, the island bay.

Licking his lips in anticipation of the first crystal draughts of the stream, Bonaventure pushed through the last of the foliage, and stepped out onto the mossy ground at the stream's banks. The sounds of gentle splashing he'd heard on his approach stopped suddenly, to be replaced by the sound of a stifled shout of alarm.

There before him, knee-deep in the water at the stream's edge, stood a vision of unearthly beauty. Wearing only a garland of flowers woven into her hair above the ears, she stood stock-still as a fawn startled in the woods, almond eyes frozen on the approaching interloper. Water streamed in rivulets from plaited strands of black hair, coursing over the gentle slopes of her breasts and down her slender waist to her legs. Her delicate hands lay still at her sides, the left holding a short-handled spear, while in the right flopped an apple-red fish, its gills rustling uselessly like a foresail under a headwind.

It was the woman from the first night's feast, the one glimpsed across the firelight. An expression triangulated somewhere between surprise, fear and pleasure flitted across her face, and Bonaventure realized he was blushing.

"Um, hello," Bonaventure mumbled, finding that he'd lost hold of every native greeting he'd been taught.

The woman cocked her head to one side, looking at him quizzically. Then, a slight smile playing across her lips, she held out the apple-red fish before her, a peace offering or gift of truce.

Smiling, and with a shrug, Bonaventure took a tentative step forwards, and accepted the gift of this island Eve, his paradisiacal Eden made complete.

Chapter Twenty-One
Of Names

THE STILL-WRITHING fish held awkwardly in his hand, Bonaventure struggled to compose some sort of intelligible greeting, scouring his scant knowledge of the island language. The native woman, despite Bonaventure's raging blush and his frantic attempts to look anywhere but upon her naked form, seemed unable to intuit his inbred modesty and discomfort at her lack of it. Standing only inches apart, a wide gulf of cultural differences separated the two, which no wordless gesture or piscine gift appeared sufficient to bridge.

Finally, inspiration struck, and shifting the desperate fish from hand to hand Bonaventure shouldered out of his wool-spun blue coat, and presented it to the woman. In part gift in recompense, in part salve for Bonaventure's wounded sense of decorum, the coat was eagerly accepted by the woman, who slipped into it as easily as a jumping dolphin could slice back under the waves. She rubbed at the texture of the coat's fabric, and made a low cooing noise over the brass buttons and stitched piping.

The woman now at least partially clothed, Bonaventure felt more at ease addressing her directly, and found that his scant resources of the native language came more freely to his tongue.

Pointing to himself with his free hand, the fish quickly approaching the point at which it would be beyond all care in the other, Bonaventure stammered through a series of syllables which meant, so far as he could tell, roughly *"me... name...,"* after which he appended "Lieutenant Hieronymus Bonaventure" in English. The woman, again cocking her head to the side, rubbed the fabric of the right arm of her new coat with her left hand and regarded him without comprehension.

"*Name,*" he said again more distinctly, "Hieronymus."

"He-ra-no..." the woman parroted, nodding at each individual syllable, before the "mus" element got the best of her.

"That's right," Bonaventure encouraged. "Hieronymus."

"Herano," the woman repeated, and then smiled. "Herano," she said once more, pointing to Bonaventure, her fingertip just inches from his chest. She turned her hand around, and pointing at her own bare breastbone answered, *"Pelani. Pelani ko Tevake wata."*

Bonaventure grinned in return.

"Well, then, that's progress, isn't it?" he said through his smile. "How do you do, Mistress Pelani?" he asked, bowing slightly at the waist.

The woman, Pelani, giggled slightly at his antics. She took a few steps backwards, raising her arms up and down, flapping the coat's edge like a bird's wings. Arms outstretched, a corner of the coat's hem caught in each hand, she spun on one heel, laughing.

"You seem to do very well indeed," Bonaventure answered himself. He reached a hand up to rub his chin contemplatively, forgetting the now-dead fish until he'd smacked himself full on the mouth with it.

Pelani, having seen the unfortunate encounter between the lips of the fish and the man, stopped in her gyrations, intrigued. From her look, and her knitted brows, it seemed as though she suspected this might be some common act among the ocean-going white men. When she saw the expression of annoyance and self-recrimination on Bonaventure's face, she broke into a long peal of laughter, followed by a lengthy string of liquid syllables and phrases, the only ones of which Bonaventure caught were "Herano".

"Yes, yes," he said, chiding himself, "laugh at the foolish foreign interloper, who prefers to kiss dead fish rather than beautiful ladies." He stopped, rifling through his sad store of native words, and came up with one which seemed appropriate.

"*Rereke,*" he said, pointing to himself again, this time with the lifeless form of the fish. "Funny."

The woman Pelani cocked an eyebrow, and then slowly nodded.

"*Rerete,*" she answered, and then resumed laughing.

Chapter Twenty-Two

Cargo, Cannon & Crew

THE MORNING AFTER Bonaventure had his chance encounter with the island woman, Pelani, one of the Spanish prisoners took a turn for the better, while the other took a definitive turn for the worse.

The majority of the ship's complement, cargo, and cannon had been transferred to the fortifications at the foot of the cliff, the bulk of the palisades complete. Last to be moved from ship to fort were the Spaniards, carried in their drowsing stupor on jury-rigged stretchers. En route, halfway between the sandy beach and the rocky tower of stone, one of the Spaniards, Alvarez, was roused from his stupor and began to shout aloud in a torrent of Spanish curses.

"Lower him to the ground," ordered Lieutenant Bonaventure, who was supervising the transfer of the prisoners while the captain arranged his quarters in the fort. "Doctor," he called to Beauregard, who walked a few yards behind, "if you could?"

The doctor approached at a leisurely pace, squinting in the morning sun, reaching the first lieutenant's side while the Spaniard struggled to sit upright.

"He appears to have awoken," Bonaventure said.

"I think I'll make the medical prognosis here, Mister Bonaventure," the doctor answered, the intended humour of his tone laced with annoyance at being called away from his botanical excursions. He bent down, eyes level with the groaning Spaniard, and reaching out prodded the still groggy man in the chest with an outstretched finger. "I do believe you're right, Mister Bonaventure. He is awake."

The Spaniard bit off another string of syllables, which Bonaventure had to assume were some sort of invective, and rose shakily to his feet. Taking a few deep breaths, he seemed to calm slightly, and turned to the first lieutenant. With a slight bow, he spoke a few words further.

"My apologies, friend," Bonaventure answered with a shrug, "but I'm afraid I haven't a clue what you're on about. Doctor?"

"I'm no help, I'm afraid. Beyond a measure of Latin and a blushing familiarity with Greek vocabulary, I must confess my linguistic skills trail my other accomplishments by a considerable margin." With a sigh, he looked off towards the trees, where his true loves grew tall and green, waiting for his return.

"Well, then," Bonaventure said. Holding his hands palm up before him, he addressed the Spaniard in slow, deliberate tones. "We... are... pleased... to... find... you... well... Mister... Alvarez."

The Spaniard's eyebrows rose at the mention of his name, and after a moment's hesitation he nodded.

"*Si, si,*" the Spaniard answered. "*Bueno.*"

"If... you'll... come... with... us... we'll... find... you... accommodation."

One eyebrow lowering, the other kept at full mast in his confusion, the Spaniard looked at Bonaventure blankly, and answered with a shrug.

"Come along, then," Bonaventure said, a wave of his hand taking in the now-ambulatory Spaniard, the pair of crewmen carrying on a stretcher his still unconscious mate, the other crewmen hauling wooden boxes of medicinal equipment and supplies, and the doctor. "Let's get this to the fortifications. With a few more trips, we should be able to transfer the rest of the equipment by nightfall."

The company continued the short distance to the fort, and returned for another load, leaving the conscious and unconscious Spaniards with Doctor Beauregard and a handful of armed Marines in the makeshift medical facilities at the fortification's centre.

By nightfall, the remainder of the ship's equipment and supplies had been transferred to the fort, Bonaventure proving as good as his word. When the last of the boxes was safely within the palisades, Bonaventure received word from the doctor that the other Spaniard, Diaz, had died in the late afternoon, never having regained consciousness.

Chapter Twenty-Three
Within the Fort

LYING ON HIS narrow cot that night, within the walls of the fort, Bonaventure's mind raced. The feeling of unease he'd been able to put off so briefly during his walk into the island's wilds had returned twofold. This disquietude, perhaps amplified by the unfortunate death of the Spanish friar, the only person who might have corroborated the other prisoner's unlikely tale of sudden madness, set his nerves aflame, and set a dozen thoughts warring for supremacy in his fevered mind. By midnight still unable to stay motionless, he breathed a laboured sigh, and climbed to his feet. Pulling on a shirt and stamping into his shoes, he walked towards the firelight at the fortification's far side.

The designers of the fort, as seamen, had built a place in which they'd feel at home and secure. It was only natural, then, that they'd construct on land a structure so close in keeping with the size and design of a seagoing vessel. Comprising almost precisely the same area in square feet as the frigate herself, all the decks taken into consideration, the fort was laid

out in a manner familiar to the frigate's crew. At the end far-
thest from the entrance, against the rocky cliff that served as
the fort's fourth wall, stood a two-level structure that housed
the captain's quarters, an officer's mess, and a largish conference room where a collection of tables, chairs, maps and
charts from the ship had been relocated. Proceeding from this
structure towards the fort's entrance one passed rows of huts
with thatched roofs, in which one or more of the ship's officers
or ranking crewmen were positioned. The doctor, the first lieutenant, and second lieutenant each had a hut to themselves,
while the remainder of the huts housed two or more men
apiece. Beyond the huts was a sturdy wooden structure, with
reinforced walls and a roof of interlaced wooden beams, in
which was kept under lock and key the ship's stores of food,
liquor, weapons, and ammunition. Beyond the stores were
strung row upon row of hammocks, in which crewmen
drowsed by night, and which were rolled up by day leaving a
parade ground of sorts for any drills the captain saw fit to
order. Finally, along the three wooden walls of the fort, were
lined guard stations and watch-fires, manned by detachments
of Royal Marines, each with musket at the ready, both to keep
the natives out and to keep the crewmen in.

It was towards one of these watch-fires that Bonaventure
walked, his stomach rebelling against him, his pulse pounding in
his ears.

"Who goes there?" came a voice from the other side of the firelight, "As if I couldn't tell from that ungainly gait."

"Mister Jeffries," Bonaventure replied with a nod. "Must you
persist in mocking me at every turn?"

"Here now, Our Hero," Jeffries answered through a toothy
grin. "If we cannot mock our betters, then what amusement
might be left to a benighted soul such as myself?"

Bonaventure rounded the fire, and found Jeffries lounging on a pile of lumber at the edge of the circle of light. A few feet away, trying desperately to stay awake, was a Royal Marine, on his feet but leaning heavily upon his musket.

"You've not come to relieve me as officer of the watch, now have you, Hero?" Jeffries went on. "Or have you only come to keep me company in my desperate solitude? Our Sergeant Higgins, here," he motioned to the Marine, "while no doubt a credit to his uniform, and a loyal servant to the Crown, is not much of a conversationalist, I'm afraid."

"Erm, what?" the Marine asked, drowsing.

"My point exactly," Jeffries answered.

"The latter, I suppose," Bonaventure replied, "though I suspect I'm more in search of company myself than fit to serve as company for another."

Jeffries narrowed his eyes, appraising his fellow officer.

"Sit down, damn it man," he said, patting the pile of lumber beside him. "You're all out of sorts, and if you must know having you hover over me so is ruining my digestion. Sit down and have out with it," he warned with a mock sneer, "or seek your blasted company elsewhere."

Answering only with a sigh, Bonaventure settled himself on the wooden pile, and began to rub his palms together.

"You're in something of an antic disposition, aren't you," Jeffries observed. "What in a place so near to Heaven on Earth could have you so unnerved?"

Bonaventure drew another from his repertoire of sighs, and shook his head slowly.

"Would that I could say," he answered in a low voice. "I'd think I were suffering some malady, some island illness, were it not just my mind and heart that are so overworked, with my physical self as hale and hearty as it's ever been. I'd say that the untimely death of our Spanish guest had set me ill at ease, were it not that I've suffered so the day through... the week past, if I'm honest."

"What, then, Hieronymus?" Jeffries asked again, laying a hand on the other's knee. "In our years together I've never known you to be so off balance."

"I wish I knew, Will," Bonaventure replied. "If pressed, I'd say it stems from our first night here on the island, something to do with that first feast, and the warriors's dance, or the old man's song, or that woman—" Here he broke off, averting his eyes.

"What woman?" Jeffries asked in slow tones, a smile creeping across his face.

"Oh, just some native I chanced to see at the feast, and across whom I stumbled again yesterday. Just a native woman."

The smile on Jeffries's face grew wider, and he began to nod.

"Ah, I see," he said, "'just a native woman,' is it? In all the time we've sailed together... How long has it been, now?"

"Three years, I suppose," Bonaventure answered absently, his gaze fixed on the flickering fire before them. "Nearly four."

"Hmmph," Jeffries grunted. "I'd have thought much longer. Much, much longer. Though perhaps it's just your interminable lectures on history, geography and your general views on life that have made it seem so. In any case, in all that time—three years, four or ten—I don't believe I've ever heard you utter the word 'woman', or any woman's name for that matter, with quite that tone of voice." He paused, rubbing his chin. "What is her name, I suppose I should ask?"

"Pelani," Bonaventure answered, in as even a voice as he could manage.

"See there," Jeffries nearly shouted, slapping Bonaventure's knee. "Did you hear that, Mister Higgins, the drops of sweet nectar fairly flowing from his lips as he uttered the word. 'Pelani', he says. No, fairly sings it: *'Pelani!'*"

"Um, what?" the Marine answered.

Jeffries ignored him.

"Let me ask you," Jeffries continued, taking a more conciliatory tone. "Do your innards feel as though they've sunk deeper into your abdomen, leaving a gaping hole there behind your navel?"

"Well, I suppose—" Bonaventure began, before Jeffries ploughed ahead.

"And do your thoughts race at every moment, pulling this way and that, leaving you scarcely able to stop and concentrate on any one thing or another?" Jeffries went on.

"You could say that I—" Bonaventure tried again.

"And, for that matter," Jeffries interrupted, "when you 'stumbled across' this woman, as you so eloquently put it, did either of these two aforementioned symptoms continue, or did they for the moment abate, to be replaced by a kind of giddy euphoria which left you still nearly speechless, but better able to concentrate your attentions on her and her alone?"

"I—" Bonaventure began.

"I knew it," Jeffries shouted, jumping to his feet and proceeding to pace back and forth before the pile of lumber. "Our brave Hero, the honourable Lieutenant Bonaventure, valiant at war, victor of countless battles, decorated repeatedly in the current unpleasantness, trustworthy friend and fearsome foe, has been laid flat on the ground by the gaze of a mere woman." He turned to the Marine, indicating Bonaventure with a wave of his hand. "Do you mark him, Mister Higgins? Our noble first lieutenant, unbeaten in battle, his heart conquered by a woman's glance."

"I can see him," Higgins answered, trying to take a more active role in the conversation.

"All right, all right, Mister Jeffries," Bonaventure answered, rising to his feet. "That's quite enough." He brushed off his pants legs, and smoothed the fabric of his sleeves. "Very amusing, I'll admit, but I'm afraid you'll have to find another target for your quips this evening. I'm sure my recent disquiet is the result of nothing so much as a lack of rest, so if you don't mind I think I'll return to my cot for some much needed sleep."

"But what about the company you sought?" Jeffries said with a smile. "Is not the company of our garrulous Mister Higgins and myself sufficient for your needs?"

"Quite sufficient, I'm sure," Bonaventure replied, nodding to Jeffries and to the Marine, who it seemed had lost interest in the conversation and directed his attention back to the fire. "But I find I've had my fill of company for the evening, and I bid you a good night."

With that, Bonaventure turned on his heel, walking away from the fire.

"Oh, Mister Bonaventure," Jeffries called out in a singsong voice when Bonaventure had gone not more than a few yards.

Bonaventure wheeled around, eyes burning.

"Yes, what is it?" he shouted back, impatient.

"Unless I misremember the design of our accommodations," Jeffries answered, "I believe that your cot lies in that direction." He pointed past the fire towards the huts beyond the rows of hammocks and the ship's store, opposite the direction that Bonaventure had been heading.

"Well, I, I was simply taking the long way round the circuit of the fortifications," Bonaventure answered in halting tones, "to burn away any of my excess energies and to make a quick accounting of our watch-fires."

"As you say," Jeffries answered back, smiling broadly. "Sleep well, and good luck with those excess energies of yours."

Fuming, his thoughts still racing and his hands clenching into impotent fists, Bonaventure stalked away into the darkness. His best revenge, he knew, was that Jeffries was now left with only

Higgins and the fire for company, but Bonaventure wasn't sure which, Higgins or the fire, would make the better conversationalist.

Chapter Twenty-Four
Industry

HAVING HARDLY SLEPT a moment all night, Bonaventure took over as officer of the watch from Midshipman Horrocks for the forenoon watch. The logbook was updated accordingly, though with fewer and scanter entries than would have been typical while at sea. Bonaventure's log entries for much of the last week had read simply *"Conditions favourable. Work continues on const. of fort and amassing of materiel."* This morning was no exception.

Feeling feverish from lack of sleep, Bonaventure spent the four hours of the watch making a circuit of the fortifications, checking on the progress of the construction, and hunting down key crew-members for their reports, staying always in motion, never still. The men were mustered for their parade inspection, as best as could be managed under the circumstances, those already dispatched to fell and plane lumber excused from the obligation. Approaching noon, when grog was customarily issued on board ship, a pint each of a mixture of rum diluted with water, there were those among the crew who opted for an extra ration of water instead, much to the amazement of the quartermaster and their mates. As the day wore on, though, the tropical sun beating down on their naked backs, more than a few of those who had mocked their more conservative fellows had reason to alter their opinions, swearing to abstain themselves for the duration. Without the cool ocean breezes to which they'd grown accustomed when at sail, the wind from over the bay baffled by the high wooden walls of the fort's palisades, even a few old salts who prided themselves on never feeling heat's bite found a new respect for the elements, their lips and throats dry and parched.

The grog distributed, and the hour of noon reached, Midshipman Daniels arrived to relieve Bonaventure as officer of the watch. Daniels, still over a barrel for his misconduct at the first night's feast, had been assigned two consecutive watches for the week past and the week to follow. Starting at noon, and running until almost sundown, he was on his feet supervising the men, and in nominal command, through the hottest parts of the day. That he missed the dinner meal, having to eat whatever was left when he was finally relieved by the officer of the so-called last dog watch at six o'clock in the evening, only compounded the punishment.

Finally at his liberty, Bonaventure found that he was as agitated and ill at ease as he'd been hours before when he'd first come on duty. Lack of sleep had left him feverish, his eyes raw red, but had not diminished the nervous energy he'd complained about to Jeffries the night before.

Bonaventure, reminded of Jeffries's jabs throughout the morning, and the sleepless night that preceded, ran through helpless, hapless defences and rebuttals in his overworked mind. It was absurd, he knew, that he should develop some manner of infatuation for any woman, much less a native of a barbaric culture such as this. He was an officer in His Majesty's Navy, for God's sake, and had a duty to uphold, and standards to measure against, none of which involved debasing himself with lustful passions at the first opportunity.

Still and all, came a persistent internal voice in reply, the tugging Bonaventure felt towards the woman Pelani did not *seem* to him debased and lustful, but seemed to him rather of a more refined nature. He found himself, against his will, remembering the delicate bow of her smile, the curve of her neck against her shoulder, the light in her eyes when he tried unsuccessfully to communicate in something approximating her own tongue. The fact that he wanted to walk into the woods that very minute, to find her and only look upon her from a distance meant that his intentions were of a more honourable stripe, he was sure.

Bonaventure shook his head. To go traipsing off across the island looking for the girl would only prove that everything Jeffries had chided him about was true, which Bonaventure simply could not accept. Better, he decided, to find some form of industry to occupy his thoughts, and to bleed off the nervous energy that sat coiled in him like a snake.

Finding the thought of construction duties, or carpenter's work, unappealing for the moment, Bonaventure instead opted for some long needed exercise. He crossed the fort to the hut where his kit had been stowed. There, hanging from a hook in the rough planed lumber of the hut wall, hung his sword.

Bonaventure had lost his original sword, a standard-issue fighting blade as specified in the Royal Navy regulations, while on a rare land campaign in Southern Italy a few years before. Along with a small detachment of able seamen and Royal Marines, Bonaventure had been taken captive in Calabria by the French under the command of General Massena, only managing to escape when the battle was virtually over. In their retreat, the then-Midshipman Bonaventure had faced down a mounted French hussar, armed only with a heavy branch torn from a burned tree trunk, and brought horse and rider to their respective knees. Keenly aware of the need to lead the men under his assumed command to freedom beyond the enemy lines,

Bonaventure had snatched up the fallen hussar's light cavalry sabre, suppressing the shudder that wracked him as he stepped over his enemy's bloodied and still body. Rejoining their company in the battle's last hours, Bonaventure and the other escaped prisoners were lucky enough to fall in with a battalion already in retreat, managing to reach the waiting British ships in the harbour before the final rout of the British and their allies by General Massena's forces.

In the few years since, Bonaventure had kept the hussar's sabre for his own, as a reminder both never to underestimate a foe, and never to forget the cost in human lives the strategies of distant commanders can bring. At times, he wondered if the Navy might not be better off if all her officers were forced at least once to endure what he had there in Calabria. His own Captain Ross, not least among them, would most assuredly benefit from the education.

Taking the sabre down from its peg, Bonaventure left his hut, returning through the fort to the sandy beaches beyond. It had been too long since he'd last drawn his sword in anything but defence, and the thought of just once enjoying the pure art of the weapon quickened his step.

Chapter Twenty-Five
Swordplay

THE SABRE'S BLADE slid from the scabbard with the whisper of steel against steel, soft as a stolen kiss. Bonaventure, stripped to the waist and barefoot on the hot sands, wearing only his threadbare breeches and the miniature globe pendant around his neck, tossed the scabbard to the ground with his shirt and shoes and cut the air before him experimentally. The sabre's hilt, warm under his hand, fit into his grip as though he'd been born for it.

He'd hoped to test his mettle against a partner, the challenge of two swords at play always more instructive than just the one, but he found himself without an available opponent. Of the ship's complement, only Lieutenant Jeffries had ever proved suitable to the task, both in temperament and in skills, but while Jeffries typically agreed to a bit of sport with Bonaventure, though sometimes reluctantly, so far this morning he was nowhere to be found. The only other crewmen currently at their liberty having proven more apt either to hack senselessly at Bonaventure's blade during their skirmishes, with no art or science to their attack, or else to cower in abject fear when Bonaventure's sword was first dragged from its scabbard, Bonaventure had no choice but to test his skills against the air itself, and whatever phantom opponents his imagination could muster.

The sabre, with its curved blade just over thirty-three inches in length and with a gently curving hilt-guard of smooth worked brass, was heavier by a matter of ounces than the spadroon he'd worn when first he'd gone to sea, though of roughly the same length. Standing before the looking glass at the haberdasher's shop years before, dressed for the first time in his midshipman's uniform with the straight officer's sword hanging at his belt, Bonaventure had felt as though the dreams of his childhood were finally coming to fruition.

Inspired by the tales heard around the family fire, both the stories of familial pride his mother told and the tales of epic mythology shared by his father, Bonaventure had early decided that a life of adventure was the only life for him. A key requisite to such a life, though, he quickly decided, was a mastery of the art of arms, most notably that of the sword. Raiding whatever library or bookseller he came across— always in secret, as he knew his parents would hardly approve—he amassed a personal syllabus of books on the subject, his aim to instruct himself in becoming a master swordsman. He'd studied his Digrassi, Blackwell, and Silver with a devotion as deep as it was pure, poring over the text and engraved images as though the mysteries of the universe were contained within them. He spent long afternoons practising his moves in the broad and empty fields near his parents's home, a length of stalk cut from the riverside rushes substituting for the elegant rapier of his imaginings.

Giles Dulac quickly put an end to that, the books and manuals, the play fighting in the fields, all of it. Dulac, a family retainer at a nearby estate, approached the young Hieronymus one autumn morning on the road and offered to instruct him in the art of the sword. Bonaventure blushed and stammered his feeble refusal, unsure how to respond. He wasn't sure what to make of the strange man, with his odd manner of speech and the severe cut of his dress, but suspected that the man was jesting, making light of his young ambitions. He'd stumbled away, mumbling his regards, and hurried from the road across the fields and back home again, Dulac's quizzical half-smile following him as he went. In the days that followed, he avoided both the road and the estate where Dulac was employed, anxious to avoid another embarrassing encounter.

A few short weeks later, though, when half-heartedly swinging at buzzing horseflies with his stalk sword in the field, he chanced to see Dulac and the young lady of his employer's household set upon by a pair of armed brigands while walking along the road from town. The girl, a few years Hieronymus's junior and the age of his younger brother, screamed in terror as the two men approached, larceny and lust driving them. Dulac, as coolly as if he were swatting at one of Hieronymus's horseflies, swung his fist in a neat arc that connected with the chin of the forward-most of the brigands, wresting the sword from the man's hand as he collapsed in an insensible heap. Turning on the second man, then, Dulac had parried a cut from the attacker's sword, and with no visible sign of effort smacked the attacker across his sword-hand with the flat of his blade. The second attacker, howling in pain, clutched at the broken bones of his hand, letting his own sword fall useless to the dust at his feet. With a casual disdain, Dulac then hurled the appropriated sword end over end into the dense foliage at the far side of the road, and taking his young charge's hand casually continued down the road towards his employer's estate.

Later, after the two would-be bandits had scurried away towards the town, the young Bonaventure, still wide-eyed with amazement, had searched in vain for long hours for the sword thrown in the foliage. He never found it, to his young and profound disappointment, but he had found something better. He had found a true fencing master.

Now, Dulac's words coming to mind unbidden, so many years later, Bonaventure balanced his weight evenly, left foot back and right foot forwards, and began his practice manoeuvres. A young island boy, coming out of the tree line heading towards the bay, stopped at the beach's edge to watch him, a solitary audience for his solitary skirmish.

Chapter Twenty-Six
Adversary

THE FOLLOWING MORNING, when Bonaventure renewed his fencing drills, he found his audience had grown considerably. In addition to the young boy who'd watched him from the shadows of the tree line the morning before, there were a dozen or so island women, an equal number of men, and a handful of children scattered around, of ages from near cradle to near grave. With an inescapable twinge, Bonaventure noted that Pelani was not among the assemblage.

Since the morning before, it now seemed to Bonaventure, he'd done precious little but intentionally not think of the island woman who'd bewitched him, intentionally not pictured her laughing face in his mind's eye, intentionally not run off across the island looking for her. It said a considerable amount about his self-control that he'd been able to perform his duties at all during that time, given the amount of attention he most definitely was not devoting to the woman Pelani.

It was unfortunate, for Bonaventure at any rate, that his old friend Jeffries was nowhere in evidence for the better part of a day and a half. Bonaventure had not seen the second lieutenant since he'd left him at the campfire, two nights before, and as a result he'd been left with little choice but to practise his fencing skills, devote himself to his duties, and sit in quiet solitude when at his liberty. When the crewmen had quit the fort near sunset to join in another of the now almost daily feasts with the native islanders, Bonaventure had been left alone with the dispirited Marine sentries and the unfortunate Midshipman Daniels as officer of the watch. He'd preferred to be alone rather than to bother them at their duties, and so had spent the night lying awake on the cot in his small hut, though he'd never admit to any such activity as pining away. He was merely contemplative, he assured himself, taking the opportunity to collect his thoughts.

Now, still not having laid eyes on Jeffries, or on Captain Ross for that matter, Bonaventure again found himself barefoot and stripped to the waist on the sandy beach, testing his cut and thrust against invisible opponents and trying to ignore the growing crowd of islanders gathered to watch at the beach's edge.

Dulac, when introducing the young Hieronymus to the true art of the sword, had insisted that he first forget the taxonomies and categorizations of attacks and parries he'd learned from his furtive studies. So far as Dulac was concerned, there was nothing essential to the art of fencing that could be captured in words, to do so in his eyes being the equivalent of pinning a butterfly to a board of cork. When you had done so, Dulac explained, you might be able to mark off the general shape of the thing you were studying, but you'd never be able to measure the thing that gave it life. The art of the sword, he told the young Bonaventure, lay in the sword itself; only the sword could teach it.

Bonaventure, shifting his weight momentarily from his left foot to his right to advance a step up the beach, swung his sabre in a tight arc, from shoulder height to waist. Then, twisting his wrist and stepping to the side in one movement, he brought the sword back around the other direction, a shadow parry. Pulling his sword hand back near his waist, the point of the sabre still before him defensively, he stepped back with his left foot, returning to his original posture and position. He repeated the exercise, once, then again, paying careful attention to the speed of the transition between movements. After twenty or so repetitions, he moved on to another exercise.

As Bonaventure practised, the words of Dulac still in his ears as strongly as if he were standing beside him, a susurration of voices rippled from the crowd at the beach's edge. Continuing in his exercises, Bonaventure was unable to prevent his curious gaze from drifting over to the native audience. So startled was he by what he saw, so quickly put on his guard, that the shadow opponent of his imaginings could easily have deflected his killing thrust and made a successful attack on the riposte.

From among the crowd of onlookers at the edge of the tree line strode the tall tattooed warrior who'd first escorted Captain Ross and the officers to the island, and who had led his fellow warriors in the martial dance at the first night's feast. No longer richly caparisoned as he'd been on that night, he was now dressed simply with an abbreviated breechcloth around his waist, a length of leather cord wrapped around his left arm from wrist to elbow, and with a six foot wooden staff in his right hand. This staff, straight and smooth as an arrow, was fire-blacked and hardened a foot down either end, the middle sections left smooth and brown. On his face he wore the same impassive sneer he'd displayed since Bonaventure had first seen him on the double-hulled canoe, cold and watchful.

Bonaventure was unsure what to expect. Was the warrior come to attack him, to prove his worth in front of his countrymen? Or was he on some errand for his island king, approaching the fort only to deliver some message? Bonaventure could not know for certain, but thought it best to continue his exercises for the moment, coolly watching for any sign of trouble from the corner of his eye. All the same, he tightened his grip on the sabre's hilt, and his next practice thrust came with unprecedented fury.

The warrior, without pausing an instant, walked halfway the distance between his fellow islanders and the position were Bonaventure stood and halted. Planting his feet wide, and raising his wooden staff overhead with a hand at either end, he threw back his head and shouted aloud.

"*Kane ko Kururangi wata,*" he bellowed. He paused, glancing first at the congregation of islanders and then at Bonaventure. "*Kane ko Kururangi wata,*" he repeated, even louder.

Then, in a smooth motion he slid his left hand along the staff to join with his right at the other end, and with a two-handed grip brought the tip of the staff whistling towards the ground, stopping just inches from the beach sand. This done, he paused for a moment, eyes wide and mouth snarling, his gaze locked on Bonaventure. He seemed to have struck a pose, a portrait of native martial fury. Grunting loudly, he swung the staff back up overhead, leapt up into the air, and landed solidly on his left foot, his right shot out to the side for balance, the staff thrust forwards in what would have been a killing blow to any living creature in reach. He paused again, holding another pose, and then moved again.

Bonaventure continued his fencing manoeuvres while watching the island warrior with wary eyes, sure of an attack at any moment. While the island warrior, who from his earlier declaration Bonaventure supposed must have been called "Kane", moved from martial pose to martial pose, Bonaventure moved through his sword forms one after another, the two men's eyes locked on one another. It was not until the island warrior had gone through some half-dozen poses and attacks, and Bonaventure was working on his low cuts at imagined legs, that Bonaventure realized what was occurring.

The native warrior, having heard from his fellow islanders about the white man's display of swordsmanship on the sands before the fort, had no doubt assumed that Bonaventure's goal was to impress upon the natives his prowess in battle. They could not have guessed about his anxieties and preoccupations, and saw only a man stripped half-naked swinging a few feet of steel in the empty air for hours on end. The warrior, then, both to deal with this possible threat by the outsiders, and to reinforce his position among his people, could only respond in kind. He'd fetched his own weapon, and come to the beach's sands to display his own warrior's worth.

When Bonaventure discovered what motivated the island warrior, he could not help but smile. For the first time, he realized he might be able to understand the mind of the native islander. Neither the angels nor demons of his fears and dreams before landfall, the people of the island were no better nor worse than the men who sailed with Bonaventure, nor the men and women they'd left behind in England. Seeing in this fierce warrior, previously so alien a creature, a motivation he might himself have experienced in the same situation, put Bonaventure somewhat at his ease, and his easy grin soon gave way to gentle laughter.

Completing a lunge, and drawing back into another shadow parry, Bonaventure paused for a moment, lifted his sword high over head and shouted back to the warrior.

"Hieronymus Bonaventure," he shouted past his smile. "Hieronymus Bonaventure."

"William Jeffries," came a weary voice from behind him, the customary sarcastic bite dulled.

Lowering his sabre, Bonaventure turned, and found the second lieutenant standing a few yards behind him. There were dark bags beneath Jeffries's eyes, and he didn't look as though he'd slept much if at all since last Bonaventure had seen him.

"Jeffries," Bonaventure answered, "what the devil happened to you?"

"The captain..." Jeffries answered, and then paused to catch his breath. Seeing the humour in his own interrupted answer, he smiled and shrugged. "Well, yes," he added tiredly, "the captain happened to me, certainly. And now he'll happen to you. We're needed in his quarters, Hero." He paused again, and added in glum tones, "Both of us."

Before Bonaventure could answer, Jeffries had turned and walked back into the fort. Snatching up his shoes and shirt, Bonaventure hurried after, pausing only to glance back over his shoulder at the island warrior, Kane. Kane, fierce pride showing on his face, stood stock still, watching his enemy retreat. Bonaventure watched the other islanders come from the tree line to cluster around their champion, and knew that so far as they were concerned, the battle of will and skill had been won, and Kane the clear winner.

Chapter Twenty-Seven
The Captain's Quarters

BONAVENTURE ARRIVED AT the two-level quarters constructed for the captain's use a few steps behind Jeffries, to find a conference already in progress. In a chair along one rough-hewn wall sat Doctor Beauregard, looking bored and impatient to return to his botanical exploration of the island. On a bench along the far wall sat the slumped form of Bernal Alvarez y Aguilar, looking tired and beleaguered, but healthier at least than he'd seemed when Bonaventure had seen him last. Pacing the floor in front of Alvarez, making a circuit from the bench to the long table in the middle of the room, piled high with nautical charts and leather-bound books, steamed Captain Ross, a red flush on his cheeks and a fire in his eyes.

"There you are, Jeffries," the captain barked on their entrance. "If you and Mister Bonaventure feel you've wasted quite enough of our time with your dawdling, then perhaps we can continue."

Bonaventure, standing to attention at the building's door, was suddenly aware of the sand particles that dusted his clothing and hair, the sad state of his breeches and shoes, the shirt-tail which he'd neglected to tuck in. He tightened the grip on his sabre's

scabbard, which he hadn't had time to sling on his belt, and waited to be addressed by his captain.

"Come in and shut the door, damn it, man," the captain fairly
shouted, glancing momentarily over at Bonaventure. "What
we've to discuss here is hardly for public consumption, now is
it?"

With a paradoxical sigh of relief at being so lambasted,
Bonaventure ducked inside, closing the door behind him, latching
it shut with a loop of hempen rope fastened to the doorframe that
pulled snug over a wooden peg on the door itself.

"You wanted to see me, sir?" Bonaventure finally said, after the
captain had spent long moments pacing the packed-dirt floor in
his silent fuming.

"Of course I did," the captain replied, as though it were the
most natural thing in the world. "You're my executive officer, are
you not? And as such, should you not be included in discussions
pertaining to threats to the ship and crew?"

Bonaventure could only nod in response. It seemed only reasonable that as first lieutenant he might be called upon to act in
such a capacity; in his last few months of service under Captain
Ross, however, he'd found that the captain increasingly kept his
own counsel in such situations, and was surprised to find that
trend here being reversed. Looking around the room, though, at
the defeated expressions on all involved, he began to suspect that
the captain was desperate for input, any input. All of the men in
the room looked as though they'd been there for some time, and
all wore expressions of wearied impatience, not least of which the
Spanish prisoner himself.

"I take it," Bonaventure continued, "that this in some way
involves the voluntarily marooned crew of the Spanish
galleon?"

"Take it you might," Doctor Beauregard answered tiredly without looking up, rubbing his palms on his thighs. "And gladly."

The captain's attention drawn to Beauregard with a glare, Jeffries caught Bonaventure's attention for a brief instant and rolled his eyes. Bonaventure nodded, understanding. The captain had been at getting information of some kind from the Spanish prisoner, with Jeffries the only qualified officer available to translate the questions and answers, and the doctor on hand to monitor Alvarez's still fragile health. From all indications, the four of them, prisoner included, had been at it for hours, perhaps even straight through since the day before. Likewise, it seemed as though they'd not made very much progress.

"That's quite enough, doctor," the captain snapped. "We've Mister Bonaventure's fresh eyes and perspective on the matter to plumb now, and we'll have them with no further interruptions."

"I'll do my best, sir," Bonaventure answered.

The captain sighed, with an uncharacteristically welcoming expression passing briefly over his face. As quickly as it had flickered across his brow, though, it was gone, replaced by the same weary determination.

"The matter, Mister Bonaventure," the captain went on, "is that this Spanish bastard has yet to answer our enquiries into the position of this island of his with any useful level of detail, and I've very nearly reached the point of ordering the lash out, and the information flayed from his hide."

Bonaventure nodded, making a noncommittal noise at the back of his throat.

"I've called upon you, then," the captain said, "to make use of several, shall we say, singular aspects of your character. While I've never had cause to mention it previously, and should likely not ever have such again, I'd point out that it has not escaped my notice that you have a certain way with men under your command."

"Sir?" Bonaventure said, not following the thread.

"I mean to say, Mister Bonaventure, that where men might follow me, and obey my commands, out of duty, respect, or fear, I find in many cases that the men in your charge follow your edicts out of something approaching fondness."

"Fondness, sir?" Bonaventure asked.

"A sort of familiarity, I suppose, or admiration for the more intangible elements of your personality. In short, Bonaventure, you have an easy way with the men, and I've seen them gladly follow orders that they might obey only under duress were they issued from another hand." The captain paused, and then added, "Perhaps even from my own."

Bonaventure blinked slowly, baffled.

"Sir, with all due respect, I'm not certain that I take your meaning."

"It's true, Hieronymus," Jeffries cut in from across the room. "I've seen it in the men's eyes. They genuinely like you, and often follow your orders simply so as not to disappoint you."

"Well, that is, I—" Bonaventure began weakly.

"Damn it, man," Doctor Beauregard interrupted, "this is no time for false modesty. Simply accept what you've been told and let's get on with it."

"Yes, let's," the captain answered, shooting a glare at the doctor. "The task before you now, whether you accept these estimations of your character or not, is this. This day, and night, and day again I suppose, has been spent in useless industry in an attempt to reason, threaten, and cajole the information we need from this man." He jabbed a finger towards the slumped and still silent figure of the Spaniard. "We have, as I mentioned, made no appreciable progress. Now, having reached the stage where I feel that more corporeal means are necessary, I'm advised by our Doctor Beauregard that such a move might not be in our best interest, the risk of killing the bastard apparently too great. As a result, I'm left with no alternative but to seek some other means."

The captain paused, hissing breath in between his teeth.

"Therefore," he continued, "I am calling upon you to advise me on what course *you* would next take, as regards your certain likeability. How might you coerce the cooperation we so desperately rely upon from this man?"

Bonaventure sighed, looking from the captain, to Alvarez, and back again.

"I take it I have permission to speak freely and openly, then?" Bonaventure asked.

"Of course," the captain answered, nodding impatiently.

"In that case," Bonaventure replied, chewing momentarily at his lower lip, "I'd have to recommend that you let this man alone."

"What?" the captain blustered.

"Just as I've said," Bonaventure continued. "This man has, if he's to be believed, lived through an experience that the majority of us here can only begin to imagine, and has seen his only companions from that period fall along the wayside. He's now left in this no doubt strange company, only a day or two past regaining his senses, and is being asked now to guide us back to the very place where it all began. You'll pardon me saying so, captain, but I'm afraid this is entirely the wrong approach. Better, I suggest, to let the man mend, body and soul, before we put these questions to him again. Then, one would hope, having come to feel more at ease in our company, and perhaps more indebted to us for his salvation, he might look more kindly on our requests for assistance, and be more forthcoming with his answers."

The captain, his pacing for the moment ceased, looked hard at Bonaventure, his eyes narrowed to appraising slits.

"Leave him alone, you say," the captain said in a low voice.

"Yes, sir," Bonaventure answered, nodding.

The captain rubbed his chin, and then banged a fist against the tabletop.

"All right, what the devil," the captain said with a shrug. "We'll leave the feckless bastard at peace for the nonce. I swear to you, though," he went on, pointing a stern finger at Bonaventure's chest, "that by the time the *Fortitude* is seaworthy again I'll have a charted course from here directly to that damned island's front door, or I'll flog the Spanish skin from his hide myself."

"Aye, sir," Bonaventure answered.

The captain strode to the far side of the room, where a rude ladder was constructed that rose to the second level of the building, his personal quarters. Without another word to any of those in the room, he climbed the rungs and was gone.

"Well, then," Jeffries said, barely above a whisper, "I suppose we're dismissed."

Bonaventure breathed a sigh of relief, and nodded his agreement. The doctor, with a weak smile to them both, hurried to unlatch the door and rushed outside, no doubt eager to return to the island woods.

"Mister Horrocks," Bonaventure called out, catching sight of the midshipman hurrying past the building's door.

The midshipman bolted over, his eyes darting in the direction of the fort's entrance every few blinks.

"Yes, sir, Mister Bonaventure?" he asked.

"Take charge of this prisoner," Bonaventure ordered, indicating the Spaniard with a nod. "Arrange for accommodations with Macallister. He knows a smattering of Spanish, I understand, and will treat him well enough if ordered."

"Aye, sir," Horrocks blurted out, his eyes pulled by some magnetic attraction from the fort's entrance.

"He's to be well treated, do you understand?" Bonaventure repeated, a bit more forcefully.

"Aye, sir," Horrocks answered. Still, the magnetic attraction of the beach beyond the entrance drew his eyes.

"Damn it, man, what is so entrancing over there, that you can't attend to your duties?" Bonaventure shouted.

"Some native girl," Horrocks replied, a blush and a smirk competing for supremacy on his smooth, young face. "She's just standing in front of the palisades, but instead of coming stripped as damn near naked as the rest of them she's wearing an officer's blues. Some of the men figure she's stolen it from somewhere, but Symmes, he thinks she found the jacket you lost on your trek the other day."

Bonaventure's heart leapt into his throat, and he pushed past Horrocks out the door. Jeffries was calling after him, saying something, but Bonaventure just waved him off, saying he'd attend to it later. Managing to hold himself to a brisk walk, running certainly beyond the bounds of decorum, Bonaventure hurried to the entrance of the fort, and looked out onto the sands beyond, where just a short time before he'd lost himself in his impromptu martial dance with the island warrior.

The crowd of his audience had gone now, the show long over, but in their place stood a striking island woman, wearing the rough shift typical on the island, but over it Hieronymus's own blue jacket.

"Pelani," Bonaventure said in a soft voice, a smile curling the edges of his mouth. Handing his sabre to a nearby crewman and ordering him to return it to the officer's hut, Bonaventure walked out from the fort and towards the woman who hadn't left his thoughts once since last he'd left her company. Wills and skills aside, this seemed another battle that Bonaventure had lost.

September, 1798

THE QUADRANGLES OF Oxford buzzed with news of the Battle of the Nile, studies and examinations forgotten amidst talk of Rear-Admiral Horatio Nelson routing the French at the Bay of Abukir, leaving the forces of Napoleon Bonaparte land-locked in North Africa.

But Hieronymus Bonaventure, just beginning his first year at Christ Church, had other things on his mind.

"You've done what?"

So distracted was Giles Dulac by Hieronymus's revelation that the pupil nearly scored a hit, but at the last instant the tutor swept his rapier in a careless arc, like someone waving away a fly, and casually parried the thrust. Hieronymus had noted, in recent months, that as his own skill with the blade improved, there was an attendant decrease in the number of hits he scored against his instructor, which tended to suggest that he'd been given an easy time of it to date. The more he learned, it seemed, the more difficult an opponent Dulac was gradually revealed to be, and

Hieronymus had wondered whether he would ever see Dulac exhibit his full and unrestrained prowess. Too, he had wondered whether he himself would ever become swordsman enough to face his instructor in a fair fight.

At the moment, however, Hieronymus gave little thought to such considerations, confident that if his abilities with the sword were not proof against Dulac's own skills, they would be more than sufficient for the task ahead of him.

"I've challenged the lackwit to a duel," Hieronymus answered, as though it were the most natural thing in the world.

Dulac gaped, mouth hanging open, looking at Hieronymus as though his student had just sprouted horns, or begun to fly around the room by flapping his arms.

"You challenged him," Dulac repeated, with evident restraint. "To a duel."

Hieronymus nodded. "Really, I saw no other option."

"Over a girl."

Hieronymus bridled. "A lady," he corrected.

"A lady," Dulac allowed, with a heavy sigh. "But a lady to whom you've scarcely spoken."

The colour rose in Hieronymus's cheeks, but after a few long eye-blinks of consideration he set his jaw in determination. "Perhaps," he said, defiantly, "but they were choice words." He tightened his grip on the rapier, and then hastened to add, "And more parley than she deigned to share with Finch, I might point out."

The particulars of the incident were simple. A group of undergraduates, including Hieronymus and another first year, Roderick Finch, had been entering the Cocoa Tree, a chocolate house whose notorious days were long behind it, while Cecilia Haldane-Smythe, the grand-niece of the Vice-Chancellor, was on the way out, escorted by her lady's companion. The doorway of the Cocoa Tree was wide, but not wide enough to allow so many bodies passage unimpeded, and so it was that Hieronymus had bumped elbows with the girl, quite indecorously. Hieronymus had mumbled a quick, shamefaced apology, and while the girl seemed scarcely to have noticed the collision had taken place, had looked at him with the barest hint of a smile, nodded, and then continued on her way.

Naturally, Hieronymus had fallen in love with her immediately, sure that in the brief moment in which their eyes met that something had passed between, something beyond words.

Later, Hieronymus had made the mistake of mentioning something to that effect to his fellows over cups of hot chocolate. Roderick Finch, barely able to contain his peals of laughter, had responded with disparaging comments, not only about Hieronymus's ability to reason, but as to the character of the girl as well.

"And that was when you challenged him to a duel."

"Exactly," Hieronymus answered. "Well, what was I to do? The lady's honour was in question."

Dulac closed his eyes for a moment, and took a deep breath, collecting himself.

"I'm not certain that I see the difficulty," Hieronymus continued, exasperated. "After all, isn't this precisely the sort of circumstances in which the utility of swordplay can be found?"

Dulac's eyes snapped open, and he fixed Hieronymus with a hard stare. Only after a considerable silence did he speak, his voice low and full of menace. "And that's why you think I've been instructing you, is it? So that you could get into brawls in chocolate houses over imagined offences to your honour? Is that really the best use to which the skills you've learned can be put?"

Hieronymus opened his mouth to answer, and then closed it again, unsure what to say.

"That's it," Dulac said, striding across the hard-packed dirt of the carriage house's floor, and unceremoniously snatching the rapier from Hieronymus's grasp. "The lesson is cancelled." Then, he returned it and his own rapier to a long leather-bound case, and fastened shut the brass latches.

Hieronymus looked at his instructor with eyes widened, trying to puzzle out the portent of Dulac's words and action. Precisely how had Hieronymus given offence, and to what degree? "Sir?" he began at last. "Do you mean to suggest that our lessons in general are at an end, or do you speak in the particular case, only?"

Dulac turned and regarded Hieronymus coolly. "That remains to be seen," he said simply, and tucked the case under his arm. "Now, kindly remove your protective gear and come with me."

Without another word, Dulac went and stood by the open door, waiting patiently while Hieronymus stripped off his gloves and plastron, and shrugged out of his canvas jacket and back into his coat. Then Hieronymus rolled gloves, mask, and plastron in his jacket, making of it a tidy bundle that he held in the crook of his elbow.

"Where are we going?" Hieronymus asked, joining Dulac at the door.

Before answering, Dulac turned on his heel and walked out into the dreary, overcast September afternoon. Hieronymus had to hurry to keep pace with him, impatient for some response.

"My employer and his family are not at home," Dulac finally explained, without turning to look at Hieronymus, but instead keeping his eyes on the road before them. "It appears that he was successful in his repeated attempts to inveigle upon the Duke of Marlborough for an invitation to Blenheim Palace, and so today and tomorrow the Fawkes family will be away in Woodstock. I am presently at loose ends, with no responsibilities to occupy my time, and this seems an excellent and fitting opportunity to show you something I have in my private rooms at the Fawkes manor."

Hieronymus felt a sudden sense of burning curiosity, leavened with unease. In the nearly six years during which he'd studied with Giles Dulac, he'd never once been within the Fawkes home, much less visited Dulac's personal rooms.

"Should I think—" Hieronymus began, but Dulac silenced him with a shake of his head, evidently deep in thought.

They walked on up the road, Dulac maintaining a fast pace and Hieronymus having to quicken his step to keep abreast of him.

"What do you think you know of duels?" Dulac finally said, glancing over at Hieronymus for a brief instant. "Have you ever seen one?"

"I saw the Chevalier d'Eon perform on a scaffold here in Oxford, two years ago," Hieronymus answered.

Dulac scoffed. "That's not duelling. That's theatre. I mean a fight between two men, each out for the other's blood, with life and death on the line."

Hieronymus lowered his eyes, sheepishly. "No," he finally admitted. Then he quickly added, "But I've read a great deal about it. And I know all about its noble tradition."

Dulac glanced sidelong at him, eyes narrowed. "Noble tradition?"

"Of course," Hieronymus said eagerly. "Stretching back to the days of myths and legends. Men who fought in single combat for the sake of honour and country."

"Such as?"

"David and Goliath. Achilles and Hector. Turnus and Aeneas."

"Honour?" Dulac repeated, disbelieving. "Those men didn't fight for honour. What you're speaking of is monomachy, when two soldiers risked their lives to spare their fellows's needless bloodshed. David fought so that the army of the Jews need not, just as Goliath fought to spare the lives and limbs of the Philistines. Achilles represented Greece, and Hector, Troy. That's quite a different thing from killing, or being killed, as little more than a pastime or sport."

Hieronymus bristled. "But what about France? You're always talking about the days before the Revolution, when men like Etienne Bonaventure bore arms for their sovereign."

"And what came of it?" Dulac asked, growing exasperated. "For all its pomp and long tradition, the Academy of Fence which Charles IX established two centuries and more ago did not survive the first days of the Revolution. And what does it matter that its last president, Augustin Rousseau, was private fencing master to the king and an unrivalled expert with the epee, when it took only a scaffold and Lady Guillotine to end his career as maître d'armes." Dulac looked over to Hieronymus, a dark expression on his features. "The age of the Musketeer has passed. This is now the age of the Spadassinicide."

Hieronymus shuddered, remembering what Dulac had told him about Citizen Boyer's group of "Bully-Killers", swordsmen in the days of the National Assembly who stood ready to duel to the death any aristocrats who might try to frustrate the tide of Revolution.

"But even those instances of monomachy you cite were vanishingly rare," Dulac went on. "The duel as it's commonly understood didn't have its origins with ancient commanders trying desperately to spare the lives of their soldiers. No, nothing so noble. Instead, it began in much meaner circumstances, with the *Lex Burgundiorum*." Dulac glanced over at Hieronymus, took in his blank expression, and gave a half-smile. "Don't tell me that your Oxford studies have yet to include the finer points of sixth-century Burgundian legal practices?"

Hieronymus shook his head, at a loss. "No. I mean, yes. I mean… I'm not at all sure what you're talking about."

Dulac chuckled. "It was the five-hundred-and-first year of the Lord, as measured by the Church, and Gundebald was then king of Burgundy. Attempting to silence the complaints of a particularly noisome bishop, Gundebald drew on pagan legal tradition, and declared the wager of battle to be a recognized judicial proceeding. His argument was that, since God directed the outcome of wars, as every victor knew, then it seemed only reasonable to assume he would do the same in private quarrels as well, and that on scales both large and small the just cause would come out in the balance. Gundebald instituted the Lex Burgundorium, and thereafter in all Burgundian lands victory in combat would serve in court as proof of integrity. Only invalids, women, men over sixty and boys under fifteen were exempt from the law. All others, in going to court, faced the possibility that their guilt or innocence, or the rightness of their suit, could be decided in a trial by battle."

"What?" Hieronymus said, disbelieving. "Do you mean a man accused of murder could defend himself in court by force of arms? Even if there were witnesses to his guilt?"

"Of course," Dulac said. "But I'll admit I'm surprised at your reaction. Though it's seldom invoked, and the last judicial duel was fought in the days of Elizabeth, the right to apply to trial by combat is still the prevailing law in Britain."

"But what if the defendant is innocent, but injured, or weak, or in some other way prevented from making a good showing of himself in combat?"

"Ah," Dulac said, raising his finger as though scenting the wind. "That's where the champions enter the picture."

They had now reached the edges of the lands owned by Geoffrey Fawkes and slipped through a gap in the hedge onto the estate proper.

"Trial by combat spread from Burgundy to neighbouring kingdoms and beyond, and in time it was the legal standard throughout Europe. And everywhere could be found the champions for hire. It was a dangerous occupation, to be sure. And one had to be careful the kind of clients for whom one agreed to act as proxy. The losing duellist wasn't as badly off as the accused, of course, who was kept out of sight on a scaffold, a noose already around his neck in the event that his proxy should lose the contest. But the losing champion would have his right arm chopped off, which seemed price enough."

Before them rose the Fawkes manor house, looking perhaps a little more ill-used than it had when Hieronymus had last seen it as a boy. They threaded their way through the garden, and Hieronymus noted the crazing on the flagstones and pavement, signs of poor repair.

"The contests would never start before noon, and the opponents would enter the area from opposite sides, the accuser from the south, the defendant from the north. After the litigants swore an oath that they carried no magic charms or potions, the marshal would command the accuser to throw down the glove, and when the defendant picked it up, the contest would begin."

They approached the rear of the house, and the servant's entrance. A pair of gardeners working on a hedgerow at the garden's edge noted their passing, but if they thought it odd to see the Latin tutor approaching the house with a young man in tow, they gave no indication.

"If the defendant could keep on his feet, and keep fighting, until the sun set and the stars came out, then he would win his suit, whether he managed to defeat the accuser or not. If one of the litigants were felled to the ground, though, his opponent would kneel on his chest and, unless asked for mercy, dispatch the loser with a single stroke of his sword. Not that mercy was a guarantee, of course. I'm reminded of the Chevalier d'Andrieux, a cold-hearted rogue if ever there was one. He won every trial he fought—except for the last, of course—and when disarming his opponents would always ask them at swordpoint to forswear God, promising them mercy if they did. When they would blaspheme, in fear of their lives, he would run them through. He said it gave him pleasure to dispatch body and soul in one."

With Dulac in the lead, the pair entered through the servant's entrance and then made their way down a narrow stairway to a long, dimly lit corridor.

It occurred to Hieronymus for the first time, as they walked through confined space beneath the house, whether he should be at all worried about what it was Dulac planned to show him, once they reached his personal rooms. He had studied with the tutor for almost six years, but how much did he really know about the man? Dulac seldom spoke about himself or his past, aside from exceedingly rare anecdotes about his experiences as a soldier, usually with Michel-Thierry Bonaventure in the DeMeuron Regiment. And he never spoke of a family, and while Hieronymus could recall Dulac once mentioning in somewhat abstract terms his devotion to someone he referred to only as the "white lady", he could not bring to mind any instance in which his tutor had expressed thoughts about a woman in any but the most chaste of terms.

Was Dulac, then, some brand of sodomite? It hardly mattered to Hieronymus in the general run of things, since he counted among his friends at Oxford any number of students who clearly preferred the company of their own sex, and he'd cared not at all upon whom his classmates directed their affections. However, if he was being escorted to the bedchambers of a sodomite who harboured a prurient interest in him, that was perhaps another matter entirely.

"It's this one," Dulac said, indicating a plain wooden door, painted black like the corridor walls, and secured with a heavy iron padlock.

Dulac rested his sword case against the wall and, pulling a rugged key from his pocket, busied himself with the lock. While he did, Hieronymus shifted his bundle under his arm, nervously.

"Erm, sir?" he began, unsure what to say next, afraid of giving offence if he was wrong in his sudden suspicions, but eager to forestall any unpleasantness if he were right.

Hieronymus was saved discovering what his next words might have been when Dulac shouldered the door open, and he caught a glint of steel inside. "Come along, young master," Dulac said, picking up his case and stepping over the threshold into his rooms. "I prefer not to leave the door open for too long, lest one of the servants wanders by and sees what's stored within."

Hieronymus almost failed to notice that Dulac clearly did not number himself amongst the servants of the household, but was too occupied by what lay before him to parse out what that might suggest about his tutor's character. Because what he saw before him was a finer collection of antique arms and armaments than he had seen outside of a museum.

"Come in, I said," Dulac repeated, setting the case down on an occasional table near the door. "And close the door behind you."

Swallowing hard, Hieronymus nodded, and willed his feet to move. As he stepped into the room itself, and got a better look at the surrounding walls, he revised his earlier estimate. This was not a finer collection than any he'd seen outside of a museum. This was the finest collection of arms he'd ever seen, full stop. Mr. Ashmole's Museum and the Montagu House had nothing to rival what he saw before him.

"How did…" Hieronymus began. "How did all of this come to be… here?"

Dulac manoeuvred past him, a slight expression of annoyance on his face, and closed the door behind them. When he latched the door, Hieronymus saw that there were padlocks positioned on the inside, as well, so that Dulac could secure the room in his absence, and also while he slept.

"This was one of the conditions of my employment," Dulac explained, crossing the floor. "Mister Fawkes was initially leery of giving me so much space, to be secured against all members of the household, himself included, but when he held it in the balance against the low fees I charge for instructing his offspring, he quickly acquiesced."

"What... what is that?" Hieronymus pointed at a wooden club, lined with what appeared to be broken pieces of smoked glass, dangling from a thong on the near wall.

"It's a *maquahuitl*," Dulac answered. "The weapon of the Aztec warrior of New Spain. The blades are obsidian, and are sharper than they look."

Aside from the narrow bed in the far corner, a small bureau, and a washbasin and mirror, there were few domestic concessions to the room, which otherwise would have been large enough to house several people comfortably, or one person in considerable luxury. Instead, the space was given over almost entirely to its martial display.

Most of the weapons, whether hung by leather thongs from hooks on the walls or arrayed in simple display-cases of wood arranged on the floor, appeared to be swords of one type or another, but many of them were varieties Hieronymus had never seen before.

"Is that a scimitar?" Hieronymus pointed to a sword with a curved, single-edge blade that tapered to a point, the hilt protected by a knuckle-bow and flat pommel. It looked like something out of Antoine Galland's Thousand and One Nights.

"A *talwar*, actually," Dulac corrected. "From India. That one"—he indicated a sword whose blade had an even deeper curve—" is a Persian *shamshir*, the sword known to the west as the 'scimitar'."

Hieronymus stepped nearer the wall, and reached out, almost touching a strangely shaped sword, its blade curved forwards instead of back, with silver worked around the guardless hilt, but pulled his hand back just before his fingers brushed the steel.

"An Ottoman *yataghan*," Dulac said, without prompting. "And next to it is a *jian*, from China." He pointed to a straight, double-edged blade, with an ivory grip and a tassel hanging from the trilobed pommel.

There were more than just swords on the walls, though. There were flags and ensigns, scraps of tapestries and miniature portraits. But everything was of a martial nature... even if that use was not immediately apparent.

"What is in there?" Hieronymus asked, indicating a long narrow case, battered and ancient, standing up in the corner.

Dulac responded with a brief shake of his head, and said simply, "Nothing of consequence. Unlike the rest, it is not mine, but merely something I am keeping for a friend."

"So all of this is yours?"

"A personal collection," Dulac allowed. "Something I do to occupy my time."

Hieronymus stopped before what seemed to be some sort of headdress, a tall, blue, conical turban that rose to a point. It was enclosed in a frame of hammered steel, onto which had been stacked metal rings of various sizes.

"A *chakram*." Dulac stepped near, and carefully lifted one of the steel rings from the turban. "In English you might call it a quoit. It's the favoured weapon of the Akali sect of Sikh warrior monks, in India. The edges are razor-sharp, and in the hands of a skilled practitioner can be extremely deadly."

Hieronymus nodded, reverentially, as Dulac held the ring out for his inspection. Then, as his tutor was returning it to its place atop the turban, he did a full revolution, looking at all four walls, his head swimming. The swords alone must have numbered in the dozens.

"And all of these are yours?" Hieronymus repeated, disbelieving.

Dulac chuckled. "With enough time and nothing more sensible with which to occupy your attentions, you'd be amazed what you can acquire."

"But... but why swords?" Hieronymus turned and looked at Dulac, his head tilted to one side, his expression inquisitive. "Is it simply your affection for fencing and swordplay, or is there some deeper meaning?"

Dulac pursed his lips, and nodded thoughtfully. "That is an insightful question, young master. And in actual fact, I'm not sure if I know the answer. I suppose it could be because the blade, in all its myriad forms, is one of the only constants, found in every human culture in one shape or another. Or perhaps it's that deep down I want to be a hero, and I know that every hero must have his sword. But where most heroes have but one—Beowulf and his Hrunting, Roland his Durandal, Siegfried his Balmung—"

"And Arthur his Excalibur?" Hieronymus asked, interrupting.

A strange light seemed to flash in Dulac's eye, and for a moment he blanched, but then it was gone as quickly as it had come. "Yes," he said, deliberately. "And Arthur had his Excalibur. But as I say, where most heroes have but one sword, I am so lacking in heroic qualities that perhaps I attempt to redress the balance by acquiring as many swords as possible."

Hieronymus nodded, and looked once more around the room. "It is a great many swords," he agreed.

"Yes. But there is only one that I wished to show you."

Hieronymus started a bit, having forgotten entirely his curiosity at why he had been brought—much less his momentary fear that Dulac had intended to seduce him. On reflection, though, perhaps his instructor had meant to seduce him, after all, but not in an amorous or carnal sense. Perhaps instead Dulac had something else in mind, something equally as uncomfortable.

Dulac stepped past Hieronymus, and walked to the far wall. There hung one of the dozen or more flags that were draped around the room. This one was white, upon which was a large monogram, picked out in black thread, composed of three interlaced letters: VOC. Above this monogram was written the motto "Terra et Mari", and below it "Fidelitas et Honor", both in black thread.

Hanging just below this flag, in an evident place of honour, was a sword. But in light of the other exotic and unusual weapons Hieronymus had seen, he found this the least impressive piece of steel so far.

It was a spadroon, the blade straight with a flat back and single edge, with a single fuller on each side. Though clean and clearly kept sharpened, the blade was pitted with age, nicks in its cutting edge suggesting heavy use. Hieronymus had seen dozens like it in the past years, as there was a spadroon of that type hanging off the belt of every third officer in His Majesty's Armed Services. It was an officer's sword, common as dirt, not just in Britain, as he understood it, but throughout Europe as well.

The way Dulac cradled it, though, it seemed to be the most prized item in his collection.

Dulac turned, and held the sword before him, reverentially.

"This," he said, lifting his eyes from the blade to meet Hieronymus's, "belonged to my friend, and your namesake, Michel-Thierry Bonaventure."

Dulac paused for a moment, and then held the spadroon out to Hieronymus, for his inspection. Hieronymus took it, wrapping his fingers around the well-worn grip, feeling the heft of it in his hand.

"I've told you about my friend, but not how he met his end. Michel-Thierry and I served four years together in the DeMeuron Regiment, having travelled together for some while before that, but on reflection I sometimes think it's something of a small miracle that he lasted as long as he did. Michel-Thierry had a positive weakness for the duel. And for women, come to that. He survived the worst encounters of our military careers, even the Battle of Ceylon, where we expelled the British forces of General Stuart from Cuddalore at considerable cost, only to die needlessly in peacetime."

Dulac crossed the floor, and sat on the edge of his narrow bed, his face lined. Hieronymus, keeping to his feet, made a few experimental lunges with the spadroon, noting that for all of its unimpressive exterior, it was a superbly balanced blade.

"The DeMeuron were based in Capetown, in southern Africa," Dulac continued, "and after completing our service in Ceylon we returned there. The DeMeuron shared garrison duty in Capetown with the French Regiment de Pondicherry, as noisome a band of cutthroats and scoundrels as ever were. And chief among the rogues was an oaf whose name was Bagot, but who preferred to be called Le Cochet. He seemed to us more a pig than cockerel, though, and so we always addressed him as Le Cochon." Dulac paused, and a slight smiled tugged up one corner of his mouth. "As always seemed to happen when we were stationed for any length of time near civilians, one of the local women had caught Michel-Thierry's eye. Her name was Henrika, and she was daughter to one of the local Dutch farmers. The Boers were always eager to entice mercenaries away from the regiments, to act as farmhands, but I doubt they were as eager for their daughters to marry them. As it happened, though, Henrika's parents were never to learn of her dalliance with Michel-Thierry."

Hieronymus raised the spadroon up before him, testing the blade with his thumb. He was surprised to find that, despite the nicks and divots, it seemed to have held its edge exceptionally well through the years.

"One night, at our liberty, we were on our way into town, where Michel-Thierry had hopes to see his lady friend, when we encountered Le Cochon and his little herd of cronies. Now, we had had periodic altercations with the Pondicherry before, and there was already bad blood between us, so when Michel-Thierry asked the French to stand aside and let them pass, it came as little surprise that they refused, vehemently, demanding instead that we step aside for them. One thing led to another, with Michel-Thierry and Le Cochon exchanging words that began hot and grew more heated as time went on, and finally Le Cochon made disparaging remarks about the probable parentage of young Ma'amselle Henrika. One thing led to another, and in short order Michel-Thierry challenged Le Cochon to a duel."

Dulac paused, and fixed Hieronymus with a meaningful stare, silent for a moment before continuing.

"I'd had enough of duelling, and so tried to talk Michel-Thierry out of it, to no avail. He was determined to expunge what he saw as a smirch on Henrika's honour, even though the poor girl never even knew what had been said of her. We never saw the girl again, for that matter, since after the challenge to duel had been issued and accepted, Michel-Thierry insisted on returning to our barracks to prepare himself. We were already considerably in our cups by that point, and so in his current state the only preparation in which Michel-Thierry could reasonably engage was to sober up, as best as possible. By the following morning, when we gathered just before sunrise in the fields beyond the garrison's stockade, I acting as Michel-Thierry's second, and a rat-faced Gascon acting as Le Cochon's, the two combatants were mostly sober, it seemed, if more than a little worse for wear. When the sun rose, the two men met each other in their shirtsleeves, chests bared to show they were not wearing anything that might ward off a thrust. Le Cochon had a cavalry sabre in his fist, Michel-Thierry his spadroon. At the cry of 'Allez!' the two closed and crossed swords."

Hieronymus tightened his grip on the spadroon's hilt, feeling his pulse begin to quicken, imagining the moment.

"In such a contest," Dulac went on, his tone weary, "if one of the duellists concedes that he is hurt, or his second notices a wound, then the duel is stopped. But with the consent of the wounded man, it could continue. So it was that when Michel-Thierry, who was as talented a swordsman as most are likely ever to see, received a cut on his upper arm from a chance blow, he insisted that the duel continue, even after I'd raised my own sword to signal Le Cochon's second to call for the blades to be struck up. Michel-Thierry could have ended the duel with nothing more serious than a slight scar and perhaps a bruise to his pride, but he would not allow Le Cochon to walk away from besmirching a woman's honour unscathed. And so the duel continued, right on 'till the end."

Dulac fell silent for a moment, eyes closed, and sighed.

"And what happened next?" Hieronymus asked, breathless with anticipation. "Who won?"

"Neither man, as it happens," Dulac said, slowly opening his eyes. "When next they closed, Michel-Thierry parried Le Cochon's thrust and, with a single blow struck the Frenchman's head from his shoulders. But Michel-Thierry's parry had not been as successful as it had initially appeared, for as Le Cochon collapsed lifeless to the ground, his sabre was dragged from his hand, its point still buried in Michel-Thierry's groin."

Hieronymus flinched, and reflexively moved to cover his privates, faced screwed up in sympathetic pain.

"Le Cochon was, I suppose, the more fortunate of the two, though when his decapitated head was later recovered, it bore an expression that suggested his mind had survived long enough to reason out what had happened to him. Michel-Thierry, for his part, took long hours to die, slowly bleeding out his life's blood, as the bile from his punctured organs poisoned him from within. When he finally died, as night fell, I'm ashamed to admit I considered it a mercy."

Dulac rose wearily to his feet, and returned to stand before Hieronymus. He indicated the sword his pupil held.

"That is all that remains of my friend, and of our friendship. After burying him there in the Cape of Good Hope, I abandoned my commission and deserted the DeMeuron Regiment. I travelled north, aimlessly, stopping in Varadeux to retrieve my collection"—he indicated the walls around him with an abbreviated wave—"before returning eventually to the British Isles, which I'd left so many years before. Once here, I made use of my facility with language to find work as a tutor in the Fawkes household."

Dulac reached out to Hieronymus, indicating the spadroon with a nod. Hieronymus, reverentially, returned it.

"I had thought that perhaps the days of the sword were behind me," Dulac said absently, examining the blade. Then he stepped to the wall, and carefully returned the spadroon to its accustomed place. "That they would become for me nothing more than relics of the past. But when I saw you playing at sword-fighting in the fields that day, I knew that those days were not entirely behind me." He paused, and in a quieter voice said, "Not entirely."

"But why?" Hieronymus asked. "Why did you choose to instruct me?"

Dulac looked to him with a somewhat wistful smile. "Perhaps because I believe no one named Bonaventure should pick up a sword unless he knows how to use it?" He narrowed his eyes, and the smile faded. "But likewise I know that no Bonaventure should ever again risk his life over some meaningless sense of honour."

Before Hieronymus could respond, Dulac reached out and laid a hand on his shoulder, fixing him with a rigid stare. Hieronymus blinked, but did not look away.

"With any luck, young master, you have a long life before you. And in that life you will love, that much is sure, and not simply a stranger into whom you collide in passing. You will love, and deeply. And there is no shame in fighting to protect those you love. But to kill, or be killed, merely to spare someone hurt feelings, or out of a misguided attempt to safeguard someone's reputation, is an offence against everything that is right and true."

Hieronymus nodded, albeit reluctantly. "Roderick Finch will laugh all the harder when I cancel our duel. I think he was half-convinced it was a jest in the first place."

Dulac smiled and tightened his grip momentarily on his pupil's shoulder. "Well, better that he laugh than that you or he, or both, should die needlessly."

"Perhaps," Hieronymus allowed. "But that will make his laughter no less grating."

Dulac's smile widened, and a sly look came into his eye. "Well, there are ways of exacting revenge that cause no permanent injury, and which run no risk to life or limb. Have I ever told you about the time that Michel-Thierry and I decided to even the score with the DeMeuron's quartermaster…?"

Part III
Arcadian Allies

Chapter Twenty-Eight
Interregnum

THE WEEKS SLIPPED by quickly, escaping notice like black birds
flying against a moonless night's sky, melting into months. The
repairs to the ship, now hoisted dry by means of a massive block
and tackle constructed at the cliff's edge, were progressing much
more slowly than the carpenter had anticipated. Few among the
crew, however, with the exception of the officers, seemed much to
mind. The captain, having been dissuaded from torturing the
Spaniard, Alvarez, to their service, had turned his attention to for-
mulating elaborate plans of action, imagining in intricate detail
his campaign against the entrenched Spaniards on that far-off isle,
wherever it might be.

Bonaventure, for his part, had spent their time of forced exile
on the island of Kovoko-ko-te'maroa plumbing unexplored
depths of his own character, in solitude, with his mates, and in the
company of certain of the islanders, the woman Pelani chief
among them. The Te'Maroans, as they preferred to be called, had
made a place for the frigate's crew on the island, albeit a temporary one, and the months past had shown a subtle blending of the
two cultures, ship and island. They remained separate peoples, to

be sure, but the edges between one group and the next, at first so distinct and marked, came in time to blur and grow indeterminate.

Alvarez, too, had found a temporary home with people not his own. At Macallister's side, he'd integrated slowly into the daily life of the crew, learning English sufficient to communicate with those around him, though his diction was sadly coloured by the more unusual speech patterns of his instructor the quartermaster. Recovering slowly from his long ordeal, he was soon assigned duties of his own, given a place in the daily warp and woof of life among the frigate's crew, and eventually emerged by inches from his shell, seeming more and more a complete man.

As the months passed, and the stars turned in their slow gyre overhead, the seasons began subtly to change. An ill wind was blowing in from the south, lowering clouds gathered on the horizon.

Chapter Twenty-Nine
Tongues

BONAVENTURE'S LEFT ARM still ached above the elbow, the ring of etched black patterned swirls only now healing from open wound to tattoo, so he went stripped to the waist and barefoot, looking for Pelani. His scant duties of the day discharged, he was eager to explore more of the island's north shore with the woman, and just as eager for any of the distractions one or the other of them might engineer along the way.

As Jeffries was always so quick to remind him, Bonaventure's experience with women before landfall on the island had been slight, to be charitable. With the exception of a few weeks spent on a launch in the company of an Italian noblewoman and her comatose and feverish husband, drifting along the Mediterranean waters awaiting some rescue, and two days and nights in Brighton with a tavern maid one uncharacteristically drunken weekend, women had always been a concept viewed only in the abstract by Bonaventure, with little practical application.

Now, gaining a wealth of experience with the concept firsthand, Bonaventure was unsure whether to attribute his feelings and impressions on the matter to his inexperience, to the novelty of his exotic partner and her surroundings, or to something innate regarding Pelani herself. Given the identical circumstances, would he feel the same about Mary, the Brighton tavern maid, were she to be whisked magically around the globe and deposited on the hot white sands and under the clear blue skies of Kovoko-ko-te'maroa, as he now felt about Pelani? Or, given the reverse, would he feel the same about Pelani were he to encounter her instead in an ale-soaked Brighton tavern, bundling in a hayloft smelling slightly of urine, rather than here in such exotic surroundings?

Bonaventure could be sure of only one thing, as Jeffries reminded him continually whenever the subject was broached: he spent too much time thinking. Even when in the throes of passion, Bonaventure felt himself tempted to consider the nature of his passions from a detached point of view, taking a perspective outside himself to consider whether what he felt and thought was genuine, or simply the product of his circumstance. Thankfully, whenever now he heard this internal voice calling him away from the more corporeal aspects of his pleasure and towards reflection, there came in response the imagined echo of Jeffries's braying laughter, mocking him for his inability simply to enjoy the moment. Leaving the two voices to fend for themselves, his own worst impulses and Jeffries's chiding response, with a light heart and clear mind Bonaventure was able to concentrate his attentions on the passions of the moment.

Bonaventure found Pelani at the stream where they'd first met, the commonest place for their frequent rendezvous. An easy smile lit up her face on his approach, and she gently folded into his embrace.

"Herano come to walk with me," she said in her native tongue, her lips brought near Bonaventure's ear.

"Yes," Bonaventure answered simply in the island language, though unsure whether she had meant the phrase to indicate a question, a statement of fact, or an instructive order. "To the north shore, to see new things."

Pelani nodded, and after nuzzling at the nape of his neck for a moment, took his hand and led him towards the north.

In the months past, Bonaventure had come to learn more and more of the native tongue, primarily from Pelani herself. The language's vocabulary was relatively small, Bonaventure having reached the point that it was a rare word he heard spoken the meaning of which he didn't know. The language's syntax, likewise, was regular in use and sensible in structure, so that he could parse the gross sense of any phrase he heard spoken. Unfortunately, just as he found himself limited in his ability to generate sentences and clauses easily to make his own meaning clear in anything but the simplest of phrases, he found that shades of meaning and subtlety often confounded him. With careful study, he was able to recognize the several meanings a phrase might suggest, as with Pelani's possible question, statement, or command, but he was usually unsure which of the possible meanings was the correct one. Still, his comprehension was improving, and he was sure with time he would master it.

Since they'd become communicative, Pelani and Bonaventure had frequently discussed both her island culture and his ship and crew. They often found, though, that there were impassable barriers between them, whether linguistic, cultural, or conceptual in nature. He might understand the words she said in the concrete, and vice versa, but the leap from the concrete to the abstract was often an unattainable one. For example, while Pelani had accepted that Bonaventure and his crew had sailed from an island on the far side of the world, she could not accept but that his island must be nearly identical in most respects to her own. The concept of "island" to her suggested a seamless abstract encompassing the sands, the trees, the crystal blue waters and brilliant blue skies, the cliffs, and so on. Other islands might vary in the placement and distribution of these qualities, but would differ only in size, not in type. The nearest Bonaventure could come to explaining England to her in those terms was to establish it as "island without crystal blue waters or warm skies or palm trees but colder and greyer and large."

The reverse was also often the case. When speaking to Bonaventure Pelani would use a single word or brief sequence of words that to her carried with it a long chain of associations, none of which were apparent to him. Such was the case now, on their way to the north shore, when Bonaventure revealed to her why they had come originally to her island, and where they planned to sail from there.

"You must not sail," she said, stopping short and pulling her hand from his grip. "Death waits in the fire."

Bonaventure was sure that he'd misunderstood, or that he'd communicated badly their intentions. Laying a soothing hand on Pelani's bare shoulder, he answered gently.

"We will sail for the island of rocks with no trees, and attack our enemies from across the world to capture their treasure. Our captain commands."

"No," Pelani shot back, shaking her head fiercely from side to side. "First volcano is a place only for fire and death, and those trapped there are death themselves, the fire burning inside them."

Bonaventure's brow furrowed.

"The island of rock with no trees is the first volcano in what way?" he asked, confused. "You know of that place?"

"Yes, yes," she answered, nodding as fiercely as before. "This is a place we know, destination of heroes in our stories and last place prison of the father of fire, forbidden to go."

The word for forbidden, *tapu*, brought Bonaventure up short. He'd heard the word used only infrequently, referring to acts or ideas the islanders considered the worst kind of blasphemy. A Spaniard describing an enemy relieving himself on the steps of the

Holy Vatican would not speak with as much fear commingled with disgust as the islanders did when discussing something that was *tapu*.

"Forbidden?" Bonaventure repeated, thoughtfully. "Why forbidden?"

"No," she said pulling away. "Forbidden even to discuss, for all but the high priest. To say will invite the fire, and risk death in the hidden place. Do not go, Herano. Do not go to the First Volcano."

Murmuring soothing words, Bonaventure drew Pelani towards him, taking her in his arms. She shivered in the warm air, her hands bunched in fists pressing into the bare skin at his back.

"Do not," she repeated softly, her cheek pressed against his chest. "Do not go."

Chapter Thirty
Wings

IT WAS CLEAR that Pelani would not easily dissuade Bonaventure from venturing to the island which she called "First Volcano", even if the decision were his to make, which it was not, and equally clear that Bonaventure could not impel Pelani to dismiss her own concerns as nothing more than received superstition. So it was that as they neared the north shore of the island, the two reluctantly settled into a variety of impasse, letting the matter drop for the moment, and with a will turning their thoughts to more pleasant topics, the easier to find common cause.

Bonaventure had never yet visited this region of the island, and at first blush it presented very little to his eyes that they had not seen before: the crystal blue skies arching overhead; the endless expanse of ocean stretching out to the horizon, limned by white breakers; white sands underfoot bordering the emerald-leaved trees where the beach met the forest, studded here and there with black rocks that rose like scattered dragon's teeth. Still and all, he had little cause for complaint, with the warm presence of Pelani close at hand.

As he surveyed the north shore, though, something caught Bonaventure's eye, and his dormant curiosity was quickly awoken.

It was a flutter of black in amongst the deep green leaves of the trees lining the beach's edge. His initial impulse, unexamined, was that it was simply a bird, one of the many that crowded the island's trees. Following close on the heels of this impression, though, was a sense of scale, and the realization that the tree upon which the dark fluttering shape perched was much further away to Bonaventure's vantage than he had originally surmised. That being the case, the bird—if bird it was—was of a considerably larger profile than any he had theretofore glimpsed on the island.

Bonaventure's first reaction was to freeze in place, shooting out his arm to arrest Pelani's progress up the beach, and then with his hand around her shoulder, to narrow his eyes and peer more intently at the dark fluttering shape. It took a moment for his eyes to resolve the shape from the shadows that surrounded it, but when they had, Bonaventure found fresh surprise. The creature was large, there was no doubt, but stranger still, it did not appear to be a bird, for all that it had wings and perched upon a high branch. It was difficult to make out many details, but the creature's limbs had more the look of a bat's leathery wings than the feathered wings of a bird, and the bulk of the creature's body seemed something close to the dimensions of Bonaventure's own torso.

Pelani, at first confused as to why Bonaventure had come to a halt, followed his gaze, and then her own eyes widened with alarm. "Herano come!" she said in a harsh whisper, grabbing hold of his elbow and tugging him back the way they had come. "We must go. Away."

Gently, Bonaventure took hold of Pelani's wrist, holding fast. "What is the matter?" He smiled slightly, and then added, with a little more acid than he'd intended, "Is the creature *tapu*?"

Pelani cocked an eyebrow, and looked at Bonaventure with a puzzled look. Then she shook her head, forcefully. "No. Not forbidden. But *dangerous.*"

Bonaventure looked from Pelani to the dark shape perched in the tree. "Dangerous, is it?" He released his hold on her wrist, and then drew the pistol that was snugged in his belt. With his other hand, he patted the hilt of the sabre that hung on his other hip. Then, in English, he said, "I shouldn't worry too much about that."

Shifting the pistol to his other hand, he reached over and threaded his fingers through Pelani's.

"Come along," he said in the island tongue, soothingly. "I want to take a closer look."

Pelani was clearly shaken, having little desire to venture any nearer the creature, but she seemed just as reluctant to leave Bonaventure's side with the creature at such close quarters, and so begrudgingly followed along in his wake.

They began some yards away from the tree where the creature perched, and inched closer as quietly as Bonaventure was able, but before they had got much nearer, the creature seemed to startle. Whether it was in response to the sound of their footfalls, or even just the noise of their breathing, or some other factor entirely, Bonaventure could not say, but the end result was the same. The creature spread its wings and dove from its perch, flapping deeper into the forest.

"Come on!" Bonaventure tugged Pelani after him, quickening his pace. "We still might be able to catch it."

They plunged into the tree line, the trunks close set around them, and pressed on, following in the direction the creature had flown, quietly as they were able.

The treetops overhead were so tightly spaced as to be virtually knit into a skein, and the little sunlight that reached the forest floor over which they walked was dappled thoroughly with shadow. Occasionally they passed through regions as dark as twilight, only to pass again through areas only partially shaded.

Pelani remained silent, but the tight grip of her fingers around Bonaventure's own, and the way that she hung back, dragging on his progress like a lowered anchor, made clear that her earlier reservations about the creature had not been abandoned.

"What is it?" Bonaventure called back over his shoulder in a low whisper, as they moved through the trackless wood. "That creature. What is it?"

Her jaw set, her lips drawn into a line, Pelani fought to control her fear. "Monster," she said simply. "Black winged monster. It migrates to our island, sometimes, but rarely stays long. It seeks its lost home, *Moukere tukoro*."

Bonaventure raised an eyebrow. The name meant "Wandering Island", as near as he could make out. "A lost home?"

Pelani gave an abbreviated nod. "Its home moves with the seasons, and the black winged monster flew away, and when he flew back, its home was nowhere to be found. So it roams the seas in search." She shook her head, expression darkening. "It is not from this world, but from beyond the land of the living, and it is danger to approach."

"Danger." Bonaventure nodded. "But not forbidden?"

A slight smile tugged the corners of Pelani's mouth. "No," she said, shaking her head. "Not forbidden."

"As I said," Bonaventure said, smiling. "Dangerous I can handle."

Finally, they reached the place where the black fluttering creature had retreated. It perched on a tree, in a twilit area, the ground beneath covered in thick shadow. It seemed not to have heard the sound of their approach, and remained on its perch, wings rustling slightly.

Seen close to, the creature was even stranger than Bonaventure had imagined. It was something like a headless bat, but of enormous size, its wing span easily measuring from the tips of Bonaventure's outstretched hands, five or six feet in all. Its hide was a uniform black, with leathery wings and menacing talons of the same shade. It had no discernable head or sensory organs, just a cavernous wound-like mouth that stretched between the joints of its two wings, opening and closing rhythmically, making an unsettling smacking sound. Periodically it emitted a strange, high-pitched whine, like the cry of a drowning animal, which set Bonaventure's teeth on edge.

"I want to get a closer look," Bonaventure said, in a barely audible whisper.

"No," Pelani said forcefully, holding her ground and tugging back her hand. "It is danger to approach."

Bonaventure smiled, releasing his hold on her hand. "You stay here, then. I will return quickly."

Pelani opened her mouth to object, but Bonaventure turned and continued before she was able to give her objection voice.

Bonaventure had no desire to harm the creature, but likewise little wish to see himself harmed, or Pelani come to that, and tightened his grip on his pistol, just in case.

He was perhaps a dozen feet from the creature, close enough that more detail about its physiognomy was now coming into view, when everything went horribly wrong.

A dried twig snapped under Bonaventure's step, and the creature immediately reacted, violently. A blood-chilling cry issued from the thing's enormous mouth, and it launched itself off its perch, directly at Bonaventure.

The creature was only an eye-blink away from striking Bonaventure with its wicked talons, and so he fired his pistol at it, however reluctantly. His shot struck the creature's body dead centre, and it fell flapping to the ground.

216 Set the Seas on Fire

For an instant, Bonaventure was sorry to have killed the thing, having only wanted a closer look. He turned back to Pelani, wearing an apologetic expression, though to whom he might apologize, he wasn't sure. Then, as he turned to step nearer the fallen creature for a closer inspection, the shadows around them erupted in noise and movement.

Dozens of the creatures, possibly more, burst out of the shadows, having previously lain unseen on the dark ground, lying flat with their wings outspread, now stirred to motion by the sound of Bonaventure's shot. Dozens of the black winged beasts or more, each with its enormous wound-like mouth opening and closing menacingly, each with its talons out and grasping, filling the air around them with the high keening of their shrieks and the dark fluttering of their wings. Dozens of the monsters, and all of them intent on one thing: the blood of Bonaventure and Pelani!

Chapter Thirty-One
Flight

So THICK WERE the bat-creatures in the air, so quickly were they upon them, that Bonaventure didn't have the opportunity to load, and only by sprinting to Pelani's side and dragging her along behind him in a pell-mell rush into the close-packed trees were they able to escape immediate death in the smacking jaws of the beasts. As it was, with the trees growing so close on all sides, the progress of the bat-creatures was somewhat retarded, but not sufficient to put the pair out of harm's way.

Bonaventure was forced to use his pistol as a club, holding the barrel and battering the things with the heavy wooden grip, while his sabre filled his other fist. Pelani, to her credit, didn't cry out or scream in terror, but seemed gripped instead by a steely resolve. As they fled through the trees, she snatched up a fallen branch, and swung with a will at the noisome monsters that flew at them from all sides.

"To the south!" Bonaventure shouted over the keening cries and flapping of the bat-creatures. He knew that to the north there lay only more forest and the beach and ocean beyond, and hoped against hope that by pressing south they would reach either his own people or Pelani's, and thereby some shelter.

They pressed on, only narrowly escaping the innumerable bites and swipes of the bat-creatures in flight, Bonaventure battering them with his pistol's butt, laying about him on all sides with his sabre, while Pelani put up a spirited defence with the heavy tree branch. The talons of one of the creatures caught in her hair, and as the creature flapped its wings and tried to take to the skies once more, its claws holding fast, Bonaventure slashed out with his sabre. The sabre glanced off the bat-creature, inflicting minimal damage, but as the arc of the blade carried it onwards it sliced through Pelani's hair, shearing off a large hunk and freeing her from the creature's grip.

Another of the bat-creatures hove into view before them, and Bonaventure battered it to one side with the butt of his pistol, but not before the creature had raked across his upper arm, drawing a pair of deep red cuts. Still another was spit on the end of his sabre, and Bonaventure lost precious moments dislodging the heavy creature from the gored blade.

It seemed that any one of the bat-creatures was scarcely a credible threat, when met properly armed and prepared, each could be felled relatively easily with a single shot or sword-thrust, and even a round walloping with the pistol's wooden butt or with the heavy branch Pelani carried was sufficient to turn them aside, at least temporarily. However, it was in their sheer numbers that the creatures presented their most significant threat. As many of them as Bonaventure and Pelani were able to cut down or knock to the ground, still more came after them, seemingly endless waves of the creatures, all leathery wings and grasping talons and wide snapping jaws.

On the pair plunged through the forests, low-hanging branches snatching at them, whipping scratches on their faces and arms, tearing ribbons from Bonaventure's shirt. And still the bat-creatures pursued, filling Bonaventure's ears with their piercing, keening cries.

Finally, when it seemed that they could go no further, and would succumb to fatigue, and then in short order to the teeth and talons of the bat-creatures, the pair burst through the trees and into a wide clearing. Immediately before them stood a cluster of huts, surrounding a central fire, whose smoke curled up, a grey ribbon against the clear blue sky. Women crouched around the fire, chatting breezily, while in the near distance a group of children played at a game of tag and chase.

"It is... Kururangi... village," Pelani just managed, panting and breathless.

"Help us!" Bonaventure shouted aloud, stumbling towards the circle of huts, glancing over his shoulder, expectantly. The bat-creatures could not be far behind now. "Help us!"

Figures rushed from the huts, as the women around the fire jumped to their feet, startled. One of the newcomers on the scene was a tall warrior, skin covered in dark spiralling tattoos, who Bonaventure recognized after a heartbeat as the warrior known as Kane.

"Pelani!" the island warrior shouted.

Just at that moment, the first wave of bat-creatures crashed through the trees, flitting into the open air of the village.

Kane shouted a curse, the wording of which Bonaventure couldn't catch but whose meaning was crystal clear. Without pausing an instant, Kane rushed to the roaring fire at the village centre, shouting out instructions to the bewildered villagers as he went. He rounded the fire, snatching up a brand from the flames and holding it overhead like a banner, and then raced towards the place where Bonaventure and Pelani had finally collapsed to the ground, overcome by exertion.

The island warrior hurled imprecations in the native tongue at the bat-creatures, intended as much to startle as to offend, and waved his fiery brand back and forth in front of him, the flame flapping like a flag, the acrid smoke curling up.

Easing Pelani to the ground, Bonaventure managed to climb up onto his knees, spent pistol in one hand, sabre in the other.

The men and women of the village wasted no time, but rose to Kane's challenge, disassembling the carefully arranged cook fire a log at a time, and rushing to stand between the village and the oncoming waves of bat-creatures. In short order, a wall of dancing flame met the winged monsters as they crashed through the tree line, the ground before them littered with the smouldering remains of their brethren who had flown too near the villagers's brands.

Bonaventure rose to his feet, a stitch in his side, his lungs burning. He sheathed his sabre at his side, and with hands that shook with fatigue loaded his pistol. His intent was to join the line of fire-wielding defenders; by the time his pistol was ready, though, the job was done, and the last of the bat-creatures had been driven away. The sounds of their flapping wings and cries could be heard echoing through the shadow-dappled woods beyond the tree line, but no more of the creatures appeared in the clearing.

Bonaventure held the pistol impotently in a white-knuckled grip.

When it was clear that the danger had passed, Kane turned from the tree line and strode towards the place where Pelani lay, Bonaventure standing over her.

"You have my thanks," Bonaventure said, reaching out a hand of greeting to the island warrior.

Kane glanced at Bonaventure, the scorn evident on his tattooed face, but ignored the proffered hand. Then Kane looked down at Pelani, his expression unreadable, and after a long silent moment, stalked away.

Bonaventure watched Kane's retreating back, thoughtfully. Then he tucked his impotent pistol back into his belt, and helped Pelani to her feet.

"Dangerous," Pelani said, breathlessly. "Not forbidden, but very, very dangerous."

Bonaventure wrapped his arm around her waist, and smiled. "Next time, I will listen more carefully!"

She returned his smile, but Bonaventure could see the care writ plainly on her face.

Chapter Thirty-Two
Cultural Divide

A FEW DAYS later, though he had regaled them with the story of his encounter with the bat-creatures, Bonaventure had yet to communicate to his captain or mates Pelani's concerns about their destination. He wasn't sure on the one hand precisely what she was trying to tell him, and on the other hand whether he'd believe her if he had understood, though admittedly given their experience with the winged monsters, he might be prepared to give her more credence than he otherwise would. Too often, the gulf of cultures separating the two lovers was forgotten, to be re-emphasized only in times like these. As close as they might often come, skin to skin and heart to heart, there was a divide separating them that could never be completely breached.

In the same way, the perceptions and precepts dividing the two cultures now sharing the island often led to conflict. When Bonaventure heard the shouts following the theft of the pistol, he was sure the conflict would lead next to bloodshed.

Since they'd first landed on the island months before, the crew had had problems with theft. Stealing anything, on board a ship at sail or at dock, was a serious offence, and an invitation to

224 <i>Set the Seas on Fire</i>

lashings at least and death at worst. Even something as petty as thieving another crewman's ration of grog was sufficient to bring down the most severe corporal punishment, a guiding principle of the Royal Navy being the sanctity of property, both that of the individual and of the ship herself.

The islanders, however, seemed not as apt to revere the notion of property. In their more casual society, things were kept in common, and as such could be taken up and used by anyone with a need for them. If an islander needed an axe, and an axe was handy, the axe was his to use. Likewise in their relationships, while a man and woman might be joined together as husband and wife, they were free to engage in whatever congress they chose, temporary coupling having no impact on the sanctity of the union. Jealousy and greed were unknown on the island, at least of course until the arrival of the *Fortitude*.

Almost immediately upon landfall, property began to go missing. Tools, nails, clothing, whatever was at hand, anything brought from the ship to the island was fair game for the islanders's grasp. Several times these thefts had almost led to blows, either between crewmen accusing one another of the thefts, or between crewmen and the islanders who they suspected of being the thieves. Luckily for the ship's crew, and the continued hospitality of the islanders, the captain was able to establish early with the island's king the need to prevent continued thefts without resorting to force of arms.

The island's king, for his part, must have been convinced the captain and his crew were deranged in some fashion, to place such a premium on things of so little significance, but he had ordered his people to leave be the things the visitors had brought to their shores. As incomprehensible as it was to the islanders, the visitors considered these trinkets and tools as parts of themselves, and would not accept their loss. The islanders, giggling behind their hands and gaping wide-eyed at the madness of the ship's crew, reluctantly agreed to try not to steal. Some thefts, of course, would be unavoidable.

It was Midshipman Symmes who precipitated the most recent crisis. Seamen were never much for swimming, seeing the ability to stay afloat as something of an unnecessary risk. If a ship were to founder and sink, with no rescue in sight, most sailors preferred the thought of following their ship down into the depths at once, to sleep in the sea's briny embrace, to the prospect of treading water needlessly for as long as their strength held out, surviving only to suffer aches and pains or to attract the attention of hungry sharks. Symmes had been instructed in this view early in his naval service, and had never previously seen any reason to doubt it.

Now, though, seeing the islanders paddle out on long boards past the protective ring of the bay to the choppy waters beyond, riding back on the crest of a wave standing upright on the board's surface, Symmes was seduced. When the clarion call of the surf was too much for him to resist, he stripped naked, piling his shoes and clothes in a neat pyramid on the beach with his pistol perched on top, and plunged splashing into the water. He had no board to stand on, and no desire to try one if he had, wanting only to test the push and pull of the waves on his body.

For the better part of an hour he splashed in the water of the bay, rarely going further than he could stand. He managed to accidentally swallow nearly his weight in salt water, and burned the fairer skin of his private areas in the hot sun. When he'd finally had enough of the water, his muscles beginning to ache, he waded from the surf and back to the shore. Drying quickly in the hot air, he pulled on his clothes, realizing only when buckling up his shoes that his pistol was nowhere to be found.

Some thefts might have been unavoidable, but the captain hardly relished the idea of an islander going armed with the crew's own weapons. Though rarely straying far from his quarters, the captain had made it abundantly and frequently clear that by no means were firearms to fall into the hands of the natives.

Face burning with fear, hardly able to breathe, Symmes rushed to the fort to report the theft, barrelling into Bonaventure at the entrance.

"Pistol stolen," he managed to wheeze before saline coughs racked his body. "At the water's edge."

Bonaventure took in Symmes's damp clothing and still-dripping wet hair with a glance, and immediately understood what had happened. He called over Troughton, the commander of the Royal Marines, and sent a miserable Symmes to fetch the captain.

"Have your men assembled," Bonaventure ordered Troughton. "A firearm had been lost to the possession of a native. The captain will no doubt want to parley with the island king, and attempt to negotiate the weapon's return, but I want parties of seamen and Marines dispatched to search for it immediately."

"Aye, sir," the Marine commander replied, and hurried to assemble his men.

Bonaventure buckled on his sabre, and snugged a pair of pistols in his belt. Looking through the fort's entrance at the lush greens of the island's wilds beyond, he gnawed at his lip. Unless they were very careful, the nightmare so long avoided might finally begin, and the dream of the last months end.

Chapter Thirty-Three
The Purloined Firearm

BONAVENTURE, ALONG WITH Midshipman Symmes, Marine Commander Troughton, and a handful of crewmen and Marines, had only just set off on their search when Midshipman Horrocks came running up behind them, calling for them to stop between panting breaths.

On joining Bonaventure's search party, Horrocks quickly explained that he had been high on the cliff-top, checking the soundness of the block-and-tackle harness mounted there. From that high vantage point, he had happened to spy a young island boy, scurrying along the beach towards the east, carrying something clutched in a two-handed grip. Naturally, he was prepared to think nothing of it, until at the final moment before turning away he saw sunlight glint sharply off the thing the boy carried, some hint of glass or metal hidden in his small, brown embrace. Curious, and knowing well the captain's prohibition of any theft by or unapproved gift to the natives, Horrocks had left his work on the cliff-top and climbed down to investigate. On reaching the fort, and hearing of the stolen pistol, he'd hurried to find the ranking officer on the search, sure the two events were related.

Bonaventure took the news with a mixture of tension and relief. On the one hand, it was reassuring to hear that the firearm might have been stolen out of something as simple as a childish prank, or childhood acquisitiveness, and that there was not some warrior fomenting an attack upon the crew somewhere in the wilds, now armed with his enemies's own weapon. On the other, the fact that the thief might well be a child did nothing to lessen the risk that someone on one side or the other, islander or crewman, might potentially be injured or killed in the search. Tensions, so long relaxed during the island stay, were strung tight again, the crewmen and Marines in the search clutching knifes, clubs, and muskets in white-knuckled grips. Cavorting with carefree natives in an Edenic paradise was all well and good, so long as one was able to maintain a distinct superiority of arms, and with the possibility of martial parity, carefree natives were quickly seen as potential threats. As a result, it was easy to imagine a scenario in which the searching Marines, panicked, might fire upon the natives, feeling their safety was in jeopardy. It was Bonaventure's duty, and fervent hope, to see that did not happen.

With Horrocks now in tow, Bonaventure led his party in the direction the midshipman had indicated, east along the beach, past the cliff, and through the wooded wilds beyond. In his months of traipsing around the island, Bonaventure had never yet explored in that direction, and a quick accounting from the search party revealed that none of them had either. The huts and gathering places they knew and had visited, arranged in indistinct clusters of family villages which seemed to blur one into the next, were all located to the north and west of the fort's position, either along the curve of the bay's shore, scattered through the woods in small clearings, or else arranged along the ocean shore on the other side of the wilds. What lay to the east besides more woods, sands, and sea, where their suspected thief might be headed, no one could say.

For the better part of an hour, the search party tore through the woods, failing to find a track or path through the wilds. With tense gazes they scanned the forests for any glint of sunlight on metal, kept careful watch on the treetops overhead up which a small boy might have scampered.

Finally, breaking through the tree line on the eastern extremity of the island, the ocean's waves pounding on the rocky coast below, they caught sight of a young boy. He was perched on an outcropping a hundred yards or so to the south of their position, peering intently down the barrel of a pistol.

"Sir," Marine Commander Troughton said softly, raising his musket to his shoulder, "I believe I can take him from here in one shot."

"Are you mad?" Bonaventure shot back, swatting down the end of the Marine's musket. "Would you simply murder the child in cold blood?"

"Begging your pardon, sir," the commander answered in brusque tones, "but the captain's orders on this point are quite clear. In the event that a native makes off with ship's weaponry of any stripe, cutlass to cannon, force is to be used to secure that weapon's return, and to mete out justice as is appropriate."

"And this is justice, in your estimation, commander?" Bonaventure replied, disbelieving. "To put down a native boy like a rabid dog, all for the sin of curiosity."

"If a murderer is simply curious about the act of killing, does that make his victim any less dead?" The Marine commander kept tight his grip on the musket, the stock still to his shoulder, while Bonaventure's hand still held fast on the barrel's end, pointing it towards the ground.

"As executive officer of the *Fortitude* I am the ranking officer on this excursion," Bonaventure hissed between his teeth, "and as such there will be no use of force until I deem it appropriate. Is that clear, commander?"

"Absolutely clear, *Lieutenant* Bonaventure," Troughton snapped back. "And in the event that you are removed from duty, say by an unforeseen injury from a stolen ship's pistol? Would that then be an appropriate moment?"

"In that instance," Bonaventure replied with a slight smile, "you would then be the ranking officer, and I'm afraid it would fall to you to make that determination."

After a tense moment, a small smile blurred the corners of Commander Troughton's hard mouth, and he relaxed his grip on the musket.

"In that case," the commander said obligingly, "I accede to your orders." He stepped smoothly to the side, away from the boy on the outcropping, effectively placing himself behind Bonaventure and leaving the first lieutenant the forward-most of the party.

Taking a deep breath, Bonaventure motioned Troughton and the rest of the party to hold their position, and slowly advanced alone down the rocky shore.

He'd managed to come within a few dozen feet of the boy before being noticed, but was worried that now he'd been seen, he might frighten the boy into rash action.

"Don't be afraid of me," Bonaventure said in gentle tones, holding his hands palms forwards at either side. He hoped that the boy would respond to his own language, even when it was spoken as inexpertly as Bonaventure did. "We are friends, and will not bring you any harm."

The boy, unspeaking, sat tensely watching Bonaventure, the pistol in his grip still pointing at his own face.

"The thing you have taken is dangerous," Bonaventure went on, taking a slow step forwards over the rocky ground. "Forbidden," he added, watching the boy's eyes widen at the sound of the word.

"If you give it to me, we can find another toy for you, a toy more suitable."

Bonaventure took yet another step forwards, hands still at his sides, eyes locked on the boy's.

The boy, who couldn't have been more than eight or nine years old, shook his head suddenly, tightening his grasp on the pistol, fingers slipping within inches of the trigger.

"Be careful," Bonaventure said as calmly as possible. "Forbidden thing," he repeated. He decided to try another tack. "What is your name, boy?"

The boy seemed to think about it, but only shook his head in answer.

"My name is Hieronymus," Bonaventure continued, the syllables of his own name sounding harsh when couched among the liquid sounds of the island language. He took two sure steps forwards, slowly. "Some of your people call me Herano," he said instead, trying for something more comprehensible to the boy.

The boy's eyes lightened, a spark of recognition blazing momentarily behind them.

"Herano?" the boy repeated.

"Yes, you have heard the name?" Bonaventure asked, stepping even closer.

Before the boy could answer, a voice called out from the rocky shore behind him.

"Kuekuae!" It sounded like a woman's voice. "Kuekuae!" came the voice again, and Bonaventure was sure he knew it.

In the next instant, Bonaventure straightened, looking past the boy to see Pelani hurrying up the rocky shore towards them, just as the boy turned, startled at her approach. As he turned, his grip slipped on the pistol as the barrel slipped down in his hand. A heartbeat later his fingers closed over the trigger, the barrel pointed directly at Bonaventure. A shot rang out, belching smoke and leaden death.

Chapter Thirty-Four
A Near Miss

BONAVENTURE PITCHED FORWARDS onto the stones, blood ribboning down the right side of his face. In a heartbeat, Marine Commander Troughton was at his side, musket primed and ready to fire. Pelani, reaching him just a few seconds after, dragged the young boy along behind, the pistol now hanging limp and harmless in his grasp.

"Sir?" the Marine commander said softly, reaching down to Bonaventure's neck with his left hand while his right kept the musket in place at his shoulder.

"Herano," Pelani said, just as softly, clutching the young boy to her side.

At the touch of the commander's fingers on his neck, Bonaventure's form shuddered, and his back rose jerkily with a jarring cough.

"You men, over here," the commander barked, motioning for two of his Marines to come lift Bonaventure up and over. As they did, the commander's gaze flitted continuously from the bloodied form of the first lieutenant, to the pistol-wielding youth, and back again, his finger taut over the musket's trigger.

Having rolled Bonaventure over onto his back, they were able to see the vivid red curtain that ran from just behind his right eye over his cheek and past his right ear. A ragged line of crimson-limned flesh stood out like a rent in a sailcloth under high winds, a cascade of red running from it down to his jaw. Eyes fluttering, he moaned, right hand twitching towards his face.

"Sir, can you hear me?" Midshipman Symmes asked, stepping forwards. His expression made it clear that he knew the lieutenant's pain, injuries, and possible death were all his fault, as surely as if he'd pulled the trigger himself.

"I..." Bonaventure began, his voice ragged. His eyes were still closed, but he rocked his head back and forth slowly as his mouth moved. "What was... I... will be... damned if that wasn't the most painful thing I've yet experienced."

His eyes fluttered open, his right eye gummed with blood.

"Ow," he added, dabbing at the side of his face with his right hand.

"Symmes, find something to staunch that wound," Troughton barked, relieved. "You men," he motioned towards the pair of Marines at Bonaventure's either side. "Help him up. It'll slow the flow of blood if his head is higher."

Lifting Bonaventure groaning to a sitting position, the Marines stepped out of the way when Symmes approached with a long strip of cloth torn from his shirt bottom. He wound it around Bonaventure's head, leaving only his left eye clear to see.

"Miss," Troughton continued, turning on Pelani, his tone harsh, "is this bastard your son?" He jabbed a finger at the young boy, catching him in the chest. The boy cowered against Pelani's side, eyes wide and tearing.

"She doesn't understand you," Bonaventure answered for her. Looking over as far as he could with his left eye, Symmes still industriously and guiltily bandaging his head, Bonaventure asked Pelani in her own language, "Who is the boy?"

"Kuekuae," she answered in kind, her concern for both boy and man obvious. "He is my cousin, uncle's son, offspring of Kupai."

"Kupai?" Bonaventure repeated back, racking his pain-addled brain to remember the names of the island notables. "You mean the high chief, your ruler?"

Pelani nodded, only answering out loud when she realized that Bonaventure couldn't see the gesture.

"Yes, Kuekuae, son of the high chief, of the Tevake clan."

"That might have made things sticky," Bonaventure muttered under his breath in English. He then looked up at Troughton, as well as he was able, and said, "It is a remarkably good thing you didn't fire on that boy, commander. He's the son of the island king."

"Damn and blast it," Troughton cursed. He nodded. "Yes, that would have been something of a cock-up. Your orders, sir?"

"Well, I think I'm well enough to walk, with assistance, and given that we've recovered the pistol with no loss of life I suggest we leave well enough alone."

As the Marine commander bristled, Symmes looked uneasily at Horrocks, neither midshipman sure how to react. That their beloved executive officer should shrug off such a grievous wound so lightly, and send off merrily on his way the one who might have killed him without giving the boy so much as a swat on the backside, was difficult for them to swallow.

"Aye, sir," Troughton and the two midshipmen answered in ragged unison. They helped Bonaventure to his feet, a midshipman at either side, and gently steered him in the direction they'd come.

"Herano," Pelani called after him, when they'd taken him no more than a handful of steps. "I will speak to Kuekuae's father, and see that he is disciplined. I am glad the loud stick did not kill you."

"I'm glad, too," he answered back in her language, unable to turn around. Step after painful step, every movement jarring his head and sending brilliant bursts of pain radiating out from the right side of his face, Bonaventure was led away, clutching the spent pistol in his now bloody right hand.

It was not until later, after an endless symphony of pain, his world tinged rose by the blood he could not blink completely from his eyes, that Bonaventure stopped to realize that his love Pelani was the niece of the island king himself, and to wonder what problems that suggested for him.

Chapter Thirty-Five
Trophies

THE CREASE WOUND healed and scarred as well as could be
expected given Doctor Beauregard's sometimes inattentive attentions, and Bonaventure found that along with his recently
tattooed arm-ring, he now had two marks to remember his time
on Kovoko-ko-te'maroa. Three, counting the slow changes
wrought on his heart by the island woman, Pelani.

In the days that followed the incident of the stolen pistol, and
the encounter on the rocky eastern shore, Bonaventure did not
stray far from the fort, choosing instead to convalesce within the
palisade walls. He rationalized this decision by telling himself that
he must rest and conserve his strength, and replenish the supply
of blood lost in the long march back to the fort and the doctor's
distracted care. If he were honest with himself, he would have
been forced to admit that he needed the time to re-evaluate his
position on the island, and in particular his relationship with the
island woman.

Bonaventure had always avoided entanglements when in port,
seeing little attraction in momentary trysts and relationships that
lasted only a single day and night. With the exception of Mary in

Brighton, he'd managed to steer clear of them, and his conscience had always been clean as a result. Now, contrary to his wishes, he'd found himself enmeshed with a woman, and while the day of the ship's departure was still weeks or months away, he would eventually have to face the reality of his situation, and the fact that he'd be leaving her and not coming back.

Or would he? While in his more reasonable moments Bonaventure knew that when the frigate's repairs were complete he'd mount her decks and sail on, never to see the shores of Kovoko-ko-te'maroa again, in the hours past midnight, unable to sleep, he'd lie awake on his cot and imagine a less probable future for himself. A future in which he stayed behind when the frigate left, made a life for himself with Pelani on the island and raised up sons and daughters tall and fine. It was a capital offence, of course, and he'd be hanged for the attempt if caught, but something in him saw a brighter life ahead if he were to try it. What was left for him, after all, if he put back out to sea? He'd had the adventures he'd left home to find, and had been disappointed to discover that they were barely a pale reflection of his childhood imaginings. Instead, his life at sea was one of almost continuous repetition and monotony, punctuated only by periodic threat of death and pain. Was he making the world a safer and purer place, ploughing the waves for king and country? Or was he merely serving the distant political aims of men he'd never meet, sequestered far away in the safe towers of Europe? What did it really matter to him in the final analysis, to Hieronymus Bonaventure, whether king or emperor ruled in France, or whether this nation or that ruled the waves? Might it not be truer to his own better nature to stay here, in this island paradise, and make a better life for himself?

But what risks he ran, setting aside thoughts of mutiny and hanging. That his love Pelani was the niece of the island's high chief had not left his thoughts since first he'd heard it. Bad enough that he ran the ragged edge of neglecting his duties in dallying with the woman, but to think that his doing so might jeopardize not only his own safety but the current circumstance of captain and crew was another thing entirely. Intellectually, Bonaventure understood the natives's views on such matters, and their inability to grasp the concept of infidelity or adultery, but at the same time some persistent voice inside him kept up a chorus reminding him what furious fathers, uncles, and brothers had done to licentious sailors at other ports of call.

Hiding in the fort, from both Pelani and her uncle king, and from his own impulses, Bonaventure rested and healed, at war with himself and his own better instincts.

Chapter Thirty-Six
Lists

A FEW DAYS later, Bonaventure sat by the watch-fire, warming himself against the chill in the night air borne in by the ocean breeze. The ragged line of serrated flesh beneath the head bandage was scabrous and tender, but hurt him less than it had the days previous. His legs folded under him, his elbows resting on his knees, he looked into the flickering heart of the watch-fire, trying to think of nothing at all.

"Begging your pardon, sir, but do you mind if we join you?"

Distracted, Bonaventure looked up to find Macallister the quartermaster standing over him, the Spaniard Alvarez only a few steps behind.

"By all means," Bonaventure answered, his voice cracking briefly on the third word. He realized it had been some time since he'd spoken, so lost in solitude and his own internal monologue had he been. He swallowed hard and managed a smile. "I've hardly any proprietary claim on this spot of sand."

"As you say, sir," Macallister answered, smiling. He dragged over a wide log from the cord of wood stacked at the edge of the firelight, sitting on one sawn end like an impromptu stool. Alvarez followed suit.

"Well," Bonaventure began, trying for a conversational tone, "it would appear as though you two have become thick as thieves, now haven't you?"

"I am not a stealer," Alvarez answered, offended, his accent thick and nearly impenetrable.

"He didn't say you were, you daft bugger," Macallister shot back with exasperated tones, raising up his arm as though to strike the Spaniard with the back of his hand. The Spaniard just smiled a toothy grin, and with a resigned sigh Macallister let his hand drop into his lap. It seemed to Bonaventure a familiar routine between the two.

"If you don't mind me saying," Macallister continued, turning back to Bonaventure and leaning towards him conspiratorially, "I'll remind you that if me and the dago bastard are as thick as all that, it's on the one hand no fault of my own, on the other hand something of a damned nuisance, and on the other hand more or less due only to yourself, sir. No offence."

"As many hands as that?" Bonaventure answered. "And no offence taken, I assure you. Sorry, Macallister, but I needed to put our Spanish friend here somewhere where he'd be relatively safe, and didn't much care for the idea of having him locked away in a wooden box of a hut for the duration of our stay here. With you, I knew that I had someone upon whose judgement and loyalty I could depend, and if nothing else that with your facility for languages you might educate him a bit in the King's English." Bonaventure paused, and smiled slyly. "Which, I take it from his timely response, you have."

"Aye, and more's the pity," Macallister answered. He glanced over at Alvarez, who sat watching the two with interest, listening carefully. "To be honest with you, he were easier to take when he didn't have a word of it, and would just follow along behind like a little dog all the day. Now, he's got just enough of it to get himself into trouble, which I spend most of my time trying to keep him out of."

"Now I am not the dog," Alvarez added, nodding.

"That much is clear," Bonaventure replied.

There followed an awkward silence, in which the three men looked from each other to the fire and back again, at a loss for what to say next.

"This island, she is good," Alvarez finally commented. "With the beautiful women."

"That she is," Macallister agreed, nodding solemnly. "There's more than one man who's added a name to his list, I can tell you."

"His list?" Bonaventure asked, arching an eyebrow. "What list?"

"Well, sir, that is," Macallister shifted under the first lieutenant's gaze. "See, some of the men, not saying just who, of course... Well, some of the men have made a habit of keeping track of the... ladies they, shall we say, meet when at port. A way of keeping score, you see."

"Keeping score," Bonaventure repeated, a note of concern creeping into his voice.

"Yes, sir," Macallister answered. His gaze moved to the fire, unable to maintain contact with Bonaventure's. "Kind of a game, you see. Something the men do to while away the long hours away from port, remembering all the women they've known. It can get to be a trial, sometimes, so long away from the company of women."

"The hand, he is not so good," Alvarez observed. Macallister shot him a withering stare.

"I don't expect that the officers do anything of the sort, now would they, sir," Macallister hurried to add, turning his back on Alvarez. "What with your refinement and all, taking your bringing up into account."

244   *Set the Seas on Fire*

"I don't know," Bonaventure answered, softening. "I wouldn't be surprised to learn that Mister Jeffries did much the same." He paused, and then added, "And, I suppose, truth be told, that I myself have something of a list."

"You, sir?" Macallister asked disbelievingly.

"Yes, me," Bonaventure replied. "Though, to be fair, my list is only two entries long."

"Two!" Macallister blurted out, eyes wide. He brought himself up short, and then hastened to continue. "Well, that is, two is nothing to sneeze at, sir. I mean, that is..."

"Yes, two," Bonaventure said. His attention was drawn from the fire to the fort's entrance, and the island beyond. "Though before coming here, the list was but a single name."

Macallister's brow furrowed for a moment, gears turning behind his eyes. Then a slow smile spread across his face, and he gave a few slow and deliberate nods.

"Ah, sir, you sly devil, you," he said. "You've found some company here on the island, have you?"

"Something like that," Bonaventure answered, averting his eyes, a blush rising on his cheek.

"Ah, sir, good for you," Macallister said. "You've got to make your hay when the sun shines, eh, sir? We'll be on our way soon enough, sooner if reports are to be believed, so there's not a bit of harm in enjoying ourselves while we're here, is there?"

"It would be good to stay," Alvarez said softly.

"What's that, Macallister?" Bonaventure asked, ignoring the Spaniard. "What reports?"

"Well, sir," the quartermaster answered. "I was just this morning talking to the ship's carpenter, and it looks as though the repairs are proceeding quicker than he'd anticipated. We may get the job done and the ship back to sea in just a matter of weeks."

"Weeks," Bonaventure repeated, deflating.

"Aye, sir," Macallister said, smiling. "It'll be nice to knock the sand from our feet, now won't it, sir? And get back to the open sea where we belong."

"It would be good to stay," Alvarez said again.

Bonaventure said nothing, staring into the heart of the fire.

Chapter Thirty-Seven
Obstacles on the Path

THE NEXT MORNING, on the doctor's advice to get some exercise after his period of convalescence, Bonaventure accompanied a water-gathering party setting out just past sunrise. Led by Midshipman Daniels, with Macallister, Alvarez, and a dozen or so crewmen in tow, the party was to carry spent barrels to the mouth of a nearby freshwater stream, perhaps only a few hundred yards's distance, and roll the barrels back to the fort once filled. Transporting the empty kegs was a matter of ease, each almost light enough for one man to carry unaided, but returning them full to the brim was another matter entirely.

Bonaventure, barefoot and with his loose sleeves rolled past his elbows, bent forwards and hefted one of the barrels up onto his shoulders, a hand on either end with the back of his head steadying the barrel's middle. Straightening somewhat, he found he was able to hold the barrel in place across his shoulders with little strain, and could stand up straight enough to see the path before him. He took a few exploratory steps, and found that the load was bearable, though he'd have to take smaller strides than usual to keep from jarring the barrel against his neck.

At a signal from Daniels, the party set out, the midshipman in the lead clearing the way with a long knife, Bonaventure following behind, and then the train of crewmen carrying barrels singly or in pairs.

They had gone about half the distance between the fort and the headwaters of the stream when Bonaventure heard Daniels call out ahead.

"You there, out of the way."

Bonaventure, who'd been concentrating his attentions on the path before him, looked up to see two people, a native man and woman, standing in close conversation on the narrow path before them. He could see that the woman was Pelani, but from his vantage point he couldn't make out who the man was. On seeing him, Pelani spoke a few quiet words to the man beside her, and then started walking along the edge of the path towards Bonaventure.

"Mister Daniels," Bonaventure said, issuing orders though the midshipman was technically in command. "You take these men on ahead. I'll catch up with you when I can." Bonaventure knelt down, and slid the barrel from his shoulders to the ground.

Macallister, who was doubled up on a single barrel with the Spaniard Alvarez just behind, gave Bonaventure a knowing wink that made the first lieutenant wince.

"We'll take that from here, sir," Macallister said. "After seeing you tote that one yourself, it doesn't seem right me and the dago here sharing a load."

Alvarez transferring the weight of their barrel into both his hands, leaning back slightly and carrying the load across his chest, Macallister came forwards and picked up the barrel Bonaventure had set on the ground.

Bonaventure opened his mouth to voice an objection, but on seeing Pelani draw nearer left the words unsaid. He simply nodded, and stepped aside to let the party pass. When the final man in the train had passed by, Pelani was at his side. The man she'd left up the track, who Bonaventure now recognized as the warrior, Kane, stood stock still, eyes fixed on Pelani.

"You still heal?" Pelani asked, reaching up a hand to gently brush the bandage wound around Bonaventure's head.

"Yes, I heal, and well," Bonaventure answered, his hand rising to graze the woman's arm with his fingertips. "I'm sorry if you worried."

"Of course I worry," she answered, sounding offended, her lower lip jutting slightly and a line appearing between her eyebrows. "So many days pass, and I did not see you."

"I was... resting," Bonaventure answered weakly. "The man who healed me ordered it."

"Hmmph," the woman replied with a grunt, an expression universal between their two cultures. With her head cocked to one side, a disbelieving look on her face, Bonaventure for a moment thought that he might have been looking at any put-off woman in Europe, seeing through a vellum-thin excuse. Still, he couldn't bring himself to voice his concerns to her, not yet at any rate.

Bonaventure, looking for an escape, glanced past Pelani's shoulder and saw the warrior, Kane, still standing a short distance up the trail, glowering at the pair of them.

"Your friend," he began, "Kane?" She nodded. "I don't think he likes that you talk to me."

"He doesn't like you at all," Pelani answered. "He thinks you'll steal me away, that I'll sail with you on your boat to the forbidden island."

Bonaventure cocked an eyebrow, surprised the idea hadn't occurred to him.

"Kane is the man who is to be my husband," Pelani continued in way of explanation. "Whose children I was to bear."

Bonaventure pulled up straight, startled.

"Come," Pelani went on without missing a beat, taking Bonaventure by the hand. "Father the high priest would talk with you."

Bonaventure was out of step with the conversation, trying desperately to keep up. As Pelani tugged at his hand, dragging him down the path away from the warrior, Kane, he stumbled after, looking from her to Kane and back again with his face screwed up in confusion.

"What? But…" he began. A dozen questions jostled behind his teeth to be the first to hit the air. The first was, "What does the high priest want with me?"

"He will explain," Pelani answered before the second question passed his lips.

"Wait a minute," Bonaventure said in English, then followed in the native tongue. "What did you mean, 'whose children I *was* to bear'?"

"I am with child, my monthly flow stopped," Pelani explained matter-of-factly. "The child is not his."

Pelani continued down the path, Bonaventure stumbling behind, numbed into silence.

Chapter Thirty-Eight
Relations

BONAVENTURE FOLLOWED PELANI to the east, to the rocky coast where he'd been shot only days before, south along the shore, reaching finally a simple wooden house built a dozen feet up the slope of a rocky cliff. At the base of the cliff, where a small boy sat playing, stretched a small beach of white sands, a few yards deep and perhaps a dozen or so yards along the shoreline. From his meagre knowledge of the island's geography, Bonaventure decided that this rocky cliff must mark the terminus of the chain at the other end of which the *Fortitude* and the fortifications were positioned.

Coming nearer, Bonaventure recognized the boy as the one who'd made off with the midshipman's pistol, Pelani's cousin who'd inadvertently fired the weapon at him. He seemed much more harmless now, playing with a stick at harpooning a little ivory-coloured whale carved of bone, that dangled from a thread tied to a low branch of the beach's single tree.

"Kuekuae is to live here, now, with the high priest," Pelani explained, leading Bonaventure around the sharp rocks at the beach's edge and onto the pure white sands. "His father, the high chief, has decided his discipline will be to learn at the feet of his uncle, apart from the rest of our people, until he has learned better to obey."

Bonaventure nodded, and then caught a thread of something that began to unravel in his mind.

"His uncle?" he repeated, and then tugged on Pelani's hand to stop her momentarily in her course. He pulled her to face him, and then asked, "The high priest is your uncle, too?"

"No," Pelani answered giggling, turning away and dragging Bonaventure the rest of the way along the beach. As they approached, an old man appeared at the door of the wooden house, and began to walk down the steps carved into the face of the rock itself. "The high priest is my father," she added, waving at the old man.

The high priest, still wearing the blue-dyed headband he'd sported when singing his strange island song during the first night feast, raised his hand in greeting, his grave expression looking like it had been carved from the stone that surrounded his home. Bonaventure, recalculating his risks on finding now he had bedded not only the niece of the island's king, but the daughter of their spiritual leader as well, managed a weak salute, and followed Pelani the remaining distance to the house.

The relationship between church and state on the island still managed to perplex Bonaventure, even after he'd grilled Pelani about it repeatedly the months past. The island culture was divided into varying layers of familial groupings, nestled like the rinds of an onion, each individual claiming membership in a series of increasingly larger classifications. The highest and most general category, not taking into account residency on the island itself, were eight clans or family groupings, which seemed to be measured by which canoe one's ancestors occupied on the original immigration to the island. Each of these eight family groups, prosaically called "canoes", had a chief and priest of their own. The chief was responsible for settling petty disputes between members of the clan, organizing the men of the clan into fishing and hunting parties, and staking out new territories in the event that the clan's village grouping required expansion. In times of war, or in instances of inter-clan conflicts, a high chief over all eight clans served as final arbiter and ruler.

Likewise, while the individual clan's priest was responsible for the general welfare of his family grouping, seeing to it that the children were raised in accordance with their faith, and taking responsibility for birth, marriage and funereal rites, a single high priest presided over all the clans of the island, whose charge was to safeguard the spiritual health of all the island's peoples.

What this high priest, whom Bonaventure had only seen on that first day, could possibly have to discuss had eluded the young officer throughout the walk with Pelani. Learning now that he had carnal knowledge of the high priest's own daughter, and that said daughter was now carrying a child most probably his, Bonaventure was able easily to float any number of possible conversation topics.

As they drew near the old man, though, Bonaventure was surprised to find that he felt no hint of threat or danger from the high priest. Though the man's face was frozen in the same immobile rictus it had worn during the first night's feast, Bonaventure was not convinced this evidenced any ill will. He'd found it rare on the island that any but children and women below a certain age were anything like expressive in their moods, and that the men and mature women of the island tended to wear the same stoic expression on all occasions. Their moods varied, and widely, that much he knew, but it seemed unpropitious on the island to communicate those feelings through facial contortions.

The high priest first took his daughter in his arms, held her tight for a long moment, and releasing her asked her to join the boy at play near the tree at the beach's far edge. With a final glance back at Bonaventure she walked away to help little Kuekuae perfect his harpooning skills, leaving the two men alone on the sands.

"Come," the old man said, waving a hand towards his home up the cliff-side. "We will talk."

Bonaventure glanced after the woman who walked away down the narrow beach, mesmerized for the moment by the rhythm of her hips and the gentle arc of her swinging arms. Still numb from the revelations of the day, his head crowded with rushing thoughts on the possible repercussions, Bonaventure turned his attention back to the old man, and dutifully climbed the steps to the wooden house. The old man followed after.

Chapter Thirty-Nine
Currents

"MY DAUGHTER IS for you, but you are not for my daughter."

Bonaventure sat in shocked silence, unsure how to respond to such a blunt announcement.

The pair of them, the young officer and the old man, sat cross-legged on the brushed wooden floor of his cliff-side house, facing one another. Through the open doorway, they could see the woman and boy playing on the sandy beach below.

"My daughter," the old man finally continued in his island tongue, when Bonaventure had failed to answer, "tells me that your ways are not our ways, but that there is a god who watches over your movements just as our gods watch over ours."

Bonaventure nodded slightly.

"Some of my people would say so," he replied.

"She tells me, too, that you are from an island on the far side of the world and have travelled far."

"Yes," Bonaventure answered simply.

"And yet, she tells me, you do not believe that our gods exist, or that their ways are made manifest in the world."

Bonaventure tensed. It was true that he and Pelani had on occasion discussed their differing views on religion and the supernatural, and that he had made plain his lack of belief in anything of the sort. Had he known that her father was the spiritual leader of her people, though, he might have chosen his words with more care. It was as though he'd decried the Mother Church to a stranger on a park bench in Rome, only to find that the stranger was the Pope himself. The audience would not affect his views on the matter, of course, but he would have preferred to be more politic in what he said, for fear of offending.

"Yes," Bonaventure reluctantly agreed, "I have said as much."

"Then I am sorry for you, man from across the world," the old man said, shaking his head. "Since I was younger than the boy now playing on my beach, I have studied the ways of the gods, the turn of the season's wheel, and the ways in which to bend the elements to my will. I have sailed beyond the horizon, and dived down to touch the ocean's floor, and seen and heard more mysteries than my people could ever imagine, but I have never yet before met a man so convinced that he lived in a purposeless world."

Bonaventure, unable to frame an appropriate response in his limited vocabulary, could only shrug in contrition.

"The gods steer our fate, like an oar turns a boat, and it is given to some to know the currents our lives will follow. Student of the gods and of the eight elements, I can read the world's currents, and have seen much that is to come."

"I am sure you believe it is so," Bonaventure began, "but I cannot—"

The old man waved him silent with a quick motion of his hand.

"How it is in your far land, I do not know," the high priest said, "but here in ours the young ones know to let the old ones talk. We have wisdom to share, and if interrupted might well drop dead of age before we finish a thought." A slight smile broke the placid calm of the old man's stoic expression, making clear that he was sharing a joke.

Bonaventure laughed nervously, and sat waiting for the old man to continue.

"My name given to me at birth is Temura, and I am the chief and principal priest," he used the native word *tohuna* here, "of the island of Kovoko-ko-te'maroa. I am son of and brother to kings, descended of a line of wise men and warriors stretching back over the horizon of time. I have studied and mastered the eight prime elements of the world, and learned to commune with the elemental forces and gods who hold men in their favour. I have studied the currents of the world's flow, both for those in my own family and for all my people, and have seen the dark days behind, and the darker days ahead. And I, Temura ko Tevake wata, *tohuna* to my people, tell you that I have seen your future, and it will not be here."

The old man stopped for a moment, head flung back, looking down his cheeks at Bonaventure, who sat quietly saying nothing. Bonaventure had no idea what was expected of him, what sort of answer he should provide. The old man solved the problem for him, by voicing the young officer's thoughts for him.

"You do not believe," the old man said simply, head rolling forwards until his eyes were level with Bonaventure's. "That is as I expected. I want you to remember the words I say to you, even if you do not believe, for one day they may be of use to you."

A squeal of childish pleasure sounded from the beach, and looking out Bonaventure could see that under Pelani's tutelage the little boy was mastering the art of hitting a circle drawn in the sand with his thrown stick from several paces away.

"Do you see my nephew, brother's-son, Kuekuae? Do you? I have seen what the future holds for him, as I have seen it for you. He will never follow after his father as high chief, nor will he ever take on my role as priest. He will end far from here, unmourned and forgotten, death coming for him on one leg flesh and one leg bone." The old man paused, and wiped a callused hand across his forehead, as though to brush off something Bonaventure couldn't see. When he continued, his gaze was fixed on the boy and his daughter playing below, a far-off look in his eye. It was almost as if he'd forgotten for the moment that Bonaventure was there, and that he was speaking only for his own benefit. "I cannot tell him, of course, or his father my brother, or his cousin my daughter. The gods steer the vessel of our lives, and it is not given to me to interfere. My role is merely to help keep my people in the boat."

The old man paused, taking a deep breath, and then turned his attention back to Bonaventure.

"In the same way, I can tell you that my daughter will live her life here, among her people, and bear her man Kane sons and daughters tall and fine." Raising his hand, he pointed a gnarled finger directly at Bonaventure. "But first, she will bear a son for you."

"A son," Bonaventure repeated, before he thought to object.

"Yes, a son, whom she'll name Herano in memory of your love," the old man answered, no hint of malice in his voice or eyes. "He will never know his father, but your seed and his mother's living memory of you will strengthen him, and he will become a fine strong man and leader of men."

Driving visions of his potential progeny from his mind, Bonaventure focused his attentions back on the moment.

"Suppose I were to believe you, Temura," he began. "What would prevent me from staying here on the island with your daughter, Pelani, to raise the child as my own?"

"My daughter is for you," the old man answered simply, "but you are not for my daughter, as I have said. There is no place for you among our people, and no home you could find here that would suit you. My daughter has asked me the same, both whether you should stay with us here, or whether she should go with you on your ship, and you must believe that I want only her happiness. I tell you, if you were to stay, it would bring both you and my daughter only sorrow, and if my daughter were to go with you, it would bring her only death."

"Death?" Bonaventure bristled. He had no intention, nor had he ever, of taking Pelani on board the *Fortitude*, whether he chose to leave the island or not, but the thought that he'd be incapable of ensuring her safety was an affront to him. "She would be safe with me, wherever she went."

"Safe with you, perhaps," the old man answered, "but she will not be able to go wherever you go. She could not follow you to the forbidden island, First Volcano, where she tells me you must sail."

"Why not?" Bonaventure shot back.

"Because anyone who sets foot on the forbidden island is giving themselves into the fire, and placing their lives into the hands of death itself."

The old man leaned forwards, placing a hand on Bonaventure's knee.

"I will tell you about the birth of the First Volcano," he said in a low voice, his eyes darting out the door to the beach and the southern sea beyond, "and then you will know why my daughter could never follow you there."

Chapter Forty
Genesis

"AT THE BEGINNING of all things," the high priest began, "before man, fish, or fowl, the Father Sky lay with the Mother Earth, and from their union were born two sons. Light and dark, they were, the two brothers, the one called Te'a and the other Tura. They were as alike as the moon overhead and the image of the moon reflected in still water, the same in appearance but one giving off the light which the other could only absorb. Together, they would be fathers to all things to come after, good and evil, and would shape the world we live in today.

"When they had grown, and had their years of exploring and adventuring, it came time for the two brothers to marry and pass on children. Together, the brothers visited their mother the Earth, to enquire where they might find suitable mates. But the Earth did not hear their calls, and answered their questions only with silence. Next, the brothers visited their father the Sky, but again, only black stillness answered their pleas for help. In the end, the brothers did only what they could, and set out each to make a wife for himself.

"Te'a, father to us all, made his wife of Stone, digging her from the arms of Mother Earth herself and shaping her to his liking. Tura, with less patience, fashioned his wife of the flickering light that burns. He fashioned his wife of Fire.

"The first children of Te'a and his wife of Stone would grow to become the gods of the winds, the waves, and the trees and of fish. Later generations, his perfect light growing dim passed from father to son, would become the first men, and would sail the seas to find their homes.

"The first children of Tura and his wife of Fire were the gods of the storms, and the sharks, and the torrential rains. Later generations, his pure darkness inculcated within them, would become the dwellers in darkness, the dwarves, and the demons who would plague men and the sons of men.

"So it went for generations, the two brothers, light and dark, ruling over their children and their children's children from their opposite two sides of the earth, north and south. The children of light and the children of dark came into conflict often, each claiming that their own high father was the stronger of the two. It was only natural that, in the end, the two brothers came into conflict.

"Tura, from his rocky home in the far South Sea, his wife of Fire at his side and his children of darkness spread around him, decided that his should be the hand that steered the course of the world. Te'a, at home in the North with his wife of Stone, heard of this and disagreed. Leading their generations of children as armies before them, the two brothers made war one on the other, each striving for control of all creation.

"The war lasted for generations, and the songs that can be sung about those times, about the brave deeds and treacheries of those years, are too numerous to sing in a lifetime. Know only that, in the end, Te'a and his children of Stone defeated Tura and his sons of Fire. Te'a, now the great father of the whole world, took his vanquished brother up in his arms and carried him defeated to his rocky home in the south of the world.

"Te'a, a final tear falling burning on his brother's raging brow, cast Tura down into the mouth of the open mountain which dominated his rocky home below. At his coming, the heart of the mountain burst into flames, Tura's wife of Fire welcoming him forever to his prison home. Te'a named the island Helekea, which means 'First Volcano,' and decreed that Tura never more would roam the Earth, but would remain trapped inside his home of fire and rock forever.

"From his home below, Tura and his wife of Fire continue to rule over their children of darkness, sending them out into the world to wreak evil on the sons of Te'a. And it is for this reason that all sons of Te'a know never to set foot on the island prison of the dark brother, First Volcano, for evil and death is there within waiting. It is forbidden, a place only for heroes of legend to test themselves, and for madmen to seek their doom."

Chapter Forty-One
Fact or Fable

"AND THAT IS why my daughter cannot sail with you," the old man concluded, finishing his tale and rising on creaking joints to his feet. "She is not a hero, like Pahne of legend, and neither is she mad."

Slowly crossing the distance that separated the two men, the high priest reached out and laid a gentle hand briefly on the head of the still-seated Bonaventure.

"Which you are," the old man added, "hero or madman, I cannot say. But I can tell you this. I have looked into your future, and seen only that you will, that you must, sail from here to the forbidden island, First Volcano. Beyond that, I cannot see what the world's currents have in store for you, except to say that I see no end for you here, no death stalking the waves in pursuit."

"What do you suggest?" Bonaventure asked, pushing to his feet to stand face to face with the man. He'd neither accepted nor rejected yet anything the old priest had said, but this one point gave him pause, whether fact or fable. "That I am not to die, but wander the waves, crewman aboard some doomed Flying Dutchman of legend?"

"No," the old man answered, shaking his head, allowing a sad smile to colour his placid features. "I say only that what death waits for you is beyond my ability to see. You will die, like all men, but not I think in this place, on these seas, and not for many long years to come."

Bonaventure locked eyes with the old man, and was surprised to hear the sound of his own pulse pounding in his ears. Visionary or charlatan, the high priest was skilled at word craft. Bonaventure willed his beating heart to slow to a normal pace, and took several deep breaths.

"I thank you for your advice," was all that occurred to him to say. When the old man answered only with silence, Bonaventure turned to leave, thinking their brief conference at an end.

"One thing further," the high priest added, placing a hand on Bonaventure's shoulder. "When you come to Helekea, the home of fire and death, remember to keep your eyes on all things, friends and enemies alike. The presence of the dark god will twist those with weak wills to his cause. All of us are equal parts fire and stone, with water inside to hold the two forces in check. On First Volcano, under the dark god Tura's gaze, the fires that burn within us all can flame higher, overcoming the stone that forms us. Such men become true children of Tura, and work his dark deeds."

"I will try to remember," Bonaventure said, not turning around. Without another word, he climbed the carved stone steps down to the beach, and taking Pelani by the hand led her away from the high priest's home.

Night fell as they walked hand in hand, covering the distance to the fort, not saying a word.

If Pelani knew what her father had told her lover, she didn't say, but something in her seemed to reflect the pained thoughts in Bonaventure's own mind. Whatever else the old man was or said, he was her father, and she was bound to follow his counsel. If

Bonaventure tried to stay on the island, court martial and hanging be damned, then she would not have him, and were he to try to take Pelani away with him on the frigate she would not go.

Coming at last to the palisade walls of the fort, Bonaventure pulled Pelani near him, resting a hand over her taut brown belly, and looked down at her with silent longing through eyes blurred with tears. Pelani, wiping her own eyes with the back of a slender hand, nestled in his grip for a long moment, and then pulled away. With a final glance, she turned and walked away into the night.

Chapter Forty-Two
Morning Muster

THE NEXT MORNING, having hardly slept a moment, Bonaventure was roused from his narrow cot by the sound of shouting and barked orders from beyond his hut's narrow walls. Eyes red and raw, he pulled on his breeches, shirt and shoes, and buckling on his sabre hurried out to see the cause of the commotion.

The crewmen in the fortifications were in a frenzy, assembling in ranks just within the palisade walls, the ship's full complement of Royal Marines armed and monitoring their progress. The ship's officers, with the exception of the just roused Bonaventure and the absent Captain Ross, were barking orders at the men under their command, urging them to move faster, assemble more quickly, and to do so in silence. The men, sullen and sleep-worn, stood in ragged ranks, as though awaiting some emergency inspection.

Bonaventure found Jeffries at the centre of the maelstrom, standing atop a scaffold, already counting off the men that had congregated before him.

"Mister Jeffries," Bonaventure began, a hint of annoyance colouring his voice, "what precisely is the matter here?"

"Blame Macallister," Jeffries answered, his face twisted into a scowl. "He's the one who brought it to my attention. Or blame yourself, for making me officer of the watch these past ungodly hours of the night." He paused and turned to face Bonaventure, an expression of sincere contrition flitting across his face. "Damn it, Hero, how was I to know to watch the bastard? Months on this blasted and blessed isle, him playing the simple fool, and I'd forgotten to keep one eye on him."

"What?" Bonaventure demanded, grabbing the other man by the shoulders. "Watch whom? What has happened?"

"The damned Spaniard," Jeffries hissed. "He's done a runner."

Bonaventure spun around, looking over the assembled men, as though he might see the Spaniard Alvarez among them and prove Jeffries wrong.

"When?" Bonaventure asked, still looking over the crew.

"Sometime in the night," Jeffries answered. "Macallister says he saw him around sundown, and not again. He figured he'd just come in late, but when Macallister woke up this morning he couldn't find the bastard anywhere."

"Damn," Bonaventure hissed. "Anyone else gone with him?"

"Not that we've been able to tell, mustering them all out like this," Jeffries replied. "From Macallister it seems that the Spanish bastard had been getting a bit agitated the past weeks, now that the *Fortitude* is near as damn it done. Seems he didn't have much love for going back to that island of his, and kept dogging on about staying put here."

Bonaventure nodded, tempted to admit that he felt much the same way himself.

"With him as our only way of finding the place, assuming he ever gives the captain the navigational data he needs," Jeffries went on, "it wasn't bloody likely he'd be left here in luxury's lap while we went off to fight his countrymen, so I guess he figured his only way out was to run."

"Damn and blast it," Bonaventure cursed.

"Hero," Jeffries continued, voice low and eyes on the ground, "it was my watch, and my fault that the Spaniard got past us. Find him or not, I'm..." He paused, and then glanced over to the pole set upright at the fort's centre, used only infrequently for discipline since they'd arrived. Jeffries swallowed hard. "I'm ready to take my lashes," he finished in a rush, "or whatever else the captain orders."

"Mister Bonaventure!" came the voice of the captain, shouting out from behind them. "If you please!"

The two lieutenants looked from one another to the advancing captain, red-faced and steaming, and back again.

"I'll go," Jeffries answered. "You know only what I've told you, and I'm better able to answer his questions."

Bonaventure nodded, and laid a comradely hand on his mate's arm.

"Mister Bonaventure, Mister Bonaventure, sir," came another voice, this time from the direction of the fort's entrance. Leaving Jeffries to scurry off to update the captain, Bonaventure turned to find Midshipman Horrocks rushing to the platform, as red-faced as the captain had been, but wheezing from exertion rather than rage.

"Mister Horrocks?" Bonaventure asked calmly as Horrocks drew near, skidding to a stop at the base of the platform.

"Your pardon, sir," Horrocks wheezed, panting, "but there's one of the locals at the door, and he don't look none too happy. All painted up and mad, with one of those war clubs in his hand and murder in his eyes."

"What does he want?" Bonaventure asked, already climbing down the scaffold.

"He says that one of their women was kidnapped in the night, a girl named Pelani. And he said it was one of our crew that done it."

Chapter Forty-Three
Pursuit

THE TWO MEN raced through the undergrowth in stony silence, warrior and officer, all attention on the task at hand. Bonaventure, drawn sabre in one hand and loaded pistol in the other, and Kane, shark-tooth-bladed war club in a white-knuckled grip, pounded through the island's wilds, fire and vengeance in their eyes.

They had nearly come to blows, there before the fort, on first seeing each other that morning. The one, island warrior, thinking that his rival had finally stolen away his betrothed, the other, naval officer, seeing through rage and fear-coloured eyes the man who would keep what he himself could never again possess. Only the thought of Pelani, held now in the desperate grasp of the fleeing Spaniard, stayed Bonaventure's hand. He'd been forced to reason with his rival, the man who had come only to kill him. The island was too large for one side or the other, islanders or crewmen, to search for the missing pair alone. Only together might they hope to find Pelani in time, before the Spaniard did something rash.

Kane, once convinced that his missing bride was not among the visitors, had reluctantly told his rival Bonaventure all that he knew. Bonaventure learned that a native woman had seen Pelani in the midnight hours, dragged away by a white-skinned visitor covered in clothing throat to foot. A knife had glinted sharply in the visitor's belt, and the native woman had seen what Pelani had once called a "loud stick" clutched tightly in his hand. The woman had roused the family village; the men set off after the pair. When Kane had heard, hours later in his distant village home, he'd arrayed himself for battle and run straight for the visitor's home, where he was sure Pelani had been brought.

Having established that they were standing in the single spot on the island on which Pelani incontrovertibly was not to be found, Kane and Bonaventure had set off at a run, heading into the woods in search of the missing woman and her captor, Bonaventure shouting back to his men that they should dispatch search parties of their own at once.

Now, hours later, scraped and bruised from branch and stone, the pair continued their desperate pursuit, checking first one spot, then another, then another and so on in fevered silence. Several times they encountered other search parties, either made up of Bonaventure's crewmates, or Kane's countrymen, or in rare cases commingled groups comprising both. In each instance, one or the other of them would question their people as appropriate, demanding any intelligence of Pelani's whereabouts. As soon as they'd got confirmation that there was no news to hear, the pair was off again at a sprint, hurrying to some other locale.

It occurred to Bonaventure, as they ran, that the Spaniard Alvarez might have been planning his flight for some weeks, even months. He'd been mostly at his liberty since released into the company of the crew, required only to perform his assigned duties and to spend each night and a portion of each day in the confines of the fort's walls, as was any crewman. In his periods of freedom, though, he might well have examined the island closely, searching out the most effective places of concealment or quickest paths of retreat. That he'd kidnapped Pelani, mere hours after first seeing her in the company of the *Fortitude's* first lieutenant, suggested only that he had waited on some opportune moment for his escape, and had seen in her a bargaining chip with which he might barter his freedom, were his plans to come to an impasse.

In his heart, Bonaventure knew that he deserved the silent scorn radiating out from his companion island warrior, Kane. As executive officer of the visiting ship, the conduct of her men, whether crew or prisoner, fell on his shoulders. As the man who held Pelani's heart and whose child even now grew within her belly, it was up to him to see to her safety and to ensure that no harm befell her, through whatever agency. That his inaction and inattention should now drive the two together, errant prisoner and woman of his heart, was no one's fault but his own.

Kane, for his part, remained silent, never bothering even to see if Bonaventure kept stride with him.

Suddenly, and without warning, Kane stopped short, holding out a hand to halt Bonaventure dead in his tracks.

"What is it?" Bonaventure asked in the native tongue, his voice hardly above a whisper.

"Hsst," Kane hissed, scowling, motioning that Bonaventure was still speaking too loudly. Dropping down into a crouch, he pulled Bonaventure down beside him and pointed towards the right of their previous course.

They had been heading to the north, to the furthermost curve of the island's shore, where sandy beaches and rocky spars were battered by heavy waves the day long. Pelani had brought Bonaventure this far along the shore once and shown him the shallow caves carved out by generations of waves in the rock face. She had told him that fairy creatures dwelt within them, pale things that could not abide the light of day. He had made a joke of her stern warnings on the dangers of the creatures, and the pair had ended in one another's arms, hours spent on the sandy beaches in their bare-skinned embrace, only the coming of high tide forcing them to leave.

From where they now crouched in the wooded undergrowth, Bonaventure and Kane could see the shadows of the black coastal rocks through the tree line, and past those the white-capped waves rolling in from the horizon. Kane pointed to the trees themselves, the curtain of green between the two searchers and the broad emptiness beyond.

"The leaves' colours ripple their distress," Kane whispered, not bothering to address Bonaventure or look at him when he spoke. "The plants are shifted away from the sun, not bent towards him as they are at this time of day. Someone passed through there, and recently."

Bonaventure followed Kane's gaze, looking in the direction he indicated, but could see nothing out of the ordinary.

"The caves of the *pakepeha*," Kane continued, speaking more to himself now than to Bonaventure. "He's taken her to the caves."

Bonaventure couldn't help but agree that the caves, shallow and narrow though they were, provided perfect concealment from a search. For the short term, at any rate, which were likely the only terms in which the Spaniard was thinking. Bonaventure nodded, and followed as Kane slowly advanced towards the tree line and the rock caves beyond.

Chapter Forty-Four
Confrontation

THE PAIR BROKE through the tree line at precisely the point Kane had earlier indicated, and found themselves within a few yards of a sloping hill of black rock that rose from the waters to a height of some thirteen or fourteen feet. These rocks, the very bones of the island herself, were the same which made up the cliff from which the frigate was now suspended, and in the side of which the island's high priest had made his home.

Where the water met the sand at the stone's edge, a narrow fissure had been worn away by centuries of swirling waves. Within was pure darkness and silence. Roughly the height of a man, the fissure was no more than two feet wide, and no more than three or four times that deep, a standing grave carved by nature into the living rock itself.

Stopping just before the fissure's entrance, the two men held fast, hands on their weapons. They were silent for long moments, straining to hear any sound of movement or breath. Finally, the island warrior called out.

"Pelani!" he shouted, directly into the mouth of the fissure.

No voice called in answer, but there came in response the sound of scuffling, a muffled scream, and the tang of metal against stone.

"They're in there," Bonaventure swore beneath his breath. He stepped forwards an inch, hands tightening on sabre and pistol.

"Alvarez," Bonaventure called out. "Release the woman," he went on in English. "Release her, and I promise that you won't be killed. I can do no more than that. Release her! Now!"

"No," came a shout in answer from within the small cave.

"He will not come out into the light," Kane said in his native tongue, lifting his war club a fraction higher.

"Damn you, Alvarez," Bonaventure shouted. "If you do not release the woman, I will kill you myself, with my own bare hands. Do you hear me? I will kill you myself!"

"I am going in," Kane said, not bothered that he couldn't understand Bonaventure's threats.

"No," Bonaventure shot back in the language of the island, grabbing Kane by the elbow. "The risk is too great to her."

Kane froze solid, a sneer on his face, looking down at the hand on his arm and back up into Bonaventure's eyes with a steely gaze.

"Who are you to say what risk is too great?" Kane spat. "What is she to you?"

"She is to be *your* wife, may your gods damn you, Kane, and mother to your children," Bonaventure hissed back. "But I tell you now, the risk is too great. I will kill him myself if he gives her so much as a tiny scratch, but if you go in after them you will be killing her yourself."

Kane snarled, eyes twitching in rage, but he did not move or speak. Finally, he gave a single deliberate nod and stepped back, waving Bonaventure to continue his negotiations.

"If he hurts her," Kane said, "*I* will kill him, and when I have done will kill you next."

"Fair enough," Bonaventure muttered in English. "You can try." Then he turned his attentions back to the cave mouth.

"Alvarez," Bonaventure called out again. "There is a native warrior here with me, and I assure you that he is no better disposed to your cause than I. Even if we were to leave you on the island, this man and his people would kill you the minute your attention was turned." He paused, and then added the lie, "And then they would eat you."

Sounds of whimpering came from within the shallow cave, racking sobs.

"I am not want to hurt anyone, Señor Bonaventure," Alvarez called out, voice strained. "But I cannot go back to that bad place island again. I cannot go."

"I understand, Alvarez," Bonaventure answered, taking another step forwards. Kane matched him, the pair drawing ever closer to the cave mouth. "But this woman has nothing to do with your concerns. Let her go, and you and I will discuss what we can do next."

"I am not foolish, you should not think," Alvarez answered. His voice was sounding louder and clear, from nearer the mouth of the fissure. "You will shoot at me the second I am in your sight."

"Alvarez," Bonaventure answered, forcing himself calm and his voice level, "I swear to you by everything I hold dear that I will not fire at you, unless you give me just cause first. Step out into the light where I can see your face, and we can talk some more."

"You will not shoot?" Alvarez asked, his voice straining.

"My word, Alvarez," Bonaventure answered. "I give you my word." Bonaventure turned his head slightly, leaving his eyes on the cave mouth, and in the native language told Kane, "I have told him we will not attack if he comes out."

Kane nodded.

"The native warrior understands, Alvarez," Bonaventure added. "You and the girl come out now, and no one will be hurt."

No voice came in answer, and a tense minute followed, but finally the profile of Pelani's face could be seen dimly in the dark mouth of the fissure, her eyes wide. Then, slowly and by inches, Alvarez and his hostage worked their way free of the narrow passage.

"All right, is good," Alvarez said, seeming to relax slightly, though his pistol was still pressed hard into Pelani's temple, his other arm around her throat. "I come out, you don't—"

Before Alvarez could utter another word, Kane flung back his arm and hurled his war club end over end through the air, the serrated shark teeth worked into the edge burying deep and precise into Alvarez's forehead.

The pistol fell unfired to the ground, Alvarez slumping after, blood streaming down his face from the open wound in his head like crimson tears, a confused expression of shock frozen on his face. Pelani stood still and tense, unharmed but frightened.

Kane walked forwards, taking Pelani into his arms. Leaving one arm encircling her back, her head pillowed on his shoulder, Kane reached down and retrieved his war club, wrenching it back and forth to work it from the grip of Alvarez's sundered skull.

Bonaventure stood stock still, working his mouth silently before he could manage to speak. He was shocked, watching the blood pool in the wet sands around Alvarez's ruined head.

"But I said..." he began in English, and then shifted to the island tongue. "Kane, I said that I'd told him we wouldn't attack."

"Yes," Kane answered simply with a nod, leading Pelani away from the body of her kidnapper, past Bonaventure down the beach. "You told him. But I never said I wouldn't attack."

Pelani, stunned into silence, allowed Kane to lead her away, leaving Bonaventure and the bloody corpse of Alvarez alone with the sand, stone, and waves.

Chapter Forty-Five
A Change of Plans

ALVAREZ WAS BURIED without honours the following morning, weighted down and dumped unceremoniously into the sea from the cliff-side. Following that, some sense of normality returned to the daily life of the crew, though it was tenuous at best, an illusion at worst.

The captain and his officers met for long hours, trying to divine their best course of action. Their only sure guide to the treasured island of the Spaniard's tale, where untold riches of gold, silk, and spices were waiting to be claimed, was now lost, and the captain was left with only the Spaniard's fragmentary story and scattered remarks to guide them. A small rocky island, some days's or even weeks's sail to the south and west, surmounted by a craggy volcano's peak. Were it the only other island on the whole sea, they could spend a lifetime searching it out fruitlessly, as small and unobtrusive as it was reported to be. Flights of birds were not likely to make their homes on so inhospitable a place, and so the old salt's trick of tracking a flying bird in its course might well be useless. Likewise, small as it was, clouds were not likely to be caught by the island-turned winds, no billowing white flags over-head announcing the presence of land below.

No, without Alvarez, it was likely the captain and her crew would never find their prize island, and the work of months would have been for naught.

A week later, the officers and crew having opted by chance or design to stay safely within the fort's walls when duties did not require them to venture out, word came from the ship's carpenter that the repairs on the *Fortitude* were very nearly complete and that she would be seaworthy in a matter of days.

Bonaventure, by the watch-fire with Jeffries and Horrocks, greeted the news of their forthcoming departure with mixed emo-tions. Since the incident at the cave's mouth, he'd not strayed a step from the fort walls, and had seen nothing of Pelani. Seeing her led away by the oddly comforting embrace of the warrior Kane, Bonaventure told himself that he'd been deluded to think that he might have made any kind of life with her. These were her people, this the man that would be her mate for life. He was sim-ply a visitor passing through, another name on a list and on to the next port of call.

Jeffries, who'd made the most of the last months with his own peculiar brand of hedonism, stared gloomily into the heart of the fire, no doubt dreading the coming protracted months away from land and the comforts of women. He'd cheer once away from port, the anticipation of the next landing enough to keep his spir-its flying, but now, in his dregs, he saw nothing but dark days ahead.

Horrocks, finally, had anticipated their impending departure, and had spent the last days in close discussions with his island informants, learning as much as he could about their music and culture in these final hours.

Night had fallen, and one of the three men around the fire was officer of the watch, though none was precisely sure which. The watches had begun to blur together—the one into the next—in the final days, and the officers had simply made a habit of always being on duty, always on hand, whatever energies for recreation, education, or exploration they might have had spent.

From the entrance to the fort came the sounds of some tumult, voices raised in challenging shouts. Bearing up lanterns, Bonaventure and the other officers hurried to the gate to see what was the cause.

In the flickering light from the torches they bore, eight men stood arrayed for battle in the sands beyond the fort's entrance, with the warrior Kane at their head. Each man carried a war club or fighting stick and a lit torch, each with the same grim expression on his face.

"Herano of the visiting ship!" Kane called out, stepping forwards with deliberate movements towards the fort, torch held high.

"I'm here, Kane," Bonaventure answered, stepping into the open, his lantern held at shoulder level. He was unarmed, his sabre hanging untouched on his hut wall's peg since the day at the cave. "What do you want?"

"I am told by my people who have spoken with your small man," Kane paused and pointed towards Horrocks, "that your navigator and guide was killed by my hand that day by the black rock."

Bonaventure considered this for a moment, and nodded.

"You might say that," he answered.

"And they say, too," Kane continued, "that you sail for the forbidden island of Helekea, to wrest some treasure from its womb, but that now you do not know your way."

"Yes," Bonaventure assented. "What is it to you?"

"In generations past, Pahne, our great hero who became a god, discovered this island and led our people from sacred Hawi'iki in the first eight canoes. My own ancestor, Teanu, sat in the prow of the canoe Kururangi on that first voyage, and knew the great Pahne as a brother."

Bonaventure made an impatient gesture, the shifting lantern sending shadows sliding across the sands and dancing across Kane's face.

"But Pahne did more than just that," Kane continued. "When his people were without fire and ate their food bloody and cold, Pahne set out to the heart of fire, Helekea, the First Volcano, and suffering many trials won the secret of fire for his people. Since then, many times, great warriors and heroes have gone to test their worth and strength in the belly of the forbidden island, but never one for many years."

Bonaventure nodded, beginning to suspect Kane's point.

"I, Kane ko Kururangi wata, son of the family Kururangi, descended from the rower Teanu who sat at the right hand of Pahne himself, have killed your only guide to the forbidden place. Therefore, I, Kane, strong of will and purpose, will lead you to the First Volcano, there to test my worth. These men," he waved his torch, indicating the seven men standing behind him, "a son from each of the eight great families of Kovoko-ko-te'maroa, will accompany me."

"Well, I suppose—" Bonaventure began, searching for an appropriate response.

Kane interrupted with a wave of his torch, ending any discussion.

"We will return on the morning eight days from now, our double-hulled canoe ready to sail alongside you. Be prepared for our coming."

At that, Kane turned and walked away, the other seven men in his train, none saying a word.

Chapter Forty-Six
Departure

ON THE MORNING of the eighth day, the *Fortitude* lowered safely onto the waves and fully restocked, the party of warriors returned, resplendent in feathered helmets and capes. After considerable speechifying on the part of the island king, and a blessing chant sung by the island priest Temura, the eight warriors pushed their long double-hulled canoe into the water of the bay and paddled out alongside the frigate.

The frigate's crew and company, already on board the *Fortitude*'s decks, watched the proceedings with a mixture of relief and longing: relief to finally be again under sail, their fortunes before them, and longing at leaving behind the only pure breed of paradise many of them had ever known.

Bonaventure, among them, stood at the quarterdeck, looking out over the waters of the bay towards the sandy beach, desperate for any sign of Pelani. Only at the last, with the frigate slowly gliding towards the bay's mouth, the warriors' canoe paddling alongside them, did he catch a glimpse of her, standing near the now-abandoned shell of the crew's fortification. Wearing his gifted blue coat, brass buttons glinting in the morning sun against the slight swell of her belly, she raised a hand overhead. In it, she held an apple-red fish, flapping out its last desperate gasps.

As Bonaventure watched, Pelani walked gracefully to the water's edge, and bending down she let the fish slip from her hands into the surf. Through the crystal blue waters, he could see the flash of red as it swam away, free beneath the waves.

Bonaventure stood in place at the quarterdeck, Pelani still standing ankle deep in the surf, neither moving until the distance between ship and island grew too great, each finally losing sight of the other.

May, 1861

GILES DULAC BATTED Hieronymus Bonaventure's clumsy attack aside in an effortless parry and, reversing the direction of his own sabre, slashed against Hieronymus's chest. Had it not been for the padded plastron, blood would have been drawn.

"Your fighting today lacks precision, to say the least," Dulac scolded, taking a few steps back on the piste and coming once more en garde. "Concentrate."

Hieronymus didn't speak in response, only nodded, teeth gritted behind his mask. He took his position opposite Dulac and waved his blade in a hasty salute.

"Begin," Dulac instructed.

Hieronymus stepped forwards, then back, then forwards again, Dulac moving to maintain the distance between them. Then Hieronymus feinted an attack, beating his front foot against the piste in an appel, but before Dulac had even responded to the feint Hieronymus snarled and slashed out wildly with his blade.

Dulac casually whipped his own sabre in a circle, changing the line of Hieronymus's attack.

"Concentrate," Dulac repeated, his tone level. "Begin."

This time, Hieronymus displayed even less technique and, with a cry of rage, simply swung his sabre in a wide arc, like a chopper swinging an axe.

With a disdainful expression on his face, Dulac met the blow with a clash of steel on steel, his own sword catching Hieronymus's near the guarded hilt, and with a flick of his wrist handily disarmed his pupil.

As Hieronymus's sabre clattered onto the hard-packed dirt floor, Dulac fixed him with a stare, eyes narrowed. "What have I said about fighting angry?"

Hieronymus didn't answer, but drew his mouth into a line.

"The appropriate emotional stance is as important as your physical posture. When you allow your feelings to override your judgement, you surrender the higher ground to your opponent."

"I know that," Hieronymus said defensively. "I'm not a child, you know."

Dulac's eyes widened, hearing the venom in Hieronymus's words, and a half-smile played at the corner of his mouth. "I may be mistaken, but allow me to venture the opinion that it is not I against whom you harbour some animosity, but some other figure in your life."

Hieronymus drew a ragged breath, his hands tightened into white-knuckled fists at his sides.

"Well," Dulac went on, cocking an eyebrow. "Am I mistaken?"

Visibly forcing himself to calm, Hieronymus shook his head. "It is my father," he said simply.

Dulac nodded. He stepped off the piste, and moved to the jug of water set on the dirt floor near the wall. "I had assumed as much," he said, as though it scarcely bore saying.

Before Dulac could utter another word, Hieronymus tore off his mask and began pacing the floor, in a state of considerable agitation.

"My mother is sick again, as I may have mentioned, and with my siblings busy with their studies and my father with his classes, I've been spending afternoons sitting with her, keeping her company. On some occasions we talk of the news of the day, and on others we simply sit in silence, but most times I read to her, and most often out of her favourite book, an antique copy of Arthur Golding's *Ovid*, which had been a gift to her from my father during their courtship. But if my father had any romantic impulse in him, in those days long gone, it has since been lost."

Hieronymus paused in his pacing and turned to face Dulac, looking for all the world like a barrister addressing himself to the court, pleading his case.

"This afternoon my father returned to the house before the accustomed hour," he continued, "having ended his classes for the day early, and upon finding me in his home, reading to his wife, he'd accused me of intentionally neglecting my studies. To which I replied that I cared not a fig's end for my studies, not with my mother's good health held in the balance. Upon which he said that were I to pursue a life of scholarship I would needs must do so with more dedication than he had seen me show to date. In response to which I simply said, 'The life of a scholar be damned, sir,' and strode from the house."

Dulac shook his head, disapprovingly. "He is your father, for all of that, and deserving of your respect."

"He doesn't want my respect," Hieronymus snapped, "he wants my obeisance."

"If so," Dulac said, reluctantly, "then he only wants what is rightfully his."

Hieronymus's cheeks went red, and his lips curled in a snarl. "Why should I be forced to obey a father's wishes, now that I am a fully grown man?"

"Not yet fully grown. Not in the eyes of the law, at any rate, and not until your twenty-first birthday next year."

Hieronymus fumed, but knew he was defeated. He would not reach his age of majority for almost a full year, and had until then no choice but to obey his father in all matters.

"It is unfair," he said, trying unsuccessfully to keep a petulant tone from creeping into his voice.

Dulac stepped forwards and held out the jug of water, a placating gesture. Hieronymus accepted it and, as he took long draughts from the jug, Dulac placed a hand on his shoulder.

"It could be worse."

"Worse?" Hieronymus scoffed. "That hardly seems likely."

Dulac smiled. "Just count yourself lucky you don't live under Roman law. In the days of the emperors, there were three age groups recognized as carrying legal incapacities. First was *infantia*, which originally obtained while the child was incapable of speech, but was later extended to the age of seven years. The next stage, *tutela impuberes*, ended at puberty, after which time the child could refuse the services of a tutor. Finally, *cura minoris* continued for males from the closing of tutela until the completion of their twenty-fifth year. So were Roman law still in force, you would have five more years before reaching your majority, and not merely one."

"Twenty-one or twenty-five," Hieronymus said with a sneer, "it is still ridiculous. These ages are only arbitrary, picked at random."

"Not so," Dulac corrected. "It is simply that the reasons have been largely forgotten to history."

"Then what is the reason, pray?" Hieronymus said, clearly disbelieving.

"Simple." Dulac hefted his sabre. "The end of childhood has everything to do with the ability to lift a sword."

Dulac turned and strode across the piste, to the far side of the carriage house where Hieronymus's sabre had fallen.

"In barbarian tribes," Dulac went on, "majority came with the ability to bear arms. It was typically thought that a boy of fifteen was of sufficient size to lift and carry a man's weapons, and so was a man. In England, the posse comitatus included every free-man capable of bearing arms, and the Assize of Arms provided for all subjects of the age of fifteen and older to be sworn to keep the peace. But by the time of the Magna Carta, the age of major-ity had been raised to twenty-one, and the later Statutum de Militibus provided that none were to be pressed into service before their twenty-first year."

Dulac bent down and picked up Hieronymus's fallen sabre.

"Why the change?" Hieronymus asked.

Dulac turned, and then tossed the sabre through the air, hilt first. Hieronymus handily snatched it from the air in a long-practised move.

"Because of the increase in the weight of arms and armour," Dulac explained. "As defences improved, and leather jerkins were replaced by shirts of mail, which were themselves superseded by suits of plate mail, the strength required to bear the weight also increased. So you remain in the eyes of the law an adolescent because, in ancient days, every man was expected to fight for the crown when called upon, and only a man of a certain age could reasonably be expected to bear the burden."

Dulac strode to the door of the carriage house and opened it onto a warm, late spring day. The chill of winter had lingered late in the year, and only now had broken, and but for a line of grey clouds that limned the southern horizon the skies were clear and blue.

"But speaking of burdens, I think we've borne our own quite long enough for today. I've yet to shake the winter's ice from my bones, and I think a walk in the sunshine might do us both some good. Come along."

Hieronymus stripped off his protective gear and bundled it under his arm, while Dulac tucked their sabres into his long leather-bound case with the brass clasps. Then the two, tutor and pupil, had left the carriage house side by side, walking out into the sunlight.

The day marked the anniversary of the birth of Queen Charlotte, and in her honour buildings throughout Oxford displayed the new Union Flag, which in their dozens snapped and rustled in the warm breeze, so that as the two walkers spoke their words were accompanied by a constant undercurrent of susurration.

"They seem never able to settle on an ensign, do they?" Dulac said absently, indicating the nearest of the flags with a nod of his head.

"Don't they?" Hieronymus said, a bit perplexed. "The previous Union Flag had been unchanged for nearly a century, and that previous for a century before."

Dulac glanced again at the flag, which since the enacting of the Act of Union at the year's beginning now incorporated the red saltire cross of Saint Patrick's flag, Ireland's symbol laid atop the white saltire cross of Saint Andrew from the Scottish flag, but below the red cross of Saint George representing England.

Dulac looked to Hieronymus, and with a half-smile said, "As long as all that?" Dulac paused, and then added, gently, "You really should obey your father's wishes. At least until you are independent of him by law."

Hieronymus's eyes flashed for an instant, but when he answered, his tone was level and calm.

"But one can't always follow orders and do what one is told, can they? Look to the example of Horatio Nelson, who disobeyed the orders of Admiral Sir Hyde Parker, Jr. in the Battle of Copenhagen, and therefore prevailed against the Danes. If he hadn't put the telescope to his blind eye, and announced that he could not see the signal to retreat, then the battle would have ended in defeat for the Royal Navy."

"Yes, but wasn't one of the ships in Nelson's vanguard commanded by William Bligh, he of the *Bounty* fame?" Dulac paused for breath, and let the name of the infamous ship linger in the air between them. "Do you suppose Bligh would take as cavalier a view towards disobeying orders, hmm?"

"The question isn't a fair one," Hieronymus said sullenly. He glanced skywards, as if for inspiration, but saw only the grey clouds beginning to roll in from the south. "There are more options than just those two, and subtler shadings of difference between blind obedience and complete disregard."

"Would you instead look to the example of Bonaparte, who last year defied the orders of the Directoire exécutif, eliminating that body and establishing in its place a Consulate, with himself given the powers of a dictator. What position would the First Consul take on following orders? Of the two, would you rather follow the example of Bligh or Bonaparte?"

"That's an end to it," Hieronymus said with a weary smile, raising his hands in mock surrender. "Any debate has reached its conclusion when one or the other party invokes the example of Bonaparte."

They walked on through the streets, talking of this and that, and as they did the clouds that had so swiftly blown up from the south now threatened to blot the whole sky. They turned a corner onto Broad Street, and as the light grew dim walked along the wide thoroughfare in the gathering gloom.

"What has become of our beautiful spring day?" Dulac said, unhappily.

"Quickly overcome by spring showers, it would appear," Hieronymus said, holding out his hand, feeling the first delicate pinpricks of sprinkling rain on his outstretched palm.

Before Dulac could answer, the rainfall suddenly surged in intensity, the shower becoming a deluge almost instantly.

"Come on," Hieronymus said, holding his bundle of fencing gear atop his head as a poor but serviceable umbrella. He grabbed Dulac's elbow and headed for the nearest doorway. "Let's get indoors while this passes!"

The pair raced up the front steps, and knocked at the heavy oaken door at the top.

"Perhaps no one is home," Hieronymus said, when after a moment there had come no answer from the other side.

"In which case their sign lies," Dulac said, pointing to the stone wall on Hieronymus's far side.

Hieronymus turned. Set in the wall, at about eye level, was a small engraved plaque, which indicated that Mr. Ashmole's Museum was open to public viewing for a nominal fee on the days and hours listed beneath.

"Sixpence a piece seems a fair enough price to escape this deluge," Dulac said.

"And at least we'll have something to look at while we wait," Hieronymus said, sodden to the bone and beginning to shiver as the temperature of the air dropped precipitously. "Assuming someone ever answers the blasted door, damn their eyes!"

It was at the crescendo of Hieronymus's imprecation that the door swung open, and the scowling visage of the Keeper appeared.

"Admittance for two?" Hieronymus said sheepishly, digging in his coat pocket for the coins.

With considerable grumbling beneath his breath, the Keeper accepted their payment and granted them access. Shaking their coats dry as best they could in the vestibule, they wiped their shoes as dry as possible and made their way into the museum. The Ashmolean was empty that afternoon, except for themselves and the Keeper, and so the pair had the run of the place.

They first found themselves in the museum's lower room. On either side rose towering pillars, supporting the high ceiling, while shelves and glass cases lined the long walls. Pupil and tutor wandered through the room, idly glancing at the items on display.

Hieronymus stopped by a case that contained the head and claw of a bird, which the sign alongside indicated were all that remained of the last dodo ever to be seen in Europe. The remainder of the specimen, so the card read, had been destroyed in the previous century, when damage from moths proved too difficult to repair.

Dulac moved along, evidently less interested in the taxidermy specimens. The tutor was brought up short, though, when he reached the display of the prize of the Ashmolean collection, the Alfred Jewel.

Hieronymus, seeing Dulac's interest, moved to stand beside his tutor and see for himself. The jewel, laid beneath glass on a bed of velvet, was about two and a half inches long, made of gold and cloisonné enamel, covered with a transparent piece of rock crystal. It bore the inscription AELFRED MEC HEHT GEWYRCAN, or "Alfred ordered me to be made", along with the image of a man in a green tunic, holding what may have been some sort of forked branch, but Hieronymus couldn't say for sure.

Leaning closer, Hieronymus read the accompanying card. It indicated that the jewel dated from the reign of the ninth-century Saxon king Alfred the Great, and had been lost until its rediscovery at the end of the seventeenth century, not four miles from Athelney in Somerset. It was thought to have been a symbol of office, either of Alfred or one of his officials, or perhaps an aestel, a book pointer sent to each bishopric when Alfred's translation of Gregory's *Pastoral Care* had been distributed.

"It says here that the figure on the Jewel is thought to represent the incarnate Wisdom of God," Hieronymus said aloud, "but that opinion is divided on the point."

Dulac examined the image closely, running his finger and thumb along the line of his jaw, almost as though appraising himself in a mirror.

Hieronymus straightened, feeling the tightness of neck and back, muscles sore from the afternoon's exertions. Then he froze as the next set of displays caught his eye. He hurried along, very nearly breathless in his eagerness.

It was a collection of ethnological materials collected on Captain James Cook's second exploratory voyage to the Pacific Ocean. The cards indicated that the collection had been presented to the Ashmolean by Johann Reinhold Forster and his son George, who had been official scientists on the voyage.

"Oh, think of it, sir," he said as Dulac came to stand beside him. "To travel to the far side of the world and back. And Cook did it, not once, but thrice."

"To be fair," Dulac pointed out, in grim humour, "not three entire trips, as he never made the return voyage on the last."

Hieronymus's eyes flashed darkly, and he glowered at his instructor. "That hardly seems a fit subject for levity," he said through gritted teeth.

"My apologies," Dulac was quick to respond, holding his hands up in supplication. "I hadn't meant any offence."

Hieronymus nodded, his expression softening fractionally, but Dulac's comments had clearly spoiled his enjoyment of the Cook display, and so he continued on to the next.

Further along was an orrery, an assemblage of brass set on a mahogany table and covered with a protective glass dome. Not to scale, the orrery displayed the Sun in the centre, and arranged around it six planets, along with their satellites—four around Jupiter and five around ringed Saturn.

Dulac joined him, and bent to examine the card. "On loan from the Vice-Chancellor, it says. Manufactured by George Adams of London."

"The Vice-Chancellor may want to ask for his money in refund," Hieronymus said. In response to Dulac's questioning glance, Hieronymus pointed at the little ivory spheres in their clockwork orbits. "Not enough planets."

Dulac looked back at the card, then regarded the engraving on the side of the orrery itself. "No date is given, but surely it was constructed before the discovery of the Georgian Planet."

"But it isn't just deficient one planet, but two," Hieronymus answered.

"An eighth?" Dulac raised an eyebrow. "Will wonders never cease?"

"Ceres," Hieronymus said, by way of explanation. "The Italian who discovered the eighth planet named it Ceres Ferdinandea, but other nations did not much care for the notion of addressing a heavenly body in honour of King Ferdinand III of Sicily. No more so than they wanted to call the seventh planet Georgium Sidus."

"And not only because *sidu* doesn't mean planet, but star?"

"I suppose," Hieronymus answered. "Though nearly everyone who pursues the study of the heavens has taken to calling the planet Uranus, following the example of Johann Elert Bode in Germany."

Dulac gave him a sidelong look. "For someone who has no interest in the life of a scholar, you have certainly amassed an impressive body of scholastic knowledge."

Hieronymus smiled sheepishly. "It isn't knowledge to which I object, sir. Only the notion that it can only be pursued from within the confines of a library." He indicated the Cook display with a wave. "The world should be our textbook and the subject of our study."

Dulac smiled. "You sound like a deist. Looking for knowledge of God in nature instead of revelation."

Hieronymus scoffed. "One of my classmates," he said, "John Duncan, agitates that the Ashmolean collection should be rededicated to the tenets of so-called 'natural theology'. Duncan hopes to conjoin in the mind of the visitor the view of natural phenomena with the devout conviction that such are the media of divine manifestation."

"And you don't share this notion, I take it?" Dulac said, though it was perfectly evident that Hieronymus didn't.

"Hardly!"

From the far side of the room came the sound of shushing, and the pair looked to see the pinched face of the Keeper at the door, motioning them to lower their voices.

"Not hardly," Hieronymus repeated, more quietly. "I see little evidence of the supernatural in nature."

"So you have decided to become a dissenter, I take it?"

Hieronymus widened his eyes in momentary alarm, and quickly shook his head. "No," he said. "That is to say, as a student at Oxford, I am of course an attending member of the Church of England."

"Naturally," Dulac said. He had to be, whether he liked it or not, attendance being as much a requirement towards getting a degree as a knowledge of Greek and Latin.

"But still and all," Hieronymus went on," I can't help but find myself inclined towards Anthony Collins's conception of free-thinking—however much I might find his defence of Necessitarianism distasteful. Reason, not mysticism, is the only way of attaining a knowledge of truth. I can't in good conscience believe anything without sufficient evidence."

Dulac shook his head, smiling indulgently. "What weak tea the 'free thinkers' of England serve. Like Collins they are, to a man, deists, always careful to profess devout belief in Christ while attacking the foundations of belief."

"Well..." Hieronymus began uneasily, shuffling his feet.

"Come now, come now. Can't we at least expect to have from these firebrands the courage of their own convictions. You'll have heard the story of Matthew Hammond?" Hieronymus allowed that he hadn't. "I can't be surprised," Dulac continued. "He's been largely forgotten by history. Hammond was a Unitarian, burned at the stake by the Bishop of Norwich for no other crime than denying the divinity of Christ. And that was before such effrontery was deemed illegal with the passage of the Blasphemy Act by Parliament, more than a century ago. Now, it is a crime merely to deny the Trinity or to question the divine inspiration of the Gospels."

Hieronymus looked around them nervously, as though afraid unseen persons might overhear.

"In France," Dulac continued, "when the Baron d'Holbach wrote his *Le Système de la nature*, he denied the existence of a deity altogether, saying that the gods are themselves nothing but the creations of ignorance and fear. And the universe, d'Holbach writes, far from being full of divine manifestation, is nothing but matter in motion. Of course he published anonymously, and had his books printed abroad in Amsterdam, so perhaps he was not much more courageous than his British counterparts, at that."

Hieronymus swallowed hard, and leaned in close, conspiratorially.

"Do you believe?" Hieronymus asked, his voice low. "In God?"

Dulac considered the question, thoughtfully.

"If you mean the idea of an old man with a beard, who sits in judgement on high... then no. If you mean whether I believe there exists an intelligence that created and directs everything... Well, I've seen little enough to suggest that such a being exists, but nothing to prove that it doesn't."

"So lacking evidence of the unseen, we lack the ability to make any claims about it," Hieronymus said.

Dulac nodded. "As for myself, I hesitate to say that all that exists is what can be seen." He paused. "I have seen things that offend reason and defy logic."

Hieronymus narrowed his gaze. "What kind of things?"

Dulac's expression darkened, and his mouth drew into a line. "What kind of things?" he repeated, his voice sounding as if it came from a distance. "Dark things. Things I won't discuss, even in the bright light of day. Just hope that you never encounter such for yourself."

As though in counterpoint to Dulac's words, a shaft of sunlight speared down from a high window, bathing the pair in warmth and light. Dulac seemed to relax visibly, and breathed a heavy sigh.

Hieronymus glanced up at the window, and saw the sun beyond, just beginning to peek through the now thinning grey clouds, which were dispersing as quickly as they had gathered.

"Come along," Dulac said, hefting the sword-case beneath his arm, "it looks as though the rain is letting up, and we've some time yet left for our fencing lesson before the day is over."

Part IV
The World Below

Chapter Forty-Seven
Under Sail

AFTER LESS THAN a day at sail, the double-hulled canoe of the island warriors, the *Tai Ke Whiki Ke Ra*, or "Shining Sun", proved too swift to sail alongside the *Fortitude*, easily outstripping the larger ship by lengths. With considerable debate, it was decided instead to bring the eight warriors and their sundry equipment aboard the frigate, and to tow their craft on a line behind. The warriors agreed to this, though reluctantly, and transferred to the frigate their food and provisions, leaving spare poles, spars, coils of rope and cord aboard the canoe.

The provisions brought on board the frigate included baskets containing leaf-wrapped bundles of freshly cooked breadfruit, sour fermented breadfruit, drinking coconuts, gourds filled with water, two domesticated pigs, three jungle fowl in basket-woven cages, and a dog that never barked. The warriors also brought with them an arsenal of arms, war clubs, fighting staves, and knives; fishing equipment, including fishhooks, lines, and nets; and cooking implements, carved stone bowls, gravel, and bundles of fresh grasses, kindling, and firewood.

This motley collection, an island village in miniature, was arranged in the forecastle of the ship. Warriors, pigs, birds, and dog, all took up residence on the deck, to the amusement of the crew. Seeing the steely gaze of the warriors, though, and the deadly grace with which they manoeuvred their weapons, none of the crew was foolhardy enough to voice their amusement, opting instead to save their jibes and jeers for a safer hour, below decks, out of earshot of the islanders.

The frigate herself, repairs complete, was in very nearly as fine a shape as she'd been when she first sailed out of the Plymouth shipyards. The ship's carpenter had well deserved the captain's confidence in his ability, the new planking and spars as straight and true as on a draughtsman's design, the difference between pristine original materials and pristine replacement virtually indistinguishable.

However, the Spanish launch, the captured ship on which the now deceased Alvarez and Diaz had been found adrift, had not survived the crew's extended stay on the departed island. It had been used as salvage early on; needed lumber and joists, which would have been the work of weeks for the ship's carpenter and his men to construct from raw materials, stripped from her hull.

The reborn frigate, with the islanders's canoe in tow, sailed towards the south and east. The island warrior Kane, standing feet planted wide on the forward-most part of the ship, kept his eyes on the waves below and the sun above, pointing unwaveringly at the far horizon.

Chapter Forty-Eight
Sea, Sun, and Stars

IN THE DAYS that followed, Bonaventure found himself returning slowly to the rhythms of shipboard life. Watches passed, marked by the ship's bells, duties to be performed and responsibilities to meet. So engrossed did he become that he was almost able to forget the woman and the life he'd left behind, on the island he'd never see again. Almost forget, that is.

As one of the crewmen with the greatest command of the island language, and the highest ranking of those, Bonaventure was selected by Captain Ross to liaise with their passengers, the eight island warriors. Aside from Kane, with whom he had had considerable and unsought experience, Bonaventure came to know the other seven only by their family affiliations, and then only dimly: Tevake, Hulana, Kienga, Tekiera, Rangi, Kaloni, Rewi. Along with Kururangi, represented ably by the warrior Kane, the eight men served as a portrait of island society in microcosm, a member of each of the eight familial clans, each the best reputed and highest regarded example of the warrior ideal from among their people.

The warriors made their place in the forecastle of the ship, day and night, preferring not to mix with the members of the frigate's crew if possible, feeding themselves from their own provisions and the fish they caught, and whiling away their time in recounting past deeds and glories, and in singing songs detailing the exploits of their heroes and gods. Kane, as he had since first coming on board the *Fortitude* on their first day at sail, stood apart both from his own countrymen and from the ship's crew, spending most of every day and the better part of every night at his post at the fore of the ship, feet planted wide apart, hands on his hips, never seeming to tire or ache, full concentration devoted to the seas, sun, and stars. When a correction in course was needed, he'd signal Bonaventure or one of the other crewmen fluent in his language, most often Horrocks, to communicate the change to the helmsman. Beyond this minor intercourse, however, he rarely spoke, silently watching the horizon.

When they'd been under sail for four days, Captain Ross began to grow concerned about Kane's navigational qualifications, and precisely how he was charting their course. With no instruments, charts, or equipment at hand, Kane seemed to be directing the ship's movement by nothing so much as his own whim. Fearing that his treasured prize, the galleon's cargo, might again be wrested from his potential grasp, Ross ordered Bonaventure to bring the matter to the island warrior, and to force him to make an accounting of his methods and goals.

With some reluctance, no love lost between him and the warrior, Bonaventure went fore that night during the second dog watch, just past sunset, to interview Kane.

"Kane, I need to speak with you," Bonaventure said, stepping around the seated warriors in the forecastle to the position where the navigator stood.

The warriors, having caught a half-dozen or so fish by trailing their lines over the side of the ship, were preparing them now to be eaten. They held the fish whole on spits over a stone bowl, in which embers burned over a bed of gravel, below which was spread wet grasses. The arrangement, embers over gravel over wet grasses over stone, ensured that the bottom surface of the bowl did not heat up to an unmanageable degree, thus preventing the ship's planks below from burning.

Kane merely nodded in silence in response to Bonaventure's greeting, shifting his gaze from seas below to stars above and back.

"Your methods of navigation," Bonaventure went on, undaunted, "are strange to us. We would know how they are used."

Kane seemed to think for a long moment, breathing deeply in through his nostrils and out through his teeth. Finally, crossing his arms over his chest, he gave a curt nod.

"Very well," he answered. "I will tell you."

Kane pointed towards the horizon, and to a bright burning star in the south-east corner of the sky.

"That star, burning there above the waters, do you see it?"

Bonaventure nodded.

"That star rolls up the sky on the wheel of the heavens over the place to which we sail," Kane continued. "To reach our destination, we must sail towards that star. When it has moved too high and too far to the side on the heavens's wheel, we then follow the next star to rise from the same point on the horizon. And then the next that follows when that one has gone on, and then the next, until the dawn."

"And then?" Bonaventure asked, suspicious.

"Then the sun will show us the way, by the path he takes across the sky. Four hand spans and three fingers from the point where the sun appears in the eastern sky is our course, twelve hand spans from the point where the sun disappears in the west at day's end."

Kane demonstrated the measurement, holding his arms out-stretched before him, fingertips pointing to the heavens and palms forwards. Thumbs pressed together and arms extended, he shifted his left hand to touch heel to heel with his right hand, then moved his right to touch thumb to thumb with his left, always only one hand at a time, the other staying immobile in its position. Moving hand to hand, he described an arc across the horizon, then looked at Bonaventure with eyebrows raised to make sure he'd been understood.

"I think I understand you," Bonaventure answered. "But should the sky be cloudy, or storms drive you off your course," he asked, "and the stars and sun obscured from view, how then would you steer?"

"The waves, they each have names," Kane answered, pointing past the prow of the ship at the waters below. "Every swell we ride can be named, every sea we sail through known by its manner."

"What do you mean, every sea we sail?" Bonaventure asked.

"There are three seas between our home of Kovoko-ko-te'maroa and the forbidden island of Helekea," Kane answered. "We are in the first now, the swells coming from islands far to the west, and from our home island itself. When we pass into the second sea, you will know it, because there we will see *ke maka.*"

"What is that?" Bonaventure asked. "*Ke maka?*" He'd not previously heard the term.

"They are the fires beneath the waves," Kane answered. He turned his attention back to the horizon, hands on his hips, giving every signal that the interview was at an end. "You will see," he added, not turning around. "When we pass the fires below the waves, we will be in the second sea we must sail, and half of our journey complete."

Bonaventure, seeing that Kane would not likely answer any more questions at the moment, gave the island warrior the ghost

of a salute, and then turned away. Passing by the other seven warriors, now eating their charred fish whole on the spit,
Bonaventure hurried to the captain's quarters to relay what he
had learned.

Chapter Forty-Nine
Fire Beneath the Waves

SEVERAL DAYS LATER, Lieutenants Bonaventure and Jeffries and Midshipman Symmes were aft in the gunroom, picking over the remains of their evening meal. The ship's cook had been grateful to see his dwindling supplies replenished with fresh game from the recently quitted island, but it came as some disappointment to the crew that what had been so sweet and succulent when prepared by the practiced hands of the island women so often failed to reach that mark under the cook's less expert guidance. The wild boar, which on the island had been roasted to perfection and served sliced directly from the fire-spit, on board ship was prepared like any other meat. Salty from the saline brine in which the cut joints were preserved, gummy and grey from the boiling it received at the cook's hands, the boar was barely even suggestive of the heavenly culinary delights the island had offered.

"Ah, my hearties," Jeffries said, pushing his wooden bowl away from him, the better part of his grey gummy meat left uneaten. "Hearts of oak, and the life of the sea. What more could a man desire, I ask you?"

Symmes answered with a mirthless laugh, gnawing on a cube of abused boar.

"We do our duty," Bonaventure said in way of reply, pushing his own meal around its bowl with the end of a wooden spoon. "That's what is expected of us."

"Truer words rarely spoken," Jeffries sang back, slapping his hands palms down on the table. "God, but we're a pitiful sight, our Hero, three gallant officers in His Royal Majesty's Navy, here moaning our sad fates into our plates, all for the sake of having to do our own duty. How many can say that they've had a reprieve of months from duty in a paradise such as that, I ask you?"

When no answer came, Jeffries reached over, pounding Symmes comradely on the shoulder.

"Ned, my boy, you tell me," he went on. "How many can say they've lived in the heart of Eden, even for a single day?"

"Not sure," the midshipman muttered, eyes still on his bowl. "Not many, I suppose."

"Not many, indeed," Jeffries answered. "And here we sit, snivelling and complaining about the food, our quarters, our duties, all sounding like lubbers first dragged on board ship by a press-gang."

"And what would you propose to change, Will?" Bonaventure asked, looking up at Jeffries from below his brows.

"Well, that is, I suppose..." Jeffries began, faltering. He broke off, and a broad grin spread across his face. "All right, you have me there. I suppose the only thing to do—"

The other two were spared the remainder of the second lieutenant's tirade by the timely interruption of Midshipman Horrocks at the gunroom's door.

"Come quick, all of you," Horrocks shouted, out of breath, not waiting before spinning on his heel and pounding back the other way. "You won't believe it," he shouted back over his shoulder, bounding up the steps to the open air above.

Pausing only to glance at one another, raised brows answered only with shrugs, the three officers followed along, fore from the gunroom and up the steps to the deck above.

On deck, what crewmen were on hand were crowded by the starboard railing, peering over the side. Kane, the warrior navigator, kept to his position in the forecastle, while the other seven warriors lounged unconcerned around the forwards part of the deck. Bonaventure, with Jeffries and Symmes at his heels, crossed to the railing, crewmen already there reluctantly stepping aside to clear a space for him. Grasping the railing, he leaned out, wondering what could possibly so have transfixed the crewmen's attention.

At first, the waters around the ship seemed completely normal, inky black under the night sky. Bonaventure was about to step away, sure that some prank was being played, when a brief flash at the edge of his vision caught his attention. The flash was followed closely by brief shouts and appreciative noises from the crewmen around him, those who had seen it pointing out the spot to those who had not.

"There, sir," a crewman to his left said, pointing to a spot some two dozen feet off the starboard bow. "It'll come again, watch."

Bonaventure looked in the indicated direction, and after a span of half a dozen breaths had seen nothing but black waves. Eyes straining, trying to divine what he was supposed to be seeing, Bonaventure was startled by the sudden appearance of a streak of ghostly glowing light, seeming to emanate from deep below the waves.

"Will you look at that?" Jeffries said.

"Have you ever seen the like?" Horrocks breathed, pressing in close.

As they watched, other streaks lit up or dimmed, accompanied by occasional flashes and larger regions of light all around. The light was a soft mix of yellow, white, and green, like nothing

Bonaventure had ever seen before. He'd heard reports from other sailors of odd patches of luminescence, which sometimes drifted on the tops of waves, and had seen it once at a distance himself, but never before had he heard of any such phenomena occurring so far below the ocean's surface. It was as though aquatic fairies were camped on the ocean floor below, the lights of their fairy fires burning through to the surface.

"I had an uncle," Symmes said, gaze transfixed by the unearthly lights, "who said he once saw something like that down a cave in France. Walls glowing, like, even in the darkness."

Bonaventure gnawed at his lip.

"I've seen fireflies that glow," Jeffries said, leaning out as far as he was able, "so I suppose some fish could as well. But if fish, why aren't they moving? And how are some areas so small and others so long?"

Bonaventure stepped back from the railing, and looked past the lounging uninterested warriors at Kane in the prow. He walked over slowly, stepping around the warriors and the gear, stopping only when he stood again at Kane's side.

"Fire beneath the waves," Bonaventure said in the island tongue.

"Yes," Kane answered, nodding but not turning around. "These are flames still burning from sparks dropped by the dark god Tura as his brother Te'a carried him across the waves to his prison home. They are scattered throughout the southern sea, but most are here."

Kane paused, glancing over briefly at Bonaventure.

"We are now in the second sea through which we must sail," Kane added. "We are halfway the distance to the forbidden island. Halfway to fire and death."

Chapter Fifty
Distant Smoke

THE MORNING OF the fourteenth day at sail, a black smudge of smoke appeared on the horizon, directly along the frigate's course. A short while later, the crewman aloft called out "Land ho!", and the rocky conical spire of an island crept into view. Bonaventure was aft on the quarterdeck alongside Macallister at the helm, and as officer of the watch made a note in the log of the sighting. Horrocks was sent to fetch the captain, and he returned minutes later, the commanding officer and the ship's surgeon in his wake.

"Mister Bonaventure," the captain said, still climbing the steps to the quarterdeck. "Your report?"

"As you can see, sir," Bonaventure answered, pointing past the prow, "we've sighted what would seem to be the island of the Spaniard's tale, which the islanders on board call Helekea."

"And that smoke?" Doctor Beauregard said, rubbing his hands together nervously. "Might the volcano have erupted? Might we be too late?"

"Unlikely, doctor," Bonaventure answered. He'd seen only one erupting volcano in his life, and that once had been experience enough for a lifetime. "Nothing in the Spaniard's account suggests that the volcano was active, as his mates were able to come and go through the island's caves and crevices unharmed. Likewise, if the volcano had spit up its molten core, the burning stone would kick up great clouds of steam on reaching the water's edge, and the black smoke we see would be fringed with white. The smoke on the horizon is more the smoke of a large wood-burning fire, though whether generated by the hand of man, or perhaps by a lightning strike or some such, I couldn't begin to guess."

"Thank you, Mister Bonaventure," Captain Ross replied, telescoping out his spyglass and scanning the horizon. "When do we make landfall, sir?"

"At present speed, captain, should the wind hold, I'd expect we'll be within range to send out a landing party in boats within a few hours."

"Agreed," the captain said with a curt nod. "Mister Bonaventure, on our arrival I want you to take command of the landing party. Select your men from among the crew, and have the commander of the Marines select a detachment of his finest."

"But the Spanish cannon, sir?" Bonaventure answered. "What about them?"

"Hmmph," Captain Ross grunted, scratching his neck. "Based on my notes, taken during our interrogation of the Spanish prisoner Alvarez, before his departure from the island he saw the ship's defences, cannon and carronades alike, removed from their forwards positions at the island's perimeter and stationed at the mouth of the north-facing cave."

"So I recall," Bonaventure replied. "In that event, should that intelligence be correct, if we were to come in wide of the island, say by tacking first to the east and then approaching the island on a south-westerly course, we could steer clear of the Spanish defensive positions and land our men in relative safety."

"Those were to be my orders," Captain Ross answered in sharp tones. He seemed to think it presumptuous for the first lieutenant to advance such a plan without invitation. Bonaventure realized that he was out of the habit of appeasing the captain's sometimes fragile ego, and had forgotten not to overstep his commanding officer's rigidly set boundaries.

"Aye, sir," Bonaventure said, snapping off a quick salute. "Mister Macallister," he went on, turning to the quartermaster, "course correction. Steer fifteen degrees to port, and hold on that course."

"Sir," Macallister answered, making the change.

"Any further orders, captain?" Bonaventure asked, trying to sound appropriately solicitous without verging over the border into obsequiousness.

"No, Mister Bonaventure," the captain replied, a somewhat haughty tone colouring his voice. "Be about your business. Doctor Beauregard, you're with me, if you please."

At that, the captain turned and climbed the steps from the quarterdeck down to the waist. The doctor followed, looking even more nervous than before, the thought of armed conflict with the Spaniards apparently more disquieting than dropping anchor off the shores of an active volcano. Bonaventure was hardly sure.

Chapter Fifty-One
Madmen or Heroes

THE JOLLY-BOAT was lowered onto the waves, and Lieutenant Bonaventure and a handpicked crew of seamen and Royal Marines, among them Lieutenant Jeffries, Midshipmen Symmes and Horrocks, and Marine Commander Troughton, clambered on board. The eight island warriors, led by Kane, had tugged the tow-line on which their own craft dragged, and bringing it along board transferred their equipment and provisions to it. That done, the two vessels, jolly-boat and double-hulled canoe, were paddled towards the waiting island.

Thus far, with the exception of the halo of black smoke which still hung around the island's summit like a dark wreath, they had been unable to see any other signs of life or habitation on its shores. From the position of the frigate, half a league or so from the shore, only rock and sand could be seen, with no indications of structure or movement.

"I'm not sure I like it," Jeffries observed warily, turned on his seat to look back over his shoulder at the approaching island.

"I'm certain that I don't," Bonaventure answered in a low voice. "We should have seen something by now."

"Perhaps they've sailed on," Symmes advanced, from his position behind Jeffries. "Thought better of staying here, and left."

"Left in what?" Bonaventure said. "From the Spaniard's report, they'd already dismantled the bulk of the galleon before he fled, and he and the lay friar absconded with their only other seagoing craft."

"What if the Spaniard lied?" Jeffries replied. "Or coloured the truth with fancy?"

"If he had, then we'd be here only on a fool's errand," Bonaventure said, gnawing at his lower lip. "No, that what we know from the Spaniard's tale matches so closely with the knowledge the islanders have of this place suggests only that he *was* here, and if we accept that much then we must accept the rest at face value."

There followed a tense silence, broken only by the sound of the oars sliding into and splashing back out of the surf.

"I still don't like it," Jeffries finally added.

From the other craft, Kane called out with a string of liquid syllables, standing surefooted on the platform lashed between the two hulls of the vessel, war club in hand.

"What's he saying?" Jeffries asked.

Horrocks and Bonaventure listened closely, straining to hear.

"It sounds as though they're describing the coming landfall," Horrocks put forth.

"No," Bonaventure answered, shaking his head. "He's reciting one of their poems, if you like, the song of Pahne and the discovery of fire. Their great hero, some island Ulysses, is said to have come to this island in the dawn of time to capture the secret of fire."

"Well, that's one way to while away the time," Jeffries said, rubbing at the back of his neck. "And what is said to have befallen this South Seas sojourner, this island Ulysses, on setting foot on these rocky shores which wait for us? One-eyed giants, perhaps, or great birds with the heads of women? No, let me guess. A woman with snakes in her hair, whose very glance is death?"

Horrocks forced a chuckle, glancing nervously over his shoulder at the rocky island. The facts of what waited before them were enough cause for concern, it seemed, without a need to retreat to fantastical horrors.

"No," Bonaventure answered humourlessly, "they say that deep within the island is a lake of fire, but that in order to reach it one must first best monsters and demons, foul misshapen things that come out of the darkness without warning."

Jeffries looked askance at Bonaventure, an eyebrow cocked.

"Well, you only asked me to report what the man was saying," Bonaventure said, defending himself, the hint of a shrug lifting his shoulders. "Those are the words of the warrior's song."

Jeffries turned back around, joining Horrocks in looking at the island, still wreathed in black smoke.

"Monsters and demons, eh?" Jeffries said. "Well, I only hope that they're half as inviting to look upon as the natives of our last port of call."

Bonaventure pointedly did not answer, but instead kept his eyes on the fast-coursing canoe paddling alongside them. The island warriors, Kane chief among them, were heroes and no doubt. He wondered if the same could be said of his own men, nervously clutching their muskets and pistols. Or of himself, who wanted only to return to the frigate and sail back to the island from which they'd come.

If only madmen and heroes ever went to Helekea, which were they?

Chapter Fifty-Two
Landfall

THE TWO CRAFT pulling within reach of a small stretch of sandy beach on the south-eastern extremity of the island, Marine Commander Troughton ordered four of his men out of the boat, to go ahead of the jolly-boat and take up defensive positions on the shore. As the men jumped overboard, splashing in knee-high water through the surf to the shore, a long, loud howl sounded from somewhere on the island ahead. Like the sound of a great animal in pain, or a predatory creature announcing his dominance.

"What the devil was that?" Jeffries hissed, tightening his grip on the pistol in his hand.

"Sounded like a lion," Symmes said in a small voice. "Or a great ape."

"But the Spaniard indicated that there were no game animals on the island," Bonaventure observed. "Nothing at all above the size of an insect."

"That was some ferocious insect, were that the case," Jeffries answered.

"Keep sharp, men," Bonaventure replied, curtailing any further discussion.

The jolly-boat and double-hulled canoe beached on the sand, the *Fortitude* crewmen were assembled in a ragged formation by their officers, with the Royal Marines in the forefront, the crewmen behind, some dozen men in all. The island warriors, for their part, stood in a wide arc, describing a semicircle, all attention on the rocks that skirted the small beach, and the towering summit above.

"What do you think, commander?" Bonaventure asked in a low voice, drawing near the commanding officer of the Marines.

"We should have expected some show of force by now, sir," he answered warily, sword drawn. "Even out of range and line of sight of their cannon, the *Fortitude* was easily in view during our approach. They must have seen us."

"If they were looking," Bonaventure said.

"And if there are any left to look," Jeffries added, checking and rechecking the action of his pistol's firing mechanism.

"But what was that howl that sounded?" Troughton asked.

Before either lieutenant could answer, there came from their left the noise of rocks falling, and the thud of feet landing on the beach. They spun round, as one, to see a strange figure of a man crouched on the sands some dozen yards away.

It was a man, or rather the ragged feral shadow of a man, naked and covered in dirt, hair and beard grown wild, eyes yellow and flashing. He crouched down in a tight ball like an animal poised to pounce, lips curled back over yellow and broken teeth, ragged-nailed hands curled into claws at his sides.

The crewmen, Marines and island warriors stood in silence for a long moment, watching the wild man and waiting for any sign of movement.

"What the devil...?" Jeffries whispered.

Without warning, the wild man rose from his crouch, a loud, ululating howl issuing from his throat, and rushed forwards madly at the assembled men, clawed hands out and grasping.

In the next moment, a hail of pistol and musket fire sounded from the assembled crewmen and Marines, catching the wild man in mid-stride and sending him spinning over the sands like a marionette on twisted strings. The firing continued even after he'd collapsed in a bloody heap on the beach, head and arms bent at improbable angles, all life fled.

"Cease fire, damn you, cease fire!" Bonaventure shouted. His was perhaps the only firearm in the party not to have been discharged. He pushed through the ranks of crewmen and Marines, and with Jeffries trailing behind him jogged the distance to the wild man's body. Bonaventure knelt down, examining the state of the body closely.

"Well, I think he's dead, Hero," Jeffries said blandly, his attempt at a joke.

"Thank you for that rare and crystal clear observation," Bonaventure spat back. With the barrel of his pistol, he lifted the dead man's head up off the sands, bringing the face into clearer view. "The question is, who is he? Or what?"

"Dweller in dark," came a voice in the island language. Looking up, startled, Bonaventure found the island warrior Kane standing beside Jeffries, an appraising look on his face. "A man made a demon by fire."

"What's he saying?" Jeffries asked, unable to follow in the island tongue.

"He's saying that this is a man turned into a demon," Bonaventure translated, turning his attention back to the corpse.

"Well, that certainly explains it."

"Look here," Bonaventure continued. Using his pistol's barrel to lift the fringe of the wild man's unruly beard, he caught a glimpse of glinting metal beneath, lying against the skin. Reaching down, a flash of mild disgust drifting across his face, he came up with a silver pendant, its rusted necklace chain snapping with a light tug.

The pendant, on examination, showed in bas-relief the image of a bearded man stripped to the waist, a great wound across his belly, his entrails spilling out and being wound round the body of a windlass.

"That makes a pretty picture, now doesn't it?" Jeffries said, looking over Bonaventure's shoulder at the design.

"It's the image of Saint Elmo," Bonaventure replied, looking from the gory depiction to the gored body lying before him. "Patron saint of sailors."

"So the wild man is a papist," Jeffries joked. "Well, I've seen Italians in similar states, I'll confess, but only after a full night of carousing."

"The wild man was a Spaniard," Bonaventure said, ignoring him. "One of the galleon's crew. A fairly highly placed one, if the quality of workmanship and likely price of this silver bauble is any indication."

Jeffries scratched his neck, an incredulous expression on his face.

"Well, this is splendid, just splendid," he finally said. He turned to Kane and placed a comradely hand on the island warrior's shoulder. Kane looked coldly on the hand, and then with narrowed eyes at Jeffries, but did not speak. "Men turned into demons, eh?" he went on. "This should be fun."

With that, Jeffries turned and walked back towards the rest of the party, whistling a humourless tune.

Chapter Fifty-Three
Manhunt

ON GUARD AGAINST any further attack, the contingent of Marines, crewmen, and island warriors slowly worked their way around the rocky shore to the north. They were under strict orders from Bonaventure that if another "wild man" were to make his presence known, he was to be captured for questioning, any shots fired to incapacitate rather than kill. Kane assured Bonaventure that the men in his train understood the proviso, but still the first lieutenant watched them with wary eyes, seeing the hunger for first blood and glory that burned within.

The black smoke, first sighted from miles off, still curled in faint wisps into the sky, seeming to originate somewhere to the north of their current position. As they marched, picking their way carefully over the razor-sharp rocks that fringed the island's shore, they heard other animalistic howls from before and behind them, often singly but on occasion answered by another howl from some other quarter of the island. Everyone in the party having had a good look at the felled wild man, there was little question among the group that these howling screams could only be coming from others like him.

The party had completed a quarter circuit of the island, a fourth of the way round its circumference, when they came upon the savaged bones of a large ship, beached on the shore. Only the keel remained, a few scant spines still affixed to it, the whole resembling nothing so much as the picked over carcass of a Christmas turkey.

"Well, we can be sure they haven't sailed on, whatever other mysteries remain," Bonaventure said, coming round the front of the ship's carcass, prodding the lumber bones with the point of his sabre.

"They made a thorough job of it, you have to give them that," Jeffries answered, giving a low whistle. "Complete scavengers."

"Come on," Bonaventure replied, turning away from the hulk and continuing up the shore. "The cargo's not with what remains of the ship, obviously."

The party continued, and a short time later, coming around a bend, caught sight in the near distance of smouldering ruins, the source of the black billowing smoke. At a barked order from Bonaventure, the company retreated behind the sheltering rocks, weapons at the ready.

"It seems a recently set fire," Symmes offered, as the officers gathered in a hasty conference, knelt down in a tight circle.

"Or a slow burning one," Jeffries answered.

"It looked to be the remains of some fortification," Troughton observed. "Not unlike what we constructed on Te'Maroa."

"I agree," Bonaventure nodded. "But why burning? Could it be some lightning strike? Or intentional?"

"We won't learn any more standing here, now will we?" Jeffries answered, straightening. "Come on, let's go see what dire fate waits for us."

Taking a few deep breaths, Bonaventure stood up straight, drawing a pistol from his belt to balance the sabre gripped in his other hand. Returning to the cusp of the bend, he joined Kane and the seven other island warriors, who crouched down, watching the smoking ruins as best they could from their position of concealment.

"Movement," Kane explained in the island language, pointing past the curve of the rocks at the ruins just inland. "Among the wood and smoke."

Bonaventure followed Kane's line of sight. He couldn't see anything himself, but knew enough to trust the island warrior's skills.

"How many?" Bonaventure asked.

Kane nudged the warrior to his right, who was further along the bend and in a better position to see. The warrior, who Bonaventure knew only as Kaloni, turned around and gave a short nod. Kane turned back to Bonaventure and held up a single finger.

"Can you take him alive?" Bonaventure asked. "I want him for questioning, and the weapons of my men can kill too easily."

Kane tilted his head to one side momentarily, seeming to consider it. Then he nodded.

"Alive," he said simply. Without another word, he set down his war club and took his fighting staff in a two-handed grip. Leaping to his feet, he raced around the curve of the bend, silent and deadly.

The other island warriors crowded together, pushing as far forwards around the bend as possible without stepping into full view, watching their countryman at work. Bonaventure, seeing past shoulders and heads as best he could, tried to follow Kane's movements.

The warrior Kane moved like a blur across the open ground separating the rocky shore from the smoking ruins beyond. The fortifications were situated some thirty or forty yards from the water, built against the craggy rock face of a hill, which rose up some twenty feet above. The base of the hill was obscured by smoke and ruins, but above, it seemed to join with others in a chain rising towards the conical summit of the island.

As soon as Kane had crossed the open ground and slipped in amongst the smoking planks and posts, he disappeared from their view. Tense moments followed, the watching warriors and lieutenant even stifling their breath in hopes of catching some sound on the wind. Bonaventure wondered how long the other warriors would wait until sending another of their number after him, but just when it seemed that Kane had been gone too long to have possibly been successful in his attempt, he returned to view, dragging the still form of another man behind. He walked crouched low, but casual in his step, as though he feared nothing else that the island might offer.

Bonaventure turned and snapped for a pair of musket-wielding Marines to approach, and positioned them around the bend to cover Kane's retreat. The two Marines knelt down—their muskets trained on the smoking ruins—cheek to jowl with the island warriors who now laughed and boasted, pointing towards Kane and trying to guess with what style he might have won this victory.

Kane reached the assembled without incident, and together with them retreated back past the bend to the safety of the rocks beyond. The man he dragged behind, twin to the wild man the party had earlier encountered, groaned weakly on the ground, twitching in painful unconsciousness.

"He is alive," Kane said simply, depositing the wild man at Bonaventure's feet. "Begin with your questions."

Bonaventure regarded Kane closely, thinking he saw the hint of a sardonic smile playing around the edges of the warrior's steely expression.

"Next time," Bonaventure replied, "I'll try to be more specific."

Watching Kane turn and walk back to his men, Bonaventure settled down to watch over the unconscious wild man, waiting impatiently for him to rouse.

Chapter Fifty-Four
Interrogation

TIED HAND AND foot with cord fetched from the jolly-boat, the captured wild man jerked to consciousness a short while later. Struggling against his bonds, he resisted Jeffries's attempts to communicate with him in his own language, answering only in inhuman grunts and moans, looking up at his captors with wild eyes.

Bonaventure, desperate for any other options, had a flask of water brought forwards and tipped it into the man's biting mouth, thinking perhaps thirst had contributed to his madness. The better part of the water dripping down the man's hairy chin and splattering muddily on his dirty chest, some of it managed to work into his throat, and the effect was immediate and positive. The wild man seemed to calm at once, bewildered, swallowing hungrily and reaching with straining lips towards the flask for another draught.

Bonaventure quickly pushed the flask forwards again, upending it into the wild man's waiting mouth. The water emptied, the captive seemed to relax against his bonds, his breathing becoming more regular and calm.

"Try again, Will," Bonaventure ordered, pulling Jeffries forwards. "See what you can do."

Jeffries nodded, and began his interrogation again.

The wild man, though calmed, still seemed confused and barely able to communicate, but at long last Jeffries was able to squeeze some useful information from him, drop by precious drop.

"He says that he is, in fact, a member of the galleon's crew," Jeffries explained to the others, when the interrogation was complete. "His story corresponds to what Alvarez told us before, up to the point where he and the priest escaped. After that, it appears that things took a turn for the worse."

"What happened?" Horrocks asked, breathless.

"Well, once the cargo and supplies were all safely down in the caves, the mouth of which is just back there," he jerked a thumb around the bend, towards the smoking ruins, "their captain started to get suspicious. Of his own men, his lieutenants, everyone. There were only two or three men he trusted, and these he kept by his side at all times. First he had the cargo of gold, silk, and spices moved further down into the arteries of the island, and once that was done, he posted these trusted men as guards at the mouth of the caves, refusing admittance to anyone else."

"What about the fires?" Bonaventure prompted. "Why burn the fort?"

"Well, it appears that was the fault of our guest here," he indicated the bound wild man, "and his friends. Left on the surface, denied access to the caves, it looks like they went a little mad. The captain and his aides stayed below ground, blocking off the caves's mouth, leaving only a narrow passage that was guarded day and night. The men above ground began to quarrel with one another, fights and scuffles breaking out almost daily. Finally, one killed another in a fit of passion, and after that it was nothing but chaos. They became nothing better than animals, Hero. Not men at all, but animals."

"And the fire?" Bonaventure repeated. "What of that?"

"The fires were set by the captain," Jeffries answered, looking over at the captive. "This man doesn't know why, but he seems to think it was to keep him, and the other animals, out. He does say, though, that in the event that one man kills another, once he has... finished with the body... he casts the remains onto the fire, that still burns now even weeks later."

"Why?" Bonaventure asked, not bothering to contemplate what state a body might be in once a wild man had "finished" with it.

"He doesn't know," Jeffries answered. "They're just driven to do so."

Bonaventure nodded and folded his arms over his chest. He stood silent for several moments, rolling the possibilities around in his thoughts.

"Well," he finally said to Jeffries and the other officers. "It looks like we've no choice but to attack the caves."

He motioned for the men to be assembled, and signalled Kane to bring round his warriors. Heroes and madmen, they would attack together.

Chapter Fifty-Five
Approach & Descent

THE APPROACH ON the caves's entrance, carefully orchestrated and perfectly manoeuvred, came with a profound sense of anti-climax. There came from the narrow opening beyond the smoking ruins no shouts of alarm, no fired shots of warning, no bellowing cannon or splintering carronade. Nothing. No sounds, no movement, no indications of any life. The attackers, fanned out across the wide open clearing, in offensive positions along the rock face on both sides of the opening, and hunched down just beyond the smouldering ruins, saw and heard nothing that suggested anything lay beyond the mouth of the caves.

"Well, this is somewhat disappointing," Jeffries shouted from his position flat against the base of the rocky hill to the left of the cave entrance. "I'd rather hoped for a bit more excitement."

Bonaventure impatiently waved him silent, and sidled up next to the island warrior Kane, who stood with his war club at the ready.

"Kane, what do you think?" he asked in the island tongue, eyes fixed on the thin patch of black darkness beyond the fire.

The warrior took a long moment to answer, unable to look away from the caves's mouth. If he had been any other man, in any other circumstance, Bonaventure might have suspected he was afraid.

"To enter the heart of the fire is no matter," Kane finally answered in a quiet voice, his expression strangely open. "Anyone may enter. Few may leave."

"Hmmph," Bonaventure grunted, gnawing at his lower lip. "So you've detected no sign of sentry within the cave mouth?"

Kane shook his head.

"What waits within," he replied, "waits below. We pass through the teeth unharmed and unbitten, to be consumed within the belly far beyond."

"Very well," Bonaventure said in English, nodding. He stood, and waved the Marine commander to his side. "Commander, call out your six best men. By all reports, there are only a bare handful of men within those caves, should they still live, and along with me six should be sufficient for the first foray."

"I'll need call only five, sir," Troughton answered, smiling grimly, "as I'll without question be the sixth."

"Four," Jeffries corrected, coming near.

"Um, three, sir," added Symmes, following behind.

Bonaventure looked from one to the other, shaking his head wearily. He thought to object, to order the other officers to stay above ground with the others, but seeing the determined expressions on their faces knew he could not.

"Very well, men," he answered with a nod. "Commander, call out *three* of your best. I imagine at least some of Kane's men will come along with us, to test their manhood or whatnot, so any more than that will be an unwieldy crew in such confined spaces."

Midshipman Horrocks approached, on seeing the impromptu conference in session.

"Mister Horrocks," Bonaventure continued, calling the young man over. "Misters Jeffries and Symmes, as well as the commander and a detachment of his men, will be descending shortly into the caves. I'm leaving you in command of the balance of our forces, to remain here on the beach to guard our rear."

"Stay on the beach, sir?" Horrocks repeated, eyebrows raised. "Oh, thank you, sir," he added, a sigh of relief deflating him. "Absolutely sir, guard your rear, you can count on me."

"Good man," Bonaventure answered with a smile. "All right, men. Have some torches assembled, and be ready to advance on my signal."

The men answered with a ragged chorus of "Aye, sir," and dispersed to attend to their business. Before a quarter of an hour had passed, the small company of men, Bonaventure in the lead, advanced slowly on the smouldering ruins, and the cave mouth beyond, ready to descend into the island's heart.

In the end, all eight of the island warriors accompanied Bonaventure and his men into the caves. The three Royal Marines selected by their commander, Finlay, Chamberlain, and Reed, muskets at the ready, completed the party.

The fifteen men, crewmen and warriors, made it past the smoking ruins and to the mouth of the caves without incident. Though more howling calls sounded from the far corners of the island, other Spaniards like their fellows descended into wild madness, there came no defending volleys from the recess of the cave. At a signal from Bonaventure, the first of the Marines, Finlay and Reed, slipped through the narrow opening into the darkness beyond, torches in one hand and muskets in the other. Kane and one of the other island warriors, Kienga, followed closely behind.

Reed, stepping briefly back into the smoky sunlight, indicated that the passage was clear and that the others could follow. In the lead, Bonaventure advanced, stepping from light into darkness, the smoke of the fired ruins behind replaced by the musty smoke of the sputtering torches held overhead.

Just within the entrance, seen by torchlight, there were signs of some recent struggle. The stones that had been gathered at the wide cave mouth, blocking off all but a narrow passage, had been disturbed, and a musket lay discarded on the hard packed dirt nearby.

Bonaventure knelt down to inspect the firearm and saw that it had not been fired, the barrel still packed and loaded.

"Hero," Jeffries said, indicating the cave wall above with his torch, "take a look at this."

Splattered on the cold stone wall, like some ghastly cave painting by primitive hands, was a spray of dried blood, stretching some several feet across and high. Bonaventure reached out a finger to test the surface, and his fingertip squelched against the still-sticky wall as he pulled it away.

"Hasn't been too long," he said in a low voice, looking from the wall to his fingertip and back again. "A matter of days, at most."

"What do you suppose happened?" asked Symmes.

"From the look of things, and the position of the discarded musket," Bonaventure answered, "I'd say that one of the posted guards was attacked, by a sabre most likely, and from behind."

"But why?" Symmes said.

"And where's the body?" Jeffries added ominously.

Bonaventure stepped further into the cave, bringing his torch low and playing its light against the hard packed dirt of the cave floor. There were minute traces of blood sprinkled on the dirt, describing a trail leading away from the entrance towards the depths of the cave.

"It would appear it was dragged within," Bonaventure answered. "To what end, I couldn't say."

The officers looked from one to another in silence, while the island warriors whispered quietly to one another behind their hands. Looking at them, Bonaventure was unsure which seemed more frightened, warriors or crewmen. Considering that the warriors seemed to know more about the caves, and what lay within, than they were willing to share, he hoped the more frightened of the party were the crewmen. If the warriors, then they were all likely in more danger than they imagined.

"Come on, men, let's go," Bonaventure finally added, turning back towards the passage leading down into the depths of the cave. "We've nothing to gain standing here in idle speculation." Bonaventure turned to the island warriors and addressed them in their own language. "Kane, let us advance, your men interspersed with mine. My men have their weapons that can fire at a distance, and your men are proficient in combat at close quarters. That way, we move on in relative safety."

Kane considered the suggestion for a long moment and then nodded his assent. Passing the instructions along to the rest of his men, Kane moved forwards to the head of the party, taking up the position just behind Bonaventure in the lead.

"All right, everyone," Bonaventure ordered. "Advance slowly, leaving at least the length of a sword thrust between you and the man ahead. I'll not have us stabbing each other in panic inadvertently, if a mouse were to run across your path. Keep careful watch and keep your ears open. Understood?"

A ripple of nods passed over the assembled crewmen, and then from the warriors when Kane had translated the commands.

"Very well," Bonaventure concluded, taking the first steps down the passageway, sabre drawn in his right hand, his left holding the torch overhead. "Be careful."

Kane following along behind, Bonaventure descended into the bowels of the island, eyes on the darkness ahead.

Chapter Fifty-Six
Into the Bowels

IT BEGAN AS a low rumbling noise from the cave walls around them. Bonaventure at first thought it was simply the sounds of their own footsteps, echoing back to them, but when they had proceeded down the passageway for another quarter of an hour he became convinced there was something else at work.

"Do you hear that?" Bonaventure whispered to Kane, walking a few strides behind.

"The song of Pahne talks of the beating heart of fire," the island warrior answered in a low voice. "I'd never thought to hear it."

"Hmm," Bonaventure hummed in reply, gnawing at his lower lip. "More likely some shifting of the stones around us, perhaps heat rising in thermal vents through passages in the stone."

Kane shook his head.

"The beating heart of fire," he repeated, and then fell silent.

Bonaventure continued on, a few dozen steps further, noticing a slight lightening in the passage before them. Suddenly, without warning, a great gust of wind blew towards them from the cave's depths, extinguishing half their torches and leaving them blinking dust and dirt from their eyes. Bonaventure had just regained his bearings, turning to get an accounting from the men, when there came from the end of the train shouts of alarm, and the sound of musket fire.

"What the devil...?" Bonaventure shouted, rushing back through the now dim light cast by the half dozen still-lit torches towards the sound. His thoughts raced to remember who was bringing up the rear. "Finlay!" he finally called out, the name coming to mind. "Finlay, report!"

There came no immediate answer, and Bonaventure had nearly reached the end of the train before someone called out in response.

"He's... he's dead, sir," came the voice of the next Marine in line, Reed. "His—" the man broke off, voice choking, unable to continue. Bonaventure reached his side, the musket in Reed's hand still smoking from the barrel, and pushed past him.

On the cave floor behind Reed, one of the island warriors, of the Tevake clan, lay bleeding into the dirt. Beyond him lay the still and battered form of another, Rangi, and beyond him in the dim light lay the outstretched body of the Royal Marine.

Kane, following along behind Bonaventure, bent to question his man Tevake, while Bonaventure snatched the torch from Reed's hand and pressed on to examine the two men beyond. Both were certainly dead, past all caring, the warrior Rangi with a broad sucking wound splitting his chest, the life left his eyes, the Marine Finlay in even worse shape. Stepping gingerly over the corpse of the warrior Rangi, Bonaventure crossed the distance to the body of the Marine, and let the torchlight play over the scene.

The Marine's head, sundered from his body, was cast some dozen feet away, lying along the cave wall further back the passage. His body, blood still fountaining from the ruined neck, lay limbs disarranged on the hard packed dirt floor. There was no sign of any attacker.

"Kane, what does your man say?" Bonaventure called out, hurrying back to the warrior's side. "Who attacked them? Who killed those two men?"

Kane leaned in close to Tevake, ear close to the injured man's lips, listening closely.

"He says that a misshapen figure swam out from the rock itself," he related, pointing towards the cave wall behind them. "He says he saw the creature only dimly, and for a moment, but that it looked to be a huge, monstrous head with man-sized limbs growing from its cheeks and jaw." He paused, listening intently. "He says that the creature first tore the head from the shoulders of the last man in line, then swiped at the next man in line, Rangi. The creature had come for him when the soldier before him turned, and fired with his loud stick at the monster. He didn't see where the monster fled, but he thinks it must have swum back into the rock."

Jeffries appeared at Bonaventure's side, pistol in hand.

"What the devil happened here?" he spat. "What's that man say?"

"Hsst," Bonaventure hissed, waving him silent. He turned back to Kane, who now held the warrior Tevake close as the life fled from his limbs. "Kane, monsters swimming from rock? Creatures with giant heads? What really happened? Who really attacked these men?"

Kane was silent for a long moment, listening to the last breath leave his countryman's body, then sang a short chant of blessing over his fallen comrade before answering.

"*Tikua*," he said simply, a word Bonaventure had not heard before. "Demons from the darkness, creatures of fire and earth." Lowering Tevake gently to the floor, Kane stood and turned to face Bonaventure. "These are just the first to fall, the first challenge of Helekea. The *tikua* will return, and there will be more besides." He pushed past Bonaventure and returned up the passageway. "Come. We have some distance to go."

When he had gone, Bonaventure moved on Reed, the smoking barrelled musket still in his hands.

"Reed, what did you see?" Bonaventure demanded, his voice grave.

"Yes, what—" Jeffries began, but Bonaventure cut him off with a glare.

"Tell me, Reed," Bonaventure ordered. "What attacked those men?"

The Marine, stony exterior cracked, whimpered as fat tears rolled down his face.

"I couldn't... I couldn't see—" he began, then stopped short. Forcibly calming, he took hold of himself, straightening up and blinking away his shameful tears. "I couldn't quite see, sir," he finally managed. "Finlay's torch must have blown out in that wind, and when I turned to fire I dropped my own. I just saw... a large shape... yes, a large shape, like some misshapen man, and hearing the others scream out I just fired on it." He paused, and then added, "In the muzzle flash of my musket, I thought I saw something, but—"

"What?" Bonaventure prompted, stepping in close. "What was it?"

Reed took a deep quavering breath, looking from Bonaventure to Jeffries, eyes twitching.

"It was some kind of monster, sir," he reluctantly answered. "Some sort of horrible monster."

Bonaventure, disbelieving, reached out and laid a hand on the Marine's shoulder. Whatever might have happened, whatever the man had seen, it had been a shock to his system; the man was barely able to remain on his feet.

"Reed, I want you to tell me honestly," Bonaventure said in softer tones. "Can you continue or should I send to the surface for a replacement?" He paused and then added, "There'll be no shame in it, if you were discharged. I won't have a shaken man as a risk to himself and to others, and would ask the same of any man here."

The Marine pulled himself up straight, wiping at his eyes and nose with the back of his sleeve. He shook his head firmly, mouth set.

"No, sir," he answered, his tone assured. "I won't let you down, sir."

Bonaventure looked him over for a few long moments and then nodded slowly.

"All right, then," he replied. "Good man." Turning, Bonaventure passed by and continued back up the passage. "Come on, men. We've still work to do. We'll tend to our dead when the moment comes, and remember them then."

Past reluctant nods and murmurs of assent, Bonaventure continued towards the front of the train, advancing down into the depths.

Chapter Fifty-Seven
The Beating Heart of Fire

FURTHER ON, THE passage walls widened apart, the ceiling growing ever higher. The torches relit, the now diminished party continued into the depths of the island, watching for any sign of the Spanish captain and his surviving men. It was assumed, though with little conviction, that it must have been one of these which attacked Reed and the two island warriors further up the passage, and so additional care was taken to guard their rear, the loss of three men too dear to repeat. What none of the crewmen would admit, though, Bonaventure least of all, was that they suspected the island warriors were right about the attack, and that they were harried by monsters in their approach.

The passageway bent around a curve ahead, and beyond a dull red light suffused through the dusty air.

"Go carefully, men," Bonaventure ordered in a voice barely above a whisper, calling back to the men behind. "We're bound to encounter the Spanish captain soon."

Bonaventure had cause to regret the prophetic nature of his words, rounding the bend in the passage.

There beyond, the dull red glow grown lighter, they found themselves facing a wide fissure in the cave floor, in which molten rock burbled and hissed. On the far side of the fissure, lit demonically by the red light below, stood an emaciated figure, naked and hairless, perched on a wide ledge above.

"The lake of fire," Kane whispered in his native tongue.

"The Spanish captain," Bonaventure replied in English, "unless I miss my guess."

"*Inglés!*" called out the strange figure on the fissure's far side, his voice croaking and hoarse. "Splendid," he continued in English. "You are my enemies, come to join me here in paradise, yes?"

Bonaventure, tossing down his torch and drawing a pistol from his belt, advanced to the edge of the molten fissure.

"Captain Bartolomé Velásquez de Leon?" he called out in a loud voice. "Have I the honour of addressing Captain Velásquez?"

The man beyond, his hair plucked out at the roots, resembling nothing so much as an animated skeleton draped in a thin layer of flesh, shook his head.

"Names have no meaning here, *Británico*," he replied in a croak. "Here at the world's heart, we are our own true selves revealed, shorn of human imperfection."

From this nearer vantage point, Bonaventure could see the red light reflected dimly from a mound at the figure's feet. What he'd taken originally to be an outcropping of stone seemed now to be, in fact, a small pile of gold.

As though in answer to an unspoken question, the man reached down, and picked up a fist-sized lump of gold metal in his thin hand.

"These, last treasures of the world above, are here revealed as an empty mockery of true worth," the man went on, leaning forwards over the lip of the ledge, demonic in the red glow from beneath. "We here offer them up to our true lord and master, and free ourselves of self-imposed bounds."

At that, the man extended his arm over the fissure's edge, and turning over his hand let the lump of gold drop with a popping hiss into the molten stone. It sank slowly from view, the red molten heat around it flaming brightly in brief sparks as it passed.

"Captain Velásquez," Bonaventure went on, training his pistol on the man, eyes darting to the corners of the cavern. He was sure this man was the maddened remnant of the Spanish captain now, but if so, where were the others? "Where are your men? Your aides brought with you below?"

The man, captain or not, tilted his head to one side in response, a confused look playing across his features.

"Men?" he repeated, and then understanding dawned. "Oh, the other servants, the weak ones." He turned, stepping away from the ledge's lip, but not before kicking in another half dozen or so golden nuggets. "They are here. They could not aid me suitably, as the master demanded, so I had to find some other use for them." He reached down, and picked up what Bonaventure first assumed was a stick. Looking closer, better able to see as the man stepped back towards the edge of the narrow ledge, he saw that he was wrong.

"One gets so hungry," the man explained, gesturing absent-mindedly with the leg bone in his hand. "The work is hard and demands sacrifice."

"Good Lord," Jeffries cursed, coming forwards to stand at Bonaventure's side. "Is that what I think—" He broke off, unable to continue.

"Yes, I believe so," Bonaventure answered gravely. "Captain Velásquez," he called out, trying to keep his gorge from rising, "if you'll only come with us, we'll see that you get the medical attention you deserve."

"No!" the man shouted fiercely, crouching down like an animal and shoving another portion of the gold pile into the fire. He paused, head cocked to one side as though listening to some unheard voice. "Yes," he added, then, "no. Very well."

The man straightened and gathered up in his arms the few remaining pieces of gold.

"I'm sorry, *Británicos*, but I must leave you now," he said, stepping towards the lip of the ledge. "My master has another use for me. But he's sending some others of his servants to greet you when I'm gone."

The skeletal man swung a foot out over the edge of the fissure.

"No!" Bonaventure cried out, looking desperately for some path around the flames, but it was too late.

The man tottered forwards, and fell face first into the molten stone, the last of the gold in his embrace.

"A man made a demon," Kane announced plainly, turning away from the fissure, facing the passage from which they'd come.

"Madness," Bonaventure cursed, spitting. "All of it."

"Listen," Kane added, laying a hand on Bonaventure's shoulder. "They are coming."

Bonaventure stared at the fissure, while the last of the man, his outstretched hand, sank beneath its molten embrace. Then he turned, bewildered, to the island warrior.

"What?" he asked, in English. He corrected himself, repeating in the island tongue, "What?"

"They come," Kane said again, pointing with his war club towards the passage curving away in the darkness. "The belly will devour us."

"Come on, let's go," Bonaventure said impatiently, stepping away from the fissure and crossing to retrieve his torch.

Before he had, before he could say another word, the monsters were upon them, coming out of the darkness and swimming out from the walls themselves.

Chapter Fifty-Eight
Monsters

THEY WERE JUST as the fallen warrior Tevake had described, though even more hideous than could have been imagined. Bonaventure knew that were he to survive he'd never see their like again, even if he lived to be 150.

There were eight of them all together, taller than a man but composed almost entirely of a monstrous head, muscular arms jutting out behind massive ears, and legs tapering down below the unimaginable jaw line. They were truly monsters, if anything was.

"*Tikua* demons," Kane called out to his fellow warriors, grasping his war club in a two-handed grip, torch dropped forgotten on the cave floor. "We must defeat them or die bravely in the attempt."

"More things in heaven and earth," Jeffries muttered below his breath, drawing near Bonaventure. "Either we've gone mad or are already in Hell."

"The answer's somewhere in between," Bonaventure hastily replied, drawing back the hammer of his pistol with his thumb, and swinging his sabre up into a defensive position before him. "If we're not mad, then Hell is surely loosed upon the Earth."

Bonaventure motioned Jeffries to take up a position at his side, then called out to the others.

"Fall back, men, but steer wide of the fissure."

The others, Marine Commander Troughton, the surviving Marines Reed and Chamberlain, and Midshipman Symmes, fell into a defensive ring with Bonaventure at its apex. Muskets and pistols were trained on the advancing creatures, those with swords clutching them in white-knuckled grips.

The island warriors, seeing the crewmen retreat, took the advantage, stepping forwards to advance on the monsters in a line.

"Damn it, Kane," Bonaventure hissed, knowing he'd be neither heard nor heeded. "There are merits besides victory and glorious death."

As though to illustrate his point, one of the monsters lumbered forwards, reaching out with massive arms and snatching the forward-most of the island warriors up off the ground. The warrior, teeth gritted and eyes flashing, lashed out uselessly with his fighting staff, continuing to struggle until the monster flung him bodily over the head of Bonaventure and his men, to land with a loathsome hiss in the molten pool behind. Finally finding his voice, the warrior screamed out, a sickening howl that was only silenced when his head sank beneath the molten surface.

Seeing their comrade fall, the other warriors pressed their attack, but more warily.

"Blast it, Hero," Jeffries shouted over to Bonaventure, "we can't let them face those bastards alone."

"He's right, sir," Symmes chimed in. "If we stand back watching, the things'll only pick us off next, one at a time."

"Our only chance is to rush them at once," Bonaventure agreed. "Try to drive a wedge between them, and then fight our way to the surface, covering our retreat."

"We're with you, sir," Troughton shouted, the other men nodding their assent.

"All right, then, damn it to Hell," Bonaventure shouted. "Attack."

Muskets firing, pistols flaring, swords swung in deadly arcs overhead, the crewmen poured forwards, Bonaventure in the lead, forcing the attack on the monsters.

Chapter Fifty-Nine
Pyrrhic Retreat

THE PARTY MADE progress towards the surface and the cave mouth, but at some considerable cost. Symmes was the first to fall, struck down by a heavy blow to the neck by one of the monstrous creatures. The island warrior Kienga fell next, pulled limb from limb by another, and Hulana, who slipped in the gore, fell under a monster's heavy tread.

Halfway to the surface, having pressed past the monsters, which now followed close on their heels, the party lost Chamberlain when a monster rammed into him, driving him with a sickening crunch into the cave wall. By that point, the warriors and crewmen had only dispatched two of the monsters, both times striking at the creatures's relatively unprotected legs, leaving them still living but immobilized. These two victories, though, had cost four of their own fellows's lives in the process, and at that rate they didn't have comrades enough to purchase the freedom even of one of them.

With only eight of their party remaining, four warriors and four crewmen, to the six monsters pursuing close behind, the arithmetic was obvious.

"Jeffries, you, the commander, and Reed go on ahead," Bonaventure ordered, skidding to a stop in the passageway and wheeling on the forms lumbering slowly towards them. The four remaining island warriors were a short distance back down the passage, as they retreated striking ineffectual blows to the creatures. "I'll stay behind with the warriors to hold them off."

"You've lost your mind, here in this madhouse," Jeffries answered, forcing a laugh. "If you think that I'd leave you behind to prove your heroic worth with these tattooed savages, leaving me to sing your praises the rest of my days, you are a madman." He stepped forwards and grabbed Bonaventure by the elbow. "We've only a short distance to go and, once outside, we'll have the rest of our landing party to aid us. To stay here, buying a few extra paces for us at the cost of your life, is a needless waste."

Troughton nodded, glancing back nervously at the rapidly approaching monsters.

"We've gained the ground we needed, sir," he said in a rush, already sidestepping in the direction of the entrance. "We'll only waste it to stand here discussing options."

Bonaventure looked from one man to the other, and then quickly nodded.

"All right," he said, waving them on. "Go ahead, I'll follow."

Turning back the way they'd come, he cupped his hands and called out to the warriors that followed.

"Kane, your worth is proved," he yelled out in the island tongue. "If we can reach the surface before the demons, my men can provide the cover we need to defeat them."

That said, he turned and sprinted up the passageway after his three crewmates. From behind, he heard a fierce war cry and then the sound of Kane shouting a single word.

"Run!"

Bonaventure ran on, the warriors racing up behind, the monsters lumbering close on their heels.

Chapter Sixty
Carnage

SEVEN OF THE eight remaining members of the party reached the surface in time, the last and eighth, the warrior Rewi, having been snatched up by the forward-most monster in the final seconds. Plunging through the narrow cave entrance into the open air, Bonaventure shouted out for his men to assemble on him and prepare to fire. What he had not expected to see in response were his men already assembled in a defensive position with their backs to the cave mouth, the open clearing before them littered with fallen bodies.

"Horrocks," Bonaventure snapped, seeing the midshipman close by. "We are pursued. Have your men turn and fire into the cave entrance at my command."

"Aye, sir," Horrocks answered wearily, bringing his men into position.

Only one of the creatures made it through the cave entrance, the hail of bullets that pocked and pitted his monstrous hide sending him falling lifeless to the ground. Lying across the cave entrance, his bloodied and battered form, repellent and misshapen as it was, must have served as some deterrent to his fellow monsters following behind, as they did not so much as peek through the entrance in the long, tense minutes that followed.

Ordering the crewmen to reload and keep careful watch on the entrance, Bonaventure drew Midshipman Horrocks to one side, demanding an accounting of what had gone on in their absence.

"Madness, sir," Horrocks answered in a strained voice, near to breaking, "pure madness. No sooner had you gone below, than one of those wild man creatures came from around a rock and threw himself at one of the men. We didn't react in time, and the thing had torn out the crewman's throat with his bare teeth before we pulled it off him. I ordered the men to fall back to the cave entrance, to guard your rear, and within moments another of the wild men appeared, then another, then another, racing towards us from all sides, practically throwing themselves into our line of fire. We barely had time to reload after each volley before another came rushing forwards. The last was just a few moments before you reappeared, so I'm not sure we've seen the last of them."

"All right, Horrocks," Bonaventure added, patting the younger man's shoulder. "Jeffries," he called out over his shoulder, "any sign of those creatures? Any more come through the cave mouth?"

"No, none," Jeffries shouted back. He had a deep gash in his side, where one of the monsters had forced him against a sharp rock outcropping in the cave wall before Bonaventure and the others had driven it off. He held his hand now pressed to his side, blood seeping out through his fingers and dripping to the sandy ground below.

"Are you fit to move?" Bonaventure called back to him, but then turned to Horrocks before Jeffries had a chance to answer. "Horrocks, are your men able to retreat? Any wounded that might need assistance?"

Horrocks shook his head, a dark expression clouding his face.

"No, sir," he answered. "The only wounded are already dead."

Bonaventure bit his lip, but nodded.

"All right, then," he continued. "We're getting the Hell out of here. You men," he pointed at a pair of seamen who seemed unharmed, "help Mister Jeffries and the other members of my party to their feet. Horrocks, you take the lead. At the first sign of any more wild men, monsters, or any damned thing at all, you shoot it. Do you understand me?"

Horrocks nodded gravely.

"Very well," Bonaventure replied. "Let's go."

Chapter Sixty-One
Exodus

REACHING THE BOATS without further incident, the surviving members of the landing party scrambled on board and pushed out into the surf, all without a word passing among them. The rowers at their oars on the jolly-boat, the three island warriors paddling their double-hulled canoe out onto the seas, the two craft set off, away from the island and towards their waiting ship.

When they'd put a few boat lengths between them and the shore, sitting in grimfaced silence, Horrocks leaned over to Bonaventure, a bewildered look in his eyes.

"What did you find down there, sir?" he asked, glancing with a shudder back towards the island. "What was that thing that followed you out?"

Bonaventure looked from Horrocks to the three crewmen who'd survived the foray, and then over at Kane and the other two warriors on their island craft.

"There was nothing down there, Horrocks," he answered in a low voice. "Nothing but madness."

"But sir... ?" Horrocks began.

"It will be my official report to the captain, Horrocks," Bonaventure continued, looking back at the rocky island behind, "that on our descent into the caves, we found the surviving Spanish crewmen dead at their own hands and the cargo irretrievably lost or destroyed." He paused, and then added, "I'm sure the reports of the others on the foray will bear this out."

Bonaventure caught the eyes of Jeffries, Troughton, and the surviving Marine Reed in turn, and each gave a slow, silent nod.

They rowed on, drawing ever nearer the frigate *Fortitude*. As they watched, the double-hulled canoe of the island warriors pulled away to the north, out of line with the jolly-boat, headed away from the frigate.

"Where are they going, sir?" one of the rowers asked, indicating the warriors with a jerk of his chin.

"Back to their homes, I expect," Bonaventure answered, respectfully. "They've done what they consider the work of heroes, harried their culture's idea of Hell and have lived to tell the tale. I expect they want nothing more than to return to their families, to their women..." He paused, a pang of regret biting him. "To return to their people," he went on, "and mourn their fallen dead."

"Christ," Jeffries cursed, but no one looked askance at his blasphemy. Holding in his life's blood with his bare hands, Jeffries hung his head, defeated. "Poor Ned. So young, so damned young."

Bonaventure had no answer to give, no moral lesson to draw from the encounter. He only sat in silence, rocking with the motion of the boat.

They carried with them back to the ship no treasure but their own wounds and the memory of their fallen dead. Captain Ross would not be pleased, his hopes for a prize ship and retirement lost, but Bonaventure couldn't care less. They'd paid for the captain's goals with their own blood, as Bonaventure had known they would, but the bill would eventually come round to Ross. No one escaped reckoning forever, that much he had learned.

They pulled on, in their silence, the survivors and the wounded, rowing towards the waiting ship.

Chapter Sixty-Two
The Course Ahead

BONAVENTURE STOOD AT the starboard rail on the quarterdeck, looking out over the seas. It was near to sunset, and dark clouds were gathering on the far horizon. At the sound of footsteps on the deck behind him, he turned to find Jeffries approaching, coming to relieve him as officer of the watch.

"You look as I feel, Hero," Jeffries said, standing alongside him at the rail.

"And how is that?" Bonaventure spoke without a trace of humour, his expression dark.

Jeffries touched a hand to his side, tenderly. "How do you think?"

Bonaventure saw the inelegant sticking of the shirt beneath the second lieutenant's hand, the stain of his lifeblood still faintly visible around the seam. "Does it hurt, Will?"

Jeffries chuckled, ruefully.

"Well, I suspect that Doctor Beauregard's attentions were not wholly on his task, his thoughts no doubt concerned with his prized botanical specimens, but even without the full brunt of his tender ministrations, I think I'll survive. The doctor assures me there is no sign of infection." He touched his side again, but too hard this time, and winced, drawing in a sharp breath that hissed through his teeth. "But yes, Hero, it still hurts like the very dickens."

Bonaventure reached out and laid a hand on Jeffries's shoulder. "You've my sympathies. Still, it could have been worse. You could have ended up like—" He bit the words off, swallowing them unspoken, and a cloud passed over his features. After a long pause, he said, "It could have been worse."

Jeffries nodded, understanding. Then he brightened, fractionally. "Have you heard? The island of the Te'Maroans is now newly christened. Captain Ross, as is his privilege and prerogative, has entered Kovoko-ko-te'maroa into the logs as Kensington Island, in honour of our gracious king."

Bonaventure cocked an eyebrow, and a slight smile tugged the corner of his mouth. "And has anyone informed the captain that King George has never resided in the walls of Kensington Palace, preferring Buckingham House, or Windsor Castle in a pinch?"

Jeffries grinned broadly and shook his head. "I doubt that any in the crew will see fit to contradict the captain in this matter."

Bonaventure shrugged. It was just as well. Cartographers could put it down as Kensington Island in as many maps and charts as they liked, but it would make no difference. To him, it would always be Kovoko-ko-te'maroa, the home he could never keep.

"Hero?" Jeffries said, breaking the long silence that stretched between them. "About the cave, and... That is... Well, I'd very much like to hear your thoughts on the things we've seen, you and I."

Bonaventure mulled it over. The things they had seen? The bird of fire that Pelani's father was able to conjure over the flames, the bat-creatures that harried him and Pelani on the island, the strange creatures who dwelt beneath the caves of the dormant volcano, and the madness that had gripped the Spanish captain and his crew. What was he to think of them? What *could* he think of them?

"I don't know, Will," he answered, at length. "I'm not sure I *have* any thoughts to share. It seems as if the things we've witnessed are... well, they just seem too oddly shaped to fit within my skull. It's as though my mind refuses to accept them, though I have the evidence of my own senses as proof." He worried at his lower lip between thumb and forefinger. "The world in which I've always lived has been an ordered one, for all its mysteries, and there is in it no place for monsters and demon-driven madmen."

"Even if you've seen them with your own eyes?"

Bonaventure nodded, sighing. "Even so." He gripped the rail tighter, and glanced over his shoulder at his friend. "I think the only thing for us, you and I, is to return to an ordered, monotonous existence, the wearing drudge of daily life. Just forget things hidden deep within the earth, forget the paradise and Hell through which we've passed these last months, and live only in the world of the mundane."

Jeffries narrowed his eyes. "And you can do that?"

Bonaventure set his jaw. "I can certainly try."

Even as he spoke, though, he couldn't help but wonder. So much of what Pelani and her father had told him, which he'd initially rejected as base superstition, had proven correct. What, then, about the other things they had reported to him? What of the old island priest telling Bonaventure that he would not die on these seas and not for many long years to come? Bonaventure knew well that there was but one sea, vast and unending. That being so, then where would his journeys carry him, and where would he finally meet his end, if not on the sea?

Lights flashed deep within the dark clouds that hulked on the horizon, followed by the faint pealing of distant thunder. A strange storm was brewing, and it looked as though it was heading their way.

April, 1802

GILES DULAC WAS waiting for him on the piste when he arrived at the carriage house for the last time, the sword-case at his feet.

"Many happy returns of the day."

"Thank you, sir," Hieronymus Bonaventure answered with a smile. "I'll admit, though, that I'm sorry to mark the occasion with our last session."

Dulac pursed his lips, and nodded thoughtfully. "So you're going, then, as planned."

"Too late to fight the French it seems," Hieronymus said, smiling, "if only by a few weeks. But I'm going, still and all."

"I wouldn't worry too much on that account. I harbour serious doubts that the First Consul will be satisfied with the state of things for long. I'm sorry to say that the Peace of Amiens will not last."

Hieronymus shrugged out of his coat as he crossed the dirt floor, hung it from a peg on the wall, and then returned to the piste.

Dulac stood motionless, his arms crossed, the sword-case at his feet still closed. "Have you spoken with your father?"

With a ragged sigh, Hieronymus shook his head, his expression black. "I tried," he said at length, "but all my father can think about is that damned and blasted Rosetta stone." He balled his hands into fists, as though desperate for something to strike. "You would think that the only incident of note to occur last month was Colonel Turner's presentation of that damned stone to the Society of Antiquaries."

A pained expression lined Hieronymus's face, and his shoulders hunched.

"It is as though…" he continued, with some difficulty, "as though the fact of his wife's death has escaped the man completely."

"When one loses the thing he cares for most in the world," Dulac said quietly, eyes closing slowly as if remembering some distant pain, "he finds solace where he can."

"I don't believe that." Hieronymus fingered the miniature globe pendant hung around his neck, eyes narrowed. "I don't believe he cares at all."

Dulac sighed, sadly. "You'll understand when you're older, I'm sorry to say." He paused. "So you are ready to go?"

Hieronymus nodded. "I've already been to see my siblings and bid them farewell, and visited the site of my mother's grave. All that is left is my appointment tomorrow morning at the haberdashers, for the final fitting of my midshipman's uniform, and I'll be ready to leave for Plymouth."

"Well," Dulac said with a sly half-smile. "You can't go to sea without a sword."

Hieronymus lowered his eyes for a moment, embarrassment pinking his cheeks. "I…" he began, shamefaced. "That is to say, after the purchase of my uniform I have only a little money left aside, and that little largely taken by carriage fare to Plymouth.

With any luck, though, I hope to find one at a pawnbroker's shop when I reach my destination. If not…" He trailed off, helplessly.

"Your first act on board ship shouldn't be to request charity," Dulac said, and bent to open the case at his feet. "It sets a poor precedent." The case opened length-wise, and Dulac took from within a sheathed sword. "I anticipated this might be a problem and brought along a remedy, just in case."

Dulac stood and held the scabbarded sword at his side.

"Your studies have ended a session earlier than you had thought, Hieronymus. There will be no more lessons from me, today or ever."

Hieronymus smiled. "Am I not asked to play the prize, as Henry VIII required?"

Dulac looked at him, surprised. "What do you think we've been doing these last weeks, fencing in shirtsleeves with bare blades? It's been ten years and not fourteen, but the fact that you can cross swords with me and survive unblooded and intact means that you've learned all that I have to teach you."

Dulac drew the sword from the scabbard, and Hieronymus could see that the long, straight blade, though pitted with age, its single edge nicked in several places, was still razor sharp.

It was Michel-Thierry Bonaventure's spadroon, prize of Dulac's collection.

"Here," Dulac said, presenting the spadroon to Hieronymus hilt first, the blade resting on his arm. "The prize is yours."

Hieronymus reached out his hand, but stopped just short of touching the hilt with his fingertips.

"I… I couldn't." He shook his head. "I couldn't possibly accept such a gift."

Dulac smiled. "Don't think of it as a gift. You're merely keeping it for a friend."

Hieronymus nodded gravely and, stretching out his hand, wrapped his fingers around the welcoming hilt of the sword.

"Thank you," he said, scarcely above a whisper.

"Carry it until you find a sword of your own," Dulac said. "And if this one does you any service in the meantime, then you'll do honour to the memory of those who carried it before you."

Hieronymus accepted the scabbard from Dulac and sheathed the blade.

"So now you'll go to places none has ever been, I take it?"

Hieronymus smiled broadly, shouldering into his coat. "And see things no one has ever seen."

"Then I envy you," Dulac said. "Or fear for you. Both, perhaps. Either way, you have my best wishes for good fortune."

Dulac extended his hand.

"Thank you," Hieronymus said with feeling, taking the proffered hand in his own.

"Go on then. Wait too long, and someone might beat you to all those undiscovered places."

Hieronymus smiled, almost unable to contain his excitement. With a final look around the bare space where he'd spent so many hours and learned so much, and a final nod to his instructor and friend, he tucked the sheathed sword under his arm and went out into the wider world, to see what he could discover.

Glossary

Able seaman: A general term referring to an experienced sailor, but not one used in reference to commissioned officers.

Ballast: Any heavy material placed in a ship's hold to improve stability. Without ballast, a typical three-masted ship would be too top-heavy to stay upright.

Called to quarters: To be called to battle stations.

Captain: The master and commander of a ship. Used to denote the officer in command, who did not in all cases hold the rank of "captain" (e.g. James Cook was a lieutenant on his first voyage to the South Pacific, but was referred to on board ship as Captain Cook).

Carronade: A short piece of ordnance, typically of large calibre, having a chamber for powder.

First lieutenant: The ship's executive officer, typically second in command.

Forecastle: A short raised deck at the forwards end of a ship.

Foremast: The forward-most mast of a ship.

Fothering: To stop a leak by running a sail beneath the ship.

Frigate: A three-masted ship of war carrying between twenty and fifty guns.

Galleon: A type of ship used as a trading vessel by the Spanish.

Grapeshot: A sort of prototypical shotgun shell, grapeshot was made up of small iron balls in a canvas bag, which scattered when fired from a cannon.

Gun deck: The deck of the ships where the majority of the guns (i.e. cannon) were kept.

Gunports: Apertures in the hull of the ship through which cannon could be aimed and fired.

Half-pay: When an officer of the Royal Navy retired, he received as his severance half of his last pay-rate per month for the remainder of his life. An officer on half-pay, however, could not be employed in the public service.

Hauled: To trim the sails, steering as closely in the direction from which the wind is blowing as possible.

Helm: The controls used to move the rudder and steer the ship.

Mainmast: On a three-masted ship, the centre mast.

Maintop: A platform midway up a mast.

Match-tubs: A tub wherein lit matches were hung upside down, ready to be used in lighting cannon.

Midshipman: A commissioned officer below lieutenant in rank.

Mizzenmast: The rearmost mast on a three-masted ship.

Orlop deck: The lowest deck of a ship, used typically for storage.

Port: When facing the fore of the ship, the direction "left".

Prize: Any enemy vessel and the cargo she carries captured by a ship and delivered to the Admiralty.

Quarterdeck: A raised portion at the rear of the ship, where the captain and other officers command the activities of the crew.

Quartermaster: A non-commissioned or "petty officer" who assists with steering the ship, signalling, and navigation.

Quartermaster's mate: A petty officer who reports to and assists the quartermaster.

Reefed: To roll or fold up all or a portion of a sail, to reduce that part exposed to the wind and diminish the ship's forwards motion.

Rigging: A term used to refer to any of the lines or ropes used on a ship, typically those which are used to position the sails.

Second lieutenant: The officer in the chain of command below the first lieutenant, the third in command.

Spars: A term used to refer to any of the poles used on the ship, and to spare lumber kept below deck as replacement.

Spyglasses: Telescopes.

Topsails: The middle of three sails on each mast, second above the deck.

Windward: In the direction from which the wind is blowing (the opposite of leeward).

Author's Notes

READERS OF MY previous novels may recall that I am the type of person who feels cheated when "The End" are the last words in a book, and who never buys a DVD if the "Special Features" are nothing more than theatrical trailers. While I feel that stories should explain themselves, I nevertheless like a little extra material to explore when I finish the story itself, a bit of behind-the-scenes business that I can dig into after the credits roll.

With that in mind, I offer the following notes.

On the Text

THIS EDITION OF *Set the Seas on Fire* is a considerably expanded and revised version of a novel originally published in a print-on-demand edition by Clockwork Storybook, a short-lived writers's collective in Texas (about which more further down), and subsequently made available online under a Creative Commons licence, both times under the same title. The present volume is some 25 per cent longer, but contains the complete text of the earlier versions.

On the Bonaventure family

THE DASHING HIERONYMUS Bonaventure, first lieutenant on the HMS *Fortitude*, is a member of a large extended family of explorers and adventurers, the Bonaventure-Carmody clan. Documented in the pages of *Cybermancy Incorporated, Here, There & Everywhere, Paragaea: A Planetary Romance*, and *End of the Century*, the family also includes time traveller Roxanne Bonaventure, Victorian-era explorer Peter R. Bonaventure, WWI-era aviator Jules Bonaventure, secret agent Diana Bonaventure, and research magician Jon Bonaventure Carmody. *Paragaea: A Planetary Romance*, to which this work is a prequel and in which Hieronymus previously appeared, relates his later adventures after falling through a traversable wormhole into another world.

The Bonaventure-Carmody clan owes much to the von Bek/Beck/Begg stories of Michael Moorcock, to the Diogenes Club stories of Kim Newman, to the superhero comics of Alan Moore, and especially to Philip José Farmer's Wold Newton stories. Any reader who enjoyed any aspect of the present volume is encouraged to seek out all of these, at once.

On the Te'Maroans

I FIRST DEVELOPED the island culture of the Te'Maroans to act as part of the backdrop for an urban fantasy shared world assembled by a Texas-based writers's collective. The shared world, like the writers's collective, was called Clockwork Storybook.

In that world, the displaced Te'Maroans had taken up residence in the fictional city of San Cibola, on the west coast of the United States. Characters like Susan Kururangi, monster hunter, and Alf Tevake, urban shaman, would occasionally make reference to the island of their grandfathers, and the myths and legends of those that had come before them. The Te'Maroans of *this* branch of the Myriad are close cousins to those in San Cibola, and this story represents, from a different vantage point, one of those legends.

As regards the language and customs of the Te'Maroans, I readily admit that I stole aspects from various Polynesian cultures, and particularly from Maori, for that of Kovoko-ko-te'maroa. But I also made up out of whole cloth as much as I stole, so I'm a liar as well as a thief.

I also stole the name of the island, at least in part. I'll not say from where, but I will say that Kovoko-ko-te'maroa is not down in any map. But then, true places never are.

On Giles Dulac

GILES DULAC'S CONNECTION to the Bonaventure family is explored in the pages of *End of the Century*, where it is revealed that he has not been entirely forthcoming to Hieronymus about his background. The question of whether he is any relation to the similarly named Jules Dulac, who appears as travelling companion to the Victorian explorer Peter R. Bonaventure in the story "Secret Histories: Peter R. Bonaventure, 1885" (originally included in *Cybermancy Incorporated*, now available online; visit http://www.chrisroberson.net/stories.html for details), is also addressed in the novel.

On Sources

THERE IS THE danger, in citing sources in an afterword, of giving the appearance of one who wishes to be impressive. As though to bolster up sagging confidence in whatever text may have preceded it, an afterword filled with scholarly citations makes a writer look like he's trying too hard to seem smart. *Look at my syllabus,* the writer says, stepping out from behind the curtain, *see how much I've read! I can't be all bad, right?*

Keeping the preceding firmly in mind, I find myself unable to resist the temptation to peek out for a moment from the messiness backstage, to give credit to the handful of books that allowed me to write this one. Bear in mind, while any plaudits for *Set the Seas on Fire* should rightly be shared with these authors, all the blame for it rests squarely on my shoulders.

My thanks, then, to the following authors, in no particular order: to Dudley Pope, for an amazingly detailed portrait of life in His Majesty's Navy during the Napoleonic Wars in his *Life in Nelson's Navy* (Bluejacket Books); to Peter Aughton, for his account of Captain James Cook's first voyage to the Pacific in *Endeavour* (The Windrush Press); to Dean King, for the handy vocabulary guide that is *A Sea of Words* (Henry Holt and Co.); to Johannes C. Andersen for *Myths and Legends of the Polynesians* (Dover) and Donald A. Mackenzie for *South Seas: Myths and Legends* (Senate), both for providing a roadmap to the myths and folklore of the South Seas; to Richard Cohen for *By the Sword* (Modern Library), for an indispensable history of the sword; and finally but not least to C.S. Forester, Rafael Sabatini, Michael Curtiz, and Errol Flynn, for pointing the way.

Chris Roberson
Austin, TX

About the Author

Chris Roberson's novels include *Here, There & Everywhere*, *The Voyage of Night Shining White*, *Paragaea: A Planetary Romance*, *X-Men: The Return*, and the forthcoming *End of the Century*, *Iron Jaw & Hummingbird*, and *The Dragon's Nine Sons*. His short stories have appeared in such magazines as *Asimov's Science Fiction*, *Postscripts*, and *Subterranean*, and in anthologies such as *Live Without a Net*, *The Many Faces of Van Helsing*, *FutureShocks*, and *Forbidden Planets*. Along with his business partner and spouse Allison Baker, he is the publisher of MonkeyBrain Books, an independent publishing house specializing in genre fiction and non-fiction genre studies, and he is the editor of the *Adventure* anthology series. He has been a finalist for the World Fantasy Award three times—once each for writing, publishing, and editing—twice a finalist for the John W. Campbell Award for Best New Writer, and twice for the Sidewise Award for Best Alternate History Short Form (winning in 2004 with his story "O One"). Chris and Allison live in Austin, Texas with their daughter Georgia.

Visit him online at
www.chrisroberson.net.

The debut of a stunning new talent in the fantasy firmament

GAIL Z. MARTIN

THE SUMMONER

Book One of the
CHRONICLES OF THE NECROMANCER

ISBN: 978-1-84416-468-4

The world of Prince Martris Drayke is thrown into sudden chaos and disorder when his brother murders their father and seizes the throne. Cast out, Martris and a small band of trusted friends are forced to flee to a neighbouring kingdom where he believes they can regroup and plot their retaliation. But if the living are arrayed against him, Martris must call on a different set of allies: the ranks of the dead...

www.solarisbooks.com

 SOLARIS FANTASY

"A finely faceted gem"

Mindy Klasky, author of *The Glasswright's Apprentice*

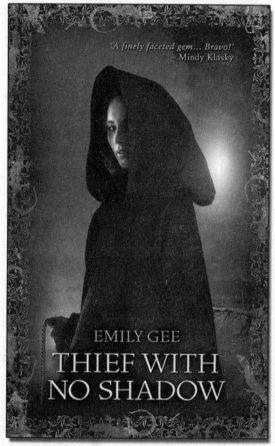

ISBN: 978-1-84416-469-1

Aided by the magic which courses through her veins, Melke is able to walk unseen by mortal eyes. When a necklace she has stolen holds the key to both saving her brother's life and breaking a terrible curse, she must steal it back from a den of fire-breathing salamanders. Things are about to get very tough for Melke, especially when she comes to realise she may have to trust the very people who were out to kill her.

www.solarisbooks.com

 SOLARIS FANTASY

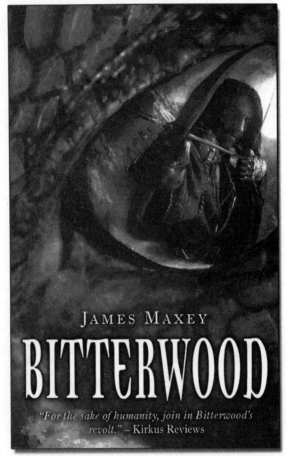